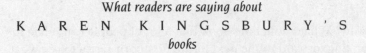

"*Forgiven* hadn't even arrived and my daughters were begging to read it before I did. I appreciate Karen's ability to write about real-life situations interwoven with biblical truth and hope."   —J.P.

"Karen's books are FANTASTIC and very inspirational! I feel lost if I don't have another one of her books to pick up after finishing the last one."   —Nancy

"Your books changed my life. Thank you for helping me to find God again. I read your last one in one day and bawled like a baby all night and all next day. GREAT, AWESOME BOOKS. I cannot wait for the next ones to come. I am off to read the Bible. Thanks again, Karen. I found GOD!"   —Kelly

"I really enjoyed this book. The families seem so real I can feel their happiness, love, and even their pain. I can't wait to get to every book in the series to see what happens next."   —Ruth

"Karen Kingsbury is an amazing author. She makes me cry during every book! She writes so powerfully! I feel like I know all of her characters personally, and it is so easy to relate to them."
—Kathryn

"Just finished *Forgiven* last night—what a book. At the end it was hard to read through my tears. I loved it. Can't wait for the next book in this series to come out. Karen, never stop writing. You are an inspiration."   —Kathie

FORGIVEN

Karen

NEW YORK TIMES
BESTSELLING AUTHOR

KINGSBURY

BAXTER FAMILY DRAMA™~FIRSTBORN SERIES #2

Tyndale House Publishers
Carol Stream, Illinois

Visit Tyndale online at tyndale.com.

Visit Karen Kingsbury's website and learn more about her Life-Changing Fiction at KarenKingsbury.com.

TYNDALE and Tyndale's quill logo are registered trademarks of Tyndale House Ministries.

Baxter Family Drama is a trademark of Tyndale House Ministries.

Forgiven

Cover designed by Jennifer Ghionzoli

Interior designed by Alyssa Force

Edited by Lorie Popp

Published in association with Alive Literary Agency, 7680 Goddard Street, Suite 200, Colorado Springs, CO 80920.

Some Scripture quotations are taken from the Holy Bible, *New International Version,*® NIV.® Copyright 1973, 1978, 1984 by Biblica, Inc.® Used by permission. All rights reserved worldwide.

Some Scripture quotations are taken from the *Holy Bible,* New Living Translation, copyright © 1996, 2004, 2007 by Tyndale House Foundation. Used by permission of Tyndale House Publishers, Carol Stream, Illinois 60188. All rights reserved.

Forgiven is a work of fiction. Where real people, events, establishments, organizations, or locales appear, they are used fictitiously. All other elements of the novel are drawn from the author's imagination.

For information about special discounts for bulk purchases, please contact Tyndale House Publishers at csresponse@tyndale.com, or call 1-855-277-9400.

Library of Congress Cataloging-in-Publication Data

Kingsbury, Karen.
    Forgiven / Karen Kingsbury.
        p. cm. — (Firstborn ; 2)
    ISBN 978-0-8423-8744-6 (sc)
    1. Women theatrical producers and directors—Fiction.   2. Children's theater—Fiction.
I. Title.
PS3561.I4873F67 2005
813'.54—dc22   2005015404

Repackage first published in 2011 under ISBN 978-1-4143-4977-0.

Printed in the United States of America

27   26   25   24   23   22   21
11   10   9   8   7   6   5

To Donald, my best friend, my Prince Charming

The years have flown past, and I'm amazed that we're into our eighteenth year of marriage. I remember our honeymoon and how you'd look at me every few hours and say, "It took so long to get here; I can't believe we're finally married!" That'll teach us to hurry time. With you, Donald, the dance is a beautiful one, sometimes slow, sometimes tapped out in a frantic pace. But I wish the music would go on forever, because every day is better than the last. Can you feel it?
How we're entering this new phase of life with teenagers?
Stay close by and keep praying!
I think we're going to need each other more
in the coming years than ever!
I love being your wife.

To Kelsey, my precious daughter

I had a sudden disconnect the other day when I took you to get your driver's permit. I glanced at the little girl beside me, half-expecting to see a ponytailed sixth grader. Because this is supposed to go on forever, right? The part where I drive you places and we hold deep, meaningful conversations about your friendships and your faith? But instead, there you sat, a willowy young woman with the future shining in your eyes. Has anyone ever been more excited to get behind the wheel of a car? Hmmm. Every minute matters, honey. I'm grateful for the relationship we've shared and the one that will take us into this next stage of your life. Don't ever forget you're a one-in-a-million girl, Kels.
I love you. Shine for Jesus!

To Tyler, my oldest son

This has been an amazing year for you, my Broadway boy! A lead part in a professional local theater company? I stand back in awe at how God has brought you from that precocious kindergartner walking around the house in an Annie wig singing "Tomorrow" at the top of your lungs to the self-possessed young man, serious about shaping your voice and your acting skills so that you can be an even brighter light for the Lord. Your song is still the sound track of our lives, Ty.
I love you. Keep singing for Him!

To Sean, my smiley boy

Everyone who sees you or gets to know you says the same thing: "That kid is always so happy!" You've been home more than four years now, but it feels like you've been here since the beginning. I love your smile and your energy, the way you listen at devotions every morning. You've blossomed in so many ways. God has big plans for you, Sean. Keep trying your best and reaching for the stars! I love you, honey.

To Josh, my soccer star

When it comes to picking teams, everyone wants you, and you're the first
to explain the reason: "God made me an athlete," you tell people. The same
is true for your brothers, but I have a feeling Jesus will use your athleticism
in a very special way. I marvel at your confidence, the easy way you have
of excelling in everything from art to keeping your room clean. But the reason
I'm most glad you're on our team is because of your desire to please the Lord.
Everyone else might be asleep, but there you are, a flashlight under the covers,
reading your Bible. Keep your determination, Josh. I love you.
Be first place for God and all the rest will come.

To EJ, my determined chosen child

Long ago, God could've led us to any of a million little boys who needed
a family. But He chose you, and we quickly did the same. You are living proof
of how love and determination, boundaries and praise can change someone
for Jesus. You have no quit in you, EJ, and I stand in awe at that. I love when
you think no one's watching and suddenly launch into a silly song or dance. My
heart delights in knowing that your talents are more than running faster than
anyone at school. You make us laugh, and one day I pray God uses
you to bring a smile to the faces of many people. I love you.
Keep smiling when no one's looking.

To Austin, my miracle boy

You will always be my little Isaac, the child we were given and then nearly lost.
But, sweet boy, you are simply growing up too fast, coming to me more often
than before with sweatpants that hit above your ankle. I thank God that
you're still a towhead, still adorable with that toothless grin of yours.
Yesterday I found a dinosaur on my bathroom floor, and I realized you'd been
in there an hour earlier. I went to move it, but then I stopped myself
and let it stay. My days of dinosaurs on the bathroom floor are numbered.
I love watching you run and gun on the basketball court, love hearing the
other coaches ask, "Hey, that blond kid who's a head taller than the
other boys, is he really in first grade?" I'm so proud of your hustle and
the way you listen to your daddy. He's the best coach of all, honey.
Now and in the years to come—whether the sport is basketball, baseball,
or walking with God. I'm so glad you're healthy and strong.
I love you.

And to God Almighty,

who has—for now—blessed me with these.

ACKNOWLEDGMENTS

No book comes together without the help of many people. The Firstborn series draws largely on my personal experiences with family and raising children, including my connection with Christian Youth Theater. We discovered CYT two years ago, and since then it has transformed our family. Kelsey and Tyler are active in CYT's plays and tour groups, and we have met many friends who will be a part of our lives forever.

CYT has been the inspiration for my plotline involving Katy Hart and her Christian Kids Theater. I have drawn from much of what I've seen play out in real life, while shaping my characters and the backdrop for my stories. Of course, all plotlines and characters remain fictitious and any resemblance to real events is purely coincidental. That said, I owe special thanks to our hardworking CYT area coordinator, Bethany Larson, and to our wonderful director, Beka Hardt, along with the families who have helped inspire me to write about kids theater. We thank God that you are in our area, helping our children have a wonderful outlet to grow and learn in theater arts.

Thanks also to my great friends at Tyndale House Publishers, including Ron Beers, Becky Nesbitt, Travis Thrasher, Anne Goldsmith, Cheryl Kerwin, Kathy Simpson, and everyone who has helped make first the Redemption series and now the Firstborn series such a success. These books are touching and changing lives, and you play a significant part in that. I'm honored to be working with you.

A big thank-you to my agent, Rick Christian, president of Alive Communications. I am amazed more as every day passes at your integrity, your talent, and your commitment to getting my Life-Changing Fiction out to people all over the world. You are a strong man of God, Rick. You care for my career as if you were personally responsible for the souls God touches through these books. Thank you for looking out for my personal time, my relationships with my husband and kids most of all. I couldn't do this without you.

As always, I couldn't do this without the help of my husband and kids, who are so good about eating tuna sandwiches and quesadillas when I'm on deadline. Thanks for understanding the sometimes-crazy life I lead and for always being my greatest support.

Thanks to my friends and family who continue to surround me with love and prayers and support. And to my mother and assistant, Anne Kingsbury, for having great sensitivity and love for my readers. Your personal touch is so precious to me . . . thank you with all my heart.

And thank You to God Almighty, the greatest Author of all—the Author of life. The gift is Yours. I pray I might have the incredible opportunity and responsibility to use it for You all the days of my life.

CHAPTER ONE

THE ANSWERS WERE INSIDE the brown paper sack. At least that's what everyone was telling him.

Dayne Matthews carried the bag inside his Malibu beach house, set it on his kitchen counter, and took a deep breath. Kelly would be gone until the next day, visiting her agent in Manhattan. Dayne had all night to sort through his questions, all night to catch even a glimpse of the peace he was missing.

He opened the bag and pulled out a thick, heavy book: *Kabbalah—Becoming Your Own God.*

Dayne ran his fingers over the cover. He'd gone to the Los Angeles Kabbalah Center a few times, and earlier today he'd stopped by and purchased the book. The Kabbalah bible. He was starting to understand the stuff, and now that he'd gotten past the guilt, past the nagging inner voice accusing him of turning his back on his parents' faith, he was ready to dive deeper.

A man in a white shirt and white pants had been working behind the counter. He hadn't seemed to recognize Dayne, but then dozens of celebrities attended the center. Famous actors probably didn't impress the guy. Why would they, when enlightenment meant shedding worldly values, exchanging them for a higher level of consciousness?

Dayne had set the book on the store's counter. "This is it, right? The big book?"

The man smiled, an otherworldly smile. "The answers to life are between the covers."

That's all Dayne needed to hear. At this point in his life, he was all questions and no answers. None at all. He was living with his current leading lady, Kelly Parker, but he didn't love her. Even so, he didn't want to break up with her. Filming for the movie started in two weeks. Cut it off with Kelly now and they could forget having any chemistry on camera.

Dayne now flipped the book over and read the inside back cover. An italicized section at the top of the page said: *Are you lacking peace? Does traditional religion leave you empty and searching? Come to the oldest truths in the world, the truths that will truly set you free.*

That's what he was missing. Freedom.

He was trapped in his life, locked in with no way out. Not in the situation with Kelly, and not with his biological family, the Baxters. They knew nothing about him because he needed to keep it that way. Otherwise the paparazzi would take away his family's freedom the way they'd taken his.

And what about his anger? The way he'd gone from a relaxed sort of guy who didn't get bothered by much to being mad all the time. Mad at his adoptive parents for sending him away to a boarding school so they could traipse around the Indonesian jungle telling people about Jesus. Mad that they died in a plane crash when he was eighteen and mad that he'd lived without any family ever since then, when the whole time he had biological parents and siblings living in Bloomington, Indiana.

That was another thing. He was angry that his parents hadn't explained the whole adoption thing to him. It wasn't enough to tell a little kid that some other mother gave birth to him. What was he supposed to make of that? If he hadn't run into Luke Baxter at his attorney's office more than a year ago, he never would've known who his biological mother was at all.

But he knew now, and because of the photographers—the parasites that stayed within breathing distance of him at all times—the Baxters might as well not exist. And that made him mad too. But nothing made him angrier than the stalker who had attacked Katy Hart and him last month, the lunatic fan who because of some wild delusion actually believed she was married to him. The woman's case was going to trial in May, and he'd have to see her again. Sit across from her while he took the witness stand. The jury better throw the book at her.

He pictured her, the way she'd jumped out of the bushes, grabbing Katy and holding the knife to her throat. After that there was no way Katy would take the starring role Dayne had offered her. She couldn't wait to get back to Bloomington, where he'd found her. But the girl had captured his heart and mind and soul. He sighed and stared out the window at the ocean beyond his backyard.

Katy Hart. Even now he couldn't forget about her.

A week ago something happened that reminded him of how the memory of her had become part of his being. His housekeeper was out sick for three days, and Dayne had tried his hand at a load of laundry. Hidden among a basketful of his white T-shirts was a pair of red Ohio State running shorts. By the time Dayne returned to the washing machine, every one of his white shirts was pink.

In a hurry to fix the problem, he grabbed one of the T-shirts and ran it under cold water. He scrubbed it with his hands and then with a washcloth and finally with a wire brush. He could get the pink out and make the T-shirt white again, he figured, if he rubbed hard enough, if he worked at it, if he put an extra dose of effort into the job. But it was impossible. The red had become part of the white, woven into every fiber.

That's how it was with Katy.

She was there when he woke up and waiting for him when he lay down at night. Sure, he had hours when she didn't come to mind, but then she'd rush back in. Never mind that she hadn't returned his phone calls or made any contact with him since she returned to Bloomington. Forget the fact that he'd probably never see her again. She was there—nothing he could do about it.

He looked at the back inside cover of the Kabbalah book again. Truths that would set him free? Yeah. He needed freedom, all right. Plenty of it. Freedom from his anger and guilt and obsession with Katy.

And maybe freedom from Kelly Parker too. Living with her was like living a lie, waking up beside her every morning, parroting *I love you*'s every night. When they were done with the film, he'd tell her good-bye. She'd be fine. Her next leading man was only a film away.

The thing was, he didn't want to wait until they were done filming. Especially when they'd be spending the first two weeks on location in the place he'd pushed for, the place he felt would give the best picture of a small town. The one location where he didn't want a girlfriend hanging on his arm.

Bloomington, Indiana.

☙

Ashley Baxter Blake had to talk to her husband.

Only Landon could fully understand the importance of the information in her hand. Information that would change all of their lives. All she had to do was find him. Because on this fall day, Landon and Cole, their son, were at Lake Monroe, taking advantage of the summerlike day Bloomington was famous for.

This was the sort of news that couldn't wait until they came home—good day or not. Of course, Cole didn't need to find out—not right away. But Landon? He deserved to know as soon as possible. She stared at the information, tried to absorb the reality of what it meant to all of them. But especially what it would mean to her husband.

He'd stood by her as far back as she could remember, through her darkest hours when she was alone and pregnant with Cole, in the days following September 11 when everything in their worlds felt upside down, and even when her health was in desperate jeopardy.

Landon had been there through all of it.

She made the decision quickly—the way she made most of her decisions. Without stopping to tidy up the kitchen or check her look in the mirror or make sure every door was locked, she snatched her keys from the kitchen desk, hooked her purse on her forearm, and hurried out to her car.

The information was still in her hand, the way it would stay until she reached the lake. On the ride there, she fought tears, refusing them because how could she be crying when she found him? They could cry later, together.

When she finally pulled into the gravel lot at the lake, she parked and ran lightly down the path to the water's edge, where she saw the shaded backs of Landon and Cole, sitting on the old red ice chest, the one with the plastic hinges and the crack along the right side.

She slowed, and when she was ten yards from them, she stopped and took in the picture of them. Landon, tall with muscled shoulders, elbows resting on his thighs, the fishing pole out in front of him; and Cole, his blond hair sticking out from under his baseball cap.

They were something together. Ashley never missed the fact, never got tired of watching the way Cole thrived in Landon's presence. She closed her eyes, and for a moment she let the breeze off the lake wash over her.

A single deep breath and she stared at the information in her hand one more time. It was really there, shouting up at her that everything was about to change. Even the picture of Cole and Landon in front of her. When she took another step, a few early fallen leaves crunched beneath her feet.

Landon turned around. "Ashley . . ." His smile lit his face. "You came!"

She hid her hand behind her back. "I, uh . . ." *Think, Ashley, think of something to say.* "It was too nice to stay home."

Cole turned around, and as he did, he dropped his fishing pole. "Mommy!" He scrambled off the ice chest, ran to her, and flung his arms around her waist. "I caught a fish! It wasn't the biggest guy in the lake, but Daddy says we can keep it and eat it for dinner!" He tugged on her arm, leading her closer to the water, and pointed at a string of fish anchored on the shore. "See it! It's the very first one, the one with the little rainbows on it."

"Wow, Coley!" She stooped down, careful to keep her hand hidden from both of her guys. "He's perfect for dinner."

Cole puffed out his chest. "That's what Daddy said."

Ashley turned to Landon. "So . . ." She couldn't last much longer. Not only did he deserve to know, but she couldn't feign conversation when all she could think about was sharing the news. She shrugged and pointed up the hill toward the parking lot and the kids' playground adjacent to it. "How 'bout you two fishermen take a break so Cole can play on the swings?"

Landon must've read her eyes because his smile faded. He looked at her as if to say, *What, Ashley? What is it now?* But none of that came from his mouth. Instead he gave a slow nod and looked at Cole. "Let's leave our gear for a few minutes, buddy. Okay?"

Cole's expression fell a little. "How 'bout we play later?"

"Well—" Landon was gentle but firm—"Mommy and I need to talk, so let's take a break. Just for a little bit."

"Okay." Cole set his face, resigned. "But the fishes stay here, right, Daddy? In this very spot?"

"Right." Landon set his pole down on the ground. He winked at Cole. "But here's the secret—the fish are always right here."

Cole found his smile as they started up the hill. "Maybe we'll catch a bigger fish 'cause this way the fishes will all get tricked that we're leaving."

"Exactly." Landon put his arm around their son and slowed so Cole could keep up.

Ashley's heartbeat kept time with her feet, thudding through her entire body. All the while she kept the hand with the news in it behind her back. When she couldn't stand the slow pace another minute, she leaned down and grinned at Cole. "Race you to the top!"

Cole jumped in the air as he took off through the trees, weaving and hopping and getting to the top a few seconds before Ashley. "You're pretty fast for a girl, Mommy." He was out of breath, giggling at her. "Maybe next time."

Landon jogged up to them just as Cole was making the comment. "I'd say she's pretty fast, period." He chuckled.

After talking for a few minutes about whether the bigger fish would come back while they were gone, Cole ran off and found a boy his age to swing with.

As soon as he was gone, Ashley looked up at Landon. Her air seemed stuck near the base of her throat, as if she could neither speak nor draw a deep breath.

"Ash—" Landon searched her face—"what is it?" Concern and surprise filled in the slight lines above his brow. "What's going on?"

She laughed, but it sounded more like a gasp. "I had to come." Her arms were shivering, even with the sun directly overhead.

She fingered the information in her hands, and then in a rush she held it out to Landon.

He glanced at it and then back at her. Then he looked down and squinted, trying to make it out. "What is it?"

"Take it." She was unable to breathe. "Read it, Landon."

"I'm trying." He took it from her and narrowed his eyes. Then, like the slow lighting of a fluorescent lightbulb, somewhere in his heart it registered. She knew this for one simple reason:

Landon was crying.

CHAPTER TWO

KATY HART HURRIED DOWN THE AISLE of Bloomington Community Church and glanced over the list of kids waiting to audition for the musical production of *Annie*. One hundred and thirty-eight names, more than at any show so far. Chaos reigned throughout the building, but Katy felt a sense of calm.

Something special was about to happen. She could feel it. Two months earlier she had been ready to accept a leading role in Dayne Matthews' upcoming film, *Dream On*, ready to leave Christian Kids Theater and start a new life. But God had showed her where she needed to be, and the answer was clearer than water. She reached her table near the front of the sanctuary and scanned the room. This was her place—she had no doubts.

And because of that, she had the feeling that this play was going to be different from the others, that her purpose as director of CKT in Bloomington was about to be made crystal clear.

"Hi, Katy!" Three girls bounced past her, arms linked. They were fourteen or fifteen, always bubbly and excited.

"Hi, girls." Katy set her clipboard down. "You ready?"

"Oh, my goodness." The one with red hair fanned herself, her words fast and breathy. "I'm scared to death. I hate auditions."

"You do not." The blonde beside her gave her a light shove. "You just told me you love your song."

"I love it, but I mean . . ." She made an exasperated sound and tossed her hands in Katy's direction. "I'm still scared to death."

The third girl had short-cropped brown hair. She leaned in and grinned. "Have you seen the new boy?" She pretended to go weak at the knees. "He's from the public school downtown." Her voice fell a few notches. "He's gorgeous, and everyone says he can sing like a dream."

"He's not as cute as Tim Reed." The blonde put her hands on her hips. "No one ever will be."

The brown-haired girl looked offended. "I'm not talking about just looks here. The new boy can sing. There's no one close."

Katy loved this part, the way the kids confided in her. She raised an eyebrow. "Well, then, I guess we'll have to see, won't we?"

The girls giggled in unison, and in a rush they were off.

Katy looked to the back of the sanctuary at the kids still streaming in, each with a number pinned to his or her shirt. She hopped onto her chair and clapped her hands, the special clap that all CKT kids were familiar with. As she finished, everyone turned and repeated the clap, leaving a silence over the room.

"Okay." Katy smiled and made eye contact around the room, spotting the Flanigans and the Reeds and a dozen other families she knew well. "Welcome, everyone. Most of you know the routine. I'll take the first group in just a little bit."

She paused and a wave of emotion welled in her chest, catching her off guard and making it hard for her to talk. It was the feeling of being home. She coughed and found her voice. "Let's pray."

They all bowed their heads, and the clusters of kids spread out across the sanctuary linked hands or put arms around each other.

Katy closed her eyes and began. "God, thank You for everyone here today. I pray You will be with the kids auditioning and help them do their very best. For You and because of You, in Jesus' name, amen."

The noise immediately picked up, but Katy didn't mind. Not really. It was a beautiful sound, the mix of kids laughing and singing and delighting in the adventure of musical theater. She squinted and tried to see past the open doorway at the back of the room. Rhonda Sanders, her best friend and assistant director, should have been here by now. Rhonda was choreographing the show, and she would take part in the casting process as well. Kids probably had her cornered in the foyer somewhere.

Heath Hudson walked up behind Katy and put his arm around her. "We've got the soundboard ready." He released her and stood inches away, his eyes on hers. "How're you doing?"

"Good." Katy gave him a warm smile. She liked Heath, liked that he was her age and one of her friends. But she had no feelings for him beyond that. Part of it was that Rhonda was crazy about him, not that he felt the same way about her.

"It's you, Katy," Heath had told her last summer. "I think God has us working together for a reason. I'll wait as long as it takes for you to feel the same way."

Yes, Heath had been openly smitten with her since they met a year earlier. He was nice and funny, a successful salesman in his late twenties with a strong faith and sense of family. But the feelings simply weren't there for her. The plan this fall was to help turn his interest toward Rhonda.

Katy touched his elbow. "Thanks for helping out."

"Of course." He shifted his weight. "I'll be here if you need anything."

"Thanks, Heath." She took a step closer to the table.

He picked up on the hint. "See ya." He waved and moved off toward the sound booth.

The moment he was gone, Nancy and Al Helmes arrived at the table. They looked happy and upbeat.

"Here we go—" Al winked—"ready or not."

The Helmeses had agreed to be the musical directors for the show, the way they had been several times in the past. The retired couple played the piano and had a knack for bringing together a chorus of kids so that it rang sweet and true as one voice. *Annie* would be challenging for many reasons, including the fact that the music called for three-part harmony in the song "Easy Street," with Miss Hannigan, Rooster, and his girlfriend.

"Where's your coffee, Nancy?" Katy leaned against the table. "Don't tell me you're sitting through three hours of auditions without coffee."

Nancy's eyes danced, and she pointed to a thermos near the piano bench. "I'm all stocked up."

"Good." Katy motioned to her list of names. "With this many kids, I might need some too." She picked up her iced tea. "It's half-sugar today. That ought to get me through!"

Nancy took a step closer. "Alice Stryker's in the lobby telling a few of the moms that Sarah Jo's a shoo-in for Annie."

"Oh no." Knots formed in Katy's stomach. Alice Stryker was the worst stage mom she'd seen in all her years with CKT. Her daughter was a sweet, quiet girl, plain and unassuming until she took the stage and began to sing. No one in CKT could sing like Sarah Jo, at least not so far. Her voice had won her the part of Becky Thatcher in the recent summer showing of *Tom Sawyer*.

But Katy could barely stand working with Sarah Jo's mother. The woman was convinced that her daughter was the next Broadway sensation, prodding and pushing Sarah Jo until the girl nearly lost all sense of enjoyment from being onstage.

Katy gripped the edge of the table. "Tell me she didn't dress Sarah Jo in a curly red wig."

Nancy laughed. "No, but you know how the woman is about costumes."

"Oh, boy." Katy shaded her eyes, massaging her temples with her thumb and forefinger. "Let me guess. She made an Annie dress for Sarah Jo."

"Something like that. Mrs. Stryker was talking about it, and then she saw Sarah Jo laughing with a few of the kids, and my gracious—" Nancy held her hand in the stop position—"you'd have thought Sarah Jo stole something. Alice ran over, snatched her by the arm, and accused her of being too silly, not serious enough. The lecture lasted three minutes, and everyone in the lobby heard."

Katy moaned. "That's so sad. The woman's out of control."

"It's not fair to Sarah Jo."

"Not at all." Katy's peaceful feeling from a few minutes ago was gone. She folded her arms and pressed them into her midsection. "I might need that coffee sooner than later."

"The good news is—" Nancy gave her a sympathetic smile— "Alice Stryker is the exception."

"True." Katy managed a weak laugh. "We can all be glad for that."

"I better get ready." Nancy waved and caught up with Al near the piano. Katy loved the older couple. They were the official CKT grandparents and a beacon of spiritual strength and experience. CKT needed them, and Katy did too. But Alice Stryker being around for another show could be a problem.

She was about to check her list of kids when she heard a familiar voice and turned to see Rhonda hurrying down the aisle next to a tall guy, who seemed to be working hard to keep up. The guy wasn't bad looking, but the minute Katy's eyes met Rhonda's, she knew that whoever he was, Rhonda wasn't interested.

"Sorry I'm late." Rhonda was breathless. She set her things down, hugged Katy, and dropped her voice to a whisper. "Wait till you get a load of this one."

As she pulled back, Katy looked at the guy. He was in his late twenties, dressed in tight jeans and a close-fitting muscle T-shirt. His hair was spiked, and despite his goofy clothes, his eyes looked friendly. She held out her hand. "I'm Katy Hart."

"Katy, ah yes." He took her hand, and his smile revealed a mouthful of bad teeth. "You're just the one I wanted to meet."

Rhonda was standing behind him now, and she leaned to the side enough to roll her eyes in Katy's direction. Then she mouthed the words *good luck* and headed off to the piano to join Al and Nancy.

"Are you . . . a friend of Rhonda's?" Katy had only a few minutes, but she didn't want to be rude. Besides, she had to know what the guy's deal was, why Rhonda hadn't even stayed around for introductions. She kept her eyes on him, giving him her complete attention.

"Actually—" he pointed a few rows over—"my sister's trying out." He gave a confident nod. "I talked her into it. We're a family of high achievers."

"Is that right?" Katy crossed her arms. "You're an actor, then?"

"No, no." He made a sound that suggested theater would be beneath him. "Stanley Gaelic. I'm an RPSer. Hitting the big time next month." He thrust his chest out. "Probably one of the best in the world."

Katy blinked. "An RPSer?"

"Oh, right." He touched Katy's arm. "I always forget. Not everyone's up to speed on their RPS knowledge." He held his left hand out, palm up, and pounded it firmly with his right fist. "You know, rock-paper-scissors."

From twenty feet away, Rhonda grinned at her and made the cuckoo sign.

"Really?" Katy shifted back to Stanley. "So you mean—" she put her hand out this time and hit it with her fist—"they have competitions for rock-paper-scissors?"

"Competitions?" Stanley rolled his eyes as if Katy might be the least informed person on the planet. "We're talking huge here, Katy. ESPN covered our last contest and, well . . ." He brought his knuckles to his lips and blew hard. "Let's just say among RPSers, you're talking to someone, you know, pretty famous."

Katy could feel herself starting to laugh. "But, Stanley—" she bit the inside of her lip—"isn't it just luck?" She pounded her open hand three times and made the scissors symbol. "It's not like there's strategy, right?"

"Luck?" Stanley's face fell. He took a half step back. "It's the ultimate athletic competition. It's all strategy. Luck has nothing to do with it." He stuck out his chest again. "It's about timing and rhythm and the ability to read a person's mind." He moved closer, his eyes locked on hers. "I'm very good at that. In fact, my mother always said I had the lion's share of talent in the family." He plucked at his shirt in a mock show of humility. "Not to brag or anything. We RPSers are a special group, you know?" He raised his brow a few times. "And from what I hear, you're a special girl."

"Right." She managed a weak chuckle. What was it about her and guys? Was this what she had to choose from? Katy caught a glimpse of Rhonda and Nancy, their heads together, giggling. She shot Rhonda a look that said she'd pay her back for this one.

Stanley was going on, something about the judges being partial to guys with nice hair.

Katy held up her hand. "Uh . . ." She looked at her watch. The kids were getting antsy, the excitement at a fever pitch. She raised her voice so he could hear her. "I'd love to hear more about it, Stan, but I need to get auditions under way here."

"Never Stan, Katy." He took firm hold of her shoulder and leaned closer. "For us RPSers there's only one Stan. Stan the Man Scissors Hand, we call him." He did an awkward bow, one that looked difficult to do in his tight jeans. "I'm Stanley. Manly Stanley, actually." He straightened. "Did I mention that I'm the Indiana state RPS champion?" He cocked his head. "You know what they say about RPS champions, don't you?"

Katy wasn't waiting to find out. "Later, Stanley." She clenched her teeth so she wouldn't fall to the floor laughing. "I need to get going."

"Right." He pointed both his index fingers at her and shot a kiss in her direction. "We'll be talking afterwards then. I'm on a tight schedule, getting ready for the national meet, you know." He held out his palm and hit it three times, ending with his hand flat. "But you're in luck. I'm off tonight."

Out of the corner of her eye, she saw Rhonda drop to the nearest seat. She was bent over laughing.

Katy's mouth hung open. "Well . . . uh, maybe not tonight." She took three steps backward. "But sometime, okay?"

"Oh." Stanley's hands fell slowly to his side, and his shoulders slumped forward a little. "My practice schedule's tight this week, but yeah, we could work something out."

"Sure." She waved her fingers at him, turned her attention back to the kids, and said in a raised voice, "Okay, everyone, I need you all quiet. The first ten get in a line here in front of the room. Let's get started."

Rhonda was already seated at the table. She was still snickering. "Sorry." She moved closer to Katy, her voice low. "About Stanley, I mean."

"Not Stanley," Katy whispered. "Manly Stanley." She kicked Rhonda under the table. "I'll pay you back. There's a neighbor of the Flanigans looking for a nice girl for their son. He's out of jail now, but at least he's driving again. Bicycles, that is."

"Oooh, the anger." Rhonda giggled. "Sorry, I couldn't resist."

The first child was taking the stage, a darling boy with a baby face and big blue eyes. A hush fell across the room, and the boy came to the end of the platform. "Hi." He flashed a gap-toothed smile at Katy. "My name's Kyle Lanham. I'm eight years old, and I'll be singing 'I'm Flying' from *Peter Pan*."

Katy positioned her yellow notepad in front of her and nodded at Kyle. One of the mothers was set up at the back of the stage. She clicked a series of buttons on the CD player, and the music started. Kids younger than eight years old couldn't audition for CKT performances, so Katy rarely expected anything spectacular from the younger set. It was enough that they were willing to get in front of an audience and sing. Rarely did one of them stand out.

But Kyle was the exception.

His voice was sweet and clear, his eyes big and full of expression. When he reached the part where he sang, "I can fly, I can fly, I can fly!" an appreciative chuckle passed over the audience behind Katy. The kid had that certain intangible—a stage presence that couldn't be manufactured.

The orphans in *Annie* were usually cast as a group of little girls. But this boy definitely deserved a callback. When he finished singing, Katy smiled at him and then on her pad scribbled, *Kyle Lanham, crowd-pleaser. Definite callback.*

Sarah Jo Stryker was in the first ten and was—as always—flawless. She sang an upbeat song, "The Wizard and I," a fun tune from the new Broadway musical *Wicked*. The entire time she sang, Katy kept asking herself the obvious question: *How can a twelve-year-old sing like that?*

Still, Sarah Jo had shot up recently and unless Katy and Rhonda and the Helmeses rethought their casting plan, Sarah Jo was too tall to play Annie. Katy could only imagine the verbal tirade that would come from Alice Stryker once that fact was revealed. Either way Sarah Jo definitely earned a callback, and Katy wrote as much on her notepad.

In the next group of ten, two girls sang "Part of Your World" from *The Little Mermaid*. Katy was pretty sure this last girl in the group was also going to sing the same song. She stood and took small steps toward the stage. She was wearing a skintight, ankle-length spandex skirt covered in scalelike sequins. She looked more like a mermaid than Ariel ever did.

The girl was tall and gangly with a mouthful of braces. As she made her way up onto the platform, the skirt kept her from taking the last step. Unable to get her foot all the way up, she toppled like a felled tree and landed on her elbows, sprawled on the stage.

A gasp came from the crowd, and Katy was on her feet, sprinting to the girl. Because of the skirt, there was no way the poor thing could get up gracefully. She could barely manage to get herself halfway into a sitting position.

"Oh, boy," Katy muttered under her breath. She was too short to help the girl, so she motioned for one of the dads sitting a few rows back. The man ran up, but still there seemed no easy way to get the girl on her feet.

"I can't believe this." Tears splashed onto the girl's cheeks. "I told my mother this would happen." Her voice was low, mortified. She closed her eyes as if maybe she would open them and the whole thing would be a bad dream.

"Honey, how about if you ease your legs behind you." Katy tried to push the girl's feet back, but because of the slippery spandex, the move sent her sprawling onto her stomach. She landed with a splat. "Oooh, sorry." Katy held her hands out and gave a wide-eyed look to the father. "I'm not sure how . . ."

Meanwhile nearly everyone in the room was silent, shocked in a way that made the drama onstage that much more horrible. Only a few kids in the back of the room were stifling a low round of giggles.

"Let's see." The dad scratched his head. "She needs her feet in front of her. Let's roll her over." He helped move her feet back around so they were now sticking straight out. This allowed her to sit up partway, though she kept sliding forward. "How 'bout I lift her." He stuck his hands beneath her arms and nodded at Katy. "Don't let her feet slide forward."

Katy acted as a brace for the girl's feet, and in a move not unlike the raising of a barn wall, he pushed her up and onto her feet. Once she was standing, Katy thanked the father, who hurried back to his seat. The audience was still silent.

"I'm going home." The girl's voice was pinched, her cheeks still wet.

"Now wait." Katy put her hands on the girl's shoulders. "You worked hard on your song, didn't you?"

The girl dragged the backs of her hands across her cheeks. "Yes. I . . . I wanted to look the part, but I told my mother the skirt was too tight."

"Okay, now listen." Katy kept her voice low. "I say you leave everyone with a different memory than the one they just watched." She forced herself to sound calm. "I'll go back to the table, and you give me the best song you've ever sung."

"Really?" The girl sniffed. She straightened her skirt and adjusted her shirt.

"Yes, really." Katy smiled. "These things happen." She motioned to the crowd. "Everyone here knows that."

The girl's eyes looked a little better. She held Katy's gaze and slowly nodded. "Okay. You're right. I want them to remember my song."

"All right, then." Katy gave the girl's shoulders a gentle squeeze. Their voices were still hushed, too quiet for the others to hear. "Good girl. I'm proud of you." Katy turned and nodded at the crowd; then she returned to her seat.

Rhonda stared at the girl and gave a slow shake of her head. In a voice that was barely audible, she said, "I didn't just see that."

"Me, either," Katy whispered. Her heart was still racing. She wanted to lead the girl off the stage and help her find a place where she could get out of that silly skirt. Instead she sat down, straightened herself, and nodded at the girl. "Go ahead, please."

A few painful seconds passed while the girl cleared her throat and glanced around the sanctuary. Then with her eyes focused on Katy's, she began. "Hi. My name's Maria Pullman. I'm thirteen years old, and I'll be singing 'Part of Your World' from *The Little Mermaid.*"

Maria's first few bars were shaky, but after that, the song filled the sanctuary, growing and building and leaving a smile on the girl's face as she finished.

As soon as the song ended, the CKT kids were on their feet, cheering for a girl most of them probably didn't know. Two fathers ran up and helped her off the stage, easing her down the stairs, where she fell into the arms of her mother and made her way slowly up the aisle and out of the sanctuary.

"Well—" Katy turned to Rhonda—"nothing will surprise me after that."

"She gets a callback, right?" Rhonda had her pen poised over her own scoring sheet.

"Absolutely." Katy looked over her shoulder, and somewhere near the back, Stanley stood and waved at her. She gave a weak wave in return and looked at Rhonda. "Manly Stanley's watching my every move." She lowered her chin. "Whadya do, tell him I had a thing for RSPers?"

Rhonda giggled. "*RPSers*. And I told him you liked guys with talent."

"Thanks." Katy elbowed her friend. "Coffee on you tonight."

Tim Reed was first up in the next set of ten and gave a flawless audition. After four more singers, it was time for the new boy, the one the girls were fussing over. He had loose brown curls that hung just over his ears, and he was tall, built like a college quarterback.

"Hi." He nodded at Katy and Rhonda. His speaking voice was so strong and smooth, Katy had no doubt the kid could sing. When he smiled, two dimples appeared beneath his bright blue eyes. "My name's Bryan Smythe. I'm sixteen, and I'll be singing 'King of New York' from *Newsies*."

From behind her, Katy could hear several girls squeal. Rhonda tapped her beneath the table and uttered a low, "Please."

Katy kept herself from rolling her eyes. It was always difficult when a cute new boy came into CKT. The girls stayed distracted for weeks before getting focused on the production. She settled back in her chair and waited. As soon as Bryan began singing, Katy had to work to keep her mouth closed. No wonder the girls couldn't keep quiet. The kid had a Josh Groban voice that could stop traffic in New York City.

When he was finished, Katy thanked him, turned toward the girls, and fanned herself. Several of them burst into laughter. "What?" She tried to look surprised. "It's hot in here!" The girls laughed again, and Katy gave them a silly, knowing look. She loved this part, playing with them, meeting them at their level.

The next three groups made it up and off the platform over the next hour. Bailey and Connor Flanigan, the kids whose family Katy lived with, both turned in their best auditions ever. It made callbacks easier when the kids clearly earned a second audition. No one could ever accuse Katy of playing favorites. In the next set of ten, four more girls sang "Part of Your World."

By the time the last girl announced it as her song, Katy cracked her neck, first one way then the other. "What's the deal with the mermaid songs?" she whispered to Rhonda.

"I feel like I'm growing fins."

"If you do—" Katy covered her mouth to keep from laughing out loud—"don't go onstage."

Rhonda smiled, and they directed their attention toward the front of the room. One of the older boys who had played key parts in several plays was up next. This time, though, he couldn't seem to find his place in the song. Twice he asked if he could start over, and both times Katy said yes. The song was "Music of the Night" from *The Phantom of the Opera*, and once the boy found his starting place, he sang five words and his voice trailed off.

He shot a helpless look at Katy. "I forgot the words." His shoulders lifted in a shrug. "Could I try once more?"

"Um . . ." The situation was a little sticky. Katy could hardly allow each of the hundred and thirty-some kids to have second and third and fourth attempts at their songs. But since he could usually sing so well, she nodded. "Once more, okay?"

"Okay." The boy rubbed the palms of his hands on his jeans. This time the music began and he found the right starting place.

But once more he lost the words halfway through the first line. A frown filled his face, and he squinted at the audience. "Does anyone know that next line?"

Katy's mouth fell open. Asking the audience for help was definitely not allowed. "Okay, thank you." She nodded to the boy. Her heart hurt for him, but she couldn't give him any more attempts. "Five-minute break, everyone."

She watched the boy take his music and walk dejectedly off the stage. And then something happened that put a lump in Katy's throat. At the bottom of the stairs, the boy was met by six of his friends, kids who had been in CKT since the beginning. Together they dashed over from where they were sitting and formed a cluster around him, hugging him and letting him know that he might've blown an audition, but they still loved him, still wanted to be his friend.

The scene made Katy's eyes water. *Okay, God, You keep showing me why I'm here and not in Hollywood. But what about my Annie? Please let there be an Annie out there somewhere.*

Do not be anxious about anything, my daughter.

The response was so quick, so certain that Katy jumped a little in her seat. The words were part of a verse in Philippians, words Katy had relied on often in her life. But the way they came to her now was more powerful than ever before, as if the Spirit of God was speaking them straight to her soul.

"You okay?" Rhonda leaned in. "I could call Manly Stanley over if you need a pick-me-up."

"Spare me." She tapped her pencil. "You notice we haven't got our Annie yet?"

Rhonda winced. "Sort of."

Katy held out one hand in front of her. "We've got girls who could sing the part, but they're too old or too tall." Now she held out the other hand. "The little girls are the perfect size, but not one of them can project."

"You worried?"

"I asked God to bring us an Annie." The kids were loud. She had to lean closer so Rhonda could hear her. "I can't have just anyone sing that part."

"And we can't give it to Bryan Smythe." Rhonda's eyes danced.

"Although—" Katy stroked her chin—"if we gave him a curly red wig . . ."

The auditions continued, and finally in the last group, a little girl with waist-length hair hopped onto the stage and grinned at Katy and Rhonda. "Hi, my name's Kelsy Bouchey. I'm ten years old, and I'll be singing 'Little Girls' from *Annie*."

Katy sat back, amused. The kids knew better than to audition with a song by the character they wanted to play. Katy had warned them again and again that such a move would limit their casting potential. Kelsy would've been wrong to sing "Tomorrow." But "Little Girls" was another story. In the play, it was sung by Miss Hannigan, so it allowed little Kelsy the chance to ham it up.

And that's exactly what she did. In a voice that was strong and sweet, she sang the song without error, showing more spunk than all the other little girls combined. When she finished, Katy was convinced beyond a doubt. She'd been right earlier that evening before auditions started. Something special had indeed happened.

They'd found their Annie.

CHAPTER THREE

ASHLEY SQUIRTED A BLOB OF GEL into the palm of her hand, rubbed it over her fingers, and then worked it into Cole's unruly hair.

"Honey, I told you we were going to Papa's house." She kept her tone even. They still needed to talk, and if it took longer than five minutes, they'd be late. Not that her father would mind, but still she was anxious for the conversation with Cole. "Why didn't you come in the first time I called you?"

"Remember that frog?" Cole squirmed as the cold gel hit his scalp. His shoulders hunched close to his ears.

Ashley stepped back and raised an eyebrow at him. "We have lots of frogs in the backyard, Cole."

"No, Mom, this is the bestest one. The one with the three rows of bumps on his back."

She wiped her hands and snatched the comb from the bathroom counter. "Uh-huh, so what happened? He jump out of the bushes and you had to chase him?"

"'Zactly, Mom!" He winced as she parted his hair and tried to make most of it lay to one side. "Were you watching? I had to catch him 'cause I haven't catched him in a whole week at least." Cole took a deep breath. "He was feeling lonely."

With that last attempt, Ashley couldn't help but smile. "Okay, little mister." She finished combing. "But you have to come the first time, okay?"

"Okay, Mommy." He batted his eyes at her, and with his blond hair now neatly combed, he was irresistibly cute. "Sorry."

Ashley sat back on her heels, bringing herself down to his level. "It's okay." She pulled him close and hugged him. "Love you, Coley."

"Love you too."

She felt someone behind her, and she turned to see Landon. He ran his hand over her shoulder. "Hi." His eyes moved to Cole. "Looks like a serious talk."

"'Cause I was late coming inside." Cole's face was still long. "But guess what?" Just as quickly his eyes danced again. "I caught the bumpy frog; you know, Daddy, the big one?"

"Really?" Landon came between the two of them and high-fived Cole. "That's the best one in the yard!"

He shrugged and gave Ashley a weak smile. "That's what I was telling Mommy."

Ashley stood and looked hard at Landon. Without words she asked him the question pressing on her mind: *Is this the time to tell Cole the news?* It had to be, really, because they were going to tell the rest of the Baxter family tonight. It was why she wanted Cole to come in a little early, so he could hear it before anyone else.

Landon gave a subtle nod and looked at Cole. "Hey, buddy, how about we go into Mommy and Daddy's room and talk for a minute."

"But . . ." Cole lifted his eyes to Ashley's. "Won't we be late?"

"No." She reached for Cole's hand and led him out of the bathroom. "We need to talk first."

Once they were in the bedroom, they sat on the edge of the bed with Cole between them. Ashley caught Landon's eyes, and she felt her insides melt. His look was a mixture of passion and pure elation. Even after a year of marriage it was hard to believe they'd come so far, that God had given them a life together, and now this—a child.

"Am I in trouble?" Cole's eyes were big and just a little watery. "Sorry about the frog, Mommy. But he had so many bumps on him and I never catched him all week, and—"

"Cole." Ashley put her hand on his knee and looked into his eyes. Her heart swelled inside her, the way it always did when her son's heart became transparent. He was such a good boy. She shook her head. "You're not in trouble, honey. We want to talk about something else."

He ran his tongue over his lips, his eyes skeptical. "Okay."

Ashley looked at Landon and motioned that it was his turn.

"We have good news, buddy." Landon put his arm around Cole. "Mommy's going to have a baby."

Cole blinked. "A baby what?"

"We don't know." Ashley lifted her shoulders twice. "A baby sister or a baby brother. Only God knows for now."

Cole's eyes got wide, and he jumped off the bed. "For me?" He looked from Ashley to Landon and back again. "A baby sister or a baby brother all for me?"

"Yes, Coley." Ashley could feel her face glowing. Cole had always wanted a sibling. But for so many years the idea had been only a dream. "All for you."

"Can we get it now? We have to go to the hospital, right? Bobby in my class had a baby sister, and his mommy and daddy got the baby at a hospital. 'Cause Milly said babies come from a store or something. Then she changed that and said babies come from a bird. A big bird." His nose wrinkled in a funny face. "Dumb girls. But Bobby and me know they come from hospitals, right?" He took a quick breath. "And hey, is this my present,

Mommy? The one from when you and daddy took the boat trip? I asked you for a baby brother or a baby sister? 'Member?"

Ashley took a slow breath. On the other side of Cole, Landon had the top of his fist near his mouth, hiding a quiet chuckle. They'd figured out the days, and Cole might have been right. The baby probably did come from their delayed honeymoon cruise. Not that she was about to say that.

She reached out and took hold of Cole's hands. "The baby isn't a souvenir, Coley. It's in Mommy's tummy, where it has to stay for another seven months. Then it'll be ready to come out."

"Oh." Cole's smile faded. "Is it cooking in there?"

Ashley shifted her lower jaw sideways and resisted a laugh. "Sort of. God's putting the baby together."

"But seven months, Mommy?" Cole's voice took on a serious whine. "That's a long time. How far is that? Christmastime?"

"No, sweetie, longer." She bit her lip. Maybe they should've told him later, so it wouldn't seem like such a long time. But if they were breaking the news to her father and siblings tonight, then Cole had to know first. "The baby won't come until April."

Cole's shoulders sank. "That's a really, really long time." He perked up some. "Hey, how'd the baby get in your tummy, anyway?"

This time Landon raised an eyebrow at her and mouthed the words *good luck.*

Thanks, she mouthed back. She tilted her head, searching for an explanation. "Well—" she felt her eyes suddenly start to dance— "God decided it was time for us to have a baby." She squeezed his hands. "That's how."

"Oh." Cole's mouth hung open for a few seconds. "I wish it would come sooner."

"Us too." Landon slapped his hands on his knees. "Babies take a lot of time, Cole."

"Okay." A grin lifted the corners of Cole's lips. "But it's really, truly coming? I'm really getting a baby brother?"

"Or a baby sister." Ashley put her hand alongside his soft little-boy cheek. "The baby could be either one."

"I bet it's a boy!" He pulled free of her, skipped around the room, and stopped near the doorway. Then he lowered his head, raced across the floor, and jumped into Landon's arms. "Know what the bestest part is, Daddy?"

Ashley studied her son in Landon's arms. *Hearing you call him Daddy . . . that's the best part.*

"What, buddy?" Landon cuddled him close to his chest. "What's the best part?"

"Well—" he did an exaggerated swallow—"'member how I didn't have you for a daddy at first?"

Landon's expression softened. He stroked Cole's back and sent a tender look toward Ashley. "I remember."

Cole put his little fingers on Landon's head and patted him. "My little brother will have you for a daddy right from the start." He smiled his sweetest smile. "That's the bestest part."

❧

Ashley's heart was full as they drove to her father's house. Cole's reaction to the news, his joy and exuberance, his tenderhearted comments were something she would treasure forever. She could already see the outlines of a new painting, one that would have an expectant mom and dad with a boy bouncing between them, caught up in the news. It would be Landon's present for when the baby came.

Now she could hardly wait to tell the others. Brooke and Kari and their families would be at dinner also. It was something they did once every month or two, so none of them was expecting the announcement from Ashley and Landon.

But her heart held other thoughts, too, thoughts of her mother. When she had Cole, the circumstances had been anything but joyful. After a year in Paris, painting and working at a small gallery, she'd come home pregnant and ashamed. Cole's birth father was a famous artist. A married artist. Ashley felt she was the bane of the Baxter family back then, and the shame she heaped on herself was enough to keep an ocean of distance between her and her mother.

Now, though, if her mom were here, they would hug and hold hands and celebrate every moment. Ashley thought about that for a moment. As difficult as things had been during her first pregnancy, her mother had still celebrated the birth of Cole. She could take comfort in that at least. For most of his early years, her mother spent more time with him than Ashley did. The two were very close.

She put her right hand over her abdomen. Not so, this little one. This child would never be held by his grandmother, never know her blue eyes or her easy smile or the gentle way she had with children. In five years, even Cole was bound to forget. It was part of the pain of losing her mother, a part that would never get easier no matter how many years passed.

The radio was playing an old love song popular back in Ashley's high school days. She stared out the window. At least she would never forget. Memories of her mother would always be alive as long as she could share them with Cole and, in time, with this new child. Tears welled in her eyes. She reached across the console and took Landon's hand. It was still light out. The sun cast a rich glow across the fields between their house and the Baxter home.

God, give Mom a window, please. Let her see how it's all working out for us.

It was something she'd wanted to believe since her mother died. That maybe God gave the residents of heaven a window to the people they'd left behind. There was nothing in Scripture opposing the idea. Hebrews 12 even talked about people on earth being surrounded by a great cloud of witnesses—witnesses who had already gone on to be with the Lord.

Landon squeezed her hand. "You okay?"

"Hmmm?" She blinked back the layer of tears and looked at him. "Yeah, fine."

"You're quiet." He had one hand on the wheel, his eyes on the road ahead.

"Thinking about tonight, the announcement." She sucked in her cheek, keeping the tears at bay. "I wish Mom were here."

He ran his thumb over the top of her hand. "Me too."

In the backseat, Cole had nodded off. The excitement of an extra bumpy frog and the news of a baby brother or sister all by five o'clock had left him more tired than usual.

Ashley glanced over her shoulder at him. "At least Cole got to know her."

Landon moved his hand and placed it over her right one, the one she still had low on her stomach. "This one will too." He lowered his chin, his eyes steady on hers for a moment. "Because you'll tell him."

Her throat was thick, but she managed a laugh. "You think it's a boy too, huh?"

"Her. You'll tell her." He chuckled. "Cole just seems to know."

Their laughter faded, and after a minute or so Ashley nodded. "You're right." She looked straight ahead. Her father's house was a few hundred yards up the road. "I was just thinking that same thing—of course I'll tell this baby and even Cole when he forgets. Still . . ." She sniffed and gave him a sad smile. "I miss her so much. I . . . I just wish she were here."

CHAPTER FOUR

FAMILY DINNERS AT THE BAXTER HOUSE were different now that Elizabeth was gone. There was no getting around the fact.

At first John tried to duplicate the sort of evening his wife would have put on. The day before having the kids over, he would buy chicken and vegetables and ingredients for Elizabeth's special sauces and rice and salad. Hours before they arrived, he'd don an apron and lay the food out on the counter. But something always went wrong—the chicken was too tough or undercooked, or the sauces clumped into a big ball.

Now they did it one of two ways. Either the girls came early and made dinner or John ordered take-out food. Tonight he had brought home six cartons of Chinese food. He had them hot and ready by the time the first group opened the front door and headed inside. John was filling a pitcher with ice water when he heard the voices of Brooke and Peter and their girls, Maddie and Hayley.

"Papa?" Maddie tore around the corner and into the kitchen,

looking for him. "Hey, there you are, Papa!" She was pure energy, dressed in a sleeveless purple polka-dot dress and purple tennis shoes. "Guess what?"

"Hey, my pretty girl! How are you?" He held out his arms and swept her up onto his hip. She was seven but still very little, small enough to hold. "How's school?"

"That's what I wanna tell you, Papa! Fridays are the best day; know why?"

"Why?" John brushed his nose against hers, something the two of them had done since she was just learning to walk. "Why are Fridays the best?"

"Because . . ." Her eyes grew so big they were nearly perfect circles. She lowered her voice, as if what she was about to say was an amazing discovery. "It's called art and recess! All in the same day!"

"Yes!" John matched her enthusiasm. "That would make Fridays best of all, wouldn't it?"

Maddie wiggled to the ground and hopped around on one foot. "I learned this today from Juliette, Papa. How to hop!" She made her eyes small and serious. "Juliette's the best hopper in room three."

"Is that right?" He leaned against the kitchen counter and crossed his arms.

"It's very right, Papa." She put her hands on her hips and kept hopping. "But I'm gonna beat Juliette pretty soon, 'cause I'm practicing, that's why."

John chuckled low and quiet. Elizabeth had loved this about Maddie—her zeal for life, her enthusiasm. Elizabeth liked to talk about how she herself had been the same way as a little girl. Often Maddie's energy had spurred Elizabeth to take her on walks or play games with her. It was a way the two of them had connected.

Brooke and Peter rounded the corner pushing Hayley in her wheelchair. Brooke gave a light laugh as she watched Maddie jumping around. "So, Dad . . . I see you're getting the full demonstration. Juliette's school of hopping—something every second grader needs to know."

They all chuckled, and even Hayley laughed. She was five now and making strides every day—though the strides had gotten smaller as time passed. Still, her near drowning of two years earlier should've killed her. Every stride by itself was a miracle.

John lowered himself in front of her wheelchair and brought her little hand to his cheek. "Hi, Hayley. Papa loves you!"

Hayley grinned big, and something about her expression looked more alert, more the way she would've looked if it hadn't been for the accident. "Love, Papa! Love!" Her words weren't perfectly clear, but they were understandable.

John kissed her forehead. Then he stood, shook Peter's hand, and hugged Brooke. Their eyes met. "How's she doing?"

"Great, Papa!" Maddie hopped over, still on one foot. "I'm gonna teach her to hop like me!"

Brooke smiled. "She's taking more steps in physical therapy. They think she'll be walking by the end of the year."

"She'll need assistance." Peter ran his fingers through Hayley's hair. "But after that, only God knows."

The front door opened again, and this time the voices belonged to Kari and Ryan. "Hi!" Kari sounded upbeat. "We're here."

"Hurry." John had laughter in his voice. "We're getting a hopping demonstration from Maddie."

Jessie raced into the kitchen and watched, mesmerized by her cousin's hopping. "I can do it too." She stood on one foot and began jumping. But at three she wasn't as balanced as Maddie. As soon as she started, she tumbled over and landed on her bottom.

Kari and Ryan joined them, with ten-month-old baby Ryan on Kari's hip.

"Here, Jessie." Maddie stopped hopping, ran to her littler cousin, and helped her to her feet. "It's easier to hop if we hold hands."

With fingers joined, the girls smiled at each other and began a sort of hopping duet. When they were done, all the adults burst into applause. John savored the moment, drawing it in the way a man in the desert draws in his first drink of water. The children made up the laughter and life of the old Baxter place. With Elizabeth gone, John lived for times like this. Otherwise the house was too quiet, nothing but memories to keep him company.

Ashley and Landon and Cole arrived then, and John caught a look in Ashley's eyes. His middle daughter had never been good at hiding her feelings, and now he could tell she had something to say. The way her eyes danced, he figured it would be good. Maybe she'd come up with another painting, another sale at the local shop. She was making a living at it now, bringing in as much money as Landon, doing something she loved and staying home with Cole at the same time.

"Chinese!" Ashley gave a weak smile. "Oh, good!"

Landon put his arm around her and gave her a gentle push. "What she means is, 'Great! We love Chinese.'"

"You do, right?" John frowned. "I thought for sure everyone loved The Mandarin Dragon's food."

The others nodded and gave shouts of approval. Only Ashley looked a little green. John let it go. Ashley had always been picky. Maybe her tastes had changed over the years. "Anyway—" he moved down the row of containers, opening each and sliding spoons into them—"dig in!"

A stack of plates stood on the end of the counter. The kids and the grandkids formed a line, and after a few minutes everyone had their food. As always, they easily fit around the Baxter dinner table. Elizabeth had seen to that. She was the one who had insisted all those years ago that they get the largest table they could find.

"So we can have the kids and the grandkids back whenever we want," she'd said at the time.

Now John watched as everyone took a seat, and he smiled to himself. *You were right, dear Elizabeth. Right again.* When everyone was settled, John reached his hand out to Kari on one side and Landon on the other. Hands were joined around the table, and John bowed his head. "Lord, we are thankful to be together, now as always. Thanks for the food and for providing every good thing." He hesitated, emotional in a way that occurred more often since Elizabeth's death. He thought of Maddie's hopping session. "And thank You for the memories we make when we're together."

Everyone but Ashley was halfway through a second round of sweet-and-sour chicken and chow-mein noodles when she pushed her full plate back and looked at Landon. At about the same time there was a lull in the conversation.

Landon cleared his throat. "Okay, everyone. We can't wait another minute."

Kari put her fork down and stared at her sister. "Wait for what?"

The scene had played out a number of times around the Baxter dinner table, announcements about one thing or another—weddings and children and other milestones in life. John felt a rush of joy. Something big was coming, and he no longer thought it had anything to do with a painting.

Ashley laughed and leaned on Landon's shoulder. "Didn't you wonder why I couldn't eat even a forkful of Chinese food?"

"Yah!" Cole raised his fork in the air. "My baby brother doesn't like Chinese food—that's why!"

A thrill ran through John, the length of his spine and all the way to his toes. "You're having a baby?" He was on his feet and moving behind Ashley and Landon.

Kari squealed and Brooke broke into applause. "It's about time!"

"That's what I said!" Cole sat up on his knees and grinned at the faces around the table. "Only now we have to wait till April."

John hugged first Ashley, then Landon. A lump formed in his throat, too thick for him to say anything except, "Congratulations!"

"Thanks, Dad." Landon twisted around and patted his arm. "I still can't believe it."

"But the baby's not a souvenir." Cole gave a serious shake of his head, and around the table the others laughed. "We'll get him at the hospital after he's done in Mommy's tummy."

The conversation continued, a chorus of happy voices and well wishes and talk about names and birth dates. All the while, John felt his emotions like whitecaps on the surface of his heart. They stayed that way the rest of the evening and after the kids had gone home.

Ashley and Landon were having a baby.

He made his way outside onto the porch and took a seat on the swing, the place where he and Elizabeth had spent so many hours together, talking about the kids and the directions they were taking. He sighed as he lowered himself onto the old wooden slats and set the swing in motion. How many hours had they spent here talking about Ashley? Worrying about her decision to go to Paris, then reeling when they received the news that she was coming home pregnant and alone. With Ashley it had never been her poor choices as a young adult that made things hardest for all of them. It had been the way she cut herself off from the family, believing herself to be the black sheep.

John squinted into the dark night. If God hadn't brought Landon into her life . . . if things hadn't played out the way they did with her health issues . . . how different these days might be for everyone. He let the swing slow to a stop, and he ran his hand over the empty seat beside him. The front porch had never felt colder. With Elizabeth there he had always been warm. The two of them would share quiet laughter and conversation, recalling times gone by and days yet ahead, praying together for the kids.

Now the front porch offered nothing but quiet and chilly breezes.

A shiver ran through him, and he pulled his sweater tighter around his body. His eyes found the sky, and he remembered something Ashley had asked before she left tonight. "Dad, how's the project coming? The one with Mom's letters?"

"Uh, right . . ." John had gulped, grabbing at something to say. "I still want to put that together for you. One of these days, for sure."

Ashley had looked impatient. "You don't have to make a scrapbook. Just give me the box, so Brooke and Kari and I can go through them. We'll copy the ones we want and make a book for everyone." She put a hand on his shoulder. "How's that sound?"

He set the swing in motion again, and her question faded. He couldn't turn the box of letters over to Ashley. What if she found something else, some letter he'd forgotten about? Finding Ashley in his closet reading the letter he'd written to Elizabeth after Luke was born was close enough. If he'd been five minutes later, the secret would've been out. Every one of his kids would've known the truth. That somewhere out there they had a sibling, a full older brother they'd never known about.

At first, after Elizabeth died, he had wanted to keep the secret because of her wishes. She hadn't ever wanted the kids to spend their lives missing a brother they might never know. And so she had convinced him to put the boy out of his mind. Together they had agreed not to talk about him, not to look for him. Especially after failing to find him a decade ago.

But now he had another reason to keep the secret. The kids were all he had, and without Elizabeth, he wasn't sure how he could make them understand. If they found out they had an older brother, they were bound to have mixed reactions. Shock, certainly, and a sense of loss. But they might even feel betrayed, both by him and Elizabeth.

And that was something he couldn't risk.

Seeing Ashley with the letter in her hand that day last summer, John had felt his heart crash to his knees. What other letters had he written to Elizabeth about their firstborn son? No, there was no way he could let Ashley have the box of letters. If it meant that much to her, he'd have to make time to go through them, find a few poignant pieces, and copy them for the girls and Luke. That way their longing for a piece of their mother's past would be met, and Ashley's interest in the box of letters would be fulfilled.

The whole thing felt nerve-racking. What if Ashley grew tired of waiting and snooped around his room again, maybe thinking she would surprise him by putting together a scrapbook of Elizabeth's letters *without* his help? He took in a deep breath and blew it out slowly.

"Elizabeth . . . I miss you." His words came as easily as breathing, and a smile tugged at his mouth. "Ashley and Landon are having a baby." He brought his lips together and waited. A chorus of distant crickets filled in the spaces, reminding him of early autumn days gone by. "Can you believe it?" The question kept him company for a few seconds, but he was still alone. The way he would be forever. He stared at his knees and felt the familiar stinging in the corners of his eyes. Then he looked to the farthest places in the sky. "God, tell her I love her."

The temperature was still dropping. John gripped the swing's thick chains and pulled himself to his feet. As he did, the phone rang. He picked up his pace as he headed into the house and answered on the third ring. "Hello?"

"John? It's Elaine. Elaine Denning." She hesitated. "I hope I'm not calling too late."

Elaine Denning? The woman had been Elizabeth's friend for many years. Over the summer she was part of a group of people he spent time with, friends who attended church together and sometimes met for cards or a picnic at Lake Monroe. He hadn't seen her in several weeks. "Hey, Elaine, how are you?"

"Good." She uttered a shy-sounding laugh. "I've been up in northern Michigan with my daughter. She just had a baby."

"Congratulations!" John smiled at the picture of Elaine helping her daughter with a newborn. But he ached at the same time. Elizabeth should've been Ashley's help when her little one came along. It was just another of the losses that never seemed to stop coming at them. He walked into the kitchen, grabbed the kettle, and began filling it at the sink. "A boy or a girl?"

"Little girl. Maisy Anne."

"You must be thrilled." He put the kettle on the stove and flipped the burner on. "She's your second grandchild, right?"

"Third. My son in Indianapolis has two little boys."

John leaned back against the kitchen counter. "My daughter Ashley told us today that she and Landon are expecting." He chuckled. "Must be the season."

"Congratulations to you too, then." A smile sounded in her voice. "Ashley deserves this. I'm happy for them."

"Me too." There was silence for a moment. A time when he should've been telling her about Elizabeth's excitement, how she was right here a few feet away, and that he'd put her on the phone now so the two of them could talk. Instead he said, "So you're back, huh?"

"Yes. A month's a long time to be gone." Her tone changed, and she sounded almost nervous. "Hey, John, I have a question for you."

"Okay." The water in the kettle was starting to boil. John pulled a mug from the cupboard and dropped a small coffee bag inside.

"Well . . . tomorrow's the farmers' market at the park downtown, not too far from the university. All the squash should be in by now and the tomatoes, and I thought . . . I wondered if you'd like to go with me."

The question stopped John where he was. He set the mug down and pictured the setting, the small makeshift booths and the bigband music that would probably play from the park stage through most of the afternoon. The smell of popcorn and sizzling sausage sticks. The farmers' market was something he and Elizabeth had visited often through the years.

When he didn't answer right away, Elaine hurried on. "Don't feel pressured, John. I mean, I know you're busy with your kids, and the weekends are tough for everyone. I was just thinking I needed to go and—"

"Elaine." His tone was kind, filled with an easy sort of humor. He had nothing on the calendar for the weekend, except church and maybe an hour's visit with one or more of his girls and their families. "I'd love to go." He chuckled. "I'm afraid I don't eat nearly enough squash or tomatoes."

The conversation lasted another minute or so, and they made plans for John to pick her up at ten o'clock the next morning.

As he hung up, John poured the boiling water into his mug and gripped the countertop. She meant nothing by it, right? Certainly Elaine would know he wasn't ready for anything close to dating. His eyes found his ring finger and the wedding band that had been there thirty-six years. In every way that mattered, he was still married. There was no room in his heart for someone new, no matter how kind or enjoyable she was to be with.

He blinked and looked at his mug. The coffee was ready, so he plucked out the bag and tossed it in the trash. Elaine Denning? Of course she wasn't interested in anything other than his company. A simple outing to the farmers' market. He remembered something from the summer, the way Ashley had bristled at the thought of his spending time with Elaine. Even in a group setting.

John downed three hard swigs of coffee and shook his head. Elaine was looking for friendship, nothing more. Anything else would've been ridiculous. He carried his mug through the kitchen to his bedroom upstairs. Then he turned on the light in the large, walk-in closet and stepped inside.

The letters were there, the box pushed to the back of the top shelf, where they'd been for the past year. The whole conversation with Elaine faded from his mind. Maybe Ashley was right. Maybe if he took the time to go through the letters, he'd come up with some part of Elizabeth that the kids could hold on to.

But even before he touched the box he was overwhelmed by a desperate sorrow so great it stopped him short. His hand fell to his side, and he hung his head. He couldn't go through the letters, not now. Maybe not for another year or more. Reading her letters—

words she'd written—and others that he'd written to her would be like intentionally putting himself in a paralyzing place of grief. A grief he was only now learning how to navigate.

He stepped back out and turned off the closet light. As he brushed his teeth and got ready for bed, he refused to think about the letters or the project Ashley wanted him to put together. He simply wasn't ready. Instead, as he climbed into bed, he was thinking about something else.

Squash and tomatoes.

CHAPTER FIVE

KATY WAS ON HER THIRD CUP OF DECAF, and still she and Rhonda hadn't made all the callbacks for the second round of auditions.

"We won't be out of here until after midnight." Katy swigged the last part of her coffee and set the cup on the table. They were sitting across from each other at a café not far from the university, a place that served coffee and sandwiches and stayed open until two in the morning. Katy figured they might need every bit of that time to get the callbacks done.

Rhonda yawned. "Good thing the kids know the calls come late."

"True." Katy sorted through the audition forms spread out in front of her. "Okay, we've taken care of callbacks for three of the lead parts."

"Annie . . ."

"Kelsy Bouchey has a big edge so far."

"Oliver Warbucks . . ."

Katy grinned. "I still like Tim Reed, but we've got four other teens coming back."

"And Miss Hannigan . . ."

Katy checked her master sheet. "Bailey Flanigan and five other girls."

"Right."

"Now let's look at the orphans. That's going to take the longest time. Choosing the right fourteen little girls oughta be a trick. And I'm pretty sure I want to add Kyle Lanham."

"Yeah." Rhonda gave a tired laugh and leaned her elbow on the table. "Have you thought about my job? I have to teach 'em to dance."

They both giggled, and Katy pulled the next audition sheet closer. As she did, from somewhere near the front door a voice called out, "Katy Hart!"

She looked up and just as quickly she wanted to crawl under the table. It was Stanley Gaelic, the rock-paper-scissors guy. She whispered to Rhonda, "Look who . . ."

Rhonda was quietly laughing too hard to talk. She pointed to the restrooms near the back of the café. "I . . ." She stood up. Her face was red now. "I have to go."

Stanley walked up and looked at Rhonda. "Oh, hey, Randy. How's it going?"

Rhonda didn't correct him. She simply gave him a quick wave and headed off, leaving Katy alone.

"Katy, imagine meeting you here." Stanley slipped into the booth across from her. "This is a hot spot for RPSers. I bet you didn't know that."

"I didn't." Katy glanced down at the audition sheets. She had no time for this, but she had the feeling Stanley wouldn't give up easily. She anchored her elbows on the table and smiled at him. "Are you meeting someone?"

Stanley surveyed the café. "Just checking if any of the guys are here." He grinned and shrugged. "They're not. Looks like it's just you and me."

"And Rhonda." Katy looked him straight in the eyes. "Remember?"

"Who?" His expression was blank; then he lit up and pointed back toward the restroom. "Randy?"

"Rhonda."

Stanley bopped himself in the forehead. "I hate it when I do that." He frowned, and for a moment she thought he might hit himself again. "An RPSer has to be an expert at memorizing details. I can't believe I forgot her name."

"It's not a big deal." Katy tapped the papers on the table and flipped her cell phone open. "Well . . . I gotta make calls."

"Is that what you're doing?" Stanley reached across the table and thumbed through the stack of papers. "Have you called my sister yet?"

Katy narrowed her eyes. Now he was getting on her nerves. "Look, Stanley, I really have to—"

At that moment, Rhonda approached and slid into the booth next to Katy. "So—" she looked more composed than before— "what did I miss?"

"Not much." For a second, Katy tried to send Rhonda a signal that it was no time to encourage Stanley to stick around. But Rhonda missed it completely.

Stanley took the chance to jump in. "I'm glad you're both here." He raised his eyebrows at Rhonda. "Which one of you wants to challenge me?" He bounced a few times, his excitement spilling into his tone. "You know . . . at rock-paper-scissors." A slight chuckle came from him. "So I can show you my stuff."

"Well, Manly Stanley." Katy glanced at Rhonda and then pulled up her sweater sleeves. Anything to get rid of him. "I think I'll give it a try."

"All right." Stanley gave a confident nod. "You know how it goes, right?" He held his left hand out, palm up. Then with his right hand he made a fist and hit his open hand three times. On the fourth he opened two fingers, making the scissors sign.

Katy twisted her expression, doing her best to look like she was concentrating, studying his every move. "I think I get it."

"It's like this." Rhonda looked at her. No question she was play-ing the moment. That much was obvious. She imitated Stanley's moves, but she ended with a flat hand—the paper symbol.

"Yeah." Katy gave a thoughtful nod. "I'm seeing it better." She shifted her attention to Stanley. "Let's play."

A gleam shone in Stanley's eyes. "I'm ready when you are."

They both held their hands out, palms up. Stanley's mouth was open a little, his eyes intense. "Ready . . . set . . . go." As he said "go," they both hit their hands three times with their fists, and when they finished, Katy made the scissors sign.

Stanley made paper.

Rhonda let out a victory shout and raised her hands in the air. "Katy's the winner!"

For an instant Stanley's face fell, and his body slumped forward. But he recovered quickly. "You might be good at this, Katy."

She patted the audition papers in front of her. "I might be, but Rhonda and I need to get back to the calls."

"Just one more?"

"No more." Katy shook her head. "Good-bye, Stanley."

He held his hand out again. "Not one more? Serious?"

"Serious." Rhonda wiggled her finger in his direction. "Bye."

He sighed. "Maybe next time, then." He pointed straight at Katy. "You've got a future. I mean that." Then he raised his fist in the air. "RPSers!"

Katy and Rhonda watched him go, and not until he was out the door did Rhonda collapse on the table and burst out laughing. "RPSers? Is he kidding?"

"No!" Katy buried her face in the crook of her arm. Rhonda's laughter was contagious. "That's how he acted when you left me with him at auditions." She rolled her eyes. "What a friend."

"Auditions!" Rhonda stopped laughing, her eyes wide. She stood and slid around to the other side of the booth, her face serious. "We have to finish callbacks."

"I've been trying to say that." Katy gave her cell phone to

Rhonda and studied the next audition sheet. "Mary Reed, she gets a callback."

"We've already called Tim." Rhonda had caught her breath, and now she looked worried. "They won't mind two calls, will they?"

"Some shows we're not as organized as others. Anyway, a callback's a callback."

"Right." Rhonda checked the list and tapped out the number on the cell phone. In a minute she'd informed the Reed family that Mary also was being called back for a second round of auditions.

The callbacks continued until eleven thirty. Only a few of the kids hadn't been home, including Sarah Jo Stryker. Katy was surprised. After the auditions for *Tom Sawyer*, Alice Stryker had answered the phone on the first ring, as if she'd been sitting next to it waiting for the call. Either way, they'd left a message. Sarah Jo would definitely be at auditions in the morning.

Katy stretched her legs out in front of her. "I can't believe we finished before midnight. Must be some kind of record."

"We need to be at the church in eight hours." Rhonda downed the last of her espresso. "If I can sleep at all after this."

Katy was about to say something about the callbacks or Stanley, but Rhonda's cell rang before she could say anything.

"Who'd be calling this late?" Rhonda frowned and flipped open the phone. "Hello?"

Almost immediately the expression on Rhonda's face changed. Her smile faded and her eyes grew wide, her expression stricken.

"What is it?" Katy leaned in, her voice a whisper. "What happened?"

Rhonda shook her head, the color draining from her cheeks. "How . . . how'd it happen?"

"What?" Katy stared at her friend.

Rhonda held up her finger. There was another stretch of silence, while her expression grew from stricken to horrified. "No." The word was more of a gasp. "No, we won't."

Katy's heart was pounding. Whatever it was, the news was bad. She held her breath, waiting for Rhonda to finish the call.

"Okay." Rhonda shaded her brow with her free hand. "Talk to you in the morning." She closed the phone and stared at Katy.

"What is it?" Katy reached out and put her hand over Rhonda's.

Rhonda's voice was breathy, filled with shock. As she spoke, tears brimmed in her eyes. "Katy . . . there's been an accident."

CHAPTER SIX

JOHN BAXTER ALMOST NEVER took a shift at St. Anne's Hospital. He was one of the senior doctors on staff at the university, with a practice that left him no time for the hospital shifts he'd had as a younger man. That night he'd already been in bed thinking about the vegetables he'd get at the farmers' market when the phone rang.

"Dr. Baxter, there's been a bad accident, at least one fatality, numerous injuries." The admitting clerk in the emergency room made a weary sound. "We have just one ER doc on staff tonight." She paused. "You have more experience than anyone else. Could you please come?"

John didn't hesitate. "I'm on my way."

He walked through the doors of the emergency room twenty minutes later. By then the ambulances had brought in both the injured and the deceased. It was standard procedure. Victims were brought to the hospital, a final determination was made, and the coroner was notified. That would give the nurses a chance to clean up the bodies, cover them as much as possible, and notify the next of kin.

In Bloomington, fatal accidents were uncommon. When they happened, they rocked the emergency room staff. John could tell that was the case as soon as he walked in. His colleagues were hurrying about in what looked like an organized state of shock.

The admitting clerk who had called John filled him in on the details. "A van full of kids was coming out of a strip mall. The driver turned right, and two seconds later a full-size pickup driven by some young guy and coming from the other direction crossed the center divider. Hit them head-on."

John cringed. A van full of kids. "Teenagers in both vehicles?"

"No." Her face was pale. "The van had four young kids, six to twelve. Two from one family, two from another."

A groan came from John. He leaned on the counter and tried to imagine the way those families' lives had changed in a single evening. "What about the truck driver?"

"We don't have the reading yet, but he was loaded. Drunk way beyond the legal limit."

"He lived?"

The clerk made a face. "He's fine. Naturally." She picked up a stack of papers and straightened them, her movements sharp, frustrated. Her eyes found John's again. "The fatality is a little boy, a six-year-old boy. The twelve-year-old is in a coma; she might not make it. They're the worst, and they're from two different families. The other two kids are in serious condition."

"Thanks." John rolled up his sleeves and entered the emergency area through the double doors. Inside, he washed his hands, taking extra time the way he always did. The news made his stomach hurt. It was why he couldn't have spent a career in the ER, even though he had started there. Back when the kids were younger, every child who came in on a stretcher had the face of Kari or the eyes of Luke. They were the age of Ashley or Erin or Brooke. One of them. And now that he had grandchildren, it was no different.

He felt a tap on his shoulder, and he turned.

"John." The ER doctor handed over a chart. "Thanks for coming. I've got a girl clinging to life, two kids in serious condition, and a mother in critical. I need you in with the mother. She's got a bleed somewhere, losing pressure fast. A transfusion's been ordered."

"How's she look?" John fell into step beside his friend and one of the most respected ER doctors on staff.

"She might make it. We knocked her out." The doctor kept his pace fast as they headed down a short hallway to the triage area. "She was hysterical, shouting something about auditions for *Annie*."

"Auditions for . . ." John looked at his friend, his heart rate suddenly twice as fast. "That's the next Christian Kids Theater show. Were the kids coming from auditions?"

"I don't know. The woman's quiet now so we can work on her."

They reached the room. John had to know if there was a connection. "What about next of kin?"

The doctor read the notes on his clipboard. "I've got the woman's husband on his way in from Indianapolis. When we reached him, we were able to get identities on the other kids. Just contacted the parents, and they're on their way."

John looked in at the still woman on the gurney. From down the hall, a lab tech rushed off the elevator with two bags of blood. John patted his friend's shoulder. The man was a regular at church. "Looks like it's time to pray."

"I've been talking to Him nonstop." He brought his lips together and shook his head. "Nights like this there's no other option."

John didn't say anything. He didn't have to. His friend had been there when he'd gone through the tough times with Landon, who had nearly died after being hurt in a fire, and with little Hayley, after her drowning accident. They exchanged a last look, and John entered the hospital room.

The tech was preparing the blood transfusion. John approached the woman, going through the initial procedures, checking her stats and her chart. Only then did he take a closer look at her. Something about her was familiar, and he considered what his friend had just said—the woman had mentioned something about *Annie* auditions. He checked her chart and felt his heart do a stutter step. The woman's daughter had played a lead part in *Tom Sawyer*, the recent summer production.

If her daughter died, the tragedy unfolding in the ER would have a wide-reaching impact. In fact, it would very likely bring the community of Bloomington to its knees.

❧

Katy and Rhonda hurried through the doors of the emergency room. Katy couldn't believe it was happening. A car accident with injured CKT kids? Something like this had never happened before, and Katy could barely breathe by the time they tore into the lobby, desperate for answers.

The call had come from Bethany Allen, the new CKT area co-ordinator, and the news was bad, horrible. From what Bethany had said, after auditions Alice Stryker had gone out for pizza and ice cream with her two kids and two other children from another CKT family. They were on their way home when they were hit head-on by a drunk driver.

Alice Stryker's husband was on his way to the hospital from a conference he'd been at in Indianapolis. He'd called Bethany asking for prayers and support.

Now Katy rushed to the front desk. "Hi." She spread her hands on the counter. "Friends of ours were brought in a little while ago. They were in a car accident. The woman's name is Alice Stry—"

"Katy!" a voice screamed from somewhere behind her, near the entrance.

She turned and saw the Hanovers running across the lobby. Their kids, Ben and Brandy, had been with Alice Stryker in the van.

Katy caught Mrs. Hanover in her arms and hugged her. "We just got here."

The woman behind the desk stood. "You're the Hanovers?"

"Yes." Mr. Hanover took a step closer. "Our kids . . . are they okay? They said to get right down here."

"Why don't you follow me." She looked at Katy and Rhonda. "We can only take immediate family back. Maybe you could wait in the lobby."

Katy felt stiff and unnatural. Her heart was racing, as if it were too afraid to slow down and listen to the news, whatever the news was. She gave a final look to Mrs. Hanover, then led Rhonda to a vinyl sofa in the waiting area. Katy sat down next to her. Her arms were shaking as she pressed her elbows into her knees and covered her face with her hands. "I can't believe this is happening."

It was then, before Rhonda could say a word, that they heard the scream. A shrill, piercing scream that exploded beyond the walls of the reception area and filled the waiting room.

Katy's hands fell to her lap, and she stared at Rhonda. But there was no need to say anything. The scream almost certainly belonged to Mrs. Hanover, and a person didn't cry out like that unless . . .

The scream came again, and this time it was a series of words. "No . . . no, please no!"

A pain started in Katy's chest and burned a trail around to her back. "Was that Mrs. Hanover?" she asked Rhonda, her voice scratchy.

Rhonda didn't say anything. She only stared at her lap and shook her head. She was still shaking it when a doctor came out and took steady steps in their direction.

Katy grabbed on to the vinyl sofa seat. "He's coming toward us."

"No." Rhonda lifted her eyes. They were wide and unblinking, scared to death.

When the doctor reached them, he said, "Katy Hart?"

She wanted to run, wanted to get in her car and speed back to the theater, back to the way things had been four hours earlier with all the kids in one place, singing and listening to their peers and dreaming of a role in *Annie*. Instead she looked up and said, "I'm Katy."

"Well . . ." The doctor crossed his arms, his lips a straight line. "Mr. Stryker and the Hanovers have asked me to talk to you."

Katy could barely concentrate. All she could think about was something her mother had always told her. That sometimes on the journey to being a grown-up, something would happen that would advance the trip a whole year in a single day. Graduation or a first speeding ticket or the first night in your own apartment. Katy pressed her elbows to her sides, bracing herself. This was one of those times.

The doctor met Katy's eyes. "Alice Stryker and both her kids are alive, but they all have serious injuries. The Hanovers' daughter, Brandy, is in serious condition. She has a punctured lung and a shattered femur. She's going to need surgery yet tonight, but we feel good about her chances. The most critical is the twelve-year-old, Sarah Jo Stryker. She has severe head injuries. The next twenty-four hours will be critical."

Katy touched her fingers to her throat. Sarah Jo had head injuries? What would that mean when she had time to recover? And what if . . . ? No, she couldn't think like that. She massaged the muscles in her neck and caught a glimpse of Rhonda. Her thumb and forefinger were pressing against her temples. Rhonda kept her head low, her eyes focused on her knees. No question she wasn't ready for whatever else might be coming.

The doctor seemed to look at something near his feet. Then he released a slow sigh, and Katy knew. She knew without a doubt that whatever news the doctor was about to share, it wouldn't be good. It wouldn't be mildly terrible. Rather it would be devastating. "I'm afraid the Hanovers' son, Ben, didn't make it. He died on the way to the hospital."

The news came at Katy like a battering ram. She bent over her knees and rocked forward. Not little Ben. Not the pixie-haired, brown-eyed kid who at six years old was only this week able to take his first CKT class. Katy closed her eyes and pictured him, sitting next to his mother at auditions earlier today, swinging his legs and grinning. Before they left he'd come up to her and tugged on her sleeve.

"Guess what?" He had been so excited he could barely get the words out. "My mommy says in two years I get to try out. Can we do *Peter Pan* in two years, Katy?"

Now there would be no *Peter Pan* for Ben, no CKT class to attend, nothing. She moaned and sat up a bit. Her body knew the way through this type of pain. Losing her boyfriend, Tad, three years earlier had prepared her for this sort of moment, but Tad had killed himself with drugs. Ben Hanover never even got the chance to live.

Rhonda was crying, her head still in her hands. Katy's eyes were dry, but only because fear and shock hadn't given sorrow the upper hand. She looked at the doctor. "How are the Hanovers?"

"Times like this are never easy." The doctor pursed his lips. "They want to be alone with their daughter."

"Of course." Katy pressed her fists against her middle, trying to relieve the tightness there. Ben was gone, and now what about the injured kids? "Have they told Brandy?"

"Not yet."

She held the doctor's eyes for a few more seconds. Then she put her hand on Rhonda's shoulder. "We'll be okay."

The doctor gave them a sad nod, turned, and walked back through the doors into the emergency room.

Another low moan came from Katy as her eyes met Rhonda's. "What're we supposed to do next?"

"I don't know."

Katy leaned back against the vinyl seat, and her eyes welled up. They'd lost little Ben, and now they would have to wait and see about Sarah Jo. The scream from a few minutes ago played again in Katy's mind. Of course the Hanovers weren't okay. They'd never be the same again.

"Alice Stryker never takes kids out after CKT." Rhonda pulled her knees up to her chest. "She's the most standoffish woman in the group, and now . . ."

"Now this."

They were quiet for a while. There was nothing to say, no words that could undo the news they'd learned. They had practical concerns too. A decision had to be made about the next day. Katy drew a long, sad-sounding breath. "What about auditions tomorrow?"

Rhonda shook her head, her eyes distant. "We can hardly cancel it now. Besides, canceling it wouldn't change anything here."

She was right. Katy thought about the options. They could cancel auditions with a round of calls in the morning. But that would send shock waves throughout the organization. They would have to reschedule the session, anyway. And with everyone knowing the truth about what happened, it would be even harder to get through.

Finally Katy pulled her cell phone from her pocket. "I'm calling Bethany. She'll know what to do."

The call was short. She explained the situation, that Ben Hanover was dead and the rest were seriously injured. "Sarah Jo's in bad shape. They'll know more in twenty-four hours."

"Okay, then." Bethany was emotional. "Go ahead with callbacks. Then you can make an announcement when auditions are finished."

"Right." Katy brushed her hair off her face. "That'll work." Tears fell onto her cheeks, and she caught them on her fingertips. "Keep praying."

Bethany's voice was thick. "I haven't stopped."

When she folded her cell phone, Katy and Rhonda bowed their heads and begged God to breathe life into Sarah Jo and the others.

After that, there was nothing to do but go home. On the way, Katy caught herself humming an old show tune, one that filled the car even as tears slid down her face. The song was "I'm Flying," a favorite from the musical *Peter Pan*, and one that all the kids liked. A few had sung it at auditions just hours ago.

But the song was especially loved by a little six-year-old boy, a boy who would never tug on her sleeve again.

CHAPTER SEVEN

DAYNE MATTHEWS MADE THE DECISION over the weekend. He would go to Bloomington a few days early, get familiar with the location, and have a little quiet time. At least that's what he was about to tell Mitch Henry, the director of *Dream On*.

He pulled into the studio parking lot and looked—for a second—at the place where the yellow Honda had parked during the summer. The place where Margie Madden—the psycho fan who called herself Chloe and Anna and probably a dozen other names—would sit for hours, watching, waiting for him. She had tried to kill him and Katy Hart on Katy's last visit to Hollywood. Now he couldn't pull into the studio lot without remembering the Madden woman and chiding himself. Why hadn't he noticed her sooner? Katy might be starring opposite him in the film if not for that woman's attack on them in Paradise Cove.

Dayne let the thought pass. He was inside in two minutes, walking down the hall to Mitch's office. The man had been hired as casting director for the film, but the big dogs with the money had put him in charge of the whole thing.

Mitch was sitting at his desk, looking at something on his computer screen. His eyes lifted as Dayne walked into the room. "Hey."

"Hi." Dayne sank into the leather love seat on the right side of the office. "Everything lined up for the location shoot?"

"Yep." He clicked his mouse a few times and spun his chair in Dayne's direction. "Reservations are in order, and we've got the outdoor areas covered with local police assistance. Which wasn't easy since we moved the schedule up a month." He gripped the arms of his chair. "Yes, we're all set in Bloomington, Indiana." His grin was more than a little sarcastic. "Just the way you wanted it."

Dayne tipped the brim of his baseball cap. "Much obliged."

"Yeah, well . . ." Mitch lowered his chin and pointed at Dayne. "Mind yourself, Matthews. I have a funny feeling about this shoot."

"You know what it is, Mitch?" Dayne stood, crossed the room, and grabbed a fast-food wrapper from his director's desk. "Indigestion. Cut back on the cheeseburgers and relax a little." He leaned closer. "The location's perfect."

"Fine." Mitch motioned to the chair across from him. "Have a seat. You didn't come here to talk about my eating habits."

"True." Dayne chuckled, took a step back, and sat down. He waited a beat, his eyes locked on Mitch's. "Okay, this is it. I'm going to Bloomington a few days early."

"A few days?"

"I'm heading out Thursday. Just to look around."

Mitch wasn't buying it. He had an eyebrow raised. "What's to see? Come on—be straight with me."

"You want the truth?" Dayne felt the smile leave his face. Maybe it was time to open up a little with Mitch. . . . "I need a few days to myself, okay?"

"I'm listening."

Dayne anchored his forearms on his knees and stared out the

window at the Hollywood hills. "I'm thinking about getting into Kabbalah."

"Madonna's church?" There was no condemnation in the director's tone. "I've heard good things about it."

"It isn't a church." He'd read half the book. Now he searched for a way to sum it up. "It's a mind-set, I guess. Avoiding negative thoughts, finding the god within yourself, that sort of thing."

"Hmmm." Mitch took a pencil from a holder near the edge of his desk and rolled it between his fingers. "You need Bloomington for that?"

Dayne clasped his hands and stared at the floor between his feet. "Things are stale with Kelly." He looked up. "I don't want it to affect the film."

"Stale?" Mitch tapped the pencil on one of the files spread out in front of him. Fine lines appeared near the corners of his eyes. "Bad timing for stale, Matthews."

"I know." He pursed his lips and exhaled. "I think a week apart would be good for us."

"Wasn't she in New York the other day?"

"Yep." He sat up straighter and squinted. "It felt good as gold having the time to myself. I need more, that's all." He shook his head. "I'm worried about the chemistry."

Mitch stuck the pencil behind his ear. "You two sizzle on the screen. You always have."

"Yeah . . . before we lived together." He hated talking about Kelly this way, but it was the truth. He'd asked her to move in with him because Katy Hart was gone from his life for good, and that left him with no one but starlets who understood his place in the public eye and everything that went with it. Even attacks by crazy fans. He forced a lighter expression. "Don't worry about it, Mitch. We'll be fine."

"*Dream On*'s a love story." The director set his elbows on his desk and let his shoulders fall forward. "I'll be looking for a lot better than *fine*. So you're going alone, leaving Thursday?"

"Right. Kelly has things to do here. She'll come with the rest of you next Monday."

Mitch studied him for half a minute. Then he took the pencil from behind his ear and pointed it at Dayne. "It's the girl, isn't it? That's why you're going early."

"It's not the girl." The words came easily, but Dayne wasn't sure whom he was trying to convince—Mitch or himself. "She has her own life. I probably won't see her the whole time I'm there."

"That's a big probably." Mitch leaned back and kicked one leg up over his other knee. His eyes didn't leave Dayne's for a moment. "Stay away from her."

"I said I wasn't going to see her." His voice was louder than before. He hated this, hated how everything he did was scrutinized and commented on. "What's the big deal?"

"The two of you are tied up in an attempted murder case—that's what." Mitch stood and slipped his hands into the pockets of his Dockers. He stayed behind his desk and paced a few steps in either direction. "We've done a brilliant job keeping her name out of the tabloids. Brilliant." Mitch threw his hands up and let out a frustrated sound. "The bloodthirsty paparazzi would have a circus if they got their hands on the real story."

"What real story?" Dayne wasn't backing down. No one would make the connection between a small-town drama instructor and the mystery girl from the incident on the beach in July.

Mitch leaned onto his desk, his arms locked at the elbow, and glared at him. "You know how it goes: 'Dayne Matthews' Mystery Girl Found! Hollywood star takes live-in leading lady on location to hook up with small-town secret lover.'" He hit his hand against the desk, his tone frustrated. "I can't have that, Dayne. The story is the movie. The fact that you're sleeping with Kelly Parker only makes it better. Real love hits the screen—that's the story."

Dayne felt the fight leave him. Mitch had a point. With the pending trial, it would be impossible to keep Katy Hart's name out of the tabloids. But clearly he would be the bigger story, as long as the two of them stayed friends, nothing more. The trial was set for May, eight months away. The defense won extra time to prepare for the insane woman's mental evaluations. He pressed his palm against his forehead. All he wanted was a chance to see Katy again. One more time. Did that have to be such a big story, so news-worthy? Was everything he did bound to make headlines?

Dayne dropped his hands to his lap and shrugged. "I'll stay away from her, Mitch. Is that what you want me to tell you?" He stood and walked to the window. A thin layer of brown smog hung over the dry brush on the hillsides. Whoever said LA was the prettiest place on earth didn't travel much. He turned and looked at his director again. "Okay? I'll stay away."

"You better." Mitch nodded toward the door. "Go have your time away, Matthews. I'll see you there next Tuesday morning, nine o'clock, in the hotel lobby. We'll have a meeting; then we'll caravan to the location spot, check it out, and make plans for Wednesday's shoot." He paused. "Maybe that Kabbalah would be good for you." He grinned, his usual sign that the air was clear and all was okay between them. He sat back down and looked at his computer screen again. "You know, take care of all those hostilities you have."

Dayne laughed. "Maybe so." He turned to leave.

Before he was out the door, Mitch said, "Hey, Matthews."

Dayne stopped and faced him once more. "Yeah?"

"I know you, okay?"

"So?" Dayne leaned against the doorframe.

"So keep under the radar. Be smarter than the tabs."

There was a look in the director's eyes, a knowing that said the man wasn't convinced about Dayne's promise. That's what he loved about working with Mitch. He demanded a lot, but when it came down to it, the guy understood he couldn't control every aspect of his life.

Dayne winked at him. "You got it." He snagged his cap from his head and waved it once. "See you next week."

Less than an hour later, when he walked through the door of his Malibu house, he saw Kelly sitting on the deck in a bikini, reading. She rose and came through the patio door. "Hi." Her swimsuit covered almost nothing, and as she stood there with her hair spilling over her tan shoulders, she looked irresistible. She set the book down on the counter. "How was your meeting?"

"Good." He stuffed his keys in his pocket and let his eyes travel slowly down the length of her. "You look amazing."

"Thanks," she said in a cutesy, confident tone. "You too."

"Hey . . ." He put his hands on her hips and kissed her. "I'm leaving a few days early for Bloomington."

She grew slowly rigid and took a step back. "By yourself?"

"Yeah. I need a few days to clear my head before filming starts."

Kelly picked up the book she'd been reading and held it up for him to see. "What about all the Kabbalah talk? I wanted to go to the service with you this weekend."

"We'll go when we get back." He took a glass from the cupboard, set it on the counter, and snagged the jug of carrot juice from the fridge. This was the part he didn't like about Kelly. Why'd she have to ask so many questions?

"Okay, then I'll go with you." She rounded the corner into the kitchen and stopped a foot from him. Her tone softened. "Maybe we could both use the time away."

Dayne ignored her. He poured the juice and returned the jug to the fridge. "Look." This time he kept his distance. Her body wasn't the distraction it had just been. "I need the time to get ready for the film. It's something I always do. A little time by myself to get in the right mind-set, make sure I'm on top of my game."

"Fine, Dayne." She slammed the book back down and crossed her arms. "I'll stop hinting around." Her expression was dark, angry, and insecure. This was the Kelly Parker he'd seen more often, not the girl with the flirty tone from a few minutes ago. "You want to see *her*. That's why you're going."

"Who?" The question was an automatic response, and right away Dayne knew it was the wrong one. They both knew who lived in Bloomington. He took a long drink of the carrot juice, his eyes still on hers.

"You know who." Her voice was thick with sarcasm. "Katy Hart. The sweet, small-town girl who should've gotten the part in *Dream On*. Her, Dayne, remember?"

He took a step closer. "I can't help it if she lives there. I haven't talked to her since she went back." This was ridiculous. He'd just had the same talk with his director. He didn't have the energy for another one. He drank the rest of his juice, set his glass down near the sink, and hesitated only a moment as he walked past Kelly. He softened his expression. "Look, this isn't about us. It's about the film. I just need time, that's all."

"Really?" She was all little girl now. Her hand caught his elbow. "You'd tell me . . . right, Dayne? If your feelings for me changed?"

What was it the Kabbalah book said about times like this? Be honest . . . there was freedom in honesty; wasn't that it? He opened his mouth to tell her that she'd hit it on the head, that, sure enough, that's exactly what had happened. He'd lost feelings for her. But instead he said, "Of course I'd tell you." Then he kissed her, hating the way his body still responded to her. After a minute, he pulled back and gave her the slightest grin. "See? Everything's fine."

"Well, then . . ." She pressed herself against him and traced her finger down the side of his face onto his chin. "Wanna take a nap?"

He shot a quick look at the clock on the microwave. It was almost eleven. "Actually, I better get my jog in." He caught her finger and kissed it, slow in a way that held promise for later. "Maybe we'll turn in early tonight."

She laughed, and he went to get his running shoes. He hadn't planned on jogging, but he didn't want to climb into bed with

Kelly either. A jog would clear his head, help him understand what he was doing, usually without too much interference from fans or paparazzi. It was a Monday morning, after all. Most of the tourists went home when summer ended, and he knew how to disguise himself like other beachgoers. Especially when he was jogging.

He slipped on a pair of shorts and a T-shirt and adjusted his North Carolina baseball cap. He also wore a pair of sunglasses. If he kept up his pace, almost no one would have time to decide whether he was or wasn't Dayne Matthews. And if the photo hounds snapped a picture of him running on the beach, so be it.

The sun was warm on his shoulders as he trudged down the sandy slope to the shore. He kept his head low, another trick he'd learned over the years. The beach was clear, just a few fishermen sitting on the distant pier. Dayne kicked into gear, his stride steady. He was fifty yards out when his mind began to clear.

What was he doing, telling Mitch and Kelly all he needed was a little time away when all he could think about was Katy Hart, seeing her again and catching up with her? Had she found someone in Bloomington by now? Did she ever think about him and how close they'd come to working together? And how was her kids' theater troupe doing?

His feet pounded out a muted rhythm on the sand, and Mitch's words came back to him. The director was right. What tabloid wouldn't have a feeding frenzy over the idea of Dayne's meeting again with the woman who'd been with him at Paradise Cove when the attack happened?

At this point the rags only knew that Dayne had been having a meeting with an unknown woman, someone he was considering for the lead role opposite him in *Dream On*, when a fan wielding a knife jumped out and threatened to kill the young actress.

The story wasn't about Katy—Mitch was right on. She wouldn't become interesting unless the paparazzi became convinced that some sort of relationship had developed between her and Dayne.

Of course, they could reach that conclusion merely by seeing Dayne with her again.

A seagull swooped low in front of him, squawking, as it headed over the gentle surf. Dayne kept running. If the magazines figured out his interest, the swarm of stories would affect the film. He wiped a layer of sweat off his forehead. Mitch thought the media attention would hurt the movie. How could the public buy into a love story between Dayne and Kelly if their real-life relationship wasn't even real?

Dayne picked up his pace. Ahead on the beach, a couple sat on a blanket, too caught up in each other to notice him. The pier was still half a mile ahead, so he kept running.

Mitch was wrong about the publicity. The old adage was still true when it came to getting media attention. Any ink was good ink. So what if they linked him to Katy, right in the middle of filming a movie with the girl he was living with? All that talk was bound to make people more interested in seeing the film.

No, it wouldn't hurt the movie, and it wouldn't hurt him. He'd ridden out the gossip on a dozen young actresses. Anything they could say about Katy Hart would never affect his place in the public eye, his stature in Hollywood. The only person it would hurt for sure was her.

Katy Hart.

She was a private girl, someone whose life didn't involve daily scrutiny or public commentary. The paparazzi would catch him talking to her and they'd start speculating: Does Dayne Matthews have a new love interest? Who is she? What's happening between the two of them? What does Kelly Parker think?

The stories would come in a barrage, several each week, splashed across every magazine in the genre. That kind of attention could ruin Katy's place in the kids' theater company. He reached the halfway mark, just before the pier, and slowed to a stop. The T-shirt was too hot for the run back, so he pulled it over his shoulders, careful not to knock off his baseball cap.

As he did, he heard a distant voice shout, "Dayne Matthews! That's Dayne Matthews!"

He didn't turn around, but he caught a glimpse. The voice came from a teenage girl standing between two adults near the Malibu Beach public parking lot. Straggling tourists, no doubt. The girl wasn't about to run after him, and the few fishermen making their way to and from the pier didn't pay any mind to a screaming out-of-towner. Even if there was a movie star on the beach.

Dayne tucked the T-shirt partway into his shorts and began jogging in the opposite direction. After a few minutes he felt his shoulders relax. The girl hadn't caused a chase to develop, and he'd been right. She wasn't following him. He gazed out at the crystal blue water as he ran.

The kindest thing he could do for Katy was to stay home next weekend and hit the Kabbalah service with Kelly. This was his life, here in Malibu. The life Katy lived in Bloomington was something he'd never know anything about. Looking her up now wouldn't change that.

He had less energy today, less spring in his step. Maybe there was more to it than Katy Hart. Maybe she was only part of it. As he finished his run and trudged back up the sand to the steps of his beachfront deck, he remembered something. Mitch and Kelly didn't know all the reasons he had for going to Bloomington. And he would go, no matter what. He would go on Thursday even if no one understood.

He would take Mitch's advice and stay low, under the paparazzi radar, making sure he was smarter than last time. The photographers wouldn't be expecting him there until Monday, the day the rest of the cast and crew flew in for the shoot. Even then there wouldn't be as many media hounds as there were in Hollywood. It was just a two-week location trip.

He would go because even if he didn't see Katy again, he could be near the people who were never far from his thoughts.

The people whom he'd seen that afternoon in the Bloomington hospital parking lot. Even if not one of them knew who he was. Those were the people Mitch and Kelly knew nothing about. His father and brother, his sisters and nieces and nephews. His family.

The Baxter family.

CHAPTER EIGHT

ASHLEY BAXTER BLAKE FOUND OUT about the accident over the weekend when her father called and asked her to pray. All day Sunday she'd wanted to go and visit the two families, see what she could do to help. But she resisted. They would have other people there, people closer to them.

Now, though, it was early Monday afternoon, and she couldn't paint or read or run errands without seeing for herself how the Strykers and Hanovers were doing. She had worked with Mrs. Hanover on the sets committee for *Tom Sawyer*, and Sarah Jo Stryker had found a special place in her heart once dress rehearsals began the week before the play.

Cole was playing at a friend's house and Landon was at work, so if she was going to make a visit to the hospital it had to be now. Without giving the idea much more thought, she grabbed her car keys and headed for the garage. She was backing out when she stopped and gazed into the gray sky. "God . . . use me." It was a prayer she uttered often now that she understood life better. God had a purpose for everything, and on this day—

as difficult as it would be—He would have a reason for her being there.

She pulled into the hospital parking lot, found a space to park, and walked into the lobby. They were in regular rooms now, and only Sarah Jo was still in intensive care, which meant limited visitors. Sometimes none. That part didn't matter, because Ashley wasn't planning to visit the injured. She wanted to see Katy Hart and the families, make sure everyone was okay and let them know she cared.

She made her way up in the elevator and past the desk. Her father had told her that while the others were improving, Sarah Jo's condition remained extremely critical. Ashley moved quietly down the hall of the intensive care unit and into the waiting room. It was empty except for Katy.

"Ashley . . ." Katy stood and hugged her. There was a catch in her voice. "You missed the crowd."

"Crowd?" Ashley sat down next to Katy and turned slightly so they were facing each other.

Katy's eyes were red-rimmed and swollen. "A bunch of the teens from CKT came down for about an hour." She shrugged and tried to smile. "Just praying, being together. Hoping they could make a difference somehow."

"Who was here?" Ashley set her bag on the floor. She still wasn't sure she should've come, but at least she was the only other one in the room. Maybe Katy needed someone to talk to.

"Tim Reed and Bailey and Connor Flanigan. Four of the Pick kids and the Shaffers."

Ashley nodded, allowing silence for a moment. Then she looked back through the door toward the hallway. "What's the latest?"

"Alice Stryker's in and out of consciousness, but they're seeing improvements. Her husband's in with her." Katy folded her hands tightly. Her knuckles looked white against her jeans.

"Actually he goes back and forth between Sarah Jo's room and his wife's."

"What about her brother, Joey?"

Katy's eyes lit up some. "He's doing better. They'll probably discharge him today." A shadow fell over her expression. "He'll stay with the Reed family so his dad can be with Alice and Sarah Jo. They don't have any other family in the area."

Ashley stared at her shoes. The poor boy. How would Cole handle that? Staying with people he didn't know, being out of touch about what was happening at the hospital, not knowing when his family would be together again or if they ever would. She shuddered and lifted her eyes to Katy's. "What about the Hanovers?"

"Brandy should be released today too. Her leg's in a cast, and she has a wrap around her rib cage. They told her about Ben last night." She shook her head. "I saw her this morning, and she was still crying. The two of them . . . they were very close."

There was only one person left to talk about. Ashley didn't want to ask, didn't want to hear that the news was bad and getting worse. Finally she couldn't wait another moment. "Sarah Jo?"

Katy opened her mouth to talk, but then she closed it. A sob came from her chest, and she looked away.

Ashley put her arms around her and hugged her, rocking her for nearly a minute. "We can't give up." Her own voice was low and filled with sorrow. "If I've learned anything from God, it's that God still works miracles."

Katy coughed and massaged her throat. "Sarah Jo's in bad shape, Ashley. Her brain swelled a lot after the accident." She coughed again. "She has brain damage."

"Still . . ." Ashley gave Katy's shoulder a gentle squeeze. "She's alive. We have to hold on to that."

"I keep seeing her up there onstage, playing Becky Thatcher, singing her heart out." Katy could talk better now, but tears flooded her eyes. "Her mother was so worried about her future."

"She sort of missed out on the moment."

"Exactly." Katy sniffed and wiped her eyes. "I've been in to see Alice a few times, and she's pretty out of it. She mumbles, but she doesn't really know where she is, what's going on. The doctors want her pretty sedated until her stats are better." A weak smile lightened Katy's expression. "So tell me about you, Ashley. What miracle did God work in your life?"

Ashley had wanted this time from the first day she met Katy. The two had a connection that she sometimes felt with other artists. So far the little time she'd shared with Katy had been spent laughing. But no friendship was ever real until it also connected in the sad times. She looked out the window and drew a slow breath. "It's a long story." She looked at Katy again. "I was the bane of the Baxter family for a lot of years."

"Really?" Katy tucked her legs up on the seat and wrapped her arms around her knees. "I never would've thought that."

Ashley smiled. "My mom died last year; you know that. I'll always be so glad things turned around before I lost her. We were very close." She settled back in her seat and found a place near the beginning of her story, back when she was the Baxter child who dressed differently and acted differently and did everything she could to resist Landon Blake's interest.

The story unfolded, all of it. Over the next hour she told Katy about leaving for Paris, meeting Jean-Claude, and seeing him even though he was married. She told her about coming home pregnant and how she and her brother, Luke—after a childhood of being close—were nearly enemies for the next few years.

She talked about Sunset Hills Adult Care Home and how her elderly friends there had changed her perspective. "Especially one woman, Irvel. She taught me how to love. Her husband had been dead for years, but every day she walked with him in her memories, thought of him, and expected him to come home again." Ashley hesitated, picturing Landon. "Irvel showed me that I wouldn't be happy until I found that kind of forever love."

"Forever love." Katy angled her head. "I guess that's what we're all looking for."

Ashley explained how the tragedy of September 11 had made her realize the truth about Landon—that he was the only man she'd ever really cared about. But that time was followed quickly by her health scare. "My health didn't matter to Landon. He wanted to marry no matter how much time we had together."

"See . . ." Katy bit her lip. "That's real love. Living in the moment, knowing that even if you only have today together, that would be enough."

"Exactly."

"I haven't found that, not yet." Katy's eyes grew distant. "I had it once . . . at least I thought I did."

A nurse stuck her head into the waiting room. "Has anyone seen Mr. Stryker?"

Katy let her feet slip down to the floor. "No, I haven't seen him. Have you tried all three rooms? He has his wife and two kids here."

"I know." The woman's forehead was lined, her expression concerned. "I've checked. If you see him, ask him to report in at the nurses' station, okay?"

"I will." Katy gulped. "Is there a change? with one of his family?"

The woman shook her head. "You need to get that information from the family." She hurried on her way.

Katy stared at Ashley. "That can't be good."

"It might be nothing. They might be ready to release Joey, and they can't do it without Mr. Stryker."

"True." Katy looked at the empty doorway. Then she turned to Ashley again. "Talking with you helps pass the time. I can't go home and wait. Not until we know something more about Sarah Jo."

Ashley shifted and remembered where they were in the conversation. "You were telling me about the one time you had that sort of forever love."

"Right. Tad was his name. We met in high school and started dating in college." Katy's anxious expression lifted as she talked about Tad and the fun they had doing theater together and how he got a big break in the movie industry. But then the tone of the story grew sad. "Hollywood changed him." She squinted at the sunlight now streaming through the window. "He died of a drug overdose three years ago."

Understanding dawned in Ashley's soul. No wonder she'd felt a connection to Katy Hart. They'd both survived loss and come out on the other side. She touched Katy's shoulder. "I'm sorry."

Katy looked at her again. "It wouldn't have worked out anyway. He partied hard on location, lots of girls and beer and obviously drugs." She allowed a sad smile. "It's left me a little jaded toward Hollywood."

"I guess."

The waiting room was quiet, warmed by the splash of sunshine. After a while, Katy said, "Can I tell you something?"

"Sure."

"Almost no one knows about this." She did a half chuckle. "Last July I went to Los Angeles and auditioned for the lead part in a movie with Dayne Matthews." Her eyes held disbelief. "I almost took the part."

"Dayne Matthews? He's one of the clients at my brother's law firm."

"Really?"

"Yeah. Luke met him a year ago when he was on location in New York."

"He's a nice guy." Katy nodded slowly and let the story unfold. She talked about getting the phone call from the casting director and heading out to Hollywood for the first read. When that was successful, she went again for an on-camera audition with Dayne. Katy's cheeks grew pink as she talked about the scene calling for a kiss and how they'd pulled it off in a way that thrilled the director.

"Kind of surreal, I bet." Ashley was caught up in the story. "Did the two of you talk much after the audition?"

"We had a picnic one·day, and—I don't know—it felt like we were getting close. Then the weirdest thing happened." Fear played in Katy's eyes, and she talked about going to the beach one evening and the crazed fan who attacked them with a knife. "I'll have to go back to Hollywood next May for the trial. The whole thing scared me to death. I turned down the part and headed home." She smiled. "Where I belong."

"Wow . . . that's amazing." Ashley tried to picture the scene at the beach. "How'd Dayne hear about you?"

"That's the strange part." A few nurses walked by in the corridor. When they'd passed, Katy continued. "The first time I saw him was right here at our theater. We were at the end of our final performance for *Charlie Brown*, and he came in and sat in the back row."

Ashley was surprised. "What was he doing here?"

"He wouldn't say." Katy reached for a bottle of water on the table beside her. "Scouting locations . . . visiting someone. I don't know."

"Have you talked to him since you've been back?" Ashley was intrigued by the story. How often did a small-town girl get a call from Hollywood?

"No." Her expression held a resolve that said she'd made up her mind. "His world could never mix with mine. Not that he was interested, really." She didn't hide the disappointment in her voice. "He's living with Kelly Parker now. She took the part I turned down."

"Oh." The intrigue faded. "I guess the tabloids are right. Wild nights, bizarre fans, and a different girl all the time. They're all the same."

Katy had a faraway look in her eyes. "I thought he was different." She smiled, but it didn't ease the sadness in her expression. "Obviously not."

Ashley looked at her watch. "I have to pick up my little boy from a friend's house pretty soon. Guess I better go."

"Thanks for keeping me company." Katy took a sip of her water and set the bottle back down. She stood and slipped her hands in the back pockets of her jeans. "The minutes feel like hours sitting here alone, just waiting."

"I'll be in touch. Maybe I can come back tomorrow."

The two hugged, and Ashley made her way past the nurses' station and down the elevator. As she walked to her car, she felt a burden lift from her shoulders. She was glad she'd come, glad she'd taken time to spend an hour at the hospital. Nothing had changed with the injured, and she hadn't been able to help with the Hanovers or the Strykers. But she'd done something else.

She'd made a friend.

※

Katy crossed the waiting room floor and stared out the window at the parking lot. She watched Ashley climb into her car and drive away. It felt good sharing an hour with her, talking about Tad and Dayne and the events that had led to her place with Christian Kids Theater. Ashley was wonderful, kind and funny with an artist's eye for detail. And she'd been through hard times herself—more than Katy would've guessed.

She turned and faced the doorway. Had the nurse found Mr. Stryker? And why was she looking for him, anyway? For the past two days she'd never gone more than an hour without an update. Usually Mr. Stryker or the Hanovers would stop in and tell her about any changes or what the doctors were hoping for.

The families had given her permission to visit any of the injured. Katy wanted to go see Sarah Jo, but the girl could have only limited stimulation. Instead she took the elevator down to the second floor and walked to Alice Stryker's room. The woman was sleeping, so Katy kept her steps as quiet as possible as she entered. Wires ran from both her arms, and a constant beeping filled the room.

Katy came up to the side of her bed and took the woman's hand. "Hello, Alice." Her voice was low and soft. "You're doing so much better. Just a few more days and you'll be up and around."

Alice moaned. She slowly moved her head from one side of the pillow to the other. "Sarah Jo . . ." Compassion rang in the woman's tone, and that brought another wave of sorrow for Katy. Why hadn't she shown that sort of compassion for Sarah Jo before the accident?

Katy leaned in a little closer. "It's okay. Sarah Jo's getting the best possible help."

Mr. Stryker entered the room then, his face lined with weariness and fear. He must've heard her, because he nodded. "She's getting wonderful help."

"Have you seen Sarah Jo?"

"Yes." He grabbed his forehead with his thumb and forefinger. His eyes shifted to Alice and then back to Katy. "Can you come out in the hall for a minute?"

Katy braced herself for whatever was coming. She followed Mr. Stryker into the hall and down a ways, out of earshot of Alice. Katy searched his eyes. "Is Sarah Jo worse?"

"Yes." He fell against the wall and dropped his head in his hands. He stayed that way for a few seconds. Then he lifted his eyes to hers. "She's in bad shape, Katy. Her brain isn't responding at all."

A heaviness settled over Katy's heart. She drew a quick breath, holding back her tears. "We can't give up."

"That's what I keep telling myself." He motioned toward Alice's room. "Let's get back inside."

They did, and Mr. Stryker moved to one side of the bed. "They're easing the sedation. Her stats are good, and she's out of danger." He brushed a section of hair off his wife's forehead and looked up at Katy. "I don't know how she's going to take the news."

An arrow of fear sliced through the moment. Katy was trying to think of something positive, something that would give them reason to believe that Sarah Jo would be all right.

But before she could, Alice Stryker moaned again. This time her eyelids moved just enough to be noticeable. "Sarah Jo . . ."

It was all she seemed to say. Despite the sedation and the trauma from the accident, did Alice know Sarah Jo was in the worst trouble?

Katy took a step back and let Mr. Stryker handle the moment. He leaned in and took Alice's hand. "Honey, I'm here. You're okay. Joey's okay too. He gets to leave the hospital today."

Alice blinked and her eyes opened partway. First in slow movements, then in faster, more anxious ones. She looked around the room until she saw her husband. "Where's . . . Sarah Jo?"

"She's here . . ." Mr. Stryker's eyes filled. He swallowed hard, struggling to keep his composure. "You were in an accident, Alice. You're in the hospital, same with the kids." He gripped the bed rail with his free hand. "Joey's okay, and . . . and they're working on Sarah Jo."

As the news reached past the drugged surface of her brain, Alice began to moan louder. She rolled her head from one side of the pillow to the other and raised her shoulders, as if she wanted out of the bed.

Mr. Stryker shot Katy a look across the bed and said, "Maybe you could go check on Sarah Jo."

Katy left, horrified. How were the two of them going to cope? If Sarah Jo's brain showed no activity, then . . .

She refused to think about it, even as she took the elevator back up to the third floor and walked down the hallway to Sarah Jo's room. A doctor and two nurses were talking in hushed tones outside her door.

"Is it okay if I—?" Katy pointed to the room. "Her father wanted me to check on her."

The doctor looked like he was about to say no, but then his

expression eased. "Please hurry. We just sent a message down to Mr. Stryker, asking him to come up." He glanced into the room at Sarah Jo and motioned for Katy to go ahead. "Just a minute or so, all right?"

"Yes. Thank you." Katy stepped inside the room and drew a soft gasp as she looked at Sarah Jo. The girl was beyond pale, her head wrapped in bandages. Because of the swelling of her face, nothing about her was recognizable. Katy shifted her gaze to the machines and saw the numbers. She knew very little about hospitals and vital statistics, but she thought Sarah Jo's blood-pressure numbers seemed low.

Suddenly the reality hit her square on. Sarah Jo was failing. She must be. Why else would the doctor and nurses be gathered around Sarah Jo's room looking somber and calling her father up to see her? Katy felt small and defeated. Since she'd gotten the news of the accident, she'd believed with all her heart that Sarah Jo would be okay. The girl had been so alive, with all of life unfolding before her.

She took a few tentative steps toward the girl's bed. "Sarah Jo . . ."

There was no response, of course. Machines were keeping her alive at this point, and even so, she looked worse than she had this morning. Katy stared at her eyelids, bruised and swollen shut. The same eyes that Katy had made up before several of the *Tom Sawyer* performances.

One conversation came back to Katy. She had been putting mascara on Sarah Jo's fine eyelashes before the last show, and the girl had smiled at her. "I've learned something being in *Tom Sawyer*."

"Really?" Katy had dabbed the mascara wand at Sarah Jo's lower lashes. "What did you learn?"

Sarah Jo held still as Katy finished with her eyes. "I learned acting can be fun." She giggled. "It can even be funny."

The conversation faded from her mind, and she gripped the edge of Sarah Jo's bed. *God, don't let her die. Please. She should be singing from a stage until she's old and gray. Please, God.*

Sometimes when Katy prayed, she could almost hear God's answer—the quiet, still resonance of a Scripture deep in her heart or silent words of wisdom spoken by her parents or the Flanigans.

But this time a song filled her heart, one that grew and worked its way through her being until it sounded ever so softly on her lips. "'Great is Thy faithfulness, O God my Father, there is no shadow of turning with Thee. . . .'"

The song came in all its fullness, the lyrics reminding her and Sarah Jo and anyone who happened into the room that God would have the final word. She had tears on her cheeks as she finished singing: "'All I have needed Thy hand hath provided—Great is Thy faithfulness, Lord, unto me!'"

There were heavy steps in the hallway, and she heard Mr. Stryker talking to the doctor. It was time for her to leave. She slipped past them and down three doors to the waiting room. She stayed there another hour, praying and remembering and begging God to give Sarah Jo a second chance at life.

During that time she heard commotion in the hallway, people hurrying in the direction of Sarah Jo's room. And at one point she heard the muffled sound of weeping. Katy blocked out all of it, refusing to believe that anything worse had happened to the sweet ingenue who'd lit up the stage last summer.

She continued believing everything would be okay, that Sarah Jo would have a miraculous change and start making improvements toward recovery, right until Mr. Stryker appeared in the doorway of the waiting room. His face was red and tearstained.

"How is she?" Katy stood and their eyes met.

He grabbed the doorframe and squeezed his eyes shut. That's when Katy figured out what had happened. The man's expression told her everything she needed to know. There would be no miraculous recovery for the girl down the hall, no improvements and no recovery.

Sarah Jo Stryker was dead.

CHAPTER NINE

THE MEETING WAS SCHEDULED for seven o'clock at the Flanigans' house—two hours for the kids of CKT to cry together and pray together. Katy had no idea how she was going to get through a minute of it.

By the time Katy left the hospital at five o'clock, Alice Stryker was awake and aware of her daughter's death. The last thing Katy heard as she left was Alice screaming about not getting the chance to say good-bye. Katy had driven home in a trance, sick to her stomach. Then she asked Jenny Flanigan if they could hold a prayer meeting at their house tonight.

She called Rhonda and Bethany, and between the three of them they divided up the names of every student in CKT and spent the next hour calling them about the vigil.

Now Katy was in her apartment over the Flanigans' garage trying to sort through all that had happened. She lay on her bed and stared at the ceiling. Saturday's callback auditions had gone well, even though she and Rhonda had been in a fog throughout the morning. When auditions were over, they told the kids about the accident. The hugs and tears then would be mirrored on a larger scale tonight.

Katy had her Bible out. She wanted to read from 2 Corinthians, the first chapter, where the Christians were told that the sufferings of Christ would overflow into their lives as surely as the comfort would. But before she could open the cover, she heard the doorbell ring.

The Shaffer family was first to arrive and the Picks after that. Again and again, as more people came, the group exchanged hugs and tears and questions. Mostly questions. What was going to happen to the drunk driver? How were the others—Joey and Alice Stryker and Brandy Hanover? And how were they supposed to go on with a show when the loss was so great?

By seven o'clock, nearly a hundred people packed into the Flanigans' giant great room. Bethany had asked Katy to lead the meeting, and now she prayed with every breath that she'd have the strength. Katy found a place on the far wall, where she could see the faces of most of those gathered. Some were crying; others had their arms around one another.

"This is a hard night for all of us." Katy felt a stinging in her eyes, but she blinked back the tears. The kids needed her to be strong. "But God promised us something about times like this." She sniffed and looked around the room. "He promised to be faithful, not to turn or change or leave us."

Bailey Flanigan raised her hand. "I don't know if I'm the only one—" she glanced at the others sitting near her—"but I feel so mad at the drunk driver." She clenched her teeth as she spoke. "It was his choice to drink and get behind the wheel, his fault." She exhaled hard, lifted her hands, and let them drop in her lap. "Sometimes I think I hate him. I guess I don't know what to do with all my anger."

"All of us have probably felt that at one time or another over the weekend." Katy's tone was kind, compassionate. She and Bailey had talked about this earlier, and Katy understood. Bailey was a person of absolutes, of black-and-white lines. Forgiveness would be an issue for her and the others as time took them beyond these early days of grief and shock. Katy looked straight at Bailey. "Anyone struggling with forgiveness can talk to me later tonight. Okay . . . anyone else have something?"

No hands shot up.

Katy spotted Tim Reed's mother crying silently in the back of the room. She and Alice worked together on the costume committee, and because their kids had had the lead roles in *Tom Sawyer*, they shared a lot of Saturdays. Katy swallowed hard, doing her best to stay composed. "We need to remember something. The Bible says God's mercies are new every morning. That's what we have to hang on to if we're going to stay strong together, if we're going to find—"

The doorbell interrupted her.

Bethany slipped out of the room, and several kids followed. After a few seconds the kids returned, their faces masked in shock. "The Hanovers are here!"

A minute later, Bethany trailed as Mr. and Mrs. Hanover and their daughter, Brandy, entered the room. Brandy was in a wheelchair, her broken leg propped up in front of her. Little Ben's funeral would take place in the morning, so no one had expected them to come.

Katy studied Brandy, the look on her face. In *Tom Sawyer* she had played Aunt Polly's irritating daughter, the one who wanted to catch Tom and turn him in.

In her eyes now there was none of the mischievous pigtailed girl she'd been in the play. She was only eleven years old, but the wisdom in her expression was that of an adult. Mr. and Mrs. Hanover anchored themselves on either side of Brandy's chair, and the three of them focused on Katy. Mr. Hanover nodded, as if to say carry on, that whatever was happening tonight—they only wanted to be a part of it.

Katy could barely speak, so she looked across the room at Tim Reed. "Did you bring your guitar? I think we should sing."

Tim left the room and returned with his guitar. They started with the CKT favorite, the song they sang in the greenroom before every performance. "'I love You, Lord, and I lift my voice . . . to worship You, O my soul, rejoice!'"

From there they sang a handful of songs that the kids had enjoyed singing whenever they were together. The last song was by Casting Crowns called "Who Am I." It brought up the point that all people are merely fading flowers, vanishing waves, or transient vapors in the wind. Around the room the kids' voices rang as one.

Katy glanced at Brandy. She had her eyes closed, but tears made steady streams down her cheeks. She held the hands of her parents on either side of her.

When Tim was done playing, Mr. Hanover cleared his throat and looked at Katy for permission to speak. She motioned for him to go ahead. The room was utterly silent as he took a few steps forward. "Many of you are probably thinking that it would be difficult to put on a play after what's happened."

There were several nods from around the room. Katy couldn't help but nod along with them. How would they get together and focus on making the production *Annie* come to life, when all around them everyone would be too sad to sing or smile?

Mr. Hanover stepped back, reached out his hand, and took Brandy's again. "We wanted to ask you—as a family—if you'd please carry on." His throat grew thick and his voice cracked. He pinched the bridge of his nose, and then he let his hand fall to his side. "Please carry on. If Ben . . . if he were here he would be sitting there opening night, front and center." A sound that was more of a cry than a laugh came from him. "The day before auditions, Ben came up to me." Mr. Hanover looked down momentarily, no doubt trying to keep his composure. He lifted his eyes again. "He told me if he was old enough, he'd wear a red wig and sing 'Tomorrow.' He told me he could probably be Annie. But he'd rather be Peter Pan."

A few soft chuckles came from the group. Everyone knew and loved Ben Hanover. The ache inside Katy was so strong, she might as well have lost her right arm. She made a fist and brought her knuckles to her forehead, seeing Ben darting around the crowd of kids and grown-ups at CKT, waiting for the years to pass so he could have a chance.

Mr. Hanover waited until the room was quiet again. Then he said, "Thank you. Thanks for treating us like family and thanks for meeting here like this tonight. CKT . . . well, it's what church is supposed to be like." He nodded to a few of the older kids scattered around the room. "You go and put on the show of your life, you hear!" His voice was intense, the tears glistening in his eyes. "On opening night, we'll be there as close to the front as we can get. And somewhere—" a sob sounded in his chest, and he covered his mouth with the back of his hand—"Ben will be watching too."

When he was finished, Katy took a step forward and held up her hand. "Let's circle the Hanovers and pray for them. I'll start, and anyone who wants to pray can pray."

They moved slowly, crippled by the grief in their hearts. But they all came, forming a cluster around the Hanovers. For fifteen minutes they prayed, asking God for peace and healing. Near the end, eight-year-old Mary Reed, Tim's sister, asked Jesus to "give Benny a hug for me because he was my friend."

They also prayed for the Stryker family, and as they did, several girls who had been Sarah Jo's friends broke down, falling to their knees and forming a weeping mound of sorrow. The circle shifted around them, and by the time they were done praying, Katy had the strangest sense: not that everything would be fine any time soon but that God would use the tragic loss of Ben Hanover and Sarah Jo Stryker to build something stronger and better out of CKT.

Tim played another round of "I Love You, Lord," then led the group in one more prayer: "Lord, please . . . let something good come from all this sadness. We understand that people die. But . . . well, we don't understand this."

As he finished, the phone rang. Jenny Flanigan was standing near the kitchen so she answered it. From across the room Katy couldn't make out what Jenny was saying, and for a moment they stood there, not sure how to end the meeting. But before Katy could think of something to say, Jenny hung up the phone, turned, and came back into the great room. She was smiling and crying at the same time.

"That was Mr. Stryker." She crooked her finger and held it against her upper lip. After a moment she moved it and looked from Katy to Bethany and around the room at the others. "They've donated Sarah Jo's eyes to a little girl in Indianapolis. The surgery is tomorrow morning, and after that . . . she'll see for the first time."

Fresh tears filled the eyes of everyone in the room. The information came just after Tim had asked God for something good to come from Sarah Jo's death. It was a high note they could take away even if many of them would cry themselves to sleep tonight.

Tim was right. None of them would ever really understand what had happened, why a drunk driver would hit a van full of kids or why two of them died. But they could understand this: somewhere in Indianapolis, for the first time ever, a little girl was going to see.

It wasn't until the next morning that Katy and the others got the details through e-mail. The operation was a success. The girl who received the transplant was about Sarah Jo's age. But that wasn't all. This girl had an outgoing personality, a love for theater, and one wish—a wish that would've been nearly impossible without vision:

That one day she might perform onstage.

CHAPTER TEN

KELLY PARKER'S TALK ABOUT KABBALAH convinced Dayne to hit a midweek class at the Learning Center in Hollywood. With the tension between Kelly and him in recent days, a night of Kabbalah would be good for him. Then maybe he'd have a sense of peace when he caught the flight to Indiana tomorrow.

One of Kelly's friends—an actress in B movies—was celebrating her birthday tonight. Kelly was still paranoid about the paparazzi, so she invited the friend and six other actresses over for a girls' night in. Another reason Dayne was glad to be going to the Learning Center.

He backed his Escalade out of the garage. The night was warm, with a breeze off the ocean, and since it was already dark, Dayne drove with all the windows down.

He'd read the Kabbalah book—as much as he could take in, anyway. There were whole sections he didn't understand, but he'd picked up this much: the wisdom of Kabbalah taught ways to attain the upper world and the source of all existence. Only by realizing one's true purpose could one attain perfection and enjoy the limits of space and time while living in the current world.

Even that part was confusing.

The traffic was light, and Dayne pushed the speed limit. Having the wind in his face felt cathartic, as if it could blow away the troubles from his mind and heart. He glanced at the seat beside him and the Kabbalah handbook he'd brought along. Whatever the upper world was, it sounded better than Los Angeles. Even on a warm, clear September night.

He flipped on the radio and switched the channel to an oldies station. "Under the Boardwalk" was halfway through. Dayne turned it up and sang along for the remainder of the song. When it was over a commercial came on, and Dayne hit the Off button. The thing was, he really didn't understand Kabbalah. That's why he was going to the class. He only knew that a couple of his best Hollywood friends had found peace in it some way or another. Peace and freedom and—who could tell?—maybe even the upper world.

Dayne rested his arm on the open-window frame. What was it he read in one of the chapters? Something about taking the first steps on the path to spiritual ascent, or was it reaching attainment of the spiritual realms? Dayne gripped the steering wheel and stared straight ahead. Maybe it was both. Whatever it was, he needed it. Otherwise the thoughts of Katy Hart would drive him crazy.

Tonight's class wore on for nearly two hours, and much of it was filled with Hebrew words Dayne didn't understand. Listening to the teacher, he could only deduct that Kabbalah—for all its good—was also very difficult to follow.

He was leaving when one of the other teachers approached him. "Too bad you got stuck with him." He pointed his thumb in the direction of the teacher Dayne had listened to all evening. "That guy makes the Kabbalah book look exciting."

Dayne gave an uneasy chuckle. "He did go on a little long."

"A little?" The man laughed. "You'll reach the upper world in no time listening to lectures like that."

For a moment, Dayne studied this teacher. Many of the Kabbalists had an otherworldly look about them, but this guy seemed funny, more real. Almost like one of the guys he might hang out with at a bar or on one of the sets. He didn't seem to be in any hurry, so Dayne decided to push for a few answers. "Can you tell me something?"

"Sure." The teacher smiled at a few pretty girls as they walked by. Then he directed his attention back to Dayne. "Anything."

"Okay." He lifted the Kabbalah book and looked at the cover. "I've been reading, but I'm not sure I really get it."

"First, I should introduce myself. I'm Abi." He gave Dayne a firm handshake. "Abi Fenister." He paused and his expression grew more serious. "Kabbalah is really pretty straightforward. There are six hundred and thirteen impure desires—those are the things that keep you from the upper world. Then you have your one hundred and twenty-five spiritual steps." His voice fell several notches. "You know why there are so many?"

"I wondered about it." Dayne liked this. The guy was breaking it down, which was all he could ask for.

"Because we're all selfish. Selfish to the core, man. I mean, big-time selfish." Abi gave an easy laugh and touched Dayne's elbow. "That's why you Hollywood guys get it so much faster. You've got it all, man—everything you could ever want. The money, the women, the cars, the fame. All of it."

Dayne wasn't sure he was following this part. He frowned, trying to understand.

"See, you actor types reach the upper world a lot faster because you give up worldliness so much easier." Abi pointed at a picture on the wall, a large headshot of one of the most famous women in the movie and music industry. "Take her for example. She drops a few million at the center every six months." Abi snapped his fingers. "Just like that, you're halfway through the steps."

Dayne looked at the picture. It made sense to him. If people could give up millions of dollars, then they were—in a sense—

dismissing fame, wealth, and materialism. All in as much time as it took to write a check. He cocked his head. "What happens then, once you give it all up?"

"Think about it. Half the impure desires involve wealth and greed." The man crossed his arms, more serious than before. "More than half. You get past that kind of hurdle and you're headed straight for the upper world."

"Which means . . . ?"

"Oneness with the creator. Freedom from self. Peace, man." He leaned against a nearby wall. "It's what you see in the eyes of all these people running around here. Amazing peace."

Dayne scratched his head. "Those spiritual laws . . . anything there about forgiveness?"

"Forgiveness?" Abi's face went blank. Then his eyes lit up again. "Forgiveness is automatic. Because Kabbalists do away with negativism. Unforgiveness is negative, so it's not an issue when you study Kabbalah." He shrugged. "You simply do away with it."

"Hmmm." Dayne gestured at a few clusters of people passing by. Most of them were dressed in white. "What's with the clothes?"

"White symbolizes purity, oneness with the god inside you." Abi waved toward the Learning Center store over his right shoulder. "You can get garments of purity before you leave tonight. In fact, the guy in there can set you up with a Kabbalah bracelet and a series of tapes." He gave Dayne a light punch on the shoulder. "Makes the learning go a lot quicker. And when you've got a hundred and twenty-five spiritual laws, quick learning can be a nice thing."

Dayne looked in the direction of the store, just off the main lobby. "Maybe I'll check it out."

"Good." Abi motioned for Dayne to follow him. They walked to the other side of the foyer where three men in suits stood behind a table, chatting with each other. "I want you to meet a few of the leaders."

Dayne asked, "Where're their white clothes?"

Abi gave him a strange look, as if the answer was too obvious to state. "They're not in a position of learning. The spiritual garments are for Kabbalists in a state of learning."

They reached the table, and Abi made the introductions. Then he said to the shortest man, the one in the center, "Do you have a donation kit? I think Mr. Matthews might be interested."

A donation kit? Dayne tried not to react negatively. Kabbalists do away with anything negative.

The short man nodded and gave Dayne a smile that took up his entire face. "We're glad to have you, Mr. Matthews. People of your stature often reach the upper world in a relatively short time."

A part of him wanted to laugh out loud. They reached the upper world quicker by writing a big check? Wasn't that a little obvious? But then he remembered the look on the first teacher's face earlier this evening. He might have been boring, but he had a look in his eyes that drew Dayne in and made him long for a way to end the emptiness in his soul. The big Hollywood names who were practicing Kabbalah had the same look, as if nothing could touch them, nothing could ruffle them.

He thought about his bank account. Maybe it was holding him back. Could he really move himself halfway to the upper world by writing a seven-figure check? He took the manila envelope and tucked it under his arm. "Can I take it home, look it over?"

"Sure." Abi's expression turned helpful. "Maybe think about the amount. Keep in mind the upper world."

"Right."

"It'll set you free, man. I'm telling you." He shook his head. "I wish I had the kind of money you movie types have." He swooped his hand in an upward arch. "Talk about soaring past half the spiritual laws."

A slow sense of joy—or maybe peace—spread through Dayne. How easy would that be? Write a check, shed some of the material wealth he'd accumulated, and in the process find himself halfway to the upper world. He could do it right now, but his first instinct was probably right. He should give it some thought, figure out exactly how much to give.

He thanked Abi and the other men. On his way out, he stopped in at the store. He purchased the white spiritual garments and the red bracelet, which offered protection and identified him as a Kabbalist, a learner of spiritual matters, a person intent on reaching the upper world.

Later, as he brought the goods into his house, he thought of his adoptive parents. They'd been sold out to a conventional religion that left them toiling for heaven's rewards. Maybe they'd reached the upper world also. But they had been so trapped by relegated teachings. Until the day they died, they'd believed they were sinners, flawed and doomed to hell if not for Jesus Christ. No matter how much they had worked—even as they died doing their work—they never attained a level of perfection or oneness with God.

But with Kabbalah, he would take on a way that his adoptive parents had missed.

He found a place in his closet for the white garments he would wear when he returned from Bloomington. Then he fastened the bracelet on his wrist. He would wear it as a reminder of what lay ahead for him. Freedom and peace and a release of all negative feelings. A journey to the upper world.

He only wished he'd found Kabbalah sooner. Of course, he was about to make up for lost time in a hurry. Yes, he wanted to think about it, but when he returned from Bloomington he was sure he'd make a significant seven-figure donation, one that would pole-vault him even more than halfway through the spiritual steps. He could hardly wait to experience the freedom and peace of that moment.

But before he could travel the journey of Kabbalah, he had a different trip to make. One that would take him to Bloomington and the life he might've lived if things had turned out differently. The trip to Indiana would give him a glimpse of a family he would've been a part of, a girl he would've loved. But it would all be make-believe, his world and theirs too different to bridge.

That was the exciting thing about Kabbalah. It would take him into a world that was real.

One that would change his life forever.

✦

The Baxter house was quiet, too quiet for eight o'clock. That was one of John's most difficult adjustments since Elizabeth's death. The rooms that housed a million memories, the walls that had heard countless conversations and witnessed celebrations and the growing of his family through the years, were now silent.

John padded through the house with a cup of lukewarm coffee. He wasn't tired, and he'd already had conversations with his youngest daughter, Erin, and his oldest, Brooke. The kids were all good about calling regularly, keeping him posted on how their family lives were going. He enjoyed the conversations, but tonight he was distracted. Tomorrow was Sarah Jo Stryker's funeral.

He hadn't known her, of course. But he'd gone to the play with Brooke's family, so he'd seen her sing, heard the gift God had given her. And now he couldn't get the loss of her life out of his mind. Her family, the kids and families at CKT—all of them were reeling, and there was nothing he could do about it.

The silence got louder. John took a sip of coffee and walked to the entertainment center in the family room. TV would be a distraction, and radio—with its commercials—would only make the house seem artificially noisy. Instead he slipped in an instrumental CD, one with sound tracks from old movies that he and Elizabeth had watched again and again. The sound was rich and full, and John breathed it in. This was better.

He picked up the newspaper and sat down at the dining room table. Last weekend's accident had held a spot on the front page ever since it happened, and today was no different. The photo halfway down was of a well-built young man in an orange jumpsuit, sitting next to an attorney at what was obviously a hearing. The headline over the accompanying story read "Drunk Driver's Tragic Past Recounted."

John sighed. So this was the guy who had drunk far too much and gone out driving last Friday night. The one who was responsible for two deaths. He looked at the picture again. *God, this one is Yours, too, no matter what he's done. Show him the way to forgiveness. Please.*

He lifted the silent prayer because it was easier than hating the young man. No answer resounded in his heart, but he felt a sense of purpose, a knowing that along the way he was supposed to pray for the boy. Clearly the kid hadn't intended to go out and kill two children. John finished what was left in his coffee cup, then held the paper up and began reading the article.

According to the story, the boy—Jeremy Fisher—was an only child whose father, an army reservist, had been called up two years earlier and assigned to a unit serving in Iraq. A few months after he left, his wife began seeing someone else.

"The marriage was already rocky," a friend was quoted as saying. "She had no intention of waiting two years for her husband to come home."

Mrs. Fisher had moved to New Mexico with an old boyfriend, leaving Jeremy at home to fend for himself.

"A history of reckless-driving and drunk-driving arrests had already severed the relationship between mother and son," a police officer said. "Left to himself, the suspect went a little wild."

Based on the list of arrests and prior convictions, Jeremy went more than a little wild. He dropped out of Clear Creek High, and over the summer he had squandered all the money his grandparents had set aside for his college education. It became increasingly clear that Jeremy had trouble with alcohol.

"Twice during the summer the suspect had been arrested for

drunk driving and ordered to attend a treatment program," the police officer said. "He attempted the program once but lasted only a few days before dropping out."

John blinked and looked around the house. It was lonely, but at least he'd lived entire decades where he was surrounded by the people he loved. How would it feel to be sixteen and living alone, knowing your mother was in another state starting a new life and your father was overseas in Iraq?

He thought of his own son, Luke, and his poor decisions a few years back. If John and Elizabeth hadn't been there for him, this story could've been Luke's. He might've dropped off the deep end if they hadn't pursued him with the relentless love of God, assuring him that they loved him and forgave him and would always have a place for him.

John looked at the article again. Where would the kid go now? The story said he was facing ten years in prison because he was a repeat offender and had ignored previous court mandates.

John shuddered. *God . . . there must be redemption for Jeremy Fisher, right? The same way there's redemption for everyone. So please . . . bring someone into his life who can show him Your love and grace and peace, someone who can let him see that even he can be forgiven.*

The phone rang, and John took a quick breath, letting the details of the article pass for now. He stood, took the phone from its base, and clicked the On button. "Hello?"

"John? It's Elaine." Her voice was upbeat but hesitant. "Just thought I'd see how your week's going." She paused. "I know Friday night was hard."

"Well, that's very thoughtful." He took the phone into the family room and sat in his comfortable recliner, the one with the full view of the fireplace wall and the photos of his kids. His heart beat a little faster as he settled back into the chair. "I'm fine. I was just reading about Jeremy Fisher, the drunk driver in the accident."

"I read it too. So sad. He's been heading for this type of disaster for a long time."

"He has." John stared at the photographs on the mantel and let his eyes settle on Luke. "I keep thinking, what if the boy's parents had been around, helping him find the way?"

"Me too." She waited again. "Hey, how are your squash and tomatoes holding out?"

"I'm eating them." John smiled and tried to figure out his feelings. He and Elaine were comfortable friends, two people who had known each other for years. So why did things between them feel different now? He leaned hard on the right arm of the chair and shifted his gaze to the front window. It was dark outside, but he could still see the shadowy branches of the old oak tree. "I had fun the other day."

"It was nice, wasn't it?" She uttered a comfortable chuckle. "Conversations with friends are precious. I learned that after my husband died."

Cancer had taken Elaine's husband years before it took Elizabeth, so if anyone understood loneliness, Elaine did. John narrowed his eyes. "I'm finding that out myself." The song in the background changed, and a familiar melody surrounded him. "Sometimes I think I'll go crazy if I have another silent night in this old house."

"Exactly." In the background, he heard the clanking of dishes. "You know what I liked about being with you the other day?"

"What?"

"I liked your honesty." Her tone was less bubbly now, more thoughtful. "You're an honest man, John Baxter. Honesty means integrity, and that's not something you find too often anymore."

John tried to remember what they'd talked about that would have given her the impression he was honest. He sat up straighter. "Thanks, Elaine. That's kind of you."

"Well, it's true. You told me your concerns for Luke living with his wife and baby in New York City and about your hopes for Ashley and Landon." Her smile was audible in her voice. "I felt like I could see their lives playing out as you talked."

"Good." His heart was still beating faster than before. "That's the way it should be with friends."

They talked some more about the drunk driver and the funeral tomorrow. Neither he nor Elaine was going, but Elaine said she would call one of her friends who had a grandchild in CKT to get a report on how the kids in the group were doing.

Finally, after ten minutes of talking, Elaine got around to what must've been the real reason for her call. "The farmers' market runs again this weekend. If you need more squash and tomatoes, I'd love to go with you."

He laughed, trying to sound relaxed and unsurprised. "I'd love that, Elaine."

After that, the conversation ran down, and John agreed to pick her up Saturday morning.

Not until he hung up did he fully exhale. It was no big deal, right? Getting a call from Elaine Denning, agreeing to a second straight Saturday of visiting the farmers' market with her? Nothing out of the ordinary, nothing to think twice about, true?

He sat motionless for a moment and let those thoughts sink in. The horrible CKT accident had distracted him from thinking too hard about what his time with Elaine meant, or whether it was introducing a new friendship or a new season in his life. The fact was, spending last Saturday with Elaine had been a breath of fresh air. She'd talked about a wide range of issues with depth and interest, and she spoke with a candor and compassion that had caused the morning to pass too quickly.

But what did that mean? And why was he feeling like he should run to his room, find his wedding album, and stare at photos of Elizabeth? As if somehow he'd betrayed her by even thinking such things. He'd known Elaine a long time, so what was the big deal? He stared out the window again. The deal was, last summer they used to visit in a group. Now they were making plans for the second straight week to spend time alone together.

He stood and switched off the music. Maybe he would turn in

early and catch up on his reading. Something to distract him. The feelings mixing around in his mind were too confusing to sort through. But he was sure of one thing: he wasn't ready to think of Elaine in a future way, wasn't even ready to imagine having another relationship like the one he'd shared with Elizabeth. But maybe—just maybe—he was ready for something else.

A friendship that would bring some life back into his days and take the edge off the terrible silence.

CHAPTER ELEVEN

ASHLEY LOVED GOING OUT on her brother-in-law's boat, but rarely did all four of their schedules line up the way they did Thursday. Sarah Jo's funeral was set for late afternoon, but this morning Ashley and Landon and Cole met Kari and Ryan and their two children at the boat docks at Lake Monroe. Cole was missing school for the occasion. A fine layer of fog hung on the lake as they pulled out the boat just before nine.

The mood was quiet, somber. They had three fishing poles on board, but even Cole wasn't his usual talkative self. He didn't know all the details of the accident, just that it had happened and that his parents had somewhere to go later because of it. He wore a bright orange life jacket, and as soon as the boat began moving, he busied himself near the bucket of worms.

"I can't imagine what the families are going through." Kari settled into a seat near the windshield, taking advantage of the windbreak while she nursed little Ryan beneath a blanket. "I'd be so mad at the drunk driver."

Ashley sat a few seats away. "I talked to Katy again the other day. There's a lot of that. People want the guy locked up for a long time after what he did."

Ryan was at the wheel of the boat, and Jessie and Landon had joined Cole near the back, studying the worms.

Jessie looked squeamish. "Does the wormy hurt on the hook?"

Landon bit his lip to hide his smile, and Ashley did the same. "God made some worms for bait, Jessie. You don't need to worry, okay?"

"Okay." Still, she took a step back.

Kari adjusted baby Ryan and looked out at the lake. "How do you get past that?" She shifted her gaze to Ashley. "I mean, how do you move on and let it go? Some kid drank too much, and that's why your child's dead. It's so wrong."

"I feel for Katy Hart." Ashley slid closer to her sister. "Those kids are all looking to her. Some of the parents too."

"It's a lot." Kari stroked the back of little Ryan's head. "You're going to the funeral?"

Ashley nodded. "Landon's going with me. Dad's watching Cole." Her throat felt scratchy, and she blinked so she wouldn't tear up. "I saw *Tom Sawyer* a few times. I can still see Sarah Jo singing next to Tim Reed, her eyes all lit up. Her voice was amazing."

Kari kissed her son's forehead. "I'll bet she's singing right now."

Tears blurred Ashley's vision, but she smiled. "I like that." She sniffed. "That's the way I'll think about it."

Their conversation fell to a comfortable silence. As they moved farther out toward the middle of the lake, they picked up speed, and a cool wind blew over them. Ashley studied Landon and Ryan. They were smiling, pointing at something on the opposite shore, and sharing an occasional laugh. The picture warmed Ashley's heart. How wonderful that they were such good friends, that they gravitated toward each other in any setting.

Cole and Jessie were sitting near the back of the boat, their feet resting on the bucket of worms. Their life jackets bunched up around their necks, but that didn't stop the animated conversation they were having. Cole's eyes were wide and serious, and every few seconds he tapped the container of worms. Jessie would nod really big or shake her head.

"I love getting together like this." Ashley raised her voice so Kari could hear her over the sound of the boat. "Makes me wish Luke and Erin lived closer."

"Me too." Kari was finished nursing, and little Ryan was sleeping in her arms. "Or that Brooke and Peter could get away and do something like this more often."

Ashley stared out at the water. After a few minutes when they'd crossed the lake and found a place near a quiet cove, Ryan cut the engine. "Okay . . . let's see what sort of fish live on this side of the lake."

Cole started to clap his hands, but he caught himself. He held his finger to his lips. "Shhh." He peered over the edge of the boat. "The fishes might get scared and leave!"

"Here, buddy, hand me your rod." Landon moved in next to Cole and gave the worm bucket a light shake. "All right, find the fattest worm and let's get started."

"You mean, I get to pick out the worm all by myself?" Cole looked the way he did on Christmas morning, eyebrows raised, energy seeping from every pore.

"Yep." Landon moved the bucket closer to Cole. "Go for it."

"Yuck!" Jessie sat next to Kari. "Someone else do mine, okay?"

"I will!" Cole had both hands in the bucket, sifting through the rich loose dirt. After a few seconds, he pulled out a worm, sized it up, and held it straight out like a trophy. "This is the fattest one, Daddy!"

Ryan took a closer look. "I think he's right. That oughta snag you the biggest fish on the lake."

Ashley wore walking shorts and a sweatshirt over her tank top. The sun was breaking through a thin layer of clouds, so she kicked her feet up and leaned back. Kari and the baby were still beside her, and they stayed that way for the next hour, watching the kids fish, and once in a while getting up to admire a catch. In all, Cole and Landon caught three fish, and Jessie and Ryan caught two.

"But one of my two is the biggest of all," Jessie was quick to point out.

"I have one with a stripe on the side." Cole stuck his hand in the bucket of fish and ran his fingers along the side of the top one. "I'd rather have a stripey one than a big one, anyway."

"Cole . . ." Ashley raised one eyebrow in his direction. "You both caught nice fish."

"Just that mine is bigger, right, Aunt Ashley?" Jessie lowered her chin and batted her eyelashes at the moms and then at Cole. "That's okay, 'cause Coley's fish is nice too." She patted him on the back. "Even if it's smaller."

Ashley covered her smile and caught Kari doing the same thing. When she was sure she wasn't going to laugh out loud, she put her arms around both kids. "The important thing is, you both caught fish and now we get fish for dinner."

Cole wrinkled his nose at Jessie, and she giggled. "It's more fun to catch 'em, I think." He grinned at his cousin, and all was well between them.

On the way back, Ryan took the long way around the lake. The sky was bluer than before, the clouds relegated to the distant horizon. Ashley took her sweatshirt off and tied it around her shoulders. The sunshine felt good on her arms and face, and she thought again about Katy Hart and all the day would hold for her.

"I think I'll call Katy when we get back." Ashley brushed a section of her dark hair off her cheeks. "They're meeting back at the theater after the funeral so the kids can talk and share with each other. Sarah Jo's family wanted a quiet gathering alone back at their house."

"Maybe you can help set up at the theater." Kari leaned closer, her voice low. Little Ryan was still sleeping but every now and then he stirred. She cradled the baby closer. "What's the situation with Katy Hart, anyway? Is she seeing someone?"

Ashley hadn't told anyone but Landon the story about Dayne Matthews. She wouldn't have said anything to the people in CKT, but her sister could know. She drew a quick breath. "A couple months ago she was sort of involved with Dayne Matthews."

"The movie star?" Kari's voice jumped a notch, and she hushed herself. "Dayne Matthews? Hollywood's Dayne Matthews?"

Ashley laughed. "Most people don't know about it." She shrugged. "I guess he came to town for some reason, research or something. He stopped at the Bloomington Community Theater and saw her. When it came time to cast his next film he had his director look into her for the lead." Ashley angled her head so the light wind hit her face square on. "She went to Los Angeles a couple times, read for the part, and was offered the role. But then some fan of Dayne's attacked them near a private beach." She shook her head. "Katy came home and never looked back."

"Wow." Kari's mouth was open. "Things like that don't just happen."

"I know." Ashley squinted against the sun as Ryan turned the boat back toward the docks. "I think she still has feelings for him. But no, about your question, Katy isn't seeing anyone. She isn't lonely. I mean, she has the CKT families, of course. I think she's good friends with the CKT choreographer, Rhonda. But there's no guy in the picture."

"Hey—" Kari shifted and adjusted the blanket over little Ryan's face so the sun wasn't directly on him—"Dayne Matthews is coming to town; did you know that?"

"He is?" Ashley sat a little straighter and crooked her elbow around the side of the boat. The spray of the water on her arm felt wonderful. "What for?"

"I read it in the paper the other day. His new movie, I guess. He wants part of it set in a small town, and he picked Bloomington."

Ashley gave her sister a wry look. "Hmmm. I'll bet he's looking for more than a small-town atmosphere."

"Katy Hart?"

"Sounds like it." She brushed the water off her arm, leaned toward the rear of the boat, and flicked it at Landon.

He grinned at her and gave her a look that said he'd get her back at some point.

Kari laughed at the two of them. "So Katy doesn't know he's coming?"

"I don't think so." She slid back to her spot near Kari. "She didn't say anything. With the accident, I doubt she's been aware of much else."

At the back end of the boat, Landon pulled a skinny worm from the bucket of dirt and took four ominous steps in her direction. Ashley let out a scream, but Kari put her finger to her lips. "Shhh." She gave a pointed look to Landon. "You wake up the baby, you get to rock him back to sleep."

Landon considered it and then took another step toward Ashley, his arm outstretched, the worm dangling from his fingers. Ashley gripped the side of the boat and leaned back, slightly over the water. Then she mouthed the word *please*.

He stopped and laughed. Behind him, Cole and Jessie both giggled and gave each other high fives. Landon turned and dropped the worm back in the bucket.

"That was close." Ashley straightened up and exhaled hard. She wagged a finger in Landon's direction, but she could feel her eyes dancing. She loved teasing him, playing with him this way.

On the other side of Kari, Ryan was at the wheel but not unaware of the worm incident. He looked over his shoulder at Ashley. "You're lucky; you deserved it."

"I guess." Ashley laughed and shot an apologetic smile at Landon. "I did get him wet, didn't I?"

After the silliness passed, Kari's expression turned pensive. "That would be so tough, being a Hollywood star."

"It would." Ashley was breathless from her antics, but she settled into her spot and looked at her sister. "You couldn't go anywhere without being noticed or followed. And forget having any sort of normal relationship."

"Was that part of the problem for Katy Hart?"

"I think so. She said something about them being from two different worlds."

Kari nodded. "It's the truth." Baby Ryan woke and stretched his arms out from beneath the blanket. Kari held him up closer to her shoulder. "Ryan and I watched a Dayne Matthews movie the other day." She chuckled. "Luke was right. The two of them do look alike."

"I remember." Ashley recalled when Luke had come home for a visit and talked about Dayne's being a client at his law firm and how some of the guys at the office saw a resemblance between the two of them. She caught the spray from the lake and dusted it over her cheeks.

"Yeah, it's pretty amazing," Kari said. "I mean, it's not exact or anything, but they could be related."

"Funny." Ashley pulled her legs up and tucked her knees beneath her chin. "When will Dayne be here?"

"Next week, I think. Filming begins Tuesday or Wednesday, according to the article."

"Hmmm." Ashley shifted her gaze to the children. They were still mesmerized by the fish in the bucket, careful to stay seated. "Should be interesting."

"You think he'll contact Katy?"

Ashley hesitated. "Let's just say I saw something in Katy's eyes when she talked about him. If he feels the same way about her, he'll contact her. Probably the first day he's here."

"True." Kari bounced little Ryan. "Why else would he come to Bloomington for his small-town shots?"

"Exactly."

They reached shore, and the guys started collecting the fishing rods and buckets. Cole and Jessie gathered their sweatshirts and empty water bottles, and the group headed onto the dock.

Cole tugged on Ryan's shirt. "Thanks for taking me, Uncle Ryan. That side of the lake is way better for fishing."

Jessie ran up beside him. "And it's way better for catching big fish—like I'm good at catching." She smiled at Cole. "Right, Coley?"

He stuck his tongue out at her and then looked at Ashley to see if she was watching. When he saw that she was, he pulled his tongue back in and smiled at Jessie. "Right, Jess, that's 'zactly right."

The adults hid their chuckles again and said their good-byes.

On the ride home, Ashley and Landon talked about Dayne Matthews and his visit and the funeral later today and how much fun it had been to spend a morning fishing on Lake Monroe. As they headed up the sidewalk toward the house, Ashley let Cole run ahead and she pulled Landon close. It was warmer than usual, and it felt wonderful to stand there in each other's arms, the sun on their faces.

"Have I told you today how much I love you?" Ashley kissed him and pulled back enough to see his eyes. "I love watching you and Cole fish."

"And I love watching you." He touched his lips to hers, lingering long enough to stir the passion within her, a passion that belonged to Landon alone. "Let's go in so you can call Katy Hart." He kissed the tip of her nose. "Let me know if I can do anything too, okay?"

She loved that about him, that he understood exactly what she was thinking. Yes, she'd wanted to pull him aside and hug him, tell him how much she cared for him. Mostly because—other than the worm incident—they'd had little contact or conversation on the boat. But he was right. Her mind was thinking ahead to Katy Hart and how she was going to handle being strong for so many children tonight.

And something else: whether Katy knew that in the middle of the sadness and tragedy, Dayne Matthews was about to walk back into her life.

CHAPTER TWELVE

DAYNE FOUND OUT ABOUT THE ACCIDENT fifteen minutes after he arrived in Bloomington. His flight had landed in Indianapolis just before five o'clock, and this time he was careful renting his car.

He used his new driver's license that showed his middle name as his first name. *Allen Matthews*, it read. Between that and his baseball cap, the guy at the rental car counter didn't seem to catch who he really was. He did one other thing differently. He picked an inexpensive four-door sedan, a car without tracking technology. The first time he'd come to Bloomington, the paparazzi had found him because of the OnStar in his rented vehicle.

Not this time.

The press wouldn't expect him in Bloomington until early next week. It was only Thursday, and when he pulled into town it wasn't quite seven o'clock. He drove to the downtown area and tried to remember where the theater was, but his mind was going in a hundred different directions. He was here again, back in the place where his family lived, where he might've grown up if things had been different. Back in Katy Hart's town.

A redbrick elementary school stretched out on the right side of the road ahead of him. He turned into the empty parking lot and killed the engine. A warm breeze moved in the trees that lined the street. Dayne closed his eyes. What was it about this place? The other time he'd been here it had felt this way too, as if he were someone else, someone completely removed from the gossip and pressure and insanity of Hollywood.

He opened the windows and breathed the Indiana air deeply. It was clean and fresh and smelled faintly of newly cut grass. Two small boys on bicycles rode past, and a few feet behind them a smiling man and woman tried to keep up. The place was a living movie set for small-town America.

Until that minute he hadn't known what he was going to do with these days. Whether he would call the Baxters and tell them the truth or drive up and down the streets he might've grown up on. But now that he was here, now that the pink streaks in the sunset were fading to dark and the September evening was cooling fast, he knew without a doubt.

He wanted to find Katy, had to find her.

She had stayed in his mind since the last time he'd seen her, since the night he'd dropped her off at her hotel and told her good-bye. Through his handful of unanswered phone calls and his days with Kelly Parker and the weeks that had passed since, Katy had hidden away in his mind waiting for the right moment to take over again.

This was that moment.

He took his cell phone from the console beside him, flipped it open, and punched in her number. Even before it rang the call went to a voice mail. He snapped it closed and set it back down. The sound of children laughing filled the distant air, and he closed his eyes again. How was he supposed to find her? He had just a few days, no time to waste. The theater was an option, of course.

On a Thursday night the group might be there rehearsing or paint-ing sets. It was possible.

But he wasn't sure how to find it, and he didn't want to waste time driving around. Then it hit him. He could call the local paper, *The Bloomington Press*, the same publication that had run the re-cent story on his location filming. Reporters worked evenings every day of the week. They'd know the address of the theater and whether a play was in the works or not.

A minute later Dayne was being connected to someone in the arts department at the newspaper's office. A tired voice came on the line. "Life Section, can I help you?"

"Yes, I'm from out of town." He leaned back against the head-rest and stared at the darkening sky. "Could you tell me where the Bloomington Community Theater is?"

The reporter didn't perk up, but he rattled off the informa-tion, and when Dayne pressed him, he provided cross streets and directions.

"Could you tell me if the Christian Kids Theater has a play going on now?"

The man hesitated. "Christian Kids Theater?"

"Yes." Dayne caught a change in the man's voice, but he couldn't read it. "They did *Tom Sawyer* over the summer."

"I know the group." The man hesitated again. "They're working on a play, yes. But most of them attended a funeral today."

Dayne's heart fell to the floor of the car. *Funeral?* He leaned for-ward and took hold of the steering wheel. "Someone . . . someone in the group?"

"You didn't hear about the accident?" The man's tone was heavy. "Terrible car wreck almost a week ago."

All Dayne could see was Katy's face, her smile, the way her eyes had shone in the moonlight on the beach at Paradise Cove. He forced himself to ask the question: "Who . . . whose funeral?"

"A little girl, twelve years old. Sarah Jo Stryker. It's been all over the papers."

Sorrow and relief took turns within Dayne. Sarah Jo Stryker? The name sounded vaguely familiar, but Dayne couldn't help but think the obvious. At least it wasn't Katy Hart. "What . . . how did it happen?"

"Drunk driver. Hit a van with one mom and four kids the night of their auditions for *Annie*. One little boy died that night, a six-year-old. Sarah Jo died on Monday."

The mix of emotions turned to one—nausea. He had arrived in town smack in the middle of one of Katy's darkest hours. She loved the kids of CKT, loved them enough that she had returned to them without looking back. They were her life, and now tragedy had ripped a hole right through the middle of it.

"Hey, thanks for the information." Dayne sighed and pinched the bridge of his nose. "What time was the funeral?"

There was a pause and in the background the rustling of paper. "Five o'clock. Not sure how long it might've lasted."

Dayne thanked the man again and closed his phone. A drunk driver had done the damage? So Bloomington wasn't Mayberry after all. But it was small and close-knit. The entire community was probably touched by the accident.

Katy would be with the kids tonight, either still at the funeral or wherever they might've gone afterwards. There was only one place he could go, the place where he had seen Katy the first time. The Bloomington Community Theater. He turned the ignition key and followed the reporter's directions.

Five minutes later he had the building in view, straight ahead of him, the same old spires and turn-of-the-century architecture. The same marquee in front.

He had expected it to be dark, the parking lot empty. But a dozen cars were parked in a cluster, and a handful of people were leaving the theater. Dayne pulled in and parked near the back of the lot. He remembered the last time he did this—when he came to Bloomington to visit his birth mother, Elizabeth Baxter, at the hospital. Something about coming to this town switched him from the one being watched to the one watching.

The people leaving the theater didn't notice him. They moved slowly, and even when he rolled his windows down he couldn't hear their conversations. Over the next ten minutes several more left through the side doors, found their cars, and drove away. Finally there were just two cars left—a red two-door in the spot closest to the road and a white Jeep. Another few minutes passed, and two girls came through the doors.

For the second time tonight, Dayne felt his heart react. One of the girls was Katy Hart—he had no doubt. He'd spent time with her, watched her film, studied her audition tape enough to recognize her leggy figure, the way she moved, the way her straight blonde hair swished around her shoulders.

They hadn't spotted him yet, hadn't had any reason to look twice at the car parked in the lot. There were small downtown businesses all around the theater. He could've been anyone, an attorney or an accountant coming to put in a few late-night hours.

From where he sat he could see Katy's face, not well enough to tell if she was crying, but well enough to know she was sad. Her slumped shoulders and the occasional way she covered her eyes with her hands told him that much. Wherever the funeral had been, the theater was where the kids and Katy had come afterwards. Minutes went by, and finally the other girl hugged Katy; then she turned, climbed into the white Jeep, and drove off.

Katy walked around her car, and as she reached for the door, Dayne opened his and got out. She turned at the sound and spotted him. At first she didn't recognize him. Her eyes grew wide with fear, and she stepped back.

"Katy, it's me." He moved toward her, and when he was halfway there, he stopped and slipped his hands into his pockets. "Dayne. Dayne Matthews."

Her hands fell slowly to her sides, and she stared at him. In the glow of the parking-lot lights, he could see the disbelief in her expression. "How . . . how did you know?"

"I didn't." He took a few more steps and stopped three feet from her. The expression on her face made his heart ache. "We're filming here next week, and I . . . I just found out about the accident."

She hung her head and gave a subtle nod. Then she looked at him and lowered her brow, confused. "But how did you know I'd be here?"

"Just a guess." He took his hands from his pockets and folded his arms. The breeze was cooler now, and a chill ran down his back. "I didn't know where to go. I . . . wanted to see the theater again."

A long sigh came from her. "The funeral was beautiful. The saddest, most beautiful thing I've ever seen."

Dayne was through with pretenses. With his eyes locked on hers, he went to her and drew her into a hug, one that tore down the walls between them. Whatever it was about Katy Hart, whenever he saw her the connection was instant. It had been that way when he first spotted her at the end of a *Charlie Brown* performance at this very theater. And it had been that way in Hollywood when she first read for the part and later when she shot a scene with him.

The hug lasted a long time, and Dayne thought maybe she was crying. Finally, he allowed some space between them. He brushed her hair off her face. "I'm sorry . . . about the girl."

Katy sniffed. "She was my lead last summer." Her eyes shifted to the theater. "She played Becky Thatcher."

"I thought her name was familiar."

"Her mother was the worst . . . the worst stage mom I'd ever had." Katy made a sound that was part sob, part sigh. "She berated that girl day after day, wanting her to work harder, sing better, talk louder." Her eyes found Dayne's again. "All so she could have a future in theater." She eased out of his arms and leaned back against her car door. "You know what she told me?"

"The mother?" Dayne planted his feet at shoulder width apart, watching the emotions play on Katy's face. Sadness and grief . . . and now a sense of awe.

"Yes. She's barely out of the hospital herself, and she came up to me and hugged me." Katy crossed her arms tight around her waist. "She told me she wants to talk to the CKT families and tell them to hold on to today." Her eyes filled with fresh tears. "Because that's all any of us have."

Dayne felt as if a lead blanket were draped across the back of his shoulders. "A little late for Sarah Jo, is that it?"

"Yes." Katy dropped her chin and gave him a sad, crooked smile. "That girl wasn't allowed to enjoy one day of CKT. It was all—" she swallowed another sob—"all about what tomorrow held."

He waited a few seconds while she wiped her eyes. Then he nodded toward the theater. "How many kids came?"

"All of them." She smiled and looked at the theater again. "We talked and prayed and sang together." A car drove by, and Katy waited until it passed. "The kids of CKT have never been closer; I can tell you that."

"What about the drunk driver? What's his story?"

"He's just a kid, eighteen. Multiple offenses." Her expression darkened. "A lot of the older kids are struggling with that part. They want the guy to pay."

"I can understand."

"Me too." She straightened and took a sharp breath. "But I'm praying they change their minds. Hate never made anything better for anyone."

Dayne let her words find their rightful place in his heart, his soul. *"Hate never made anything better for anyone."* That was true, wasn't it? How many people had he hated or been angry at lately? His adoptive parents, his birth parents, the crazy murderous fan. Even God. All of them had harmed him in some way. He fingered the red bracelet on his wrist. That was the whole point of Kabbalah, wasn't it? Releasing negative emotions, moving on to the upper world?

"What's that?" Katy pointed to the red band around his wrist. She took hold of his hand and lifted it so she could see it better.

"A reminder, I guess." He wanted to hug her again, but he resisted.

"There're so many bracelets out now, you never know. Lance Armstrong has his yellow band, and there're a dozen different What Would Jesus Do bracelets." She released his hand. "What's it for?"

"It reminds me of what I'm going to do when I get back home."

"Which is?"

"Get closer to God." Dayne intended to sound more confident, but it was the first time he'd told anyone. Somehow putting the words together made him sound unsure—doubtful even. "Some of my friends are into Kabbalah, kind of a spiritual journey." He shrugged. "I'm interested—that's all I know."

"Kabbalah?" Alarm colored her eyes. "Weren't your parents missionaries? Christian missionaries?"

"They were." He gave her a serious sort of grin. "A lot of good it did them."

"So what exactly is Kabbalah?"

"It helps people get rid of negative emotions and find oneness with the creator."

"Hmmm." She sucked on the inside of her cheek, then clucked her tongue against the roof of her mouth. "I guess I didn't know you were searching."

He looked straight to the places his heart always found with her. "I wasn't. Not until you left." And just like that it was out there—the way he felt, the way he cared. The way he could never come close to getting her out of his mind. For a long time he said nothing. Then, his eyes still locked on hers, he said, "Don't you ever think about it, Katy? What might've been?"

She moved closer to him again and touched his arm. "I think of you, Dayne."

For a moment he considered kissing her. She was so close,

and with the truth laid out for both of them, the idea felt right. He steadied himself, keeping his distance this time. Then it hit him. No matter how right kissing her might feel, the timing was wrong. He crossed his arms and studied her. "How do you think of me?"

A different kind of sadness became clear in her eyes. "As someone I could never have loved." She tried to smile but failed. "I couldn't, Dayne. Our worlds are too different."

So there it was—the real reason. Nothing had changed. The fact that he'd shown up in Bloomington early or that they were standing in the theater parking lot on a September evening didn't erase the facts. He pulled on his acting face and chuckled. "Well, then—" he glanced over his shoulder—"I guess we should be glad there's no media out tonight."

"Right." She leaned back against the car again. "So you picked Bloomington, huh?"

"How could I not?" He was teasing her now, finding his way out of the emotional depths they'd been swimming in a few minutes earlier. He gestured to the horizon. "As far as I can see, Bloomington defines not just small-town America but America itself." He winked at Katy. "It's the perfect place."

"When do you start working?"

"Working?" Dayne pointed to himself. "Did I say I was working on the film? I brought it here, but actually—" he gave her another smile—"I'm thinking of quitting my day job."

She almost laughed, but the sadness from earlier still hung over her. "Then what'll you do?"

"Paint sets, you know, backdrops for community theater. That sort of thing." He pointed his thumb at the theater. "Think they're hiring?"

"I know I'm not." Another car passed by, this one with a rap song blaring. When it was gone, she gave him a partial grin. "I've got Ashley Baxter Blake, world famous painter, doing my sets."

"Ashley Baxter Blake?" Dayne felt the blood drain from his face.

Katy Hart had befriended his birth sister, one of the Baxter family? He could hardly believe it. If he hung around Katy and the theater long enough was it possible he might meet her, make a connection with her? The air was getting colder, and his knees began to shake. "Her mom died of cancer, right?"

"Right." Her eyes moved from curious to suspicious. "How'd you know that?"

For an instant, Dayne panicked. He hadn't thought about an answer, but the words came to him easily. "I heard about it last time I was here. Someone must've told me."

"Oh." Katy didn't question him. Maybe she was too distracted by the events of the day or too emotionally drained. "Ashley's amazing. The other CKT offices around the country want her to paint sets for them too—" she smiled—"not that she has time."

Dayne was still dizzy with the information, but he kept his composure. "Are you saying you don't have an opening for a sets painter?" He crossed his arms again. "I was really looking forward to a career change."

She giggled, despite the tearstains on her cheeks. "Maybe Ashley needs an assistant."

They talked about sets for a few more minutes, and then Dayne fell quiet. He'd come this far. He could ask to see her, couldn't he? "Hey . . ." His tone changed, and the humor faded. "I'm not busy until Tuesday morning. Can we spend some time together tomorrow? go for a walk somewhere maybe?"

The conflict played out in her expression. "Dayne, you have a girlfriend." Katy looked down at her feet and then lifted her eyes to his again. "I read the tabloids more than before. I like you a lot, but . . . we're so different."

Dayne tried to think of a comeback, but he had none. She was right. Their worlds were different, yes. But it was more than that. She was driven by morals and values and faith. He was just finding faith and living with Kelly Parker in the meantime. He had no right to mess with Katy's feelings. Still . . .

He took her hands in his. "I like you, Katy. I want to be your friend." He gave her a defeated grin. "Can't I have a friend in Bloomington, Indiana?"

Katy ran her thumbs over his hands, her eyes never leaving his. "Is that really all you want?"

Her question was deeper than it sounded; the look on her face told him as much. In that moment he made a decision. He wouldn't lie to her—not now or ever again. She deserved the truth, and if he gave it to her, whatever they shared, for however long they shared it, they'd both be better off in the process.

"No." He gave her hands a gentle squeeze. "That's not all I want. But it'll have to be enough."

Even in the dimly lit parking lot, he could see her blush, see the way his honesty affected her.

She looked away, but she didn't let go of his hands. "So . . . we see each other for a few days." Her voice was softer than before, scratchier. "What for? Why?"

"Because we can." He tapped her shoe with his and felt the corners of his mouth inch up. "Because it might give me an edge if I ever need a job as a set painter in Bloomington."

She couldn't contain a quick laugh.

Then without either of them saying another word, he pulled her into his arms and held her, running his hand over her back. "I want to spend a day with you, Katy. Before the rest of the crew arrives and everything changes again." He leaned back and searched her eyes. "Please?"

She thought for a while, glancing from the theater back to him again. When she finally nodded, she looked almost defeated. "Okay." She released his hands and took a step toward her car. "You still have my number?"

"Of course."

"Call me in the morning." She lowered her chin. Somehow she seemed shier than before. "We can go to Lake Monroe. We can take a walk around the shoreline."

They said their good-byes, and Katy walked around her car toward the theater again. "I left something inside."

"Want me to go with you?"

"That's okay." She raised her hand and gave him a small wave with her fingers. "Call me tomorrow."

He nodded and waved back at her. Then—feeling better than he'd felt in months—he climbed into his car and drove off toward the Holiday Inn at the edge of town. He'd registered under a false name, so he didn't expect any public scene at the check-in desk. No, he'd have all night to wonder about their conversation and the newest connection to Ashley Baxter Blake and the way Katy's hands had felt in his.

And the best part of all.

The fact that come morning he'd have an entire day with Katy in a place that might've been his if things had been different. A day when he wouldn't be Dayne Matthews, Hollywood star. Rather he would be something better and more difficult all at once.

Katy Hart's friend.

❧

Katy watched Dayne drive away, and she had the strangest feeling—as if he were taking a piece of her heart with him. That was ridiculous, of course, because even now, even in the midst of her saddest day since she'd lived in Bloomington, a day when seeing him had taken her breath away, she still knew the truth.

The two of them could have nothing together—not even a friendship. Yes, he was in Bloomington for a couple of weeks. But after that he'd go home to Los Angeles and slip back into his strange and unusual lifestyle. Paparazzi would follow him everywhere he went, and every week pictures of him and Kelly Parker would be on the cover of another magazine, shouting about how close they were, how in love.

Katy pulled her navy sweater tighter around herself as she

headed into the theater. Dayne wasn't in love with Kelly Parker. She could see that as easily as if he'd pasted the news on his forehead. Never mind that the world saw him as Dayne Matthews—cool, confident, movie star. She could see the truth. Dayne was confused and searching and unsure about what to do next.

Searching for God? She frowned as she slipped her key in the door, opened it, and turned on the lobby lights. The red bracelet looked familiar, but she couldn't place it. Several big-name Hollywood stars were part of the Kabbalah movement. Dayne had mentioned it, but she hoped his search wasn't leading him in that direction. From the little she'd heard about the group, it was almost cultlike. She hoped Dayne had enough training when he was a young boy to stay away from anything like that. She'd ask Jim and Jenny Flanigan. She knew they had once taken a course on modern religions, so they'd know about Kabbalah.

Not until she was inside the theater house area and sitting in her favorite spot—third row, center section, end of the aisle—did she let herself exhale. How had she missed the fact that Dayne was coming to Bloomington to film the location scenes for his movie? He'd talked about it back when she was reading for the part, but once she was out of it, she figured he'd find somewhere else.

Seeing him tonight, watching him walk up to her was like something from a dream. And she did dream about him, more often than she talked about or admitted to herself. He might as well live on Mars for how different their lives were. It was the reason she hadn't returned his phone calls. There was no point holding on to whatever it was she'd felt with him last summer. *Put him out of your mind*, she'd told herself a hundred times. Then maybe her feelings for him would fade.

But she'd been wrong.

That much was clear the minute she saw him in the parking lot. He had obviously waited, waited until Rhonda and the others were gone. Whatever time they shared while he was in Bloomington would be kept between the two of them. She gripped the cool wood seat and stared at the empty stage. It was dark and shadowy, like her motives for agreeing to see Dayne in the morning.

Every bit of her common sense told her to tell him no. But common sense had nothing to say about the way he made her feel when they were together. The connection was strong, immediate, the way it had been the first time she talked with him at the Los Angeles studio. In the end she figured it couldn't hurt. Spending a day with Dayne would make it harder to forget him, but it would be nice all the same. Walking with him, talking about his life and his curiosity about faith. Sharing about the accident and the funeral.

She could use a day like that, even if it never happened again.

A draft came over her, and she squinted into the darkness. The heavy velvet curtain swayed ever so slightly, and shadows danced on the stage. She'd told Dayne the truth about coming back inside the theater.

She'd forgotten to have her own private good-bye where Sarah Jo Stryker was concerned.

The funeral had been beautiful. Several people spoke, and at the end, Alice Stryker made her way to the podium and told everyone in attendance to live for the day.

"You can't find your way back to yesterday," she told them. Tears streamed down her cheeks as she talked, but her voice was clear. "And you can't know what tomorrow will bring." She paused and looked around the room at the faces of parents and children who had become important to Sarah Jo in such a short time. "But you have today. Make the most of every minute, because . . . because . . . well, it might be your last."

Pastor Mark Atteberry had given the eulogy. He talked about Sarah Jo finding her place in the choir of heaven, singing for Jesus, bringing a smile to His face.

The memory of the funeral service faded, and Katy swallowed back her emotion. Pastor Mark was right. Sarah Jo was happy and free now, happier about singing than ever before. But that didn't make her loss any easier to bear.

Katy stared at the stage, and her vision blurred. She was no longer sitting in a cold, dark theater by herself. Rather she was surrounded by fans, watching Sarah Jo take the stage on closing night. Her voice had a way of knocking people back in their seats, awestruck that so beautiful a sound could come from such a young girl. But that wasn't all. In the time it took her to work through rehearsals and complete the run of the show with CKT, something had changed in Sarah Jo's eyes.

On closing night for *Tom Sawyer*, Katy had seen it clearly. Sarah Jo had learned to love singing. No matter what her mother thought or how she'd been trained to think of every performance as a stepping-stone to something bigger and better, Sarah Jo sang that last night with reckless abandon, with all her heart, as if it were the final performance of her life.

Which it was.

Trails of hot tears pressed their way down Katy's cheeks, and she didn't stop them. Whenever she was alone in this place she would always see Sarah Jo the way she looked that night, her eyes shining, voice ringing out for all of heaven to hear. But everyone would have to live with the saddest truth of all. Forevermore, the rich sound of CKT would have one less voice in its mix.

And the song would never be the same again.

❧

Jeremy Fisher was alone in his jail cell, hunched over on a narrow wooden bench. His fingers shook, rustling the old newspaper the warden had given to him. Now—as they'd been for the past hour—his eyes were stuck on a front-page headline that read "Drunk Driver's Tragic Past Recounted."

Three times he'd let his eyes drop farther down the page into the article that told his story. But most of the time he just stared at the headline and tried to remember how to swallow, how to breathe.

Drunk driver? Was that really him, the one who had slammed his truck into a van full of little kids? He shuddered, and nausea welled up inside him. The cell smelled of urine and sweat, a constant reminder that yes, he really was that drunk driver. And this was his new reality.

His dad knew part of the truth now, but it didn't matter. The old man was serving as an army commander in Iraq. Jeremy guessed he could get a leave if he wanted to, but he'd only wired a simple message saying he'd be home in three months. They could deal with it then. In the meantime there was no money, no one to bail him out or get him a lawyer.

Not that he deserved one.

He pushed his fingers up his forehead into the mass of brown curls. Since the accident, a million times each day he tried to remember what had happened, why he'd drunk so much in the first place and how come he'd thought he could make it home. But it was like it had happened to someone else altogether.

It wasn't just the memories from that night that were gone. He couldn't piece together anything from the week leading up to the accident, and he understood why. He'd been stone drunk for all of it, drunk to the point of blacking out.

A public defender had been by to see him today, and he'd said something that stayed with Jeremy. "Maybe you were trying to kill yourself." The attorney was matter-of-fact. "Ever think about that?"

Jeremy hadn't thought about it until then, but now that he had time to mull over the idea, the guy probably had a point. Or maybe he wasn't trying to kill himself; maybe he was just trying to erase the loneliness. Not that he'd ever tell anyone else that. Loneliness sounded like an excuse, and there was no excuse for what he'd done. None whatsoever.

So what if his father had been called up in the first batch of reservists? Never mind the fact that less than a year before that he'd been laid off from his job as a sheet-metal worker, or that his mother had run off to New Mexico with an old boyfriend a few months after his father left. Lots of high school kids lived with little or no contact with their parents. So why had he started partying so hard? And why had he dropped out of school without telling his father?

The old man had e-mailed him every few days, but Jeremy never told him the truth. Not that he'd struggled in school or that he'd dropped out or that he couldn't find his way from morning to night without drinking so much that he was surprised when he woke up each day.

Even now, his dad didn't know all the details. He knew Jeremy had been arrested for drunk driving but not that two kids had died.

The nausea doubled.

Two kids. A little boy, six years old, and a girl—barely twelve. He'd driven his truck over the yellow line and shattered two families forever. He stood and moved to the bars that held him inside the cell. His fingers wrapped around the cold metal, and he hung his head. The system could spare him a trial. He was guilty as sin, guilty with no hope of forgiveness.

Whether they set him free or locked him up forever, the jail bars would stay with him. Each morning and at every breakfast, every time he climbed into his old jeans or brushed his teeth, every bit of every day the truth would stay with him like a demon on his shoulder.

He was a murderer.

Two kids were dead because of him.

A trial wouldn't prove anything, it wouldn't make things right for him and his father, and it wouldn't bring healing to the families who'd lost so much. It wouldn't bring the kids back. He banged his head softly on the cell bars and gritted his teeth. A trial would never be enough and neither would a life sentence.

Only one thing would bring him release at this point—the one thing he'd hoped for since he sobered up that terrible Saturday morning. The only thing that would make everything right again.

His quick and certain death.

CHAPTER THIRTEEN

THE DAY AFTER SARAH JO'S FUNERAL, Clear Creek High happened to have a late start scheduled. Jenny Flanigan was grateful. In the haze of sorrow and grief from the past week, she'd spent almost no time alone with Bailey. They'd been together in groups, and dozens of CKT kids had hung out at their house every day since Monday. But she and Bailey had a closer relationship than most mothers and daughters. They needed their time together.

Now it was eight thirty, and the boys were off to elementary school. Bailey came downstairs, dressed in jeans and a long-sleeved shirt, her hair curled. "Hi, Mom."

"Hi." Jenny was sipping coffee, sitting at one of the barstools along the kitchen island. She studied her daughter and felt a small burst of happiness. The circles under her eyes told how hard she'd cried the day before, but this morning her eyes held something they hadn't for a week.

Fresh hope.

Bailey poured a bowl of cereal and sat at the bar next to Jenny.

"I wish every day was a late start." She blew at a wisp of hair and smiled. "I could get used to sleeping in until seven."

Jenny slid her fingers around the warm coffee mug. "You doing okay?"

Bailey finished her bite of Corn Chex and nodded. "Better." She glanced out the back kitchen window to the view of their pool. "Sad as it still is, it felt good spending a week with my CKT friends." She looked at Jenny and rolled her eyes. "Took me out of the real-life drama at school."

"What do you hear?" Jenny leaned onto the counter, watching her daughter's eyes. Bailey told her everything. She knew who was seeing whom and which freshman was making the decision to drink or smoke marijuana. She and Bailey shared a code of honor, a trust that what they talked about stayed between them.

"Okay, get this." Bailey shook her head and ate a quick bite of cereal. "Melissa's mom had a few of the cheerleaders over the other night." Bailey waved her hand in the air above her. "Every one of their mothers thought it was this innocent sleepover, right? Well—" she paused—"the girls snuck into Melissa's mom's vodka, and they all took turns doing shots."

"On a school night?" Jenny felt her stomach turn. "Which girls?"

"The usual drinkers, you know, half the cheerleader squad. But this time Abbie joined them." Bailey's expression fell. "Mom, she's so stupid. She'd never had alcohol before."

The sick feeling doubled. "Why did she?"

"She says it's 'cause I wasn't there." Bailey stirred her cereal. "If I was there she wouldn't have. So I feel terrible, but what could I do? I had Sarah Jo's funeral."

"Honey . . ." Jenny put her hand on Bailey's shoulder. "You don't have to think like that. Abbie can't have you by her side every minute. At some point these kids have to make the right decisions on their own."

"I know." She planted her elbow on the counter and sighed. "Why do they think drinking's so great?"

Conversations like this one happened more often with Bailey, and lately Jenny had wondered if she was making the right decision by keeping quiet about what she knew. She and Jim had talked about it, agonizing over the fact that if Bailey was out drinking they'd want someone to tell them. Still, at this age, most kids—kids without a strong family faith and even some with a strong faith—were lying to their parents. And the parents seemed to prefer being in the dark to knowing the truth about what their teenagers were doing.

Bailey went on. "Look how stupid they're being, Mom. And they don't even care." She exhaled hard. "Sometimes it seems that by next year, Tanner and I will be the only ones not throwing our lives away. I mean, what's the big deal about drinking?"

"Especially after the accident." Jenny sat straighter and finished what was left of her coffee. "Alcohol killed those kids, after all."

Her eyes flashed at that. "No, Mom. Alcohol didn't kill them. Jeremy Fisher did."

"The drunk driver."

"Yes." Anger colored her tone, and she clenched her fists. "Some of the other kids at CKT and I want to do something, make an example of him."

Bailey was right, of course. Jeremy Fisher needed to be punished. But the anger in Bailey's voice worried Jenny. Bailey sounded as if the only solution for the young man was a cold, hard, determined revenge.

Jenny stood, walked to the kitchen sink, and rinsed her coffee mug. "Bailey . . ."

"What?" There was still an edge to her voice.

Jenny looked over her shoulder. "Leave room for God to deal with Jeremy Fisher."

Bailey's shoulders dropped a few inches. "Meaning we shouldn't try to keep him in jail? Mom, if he drives a car again, he'll kill someone else."

Jenny turned and leaned against the sink. "I'm not saying we should look the other way." Her voice was calm. Justice and grace were hard concepts for anyone, especially for a person young in her faith. "I just think it isn't healthy to harbor a lot of hatred toward the drunk driver. God would want you to spend your time loving the people he hurt or being an example for kids like Abbie." She hesitated. "Don't you think?"

Bailey shrugged. She held the cereal bowl to her lips and drank what was left of the milk. When she was finished she cocked her head, her eyes filled with steely determination. "I think all that. But I think he should be punished too." She stood, left her bowl on the bar, and grabbed an apple from the fruit basket near the refrigerator.

Jenny watched her daughter for a few moments. This wasn't the time to push the issue. Instead she drew a slow breath. "You and Tim have talked a lot this week."

"I know." She took a bite of the apple, her expression pensive. After she'd chewed and swallowed it she nodded. "About that Tim Reed." She grinned, the anger from a few seconds earlier gone. "Sometimes I think I like him so much. Other times—" she lowered the apple and looked at the ceiling—"other times all I can see is Tanner smiling at me across the commons area at school."

Tanner Williams had been Bailey's friend since fourth grade, and now that they were in high school, his interest in her was at an all-time high. He was a good kid, quarterback of the football team, one of the few who didn't drink or smoke. He and Bailey had gone to homecoming together.

Jenny wasn't sure which Bailey liked more about Tanner. The fact that he had stolen her heart when she was only ten years old or the idea that he was safe.

Bailey looked at her. "Tanner called last night. We talked for almost an hour."

"Was that a good thing?" Jenny didn't want to push. The relationship she shared with Bailey was something her daughter had always wanted. No prodding or digging for information was

needed on Jenny's part. Bailey shared the details of her life will-
ingly, and when people asked her who her best friend was, she
always said the same thing: "My mom."

Now Bailey grinned. "Very good."

The doorbell rang, and then they heard the door open. "Hi,
it's me!"

"Cody," Jenny whispered to her daughter.

"I know." She raised her eyebrows and straightened her shirt.
He rounded the corner and waved at them. He wore Wrangler
jeans and a white T-shirt. His dark hair was short, and his dimples
seemed to cut all the way through his cheeks when he smiled.

Bailey met him halfway and gave him a quick hug. "You haven't
been by for a while."

"I knew you were busy." He looked at Jenny. "The accident and
all." His expression was respectfully somber. "The girl's funeral
was yesterday, right?"

"Yes." Bailey returned to her spot at the bar. She anchored her
feet on the highest rung. No matter what she said about Tanner
or Tim, she still had a crush on Cody Coleman. He'd lived with
them for three weeks at the end of his freshman year, back when
his mother wasn't able to care for him. He would always feel like
part of the family. Bailey gripped her knees, her eyes still on him.
"It was so sad."

"I bet." Cody opened the fridge and found the milk. He poured
a glass and faced Jenny. "Makes me hate drinking; I can tell you
that much."

"I hate it too." Bailey had the angry look again. "It makes all of
us hate it. The guy should stay in jail forever after what he did."

For a moment, Cody looked concerned, as if maybe some of
Bailey's intensity might be focused on him. Then his expression
changed, and he crossed the room and took the stool next to
Bailey's. "Hey—" he looked around her to Jenny—"when can I
have my old couch back?"

"Your old couch?" Jenny laughed. "Cody, you're always welcome here. You know that. It's your mother you need to check with." She paused, her tone more serious. "She's okay, right?"

"Yeah, she's fine." He grinned at the two of them. "My mom needs me. I just wanna make sure I'm still part of the family."

Jenny watched him and breathed a prayer of thanks. *God . . . he's come so far. Thank You for changing his heart.*

She felt a lump in her throat at the memory of all he'd been and all he was today. Cody had come to them as a freshman with nowhere to turn, someone who drank heavy amounts every day. Now he was a junior, the most talented receiver on Jim's team at Clear Creek. He would always be an alcoholic, but it had been a year since he'd touched a drink. Jenny watched him stretch out his legs. God was beyond faithful, always, all the time.

"You're still part of the family, Cody." Jenny walked past Bailey and patted Cody on the back as she made her way to the dishwasher. A few bowls were stacked around the sink, so she loaded them. Then she turned around and faced him. "Your mother's staying away from drinking?"

The shadows in Cody's eyes told the answer before he could speak. He shrugged. "Most of the time." He pursed his lips, and the muscles in his jaw flexed a few times. "I'm always on her, telling her to get to her meetings."

Jenny nodded. "That's all you can do."

"That and pray, right?" Cody's eyes got big. "Speaking of which, I wanna go back to church with you guys again. That big place across town won't cut it for me." He grinned. "Lots of girls, but not enough God. Know what I mean?"

"I do." Jenny loved that Cody felt this comfortable around them, at ease enough to share exactly what was on his heart and mind. After a lifetime of doubting God, he'd been trying churches for the last month. She wasn't sure how much he understood or whether he was ready to make a commitment, but at least he was interested. "We go Saturdays at 5:30. Just show up at five and you can come whenever you want."

"Good." Cody looked at Bailey. His tone was sensitive, as if he suddenly remembered the funeral again. "You okay?"

"Mmm-hmm." She smiled. "I know where Sarah Jo Stryker is. She asked Jesus into her heart after *Tom Sawyer* finished last summer."

He tapped her knee. "Good girl, Bailey. You tell everyone about Jesus. I wish I would've known what you know about God when I was your age."

She looked deep into his eyes for a moment. "I wish that, too, Cody." Bailey was always quieter around him. As if she was reluctant to say something immature. The corners of her mouth lifted, even as shyness came over her. "The good news is, He's always known you."

"Right." Cody stood and stretched his hands over his head. "And one of these days I might actually find Him too." He motioned toward the family room. "Can I check out ESPN?"

"Go ahead." Jenny snagged the newspaper from the farthest kitchen counter. "Bailey has to finish the dishes, and I have the paper to read." She gave her daughter a pointed look. "Okay, miss, let's take care of your bowl and the pans from last night."

"Ugh." Bailey made a face. As close as they were, she struggled with helping around the house. She was always being reminded to do the dishes or clean her room or help fold laundry. When Cody was out of earshot, she looked over her shoulder at Jenny, her eyes all lit up. Then she mouthed the words *he's so gorgeous!*

Jenny rolled her eyes this time. She gave a mock stern look to her daughter and pointed at the sink. "Enough boy talk," she whispered. "Do the dishes."

Bailey laughed, and Jenny opened the paper. A story on the front page detailed Sarah Jo's funeral and the hundreds of students and families who remembered her. Jenny read it. Amazing how much that girl had touched the community. Her story about how she had sung so beautifully in *Tom Sawyer* had been run and rerun in the paper and played on local television news.

The part that stuck out today was at the end of the article. Katy Hart was quoted as saying, "Sarah Jo's song will play out forever and ever because she believed in Jesus Christ. That's the way it is with people who have Him as their Savior."

Jenny loved that about the local paper. This was middle America, and the reporters weren't afraid to tell it like it was. Even if the truth involved Jesus. Jenny turned the page and drifted past articles on a new local park and the funding needed for a new grade school.

She turned to the Life Section next, and halfway down the page something caught her attention. The headline read "Dayne Matthews and Crew Slated to Start Local Filming." This was the first she'd heard of Dayne Matthews coming to town. The article was brief, stating that the cast and crew for Dayne's upcoming film, *Dream On*, would arrive in town on Monday and begin filming on Wednesday. The location shooting was scheduled to last two weeks.

An hour later, after Bailey had gotten a ride to school with Cody, Katy came down from her garage apartment. She looked ready to head out somewhere. Like Bailey, her eyes were still a little swollen.

Jenny held up the kettle. "Coffee?"

"Not today." Katy slung her bag over her shoulder. "I have a meeting."

Jenny lowered her chin. "With Dayne Matthews?"

Katy didn't set her bag down or jerk back. But something subtle in her eyes gave her away. She blinked. "You know?"

"I know he'll be here by Tuesday." She motioned to the folded newspaper. "I figured he might've come in a few days early."

"He did." Katy took her cell phone from her bag and set the bag on the desk. Then she came to Jenny, her eyes dark. "I saw him last night. After everyone left the theater. He'd heard about Sarah Jo's funeral and didn't know where to find me. He drove to the theater on a hunch and because he wanted to see it again. We talked for a while." She made a face that said she was uncomfortable with the situation. "He wants to see me today."

Jenny kept from showing any disapproval. She didn't know Dayne Matthews, but she knew the sort of life he lived. It wasn't a life Katy wanted any part of, here or in Hollywood. She kept her tone even. "What did you tell him?"

"I told him yes. I'm picking him up at his hotel and taking him to Lake Monroe." Katy studied the folded newspaper. "He seems different, Jenny. I think he wants to change. He's even searching for God." She paused. "What do you know about Kabbalah?"

"Hmmm." Jenny worked to keep the alarm from her voice. "A lot of Hollywood actors are into it. To be honest, Katy, that's some scary stuff. Have you researched it?"

"Not yet."

"They believe they can attain equality with God." One of Jim and Ryan's former NFL teammates had gotten into it. She and Jim had taken a modern religion class at church so they could talk to the player about God's real plan for life and spirituality. She still remembered the basic flaws in the Kabbalah teachings. "It's very contrary to Scripture."

"I didn't know that." Katy opened the paper and scanned the page until she saw the article. After a minute she said, "He'll be here for two weeks still; that's what the story says." She set the paper down. "I'll research Kabbalah and talk to him. I know it has to be a lot different than how he was raised."

"How was he raised?"

"By missionary parents."

Jenny smiled. "Then I'd say it's a lot different." She paused, letting Katy get her bearings. "Do you have feelings for him?"

Katy sighed and clutched her cell phone between her hands. "I've spent all night asking myself that." She glanced at the newspaper on the counter again. "He's a public figure, Jenny. There couldn't be any future with him." She looked up. "But there are feelings. For both of us."

Her cell phone rang, and for a moment their eyes locked and Katy did nothing. Then in a rush she flipped it open and said, "Hello?"

Jenny watched her expression change, and she knew. It was Dayne; it had to be. She'd never seen Katy respond that way before. She raised her eyebrows at Katy. "Dayne?"

Without breaking the conversation, Katy nodded. Then, still talking, she picked up her bag, waved at Jenny, and left through the front door. At the same time, Jim bounded in through the back door. He had gotten up early to tackle a persistent spread of blackberry bushes. They grew up around the back fence every year, and every fall Jim cut them down to the roots.

It was hard work, but he loved it. He was in his element outdoors, and every year he talked about selling everything, moving to Montana, and buying a thousand-acre horse ranch. Jenny would listen patiently, then remind him that the football season was under way, or just around the corner, or that spring weightlifting and quarterback camps had started.

And always he would laugh and tell her he was only kidding. He couldn't leave the kids at Clear Creek, not when they were still building such a successful program. The head coach was Ryan Taylor, and Jim was his top assistant. Jim's time was spent tending to their real-estate investments from his old NFL days, meeting with other coaches and kids for prayer and Bible studies, and coaching the Clear Creek Cougars.

There didn't seem to be any change on the horizon.

He came up behind her, wrapping his arms around her shoulders. "Mission accomplished! No more blackberry bushes."

She breathed in the smell of him, musky dirt and faded aftershave. "Until next year."

"Right." Some of his enthusiasm faded. "Until next year."

"Ahhh, honey—" she turned and slipped her hands around to the small of his back—"I didn't mean to ruin the moment."

"No." He was playing with her, trying to sound like a victim.

"It's okay. I spend three hours in the fields and you shoot me down."

She giggled. "I love that you tease me." She pulled him closer. "Isn't it fun? Being married like this?"

He brought his lips to hers and kissed her, long and slow. His chest still heaved from the field work and the fact that he'd probably jogged the whole way across their several acres to the house.

When they came up for air, he grinned at her and traced her upper lip with his finger. "I still can't believe you said yes."

"I can't believe you asked."

They kissed again, and he gave her another hug before moving on to the cupboard. "I'm starved." He found a box of Cheerios and set it on the counter. "How was Bailey this morning?"

"Better." Jenny sat on a barstool. She rested her elbow on the granite top and rested her chin in her hand. "The CKT kids are going to be okay. Things like this only bring those kinds of kids closer together."

"Mmmm, you're right." He poured a bowl of cereal and topped it with milk. Then he took the stool beside her. "Is she still angry about the drunk driver?"

"Furious." Jenny shuddered. "It scares me a little."

He put his spoon down and set his hand on her shoulder. "She'll be all right. It's normal to feel that way."

"I guess." She met his eyes. "Dayne Matthews is coming to town. Did you see that in the paper?"

"Yesterday." He took a bite, his attention still on her.

"It was in again today." She sat up and laid her forearms on the counter. "Katy's spending today with him."

"Really?" Jim finished chewing, but there was worry in his eyes. "Is that a good thing?"

"I don't know." Jenny sighed. She reached out and took hold of his free hand. "Do you know how much I love you, Mr. Flanigan?"

"More now that the blackberry bushes are down?" His eyes twinkled, and he chuckled despite the bite of cereal in his mouth.

"Well, yes. A little more, maybe." She laughed. "No, seriously. I would hate to be single again. I think about Bailey and Katy, and all I want for them is this."

"Cheerios in the morning?"

She gave him a teasing look, took the spoon from him, and set it in his bowl. Then she stood and framed his face with her hands. "This, Jim. I want them to find someone who loves God first and them second."

"Doesn't sound very romantic, does it?" He made a funny face at her.

"It is, though." She leaned in and kissed him. "What we have is everything romance and marriage are supposed to be. But it's rare, Jim. A few people find it, and that's all." She searched his eyes, and in them she saw that he understood. "I want this for Katy and Bailey, because they deserve this type of love. It's what they've prayed for all their lives."

Jim raised one eyebrow. "Bailey's a little young, don't you think?"

She gave him a playful whack on the shoulder. "Not yet, but soon. You know what I mean. The years go way too fast. Sometimes I see her look at Cody Coleman or Tanner Williams, and I wonder if any of the guys she knows could ever grow up to love her the way you love me. The way you love God."

"Honey—" he kissed first her right cheek, then her left—"God figured things out for the two of us." He angled his head, and a lighthearted knowing look filled his eyes. "He'll figure things out for them too."

"Even for Katy?" Jenny knew better than to doubt. But Dayne Matthews? What girl could resist a guy like him? Even if being with him made no practical sense at all?

Jim pushed his cereal bowl to the side and pulled her close. They kissed, and then he whispered low to her, "Yes, love. Even for Katy."

Something in his tone told her that he was right—she had nothing to worry about. Wherever Katy and Dayne spent the day,

God would be there. And He would give Katy the same sense He'd given her. Sense enough to recognize when a man was the best thing to come her way.

And sense enough to run like crazy when he wasn't.

CHAPTER FOURTEEN

DAYNE AND KATY WERE ONLY a hundred yards into the lake trail when Dayne changed the conversation from talk about the weather and the water and the benefits of living along the shore. He couldn't keep things surface between them, not when every step he took felt like a dream.

They wore T-shirts and jeans, with sweatshirts tied around their waists in case a wind came up over the water. But a tornado could pass by and he wouldn't notice. Not when he was completely consumed with her. How could he be here in Bloomington, hiking a dirt trail around a pristine lake with Katy Hart at his side? It didn't seem real, like something from a dream or a movie. With every minute that passed he felt more taken by her, more aware of her presence. She was everything he'd ever wanted, even if he could never have her.

But now, as they hit the official trailhead and tossed their empty Starbucks cups into a trash can, he had questions. "So what've you been doing, Katy? Seeing anyone?"

He expected her to look away or tell him that she'd fallen in love. That would help explain why she hadn't returned his calls. But instead she giggled, and her arm brushed against his. As laughter filled her eyes, she looked more beautiful than he'd ever realized before.

"Either you're dating a comedian—" he was comfortable with her, his words unhurried—"or I missed something."

"You missed the RPSer." She caught her breath and grinned at him. "I met him the night of auditions. He was ready to get married the next day, I think."

"Really?" Dayne could see she was joking and that she had no interest in the guy. Still, he hated the idea of someone else moving in on her. "What's an RPSer?"

"That's what I asked." She stopped and turned toward him. "The guy's an expert at rock-paper-scissors." She held out her hand and pounded it with her other fist. "Remember that game kids played at school way back when?" She shook her head. "All he could talk about was strategy and talent and whether I'd caught him in the finals on ESPN."

"You didn't, right?"

"Of course not." She made a face at him. "I thought the guy was joking. An RPSer? I tell you, Dayne, the pickings are slim here in Bloomington."

He stopped and waited until she did the same and their eyes met. The mood between them changed, and Dayne was glad. He might have only one day to tell her how he felt. He didn't want to spend the whole time joking around. "Can I tell you something, Katy?"

"What?" Her eyes held his, waiting.

"They're slim in Hollywood too."

"Well . . ." A wall went up in her eyes. She gave him a smile that told him she wasn't ready to bare her heart. Not yet, anyway. "Good thing you have Kelly, then, huh?"

He opened his mouth, but nothing came out. Touché, he wanted to tell her. Instead he winced. "Yeah." He set his feet in motion again, and she fell in beside him. "Good thing."

They walked a little more, and then Katy glanced at him. "Tell me about your parents. I have a friend whose parents are missionaries. She says it's sort of like being a pastor's kid. Lots of scrutiny, that type of thing."

For all the connections he had in the entertainment industry and all the people he talked with on a daily basis, this was one topic that never came up. The story of his parents and him, the tale of his childhood. But it wasn't the time to talk about that, was it? Katy wouldn't want all the details. She was only trying to be friendly.

He made flirty eyes at her. "Yeah, we missionary kids were a lot of work—I can tell you that. Getting our languages mixed up and never knowing first thing in the morning if we should eat or hit the fund-raising trail."

She laughed but only briefly. "Come on. I'm serious, Dayne. What was it like?"

Her questions had a way of peeling back the layers, exposing another time and place when he was just a kid being raised by strangers because his parents were busy telling people about Jesus. He really didn't want to talk about it, but they had all afternoon. Clouds had rolled in overhead, and the trees that lined the path cast dark shadows on the trail. He caught her eyes. "You really want to know?"

"Yes." They slowed their pace. "Can you remember anything else? Before they were missionaries, you know, when you were really young?"

"Funny, I've asked myself that." He kicked at a few loose rocks and slid his hands into his pockets. "But there's nothing. They signed up for work in Indonesia when I wasn't quite four years old."

The look in Katy's eyes told him she disapproved. "You were just a baby."

"I was old enough for boarding school." He wanted to keep the story light, but it didn't feel that way. Not after stuffing the details in the dark places of his heart for so many years. He had the outside edge of the trail, and he looked past her through the trees to the lake. "Actually, it was a nice place. Clean and safe, good people working there."

His story began to unfold, slowly at first and then with more imagery and detail. He was six when he realized that he and the others in his class didn't live like other American kids.

Dayne and his parents went back home on furlough that year and had three months in Detroit, Michigan, attending the church that supported them. That Christmas, one of the boys in his Sunday school class talked about playing family games at the dinner table each night.

"At school, you mean?" Dayne sat cross-legged in the circle, confused. "Dinner happens at school, right?"

The other children gave him funny looks, and one little girl laughed out loud. "No, silly," she said. "Dinner happens at home with your mommy and daddy."

Apparently the Sunday school teacher knew about Dayne's background, because she took control of the moment. "Children, some boys and girls live with their friends and their teachers. It's called boarding school." She smiled at Dayne. "That's where you live, right?"

He nodded, but he felt strange and different.

The teacher went on. "Dayne's parents go around the jungles of Indonesia—far, far away from the United States—and they tell people about Jesus."

One of the girls said it best, said something that had stayed with Dayne ever since. No matter how far he traveled from that time, he could still hear what she said next: "Why don't his mommy and daddy stay home and teach *him* about Jesus? That way they could play games at the dinner table."

Indeed.

His next memory came from sometime around his ninth birthday. His parents tried to make it back for the occasion, but they rarely did. They would come a few weeks before or a month after, but almost never during the week of his birthday. The dorm mother had brought a handful of kids out onto the lawn so they could play and sing happy birthday to Dayne.

But he wanted his parents, wanted them in the worst way.

He pulled the dorm mother aside. "I don't want everyone to sing this year."

"Why, Dayne, what do you want?" She was a round woman with a friendly face and warm eyes. "Want me to bake you a chocolate cake?"

"No thank you." He squirmed a little. "I want my mom and dad, if that's okay."

"Now, honey, you know they're not coming." She smoothed his hair back from his forehead. "They're probably in the middle of a Bible study with the jungle people."

Even at the time her answer sounded strange. "Why would they be hanging out with jungle people, when they could be home with me?"

"Well, Dayne—" the woman looked troubled—"your parents have made a promise to tell the people in the Indonesian jungles about Jesus. It's their passion and purpose in life."

That afternoon was a turning point for Dayne. He might have been only nine years old, but he could see past the dorm mother's explanation. His mom and dad were parents. Shouldn't that be their passion and purpose in life?

From then on, Dayne thought so. Once when he was twelve and his parents were visiting, he told them what he thought. "God wants you to tell people about Jesus, right?"

"Right." His parents sat together on a bench, holding hands. His father smiled at him. "That's what we're building our lives around."

He tried to keep his tone even, but his anger got the better of him. "Then how come you haven't told me about Jesus?"

His mother let out a soft gasp. "Of course we've told you, Dayne."

"No. I know who Jesus is because of my classes. But I don't understand Him. Not even the basics about Him." He lowered his brow, studying his parents. "Doesn't that bother you a little?"

"Son, we can change that right now." His father looked at his wife, and they gave each other a nod. "Go get your Bible and we'll take a look at the book of John."

Dayne left but he didn't come back with a Bible. He came back with a baseball. With so little time to spend with his parents, he wasn't about to waste one of their afternoons talking about Jesus. He'd only wanted to make a point, and by the look in his parents' eyes when they left the next day, his point had been made.

"We might be far away, Dayne," his mother told him when she left, "but we think about you and pray for you every day."

Her comment made him sick to his stomach. He didn't want her thoughts and prayers. Even as a preteen he wanted her hugs and her time, her attention in the evenings, and her advice on everything from the plays he was interested in to the girls who seemed to notice him more often now.

He wanted parents, not distant missionaries, praying for him and thinking of him.

But his parents were determined to finish the work God had given them. They spent more time in the jungles as he got older, visiting him sometimes only three times in a given year. Left on his own, Dayne became best friends with another drama student, a guy named Bob Asher. Like him, Bob had no siblings, and he'd been raised at the boarding school since he was old enough to walk.

Bob had the best attitude of anyone at the school. If his parents missed a visit, he'd shrug and smile. "So what? So we don't see our parents much. At least we see 'em sometimes."

Bob helped temper Dayne's feelings, and through middle school and high school, the two could always be found together. But long before graduation, it was clear they were headed in different directions. Dayne wanted to act, but Bob had a craving for the faith of his parents. He wanted to preach, tell people the good news about Jesus the way his parents had.

"Don't you see?" Dayne told him one day. "Your parents picked Jesus over you. Doesn't that make you mad?"

"They made a sacrifice."

"We all did. Only no one asked us about it—the sacrifice just happened. It became part of our lives!" Dayne hated the way so many kids at the school knew exactly what to say, how to justify the life they lived. But he couldn't hate Bob. "Don't you see it, Asher? We never got a vote. Aren't you bugged by that?"

"Not if it's what God wants. . . ."

The debate raged, especially as Dayne's senior year drew to a close. He had applied to UCLA, hoping to earn a drama degree. The school had great credentials, but even better it would take him away from Indonesia and the truth that his parents still weren't available for him.

The day he received his acceptance letter from UCLA was the day he realized it was too late. He was eighteen, about to graduate from high school. His childhood had passed, and to show for it, he and his parents had only a handful of hurried memories.

Dayne's and Katy's pace around the lake was still slow, and Dayne let the story sit for a minute. "The plane crash came in April that year. They were planning another furlough, two months to help me get situated in college." He bit the inside of his cheek and stared at the water. "The dorm mother—the same one who'd been there back when I was nine years old—was the one who told me."

They came to a stop, and Katy studied him, looked deep into his eyes. "I'm sorry, Dayne."

"It was a long time ago." He scattered some gravel with the toe of his tennis shoe. "Those single-engine jungle planes go down all the time." He found a smile for her, but it didn't come from his heart. "Hey—" he uttered a dry chuckle—"they were doing God's work, right? What could be wrong with that?"

"Can I tell you something?" She cupped his elbow with her hand. "I think God's work would've been staying home with you."

"I think so too." The touch of her fingers against his arm made him hesitate before speaking. What was it about her? How come he felt like he'd known her all his life? And what about the rest of the story? Could he trust her with the truth? In the distance thunder sounded, and they started walking again. "You know what I found out last year, eighteen years after they died?"

She gave him a sad look. "That they regretted leaving you?"

"No." He wanted to pull her into a hug. Saying that made her seem perfect, not for the other hundred reasons he liked her, but because she clearly ached along with him over the loss of any normal sort of childhood. He cleared his throat. He could trust her. "I found out that I was adopted."

"Seriously?" She stopped and leaned against the nearest tree. "I never knew that."

"Hardly anyone does." He took a spot against another tree, one opposite her. "The tabloids would have a field day with it. They'd find my birth parents and print every picture ever taken. Then they'd start digging for dirt until the papers were covered with it." He laughed, but the sound was more disgust than humor. "Everyone has dirt if the tabloids get free rein on them."

"You're probably right."

"I know I am." His voice softened. "I have a friend in Hollywood, an actor. The tabs found out that his father was in prison, and they ran the story under huge headlines, made up some of the crimes, and exaggerated every other detail. Now the guy's marked for life." He shook his head. "I don't ever want them knowing I'm adopted. My birth parents have the right to their privacy."

She was quiet, looking at the lake, her expression pensive. After a while she turned her attention to him again. "Do you know who they are? your birth parents?"

He angled his head, wondering if she could tell. "Why do you ask?"

"Because most adopted people talk about their birth mother." She shifted her position, still leaning against the tree. "You talk about your birth parents."

He nodded. "You're a good listener, Katy Hart." He told her about hiring a private investigator and figuring it out. "My birth parents were young, unmarried. From everything I can tell, they weren't allowed to keep me."

Her eyes widened. "So you've met them?"

"Not really." The tree he was propped up against was digging into his back. He tucked his hands behind himself and smiled at her. "Let's just say I found closure."

Katy looked doubtful, but she didn't push the issue. "How'd you figure it out? that you were adopted?"

Images of Luke Baxter came to mind, the way Dayne had happened upon his office and the myriad of family pictures around his desk. If Luke hadn't worked at his attorney's office, he might never have known. He studied Katy, saw the integrity in her eyes and face. She was safe, definitely. Still, it wasn't the time. "I found a framed photograph in my storage unit. It . . . it looked familiar so I picked it up. Underneath it were all these documents, papers on my adoption."

"Wow. How weird would that be?"

"It was." He took a deep breath. "I found out my birth mother had written me a letter on the back side of the photo I'd found in my storage unit." He let his head rest on the tree as he watched her through narrowed eyes. "I haven't read it yet."

"Why not?"

"I guess I was angry. I mean, why didn't she fight her parents? And if she had to give me up, why'd she let a couple of missionaries adopt me?" He chuckled, trying to keep the conversation light. "Her picture's still there in the storage unit. I could read it whenever I want, I guess."

"So your parents, your adoptive parents, never told you?"

"They did once. After I found my birth mother's photo, I

remembered seeing it before. I was in primary school, about six, when my parents showed it to me. They told me she was the woman who gave birth to me. But they never came out and said I was adopted. They never brought it up again, and I forgot about ever seeing the picture. I really had no idea I was adopted until last year."

He took a breath. That was all he could say. The Baxters lived too close to bring them up now. No, the identity of his birth family would remain a secret unless somehow fate brought them together. Even so, he was determined it wouldn't happen now or on this trip. Not with the media about to descend on Bloomington because of his location shoot.

The one thing he hadn't considered was that Katy might have a connection to one of his sisters. But even if he had the chance to meet Ashley Baxter Blake, he would say nothing. He had his life, and they had theirs. It was better for all of them if things stayed that way.

Katy pulled away from the tree and peered up through the branches. "Looks like rain."

"It does." Dayne found his place beside her, and they picked up their pace. "This trail is great. It's perfect for talking."

"I think so." She smiled at him. "I've walked it with Rhonda a few times."

"Rhonda?" He was glad the talk of his adoption was past.

"You've seen her." Her voice held a subtle teasing. "Remember, Dayne? When you dropped in on us the last night of *Charlie Brown*?" She gave him a knowing look. "Rhonda's my choreographer. She's the one who spotted you that night." Katy laughed. "She came running up and told me Dayne Matthews had stopped in to see a few minutes of the show. I thought she was crazy."

He chuckled. "I wish I could've seen that."

"I still don't know why you were there that night."

Panic knocked at the windows of Dayne's soul, but he didn't flinch. "Research."

Katy looked doubtful, but she stared straight ahead and kept walking. A light rain began to fall, and she glanced up. "I think we're in trouble."

"Nah." Dayne said. "Probably just a passing cloud."

But before he finished his sentence, the rain got harder.

"Dayne . . ." Katy grinned at him. The rain was plastering her hair against her head now. "You haven't been in an Indiana downpour, have you?"

"Not lately." He took her hand and ran with her to a tree a few feet ahead. The branches above them were thick, but not thick enough to keep the rain from drenching them. "How long would it take to get back if we ran for it?" Dayne raised his voice so she could hear him over the sound of the storm.

"Too long." She laughed and wiped a layer of water off her face with her free hand. "Either way the trees aren't much help. We might as well start back."

Thunder rumbled in the distance, and Dayne looked up. "Maybe you're right."

He turned back the way they'd come and led her down the path. They moved quickly, half-running. Along the way they joked about the storm and how wet they were getting. The only thing they didn't talk about was the obvious.

He was still holding her hand.

CHAPTER FIFTEEN

KATY LET GO OF DAYNE'S HAND when they reached her car. Inside, they looked at each other and laughed even harder. Her hair hung in a wet sheet around her shoulders and the sides of her face, and she rested her forehead on the steering wheel. "Well . . ." She was out of breath, exhilarated from the cool rain and the half run back to the parking lot. "Next time I'll check the forecast before suggesting a hike around the lake."

"You know what?" Dayne turned sideways and leaned against the passenger door.

"What?" Her sides were still heaving, her heart rate returning to normal. She looked at him, at the way his eyes appeared bluer than before.

"If the forecast says rain . . . call me." He shook his head and sprayed water on his lap. "That was the most fun I've had in a long time."

She could breathe normally now, and the laughter from a moment ago faded. She smiled at him. "It was, huh?"

"Yes." He looked at his watch. "Wanna get lunch?"

Katy thought about it. The reason the day had been so much

fun was because nothing about it had been real. The real Dayne Matthews would always have a photographer or two trailing him. Maybe even some demented fan. But here, on the shores of Lake Monroe, they'd stolen a day from everyone who wanted a piece of him. Going to lunch in a public place might change everything.

He must've guessed what she was thinking. "How about the university? A couple of drenched people should be able to get a salad at the cafeteria without anyone getting starstruck, right?"

"Hmmm." He had a point. She'd been on campus a few times as a guest at one drama class or another. The place was busy and hectic. They could grab lunch, find a table out of the way, and probably stay unnoticed. "All right." She gave him another smile as she turned the key and started the engine. "Let's try."

The afternoon turned out to be perfect. Sunshine broke through the clouds even before they reached the campus. They ate without anyone looking twice at Dayne, and when they were done, they walked from the cafeteria toward the football stadium.

"We needed this." Dayne held his arms out in front of him. "I was beginning to think I'd never get dry."

"I still can't believe it." She looked over her shoulder. "No one figuring out who you are."

He laughed and glanced down at himself. "I look like a drowned rat."

That wasn't exactly true. Katy stopped herself from gazing at him longer than necessary. He looked wonderful, his muscles more clearly defined beneath his damp T-shirt.

The conversation between them continued, but Katy could barely keep up. She kept asking herself the same questions. Why was he here? What were they doing? And what could possibly come from allowing themselves a day like this? Was it simply a means to an end, a chance to follow their feelings regardless of the fact that very soon the moment would pass and they might never have this again?

Katy hugged herself as they walked. She wanted to hold his

hand, wanted to feel the way she had as they hurried around the lake in the pouring rain. If he would've stopped halfway back and kissed her, she wouldn't have told him no. And what did that say about her?

She had no answers for herself, so she shut the questions from her mind. They were almost to the football stadium, the sun warm on their bodies and faces.

He slowed and stared up at the structure. "It's huge."

"Football's huge here." She shaded her eyes so she could see it better. "In Bloomington the quarterback and coach are more famous than anyone from Hollywood."

He nodded. "I like that." A gate was open in front of them. "Can we go in?"

"Probably." She took the lead, heading for the stadium entrance. "They're getting it ready for tomorrow's home game."

From somewhere inside the gates, a band broke into song, and Dayne felt his eyes light up. "Band practice!"

"Yep." She giggled at him. Was he that removed from life's ordinary pleasures? "Happens just about every day."

They went inside and climbed a long flight of stairs. Workers were painting lines on the grassy field below, and in one end zone the Indiana marching band was in formation, belting out the school's fight song.

"This is great!" He took her hand and headed up another set of stairs. When they were near the top, he sat down and she took the spot beside him.

With no one around, it felt perfectly normal to be holding his hand. They listened, and when the song was done, he turned to her. "Do you know how lucky you are?"

A gentle breeze blew over them, and Katy ran her free hand through her hair. "Lucky?"

"Yes." He lifted her fingers to his lips, gently kissed the back of her hand, and then lowered it to the narrow place between them. His eyes never left hers the whole time. "Your life is so . . . so normal, Katy. You have the lake and the parks and the university. People living and working and raising families, with none of the strangeness I deal with every day."

Her stomach still had butterflies from the way he'd kissed her hand, but she tried to focus on what he'd said. He was right. The idea that privacy and open spaces and breathing the fresh Bloomington air were, in themselves, privileges. "I never thought of it that way."

He searched her face, and she knew. She knew long before he moved closer that he was going to kiss her. They were in a world of their own, one that wouldn't last much longer. But the feelings were there for both of them. Then, in the sweetest instant, his lips touched hers. The kiss wasn't forced or overly passionate. It was less than the kiss they'd shared in her Hollywood audition. But it melted her heart, and without thinking she slipped her arm around his waist and kept it there, even when he drew back slightly.

"Are you okay?" His voice was low, soothing. Meant for her alone.

"Yeah." She pressed her cheek against his and felt his arm come around her. "I'm okay."

He brought his hand up alongside her face and turned her so she faced him again. "How do I find myself here for good, Katy?" He kissed her again, tentative and slow. "How do I do it?"

She shook her head. "That's just it . . ." From the fountains of joy that welled in her heart, she felt a piercing pain, a sorrow that would last long after he had returned to California. "You can't, Dayne. The world will keep you right where you are."

"What if I don't want it? What if I walk away from it all tomorrow?"

She smiled. "You won't. We both know that. You have contracts and promises and obligations." Tears stung at her eyes, but she dodged them with a laugh. "Wherever you go, you'll still be Dayne Matthews."

"And you—" he traced her profile with his finger, his touch as soft as silk—"will be the only girl who's ever found a way past the surface." He cupped the side of her face. "I want more than today, Katy. I want every day this week and the next and for months and years after that."

She gave him a sad smile. "It doesn't matter what either of us wants." A flock of geese flew overhead, and she glanced up. His hand was still framing her face, and she found his eyes again. "It doesn't matter."

"The world thinks people like me can have whatever we want, anything money can buy." He gave a bitter laugh and let his hand fall to hers. "But I can't do anything, pay any amount to have this . . ." He waved his other hand toward the football field and the campus beyond. Then he looked deeply at her again. "Or to have you."

Katy was breathless. She hadn't expected the afternoon to end this way, with such honesty and emotion. But she regretted none of it. Not after what had happened to Sarah Jo Stryker and Ben Hanover. She brought her lips to his this time, and again the kiss was sweeter than any she'd known. When she pulled back, she felt the heat in her cheeks. "I didn't think we'd do this, wind up like this."

"Me, either."

"If you'd asked me a week ago—" her voice was soft, little more than a whisper—"I would've said, 'Why bother?'" She snuggled up against him and stared out at the band. They were warming up for another song. "But after Sarah Jo died, I realized something. If you have feelings for someone, you're better off to tell them. That way . . . if tomorrow doesn't come, there are no regrets to sort through, no question marks."

"I like that." He slid his fingers between hers, their shoulders touching as they watched the band director raise his arms, leading the members in an upbeat salsa number. "I like it a lot. No question marks."

"Yes." She sighed. "But it doesn't change anything else, does it?"

"No." He stood and pulled her to her feet. Then he put his arms around her waist, and she took hold of his shoulders. They kissed again, still nothing too involved. "You have practice in an hour."

"I do." She didn't want the moment to end, but it had to. The clock was pushing them mercilessly toward the hour of reckoning, toward the reality each of them had chosen. Hers in small-town America where life was rich and somewhat less complicated. His in the limelight of Hollywood. She ran her fingers over his red bracelet, the one he still wore.

"I'm still looking into Kabbalah."

She narrowed her eyes, seeing her way to the deeper parts of him. "I think the answers you're looking for are somewhere else, Dayne."

"Maybe they're right here." He kissed her once more. He seemed intoxicated with her, the same way she felt about him.

"Maybe." She smiled. "But we'll talk about that later."

"Hey . . ." He still held her, but the pensive look from a moment ago lifted. "Can I come? to rehearsal?"

"Dayne . . ." She gazed up at the clear sky. How could she discourage him when everything in her wanted to tell him yes? Finally she said the obvious. "Everyone will know."

"Not necessarily. I'll wear a sweatshirt and a baseball cap." He hugged her to himself, and they swayed for a few seconds. "Please, Katy, let me come. I'll leave if things get weird."

She thought about it until the salsa song was finished. Maybe he was right. What would it hurt? He was due in town in a few days, anyway. Then it wouldn't even be unusual that he might stop in at a local theater rehearsal. Rhonda wouldn't be surprised, certainly. Not Ashley Baxter Blake either or Jenny Flanigan. Enough people knew about their connection to make it possible, right?

"Okay." She stepped back and shook her head at him. "I can't tell you no."

He held her hand all the way down the stadium steps and raced her back to the cafeteria. When they reached the grassy lawn on the other side, he tripped and landed on his hands and knees, but he sat up and snagged her ankles as she tried to pass him. "Not so fast."

"Hey . . . you're cheating." She pulled him to his feet, and by the time they reached her car, they were laughing as hard as they had after the rainstorm.

They were still breathless as she pulled out of the parking lot and headed toward his hotel. She stayed outside while he ran in and grabbed a sweatshirt and baseball cap. Apparently no one in the lobby recognized him, because he dashed back out and waved as he headed for his rental car. He was driving since she wasn't sure how long she'd have to stay at rehearsal that night. But as he followed her to Bloomington Community Church, the place where CKT held most of its rehearsals, Katy could feel something inside her begin to change. They had found their way to a place that didn't really exist, and now it was time to take the first step back into reality.

As soon as she parked her car, he climbed out of his and into her passenger seat. He pulled on the sweatshirt and donned the baseball cap. Then he winked at her. "See? Dayne who?"

"Dayne, you're gonna get caught." She grabbed her bag from the backseat.

"Let me go first. I'll find a place inside, and no one will ever know the difference." He hesitated as his eyes held hers. He looked like he wanted to kiss her again, but he didn't. She had more to lose than he did, her reputation and her privacy. The paparazzi didn't seem to be in Bloomington yet, but just in case, she appreciated the way he held back. He tipped the brim of his baseball cap in her direction, opened the car door, and bounded across the parking lot.

She waited until he was inside before taking a deep breath and checking her look in the mirror. What had just happened to her? Had she really spent the day with Dayne Matthews, walking around the lake and getting caught in a downpour, traversing the pathways at Indiana University, and kissing him at the top of the football stadium?

The better question was this: how was she going to pull sixty grieving kids together so they could focus on the rehearsal? There was only one way—the way she'd come to count on more with every year. She closed her eyes and gripped the steering wheel. *God, I'm not sure about today or why it happened. But I meant what I said. I want Dayne to know how I feel, even if we never have a day like this again.* She sighed and opened her eyes.

Kids were arriving, and several cars were pulling into the lot. She had only a few more minutes.

Lord, show me why he's here, why he walked back into my life. I won't take a step toward his world, and he can't take a step toward mine. So why, Lord . . . ?

She was quiet, and she felt a stirring in her heart, something slow and soft like the gentlest breeze. *Precious daughter, make the most of every opportunity.*

A chill ran down her arms, and she let go of the steering wheel. There were times when she could hear God so clearly, His voice seemed almost audible.

This was one of those times.

Okay, God, fine . . . but what sort of opportunity is it? An opportunity for me or for him? She blinked, the possibilities close around her. *Or is it an opportunity for both of us?*

She waited, but this time no still, small voice blew whispers across her soul. God had a reason for their meeting—that's all she was sure about. Now she could only hope that one day she might know what that reason was.

Even if it took years to figure it out.

CHAPTER SIXTEEN

THERE WAS ONLY ONE PLACE Ashley wanted to be this Friday night.

After attending the funeral and knowing what lay ahead for the members of CKT, she and Landon and Cole had decided that they would watch tonight's *Annie* rehearsal.

Cole was fascinated by the music and chaos and the idea of kids becoming characters on a stage. But mostly he and Landon came for support, so Ashley would have someone to sit with. The sets committee would meet near the end of practice. Her real reason for coming was to watch Katy Hart work her magic with the kids, even now, in their season of sorrow.

The three of them arrived ten minutes after practice started, and they found seats on the left side of the sanctuary, near the back.

Katy was up front, explaining about what would happen next. "We've all been through a loss." She kept her voice kind and even, making eye contact with each of the students. "Now we need to take hold of that loss and move it off center stage. The community will be especially aware of our struggles, and they'll expect less from this production."

Ashley felt a lump in her throat. She reached for Landon's hand.

Katy stepped closer to the kids. "I think Sarah Jo would expect *more* from it." She hesitated, as if maybe she was too choked up to finish her sentence right away. "And that's what we're going to give. More than ever, so that Sarah Jo and Ben would be proud of our efforts."

She continued, giving directions to the various groups of actors and singers and dancers. Some would meet with Nancy and Al Helmes, learning parts for the opening song. Others would gather with Rhonda for instruction on the dance number in "It's the Hard-Knock Life."

When they all had their assignments, Katy spotted Ashley near the back and hurried up the aisle. "Ashley!" Ashley stood and the two hugged. "Will you help us with sets again?"

"Of course." She sat back down and pointed to Landon. "I've got my helper back. That's what counts."

"And me!" Cole raised his hand. "I'll help too!"

"Good." Katy grinned and gave Cole a high five. Then her expression fell. She looked at Ashley. "Will you pray about something?"

"Of course." Ashley looked at Landon, and he nodded in agreement. "What's up?"

"It's the older kids." She leaned against the back of the next pew, her eyes sadder than before. "They want to circulate a petition in the community. Find a way to make the drunk driver get the most severe punishment."

Ashley was confused. "I can see that. He's a repeat offender, right?"

"He is." She caught her long hair with one hand and pulled it over her right shoulder. "He should be punished. I have nothing against that." The kids were noisy in the background. "But the guy was just a kid himself. Still young enough to be part of CKT if things had been different."

"I read a story about him." Landon eased Cole to the other side so they could talk. "He's just eighteen."

"Exactly." Katy thought for a minute. "I keep thinking—who's going to tell him the truth? That Jesus died for him too. Who's going to give him a reason to change, you know?"

Ashley hadn't thought of that before. There were so many unfair things in life. The way Jean-Claude had left her alone after finding out she was pregnant, the steroid user who killed Kari's first husband, little Hayley's near drowning. "You want the kids to forgive him—is that it?"

"I guess so." Katy's eyes were damp. "They're so mad at him. A group like ours has to be capable of more than anger."

Ashley felt for her new friend, for the task that lay ahead of her. "I'll pray."

"Thanks." She pointed at the group of kids still gathered near the front of the sanctuary. "Duty calls."

"Hey, Katy."

She stopped and turned around.

"Landon and Cole are leaving early. Can you give me a ride home?"

"Hmmm—" she winced—"the creative team is meeting for an hour after practice. But I'm sure one of the other moms can do it."

"Okay, I'll ask one of them." Katy was right; the sets committee would have someone going her way.

After an hour of watching thirteen girls and little Kyle Lanham singing on their knees with wash buckets in the orphanage scene, Landon gave her a light kiss and said, "I'm taking him home."

Cole still looked interested, but he was yawning. Ashley reached over and took his hand. "What do you think of this? Hard work, huh?"

"Lots." Cole's eyes were big. "It's like baseball practice."

"Maybe you'll be onstage one day, Coley." She wrinkled her nose at him.

"Nah." He stood and took Landon's hand. "I'm a baseball guy, Mommy."

Landon bent down and kissed the top of Cole's head. "That's my boy." He gave Ashley a crooked grin. "See you at home."

When her boys were gone, Ashley set her forearms on the pew in front of her and rested her chin on her wrist. Katy and Rhonda were in the middle of the little girls, trying to think of choreography to fill in for the part of the song when there weren't any words.

"We could have four girls cartwheel across the stage from opposite directions." Rhonda stepped back and surveyed the open space. "Sort of the orphanage-gone-crazy look."

As a way of trying it out, Rhonda organized the little girls on both sides of the stage and had them pretend to shake blankets and make beds, all to the music Al Helmes was playing on the piano. Then she and Katy did cartwheels from either side of the stage, crossing in the middle and winding up with their hands in the air, right on beat.

The little girls went wild, clapping and screaming and volunteering to do the cartwheels. Katy adjusted her shirt and shooed them back, laughing right along with them. The progress continued, and after thirty more minutes, the scene began to take shape. The girls not only did cartwheels toward each other, but afterwards, two of the smaller girls formed a single cartwheel, with each girl holding on to the ankles of the other.

Katy caught the feet of one of the girls just as she was about to tumble off the stage. "This way we can take the act on the road and open for circuses." She spread her free hand out in front of her. "All over America!"

Everyone laughed, and Katy reworked the double cartwheel.

Ashley loved the atmosphere. It wasn't so different from painting, really. She took an empty canvas, and with mere pastels and watercolors, with oils and a handful of brushes, she could bring a scene to life. Landon liked to tell her that when he looked at one of her paintings, he could feel the breeze, smell the flowers. They were that real.

That's the way it was with theater. The stage was the canvas, and someone with Katy Hart's talent could use a handful of kids and bring a scene to life. She leaned back in the pew and looked around the sanctuary. Other parents sat in small clusters, quietly knitting or watching the rehearsal.

Ashley was just about to return her attention to the front of the huge room when she spotted a guy sitting at the back of the right side of the church. Even from across the room, the man looked familiar, and Ashley squinted. He wore a sweatshirt and a baseball cap, and he was completely caught up in watching the scene come together.

Or maybe he was completely caught up in watching Katy Hart.

Ashley studied him for a moment longer, and then it hit her. She drew a quiet gasp and resisted the urge to cover her mouth. It wasn't just any old guy watching rehearsal—the man was Dayne Matthews. He had the same look. And of course it made sense. Dayne was scheduled to be in town on Tuesday. Why wouldn't he come a few days early? He and Katy had shared something special, right? Wasn't that what Katy had said a few days ago at the hospital?

The idea was alluring. Dayne Matthews, hiding near the back of the sanctuary so he could be near Katy. Ashley shifted her position and looked at the front of the room again. She didn't want to be caught staring at him. No doubt he got enough of that in Los Angeles. She wasn't one to get starstruck or want autographs from famous people, but she wanted to meet Dayne. If nothing more than to see the real side of him, the side the public knew nothing about.

Katy was now organizing all the kids onstage for the opening scene when Annie sings "Maybe" while the other orphans try to sleep. With everyone focused on that, Ashley rose and walked quietly around the back of the sanctuary to where Dayne was sitting. The closer she got, the more sure she was. He was Dayne Matthews, no doubt.

Katy had a rule about rehearsals. Anyone could come, but they had to stay quiet. Because of that, Ashley slipped into the pew beside Dayne and smiled when he jumped back a little. "Hi." She kept her voice to a whisper and held out her hand. "I'm Ashley Blake. You're a friend of Katy's, right?"

Only then did she doubt her actions. Dayne looked like an animal caught in a trap. Swallowing hard, he glanced over his shoulder at the back door of the sanctuary. When he looked at her, his mouth hung open for a moment. Finally he shook her hand and let his linger. Not in a way that showed interest in her, but in a way that conveyed surprise and something else . . . shock maybe.

"I'm David Marshall."

David Marshall? Ashley forced her lips into a straight line and refused to smile. Fine. If he needed to keep his cover, she wouldn't say anything. Not yet, anyway. It would be better to get to know him. Then she could tell him later that he didn't have to lie anymore. She already knew who he was.

And of all people, she'd be the last one to ruin his cover. Especially when he looked like such a nice guy. Up close she could see what she'd heard the others in her family talk about. The resemblance was uncanny. It set her at ease, made her feel like she'd known him all her life.

Never mind that he was a big star. Here in the back of the Bloomington Community Church sanctuary, he looked just like her brother, Luke.

CHAPTER SEVENTEEN

DAYNE COULDN'T BELIEVE IT WAS HAPPENING.

He'd thought about the possibility, sure. If he was going to hang out at the CKT rehearsal, there was a chance he'd see his sister. But never for a minute did he think that she'd walk up and take the seat beside him. His mouth was dry, and he was still trying to find a way to get through the introductions.

He was sitting beside his sister! He released her hand and tried not to stare at her. "You . . . you have a child in the play?" It was something to say, a way to direct the focus somewhere other than on himself. He pointed to the makeshift stage up front. "They're doing a great job."

Ashley rested her shoulder against the pew so she was facing him. For a few seconds she watched the rehearsal, but she shook her head. "No. No kids in the play." She smiled at him, making sure to keep her voice low. "I paint sets for CKT."

He was finding his way back to stable ground, gaining his composure. "Katy tells me you're very talented." He gave a slight shake of his head. "World-renowned famous artist."

"I wouldn't say that." She laughed and looked at him a little longer. "My work does well locally and in New York."

"And definitely here."

They whispered for a few more minutes, agreeing that the orphanage scenes were coming together beautifully.

He couldn't tell from her tone whether she suspected who he really was or not. He figured not, since most people wouldn't play along with his false identity.

Once he'd taken a flight home from London and sat in coach, just so he could blend in better. A woman in front of him turned around to ask him for the in-flight media guide, and she stopped midsentence. "Did anyone ever tell you that you look just like Dayne Matthews?"

He'd given her a polite smile and handed her the magazine. "Thanks." He nodded. "I get that a lot."

"But . . . well . . ." The woman looked awkward, twisted all the way around in her seat. "You're not him, right?"

"Right." He laughed and pointed toward first class. "If I were Dayne Matthews, wouldn't I be sitting up there?"

The trick had worked, but only sort of. At the end of the eight-hour flight, the woman was still casting strange looks at him. By the time they got off the plane, she was whispering to the woman next to her, and it was clear that neither of them believed he was anyone other than the Hollywood actor.

But here, with Ashley, he didn't sense that. She seemed content to think he was David Marshall, Katy's friend, come to watch a rehearsal.

"I love watching Katy work." Ashley faced forward, but she leaned close enough for him to hear her. "She's brilliant with these kids."

"She is." He could barely focus on what Ashley was saying. The whole time he kept wanting to stand up and shout the truth: *You're my sister, Ashley. Come here and hug me.*

But he couldn't, not now or ever. As long as the paparazzi

were intent on taking bites out of his private life, chewing them up and spitting them out for all the world to see, he could never involve the Baxters in his life. But who would've ever thought he'd have this chance—a time to sit beside his sister and talk to her? And what if his parents had been able to keep him? This beautiful young woman would've been one of his closest friends, someone he'd have a lifetime of memories with.

She stood and shook his hand again. "Good to meet you. Any friend of Katy's is a friend of everyone here." She smiled at him. "I'm glad you could be here."

Around the room the kids were moving away from the stage for a break and scattering into the audience. Dayne couldn't remember anything she'd just said. He blinked.

"My committee's meeting." Ashley motioned to the front of the room. "We have to figure out how to make a grand staircase fit into an orphanage." Her laughter was familiar, and Dayne figured out why. It sounded vaguely like his own. Ashley waved to him as she headed down the aisle. "Nice talking to you."

"You too." He sat back, dazed, and watched her walk away. How was he going to return to Hollywood and leave everything he'd found here in Bloomington in only one day?

Katy pulled away from the group and came up another aisle. In a move that was discreet but clearly planned, she skittered along the back of the church and approached him. She didn't look too worried about whether anyone would see her talking to him. "I think you're right. The disguise works." She took the place where Ashley had been sitting. "Anyone figure it out yet?"

"No." He looked to the left side of the church. Ashley was sitting with a group of women, using her hands to describe something to them. He looked back at Katy, and he stopped himself from reaching for her hand. "I met Ashley."

"I saw that." Her eyes danced, telling him that she was still thinking about their day together, just like he was. "What'd you tell her?"

"I said I was David Marshall. One of your friends."

Katy laughed. "I don't know, Dayne. Ashley's a pretty smart girl."

He heard something in Katy's tone and lowered his chin, catching her at eye level. "Meaning?"

"Meaning I told her about last summer." Katy tilted her head. "I think you're right, though. She doesn't look like she figured out who you are."

"Yeah, she would've said something." He let himself get lost in Katy's eyes for a minute. "You're great with the kids."

"Really?" Her expression lit up.

"I can't wait to see it opening night."

With that, reality colored her eyes, and her face fell a little. "You'll be back home. You know that."

"Maybe not." He reached out and brushed her fingers with his. "Maybe I'll go into hiding and stay for the next few months. One way or another I'll be here opening night. I promise."

Katy drew a long breath, and in it Dayne thought he could read her thoughts. How great it would be if he really could run away and hide out in Bloomington. Even until the show opened. But she said nothing. Instead she stood and smiled at him. "I'm glad you came today."

"Me too."

"I have to get back to the kids, and when we're done I have a meeting."

He wasn't willing to let her go that easily. His eyes searched hers and kept her from leaving. "What about tomorrow?"

"Rehearsal ten to two." She frowned.

"Okay, so how about I meet you at your house? You jog, right?"

"Sometimes." She giggled. "I tell myself I'm supposed to."

"Let's take a jog before practice. You pick the distance."

She hesitated, and her look told him how impossible it was for her to resist him. She took a few steps back and gave him the slightest nod. "Call me."

"I will." He sat back and felt the victory. One more day. Fate would give them one more day to live outside the scrutiny of the ravenous press.

The rehearsal went on, but Dayne couldn't leave. Even if Katy wasn't able to talk to him again for the rest of the night, he would stay. Watching her was like watching a movie he couldn't pull himself away from. She stayed in his mind and made him wonder how he was ever going to get along without her.

When he did look away, his eyes would find Ashley Baxter Blake. He was glancing at her when the members of her committee bowed their heads in what looked like a group prayer. Dayne felt the slightest irritation. His adoptive parents and Elizabeth Baxter and Katy Hart. Now his birth sister Ashley. Had all of them found some sort of direction in following Jesus Christ? And what about Kabbalah? Why were none of them interested in reaching the upper world?

Dayne let the thought pass.

As Ashley stood and separated from the group, she smiled at him. Then she made her way around the pews and over to him. "Hey." She clutched a bag in one hand and a piece of paper in the other. "Rehearsal's almost over, and Katy's staying for another hour. I don't live far from here . . . would you mind giving me a ride?"

Panic danced around him again. Could he give his sister a ride home without begging her for the chance to come inside and meet her husband, her family? He felt the ache welling inside him, but he had no choice. None at all. He grinned at her. "Sure." He looked at his watch. "I was just leaving."

He rose and cast one last look at Katy. She was working with a group of kids, talking to them, nodding, and shifting her attention from one to another. He walked out without her noticing him.

As he and Ashley left the church, she talked about the direction they'd decided for the sets. "The stairs work." She kept up with him as they crossed the parking lot. "We'll keep them onstage, and they'll give us a way to showcase the orphans during their songs.

"Right." He opened the car door for her and noticed something he hadn't before. His hands were shaking. *Come on, Matthews; pull out your acting skills. She can't figure it out.* "Sounds great," he said as he got in the car.

They were halfway to her house, with her giving him directions, when Ashley stopped talking about sets and asked, "Where are you from, anyway?"

He hadn't expected the question. It took him a few heartbeats to recover. "Out of town." Yeah, that was it. "Indianapolis."

"So—" she studied him—"how'd you meet Katy?"

"Well . . ." He laughed, but he was buying time. "It's a long story."

Ashley looked straight ahead and motioned to the next street. "Turn left here."

He did as she asked. If he was going to survive the conversation, he had to take the lead. "How long have you lived here? in Bloomington?"

"All my life." She let her head fall back against the headrest. "I spent a little time in Paris, but otherwise, I've been right here."

"Are you married?" Dayne knew that she was. The private investigator had found out that much—he had five siblings, and the last of them to marry was Ashley. Her wedding took place the previous summer, just before his visit to Bloomington.

"I am." She angled herself so she could see him better. "We have a little boy, Cole. He's the love of our lives."

The ache grew. "You're lucky." He refused the emotions that surged in his heart. "Family is important."

She was quiet for a minute, telling him to take another left and then a right. When they finally pulled up in front of her modest house, she seemed in no hurry to get out. She folded her hands in her lap and sized him up. "Dayne . . . I know who you are."

He wasn't sure what to do next. Should he pretend he hadn't heard her? tell her he had places to go and that he couldn't talk? Looking at her was like seeing a part of himself in the mirror.

She looked like Luke, and Luke looked like him. But he hadn't thought it would be so obvious to her.

Maybe John Baxter had told all the kids the truth—that they had an older brother and that he might come looking for them someday. Or maybe she'd spotted him last year at the hospital, after all. Maybe Elizabeth had told them about meeting him. In that moment the last thing on his mind was the fact that he was a Hollywood movie star. He was Ashley Baxter Blake's brother, and she knew it just the same as he did.

In that case . . . in that case he was about to become part of the Baxter family whether it was the smart thing or not. He shook his head, his eyes wide, unblinking. "What . . . what do you mean?"

She smiled and patted his hand. "I know you're Dayne Matthews."

Just like that the moment changed. He realized he'd been holding his breath, and now he exhaled, consumed by relief and regret in equal amounts. She was waiting for him to say something, so he chuckled and gave her a slight nod. "Katy told you, didn't she?"

"She told me about last summer." Ashley watched him. "When I saw you back there, I knew. I read the papers. I know you're supposed to be in town next week."

"So . . ." He lifted his hands and let them drop again. Who cared if she knew he was Dayne Matthews? He had thought she meant the other part, the fact that he was her brother. If she didn't know that . . . then, well, maybe she never would. He grinned, but he felt empty, defeated. "Thanks for not saying anything back there."

"No problem." Ashley hesitated. "I guess things will be different for you next week when the filming begins."

"A lot different." Inside, a part of him screamed to tell her the truth. *I'm your brother, Ashley. We have the same parents!* But he squashed his feelings and smiled. "That's why tonight was so special."

"I won't say anything." She smiled at him again, opened the car door, and climbed out. She ducked to look through the window. "Thanks for the ride, Dayne. It was nice meeting you."

"Nice meeting you too . . ." His last words were still dying on his lips as she turned and walked up the sidewalk and through the front door of the house where she and her husband lived with the little boy they loved. Cole, right? Wasn't that his name? The boy would be his nephew, a child Dayne would never meet, never know.

His eyes blurred. The film crew would arrive in Bloomington on Monday, and after that he wouldn't have another moment like this, another chance to sit beside his sister and tell her the truth about who he was. If he couldn't do it now, if he wouldn't do it now, then he never would. He had promised himself he'd do everything in his power to keep the Baxters out of the limelight, but now . . . letting Ashley walk inside without telling her . . . it was one of the hardest things he'd ever done.

He looked at her house as he pulled away. He couldn't help but think of something sad, something that made the ache inside him worse than ever. The time he'd just shared with his sister might be the only time he'd ever share with her. As long as they both lived.

In fact, it was possible he'd never see her again.

And that was the saddest thing of all.

CHAPTER EIGHTEEN

RAIN WAS IN THE FORECAST AGAIN, but the morning was clear and cool. John Baxter had picked up Elaine Denning at six o'clock this morning for a second trip to the farmers' market. He had enjoyed the squash and tomatoes, for sure. But he still had some left. If he was honest with himself, his reason for agreeing to go this time was less about the vegetables than it was about spending time with a friend. And Elaine was turning into an important friend with every passing day.

They'd talked on the phone several times this week, working past the formalities and shallow conversations to a place of talking about their children and their loneliness. "Sometimes," Elaine had told him last night, "I can't believe God took my husband from me. I almost want to be mad at Him."

"I know." John had closed his eyes, not wanting to admit the truth about the matter. "My kids all think I'm strong, that I'm a rock living here by myself, able to carry on in every area that once belonged to Elizabeth. But most of the time I feel like lying down and never getting up, as if when God took her, He cut my legs out from under me."

Conversations like that one had worked a closeness between them. John had enough alone time to examine his feelings, and what he felt for Elaine was nothing more than companionship. Elaine was his friend. Neither of them was looking for love to replace what they'd had with their spouse. He could live the rest of his days looking, and he'd never find what he had shared with Elizabeth.

Still, the kids were grown and busy with their families. Having a friend was a good thing, and today he felt fresh and alive as he walked beside Elaine down the aisles of the market. Even so, something bothered him. Over and over, Elaine had commented on his honesty, how rare it was to find a man of his integrity. And each time she said that, he wanted to tell her she was wrong.

He was hiding the fact that he had six children. Hiding it from his family and his coworkers and now from her. The more time that passed, the more John thought about it, and today he was determined. It was time to tell someone, and Elaine was the closest friend he had outside of his relationships with his kids.

They bought coffee and a few baskets of blueberries and sat at a picnic table a little ways from the chaos of the market. John breathed in the morning air and smiled at her. "I still need my squash and tomatoes."

"You do." She picked at the blueberries and popped a few in her mouth. Then she waggled her finger at him. "They're good for you. Everyone should come here Saturday morning."

Something about her comment made him sad. It was what Elizabeth would've said. Fresh fruit, vegetables—they were the stuff she always tried to feed him and the kids as they were raising their family. It had only been in the past year that he'd gotten away from buying fresh foods. Frozen dinners and fast food were easier than cooking for himself.

He took a sip of his coffee and smiled at her. "I felt healthier this past week than I have in months."

"Good." She took a few more berries and chewed them slowly. "I'm glad the week's over. I couldn't stand another sad story about CKT in the papers."

"It was hard. Ashley went to the funeral. She said it was a celebration, but still it was one of the hardest days she's had." He leaned on the picnic table and watched a family passing by. The four children tugged on their parents, running ahead and skipping with glee over the prospect of being out at the marketplace. He narrowed his eyes, and for a moment the family was his, he and Elizabeth and their five kids. . . .

Only he didn't have five kids, did he?

"Elaine—" he switched his attention to her—"I have to tell you something. Something I've wanted to say for a few days now."

Her expression changed. "If it's about this . . . about being with me, then I understand." She shook her head. "I don't want you to feel funny about coming out with me like this or—"

"Elaine." He leaned closer, hoping that his eyes were as tender as his voice. "I'm enjoying my time with you. That's not what I want to talk about."

"Oh." She laughed, and her cheeks grew a shade redder. "I just . . . well, I don't want you to feel awkward."

"I need friends. You do too." He sat up straighter. "Nothing awkward about that."

"Okay, good." She stirred her coffee. "What did you want to talk about?"

He exhaled, amazed at himself. All those years and he and Elizabeth never told anyone, not even Pastor Mark. But now, he wanted someone to know. He wanted Elaine to hear the story. He couldn't have her thinking that he was a man of integrity, telling the truth all the time, if he couldn't be straight about this. But there was more to it than that. He wanted her opinion, her feedback. Because Elizabeth's letters still sat on the top shelf of his closet, and he still wondered about what to tell the kids.

Without someone to talk to, he wasn't sure what to do. He

took a swig of his coffee and pursed his lips. "Elizabeth and I didn't have five children."

A pair of blue jays hopped close to the table, then flew away between two nearby maple trees.

Elaine uttered a confused laugh. "John, what do you mean?"

He looked down for a moment and then forced himself to make eye contact with her. "We had six." He paused, giving her time for the truth to sink in. "Elizabeth got pregnant when we were dating. We weren't that young, really. But her parents wouldn't consider letting her keep the baby. She was unmarried and pregnant, so they sent her away."

Across from him, Elaine's mouth hung open. "You're serious."

"Yes." He felt better already, just being able to talk about it. "Her parents knew, but mine didn't. We never told anyone else, not through all the years of marriage and raising children. Our other kids have no idea."

"Elizabeth gave the baby up for adoption—is that what you're saying?"

"She had no choice." He wrapped his fingers around his warm cup and squinted against the morning sunlight. The noise of the farmers' market faded into the background. "The baby was a boy. Our firstborn son." He watched her reaction, looking for shock or judgment. There was none. "When Elizabeth was sick with cancer the first time, we tried to find him." He worked the muscles in his jaw, the disappointment over that time still raw. "The records were sealed. We got nowhere."

"Wow." Elaine set her coffee down and stared at him, her eyes full of amazement. "Elizabeth and I spent all those hours together, working with cancer patients, visiting them. I never knew."

"That was our promise." A brilliant red leaf drifted down and landed on the table beside him. The trees all around were beginning to turn colors, bright reds and pretty yellows. He dusted the leaf onto the ground. "We would go years not talking about it even with each other. Most of the time we tried to believe we'd never had him. But when the cancer came back—" he glanced at his wedding ring—"finding our firstborn son was the most important thing in the world to Elizabeth."

A shadow fell over Elaine's face. "You didn't find him?"

"No." John's heart hurt, remembering those final days with Elizabeth. "She kept praying, believing God would let her meet him before she died. She wanted it so badly that right at the end she actually convinced herself it had happened. She was . . . she was delusional, fading away a little more with every hour. But in her mind, he'd found her; he'd walked into her hospital room and told her he understood why she'd given him up." He breathed in through his nose, willing himself not to let the memories get to him.

"So, she had peace." Elaine's voice was clear and kind. "God in all His mercy gave her that. I think it's wonderful."

"That's what I told myself. Never mind that it wasn't true. At least she thought it was. It's like you said. The delusion allowed her to die at peace with all of us."

"Did the other kids . . . did they wonder what she was talking about?"

"No. They weren't in the room when we had the conversation. We'd just returned from dinner, and they were visiting in the hall, giving us a few minutes together before coming in." He hesitated, wishing he could go back to that moment once more. "Everyone knew they were her final hours."

"And—" Elaine lowered her voice, looking to the distant places of his soul—"why are you telling me?"

He took another drink of his coffee. "You keep saying how honest I am, how I'm a man of integrity." He shrugged one shoulder. "I guess I wanted it to be true."

She watched him for a moment, and then she shook her head. "No, John. That's not why you told me."

He chuckled and popped a few blueberries into his mouth. "Okay, then why did I tell you?"

"Because you don't have closure." She angled her head, her smile as genuine as the fall morning. "You don't, do you?"

"No." He sighed. He watched a squirrel grab hold of a nut and race up the side of one of the distant maples. His eyes found hers again. "No, I don't have closure."

"Elizabeth wanted to find him, and she didn't. Now it's up to you."

"That's just it." John swished the coffee around in his cup. "I can't look for him without telling the others. And Elizabeth and I were always set on not telling them. Not giving them a reason to spend a lifetime wondering, the way we had done."

Elaine agreed. "I see that." A group of older kids jogged by on the sidewalk. Their shirts all read Clear Creek Cross-Country. Elaine waited until they were gone. "What would Elizabeth want now? now that she's gone and he was never really found?"

"That's what I don't know."

"That's why you told me." She smiled and patted his hand. The sensation was nice but slightly awkward. He was glad when she drew back and took another sip of her drink. "You need someone to help you decide what to do next."

That was it exactly. Somewhere in the world, a boy had grown up without his birth parents, without the Baxter family. If Elizabeth wanted to find him, then that was the least he could do for her. "I would start looking tomorrow if it weren't for the kids." He anchored his elbows on the table and locked his fingers together. "I keep wondering what might matter to her more—finding our firstborn or keeping the truth about him from the other kids."

Elaine thought for a minute. "Didn't you say Elizabeth left a box of letters?"

"Yes." They'd talked about it a few days ago. "They're the ones Ashley wants copied. She keeps waiting for me to present each of the kids with a scrapbook of their mother's letters." His voice grew gravelly thinking about it. "I can barely look at the box without wanting to shut off the lights and cry for a month."

"I know." Elaine gripped the edge of the bench she was sitting on. "I felt like that for years afterwards. I still do."

"So . . . what's the answer?"

"Maybe the answer's in the letters. I bet somewhere in there you'll find what you need to do. Whether you should try and locate this young man or let him go for all time. And once you know that answer, you'll know the other one—what Elizabeth would want you to tell the kids."

A release came over him, as if somehow she had freed him to move ahead in the matter. "The letters, huh?"

"Yes, John." Elaine stood and collected the berries, waiting while he moved around the table and joined her. "And something else."

They were face-to-face, and he realized that she was shorter than Elizabeth. "What else?"

"Don't be afraid to cry. Even for a month."

Elaine's advice played in John's mind for the next half hour, while they bought squash and tomatoes again, and as he dropped her off at her house. Now he was home, and he set the box of vegetables on the kitchen counter and washed his hands.

The answer was in the letters.

It was true—that's where he was bound to find out what Elizabeth would've done, what she would've wanted him to do. Even after a beautiful morning of sharing conversation with a woman who was becoming a better friend with every passing day, there was no denying the loneliness.

The quiet of the house suffocated him with it.

Going through Elizabeth's letters would only make him feel worse in some ways. But Elaine was right. There were letters in that box from Elizabeth to him and from him to her. Letters from when she had been forced to move away and have the baby on her own, without so much as a visit from him. And letters where he told her how he'd felt and how no one could keep them from each other once she returned.

There were the other letters, too, the ones Elizabeth had written for him and for their firstborn child just before she died. Maybe something in that letter would tell him what he should do next. He steeled himself against the past and went upstairs to his room—their room.

He turned on the lights in the bedroom and then in the closet. Without thinking too hard about the task that lay ahead, he pulled the box of letters from the top shelf, carried it across the room, and set it on the floor at the foot of the bed. Then he dug around in a bottom cubby near the back of the closet and found the hidden manila envelope, the one that contained a copy of the letter Elizabeth had written to the five kids and the one she'd written to him. And finally the last one—the one marked *Firstborn*.

Before opening it, he sat on the edge of his bed and sifted through the box. Not far from the top was a letter she'd written to him after getting her final cancer diagnosis. He unfolded the paper and let his eyes find their way down the page.

> John, darling . . .
> I'm tired so I decided to take a nap. We need to talk tonight.
> I'm consumed with finding our firstborn son, absolutely consumed.
> I believe God's telling me to try my hardest on this. I think I'm
> supposed to meet him. It's my only prayer. We'll talk later.
>
> Lovingly,
> Elizabeth

The tears came unbidden. He read the letter again and remembered the first time he'd seen it. Tucked beneath a tube of toothpaste in their bathroom, where she'd known he would find it. He had read the letter, folded it, and slipped it into the box in the closet. Then, quietly so he wouldn't wake her, he'd climbed into bed beside her and held her until she woke up. When she did, the idea of finding their son was still the first thing on her mind.

He blinked, and a batch of teardrops slid down his face, onto the folded letter. *God, what am I supposed to do? She thought You'd bring our firstborn to her, but You didn't. Am I supposed to walk away from this? let it go?*

No answers blew across his hurting heart. He tucked the letter along one side of the box and found the one he'd hidden before, the one Elizabeth had written to him after Luke's birth. He worked his way through five letters before he set them down, stood, and went to the window. It was still early in the morning, just past eight o'clock. But it felt like the darkest hour of night inside their bedroom.

John opened the blinds and peered out. Five letters—that was enough. All he could take for one day. He sniffed and pressed his palm against the cool glass pane. Besides, he didn't need more than that to know the answer. It was as clear as it was right, and it brought with it a sense of peace that he hadn't felt since Elizabeth's death.

He stared past their land to the open sky beyond. It was time to start looking. With everything he had, he would search for the young man, and one day—no matter how many months or years it took—he would find him. If he needed to hire one private investigator or two or a whole crew, he would do so. He wouldn't tell his other children, of course. Not until his search was successful. And it would be successful. Elizabeth's dying wish had been to find their firstborn son.

Now it would be his.

CHAPTER NINETEEN

KATY WAS MORE NERVOUS than she'd been since high school when the track star asked her out and her father insisted on meeting him first. Dayne had called, and she'd given him directions to the Flanigan house.

Ashley knew he was in town; she'd guessed as much. But so far the press hadn't found out. One more day together wouldn't hurt, only now he was coming to the Flanigans', and he wanted to meet Jenny and Jim.

"They're the closest thing you have to family here." He was adamant. "I don't care if they know who I am."

She didn't either, not really.

Jim had taken the four younger boys to the lumber store, and Bailey and Connor were downstairs in the kitchen, eating and getting ready for rehearsal. In *Annie*, Bailey was one of the servants, and Connor had the part of Bert Healy. Both kids were happy with their roles, excited about how rehearsal had gone the night before.

Katy couldn't stop moving. She paced to the front door, scanned the driveway, and then returned to the kitchen.

Finally on her next trip to the front door Jenny came up beside her. She brought her head close to Katy's and peered out the window with her. "Looking for someone?"

"Jenny!" She took hold of her friend's shoulders and kept her voice a rough whisper. "Dayne's coming here. I just got off the phone with him!"

"Hmmm." Jenny checked her watch. "Does he know about us? that we know about him?"

"Yes." Her heart raced and she tugged at her shorts. The plan hadn't changed. They were supposed to jog, and she'd chosen the distance. Nearly two miles to the new park down the street. She released Jenny's shoulders and paced to the hallway and back. "What about Bailey and Connor?"

"You don't want them to know?" Jenny looked like she was trying to keep up.

"No. I don't want the CKT kids knowing about him."

Jenny gave her a strange, knowing look. She nodded and headed toward the kitchen. "I'll take care of it."

Katy looked out the window and saw Dayne's rental car pull into the driveway. Why was she so nervous? They were almost out of time, weren't they? He would meet his film crew on Tuesday, and then they could go back to pretending these days had never happened.

Was she really worried that Bailey and Connor would find out? that they'd tell the rest of the CKT kids? Or was she worried about what Rhonda and the other adults would think?

Somehow Rhonda hadn't noticed Dayne last night. But she was bound to figure it out if he came again, and then what? Maybe she didn't want Rhonda pointing out the obvious, that the drudgery of singleness wasn't solved by spending time where a person was certain—convinced—that God didn't want her.

Katy pursed her lips and blew out. This wasn't the time to think so deeply about it. Dayne was an acquaintance, a pal. That's all he could ever be. She watched him walk up to the front door, watched the way his long legs moved with a practiced confidence. She took a step back and swallowed hard. Who was she kidding? Right or wrong, her feelings for him went way beyond friendship. If she could've made these days last another week or a month or a year, she would've.

He spotted her through the small windows at the sides of the door and smiled.

She waved and rushed to open the door. *Slow, Katy.* She blew out again. *Slow down.* She ushered him inside and smiled. "Hi. I've got the route all picked out."

"Okay." Something in his expression told her that maybe he wanted to hug her, but he kept his distance. "Can I come in for a minute?"

"Dayne—" she lowered her voice—"the kids don't know about you. I . . . I think it's better if they don't."

"They won't think it's me—the real me." He grinned. Bloomington seemed to be good for him. He looked more relaxed, less worried about people finding out who he was. Maybe it was just the relief of getting around town without photographers following him everywhere. "Come on . . . where're Jim and Jenny?"

"Jim's at the store with the little boys." She smoothed the wrinkles from her T-shirt. She was about to suggest leaving right away when he headed down the hallway. "Hey," she called after him. When he didn't stop, she groaned and followed him into the kitchen.

Jenny was at the stove, making oatmeal. She gave them both a wave. "Hi." Then she turned to the kids, who had stopped unloading the dishwasher to turn and look at Katy and Dayne. "Bailey . . . Connor, this is Katy's friend." She directed the next part to Katy. "You're going jogging, right?"

"Right." Katy couldn't slow her racing heart. She was grateful for Jenny, relieved at the way she'd diverted the attention.

Connor said hello as he was turning back to the dishes. But

Bailey's glance lingered a little longer as she looked from Dayne to Katy and back again. Finally she said hi and returned to helping her brother.

Jenny stirred the pot a few times and adjusted one of the burners. Then she followed Katy and Dayne back toward the front door. When they were out of earshot of the kids, Jenny wiped her palms on her jeans and held out her hand. "Dayne, nice to meet you. I'd ask you to stay for oatmeal, but it looks like you have plans."

"We do." He gave her a crooked smile. "Thanks for the offer, though. And hey, your kids are cute."

"Thanks." She looked at Katy. "I don't think they picked up on who he was."

"It doesn't really matter." Dayne smiled. "I don't think they'd alert the media."

Katy shifted her weight to the other foot. They needed to get going. They had barely an hour for the jog as it was. "I'm more worried about the people at CKT. If they find out, the media won't be far off."

"They're not far off, anyway." Dayne bumped her shoulder with his and winked at her. "We both know that."

"Well, anyway—" Jenny smiled at him—"enjoy your jog." Her eyes took on a more serious look. "From what Katy says, you don't have a chance like this all that often."

"I don't." He glanced back at Katy, and she felt her insides melt.

She looked away, fighting her feelings for him, feelings she had been denying one way or another since he'd arrived in town on Thursday evening. If she stood there another minute, she would scream. The combination of hoping Bailey and Connor hadn't guessed who he was, the small talk in the foyer, and the knowledge that after today they might never be alone like this again was about to drive her crazy.

"Okay . . ." Katy took his hand. "We're leaving. We'll never make it to the park if we don't go now."

Dayne held his free hand up and raised his brow in Jenny's direction as they neared the front door. "Thanks for the oatmeal offer." They were halfway outside when he yelled back, "Maybe next time."

Katy pointed down the street toward a grove of trees a block away. "Follow me." She started at a sprint and held that pace until they reached the trees and she couldn't breathe. She stopped and grabbed her side. "Yikes . . ." She bent over, her lungs burning.

"Hey." He was out of breath, too, but not like her. He came up beside her and put his hand on her back. "What're you running from?"

She straightened and looked into his eyes. From him, right? Wasn't that why she couldn't stand still all morning, couldn't handle the thought of Bailey or Connor or any of the kids knowing about him? She took two quick breaths and shook her head. "I . . . I don't know."

"Yes you do." There was anger in his eyes now, anger and hurt and confusion. He took a step closer, seeing past her words. "You're running from me."

"No." She looked down and dug her fists into her waist. Then she backed up, her eyes still focused on the sidewalk beneath her feet. "No, that's not it, Dayne. I—"

He followed her and caught her arm. "Katy. Look at me."

She didn't want to, but he left her no choice. The pain in his voice was there for both of them to hear. Her eyes lifted to his. "What?"

"You're running from me, right? That's why you didn't want the kids to see me. You don't want people to know. I haven't even gone back to Hollywood and already you're running."

His answer was dead-on; she knew it as soon as he spoke the words. The fight left her, and she allowed herself to get lost in his eyes. "It's all make-believe, Dayne." Her voice mixed with the rustling of leaves overhead. "The more people who know, the harder it'll be to let go." The intensity in her tone increased. "Don't you see?" She pressed her fingers to her chest. "You'll go back to your world, and anyone who knows about this . . . about us . . . will see right through me."

"See right through you?" His expression twisted, and his tone was baffled.

"Yes." She wasn't out of breath anymore, but her chest was still heaving, her entire body caught in the emotions of the moment. "They'll see that I've fallen for you."

She expected him to freeze up, distance himself from her, and promise her that he wouldn't make it any more difficult than it already was. Instead, the darkness on his face lifted, and he held out his arms to her. "You have?"

"Dayne." His name came out sounding more like a moan. "Let's just pretend, okay? I like it better that way. We can jog and laugh and talk, and later you'll go your way and I'll go mine. I'll read in the papers about your movie and how well the shooting went, and someday, years from now, we can both look back and smile about the few days we had together."

He took hold of the sides of her T-shirt and brought her closer to him. His eyes burned straight through her. "I can't."

"How come?" There was a whine in her voice, a desperation. She never should've told him how she was feeling. It was enough what she'd told him yesterday, that she cared and that she enjoyed spending time with him. Her mistake had been in kissing him, because ever since then that's all she'd been able to think about. Through rehearsals and choreographing the orphan scenes, through the whole restless night right up until this instant, it consumed her. But it wasn't what she wanted. She wanted the laughter and the rain and the walk around Lake Monroe.

He was still holding on to her shirt, still searching her eyes.

She gave a hard shake of her head. "Why can't we pretend? We both know it's almost over." She waved her hand in the air. "Whatever this is."

"We can't pretend." He pulled her still closer, his voice soft and low. "Because I've fallen too. I fell last summer."

"Dayne, no . . ."

For a moment, she pictured Kelly Parker. What would she think if she knew Dayne was standing inches from her in a secluded grove of trees? Or that he'd just confessed to feelings for her that would put Kelly's future with him in jeopardy? She squeezed her eyes shut. No. She wouldn't think about Kelly Parker. This wasn't about Kelly or Dayne or any sense of what tomorrow held. It was simply a moment between two people who could never be together.

A cool wind played in the trees overhead, and thunder sounded in the distance. Rain might be coming again, but she didn't care. Because even as she was convincing herself of all the reasons she should keep running, she felt him draw her near.

Before she could stop herself, she was in his arms. In his arms and finding her way back to the sweetest place, to his warm embrace and his lips against hers. Because this wasn't acting or some weird Hollywood thing. It was real and true, and as she returned his kiss, she knew she was wrong. She had told herself she wanted to forget that they'd ever done this. But as the kiss continued, she could only hope one thing: that she would remember it forever.

When he pulled back, he brushed his knuckles against her cheeks. "I don't know how we're going to find ourselves through the maze of whatever happens next." He brushed his lips against her cheeks, her mouth. "But I can tell you one thing, Katy Hart." His voice was a caress against her face. "This isn't pretend."

They kissed once more, and then he nuzzled his face against hers. "Now . . . about that race you started." He nodded toward the other side of the trees, at the park that lay stretched out beyond. "Let's see if we can even our pace a little."

She laughed and they set out together, side by side on the trail until they came to the park. The clouds were darker than before, and she gave him a soft push. "If it rains on us, it's all your fault."

"Mine?" He pointed at himself. "Okay, Miss Katy, then you better keep up. I can't take the blame if you come home drenched again."

They ran faster on the way home and didn't stop until they were a few houses from the Flanigans'. The houses in their neighborhood each had five or more acres, so they still had a ways to go, but the rain looked like it would pass.

When they finally reached his car, she leaned on the hood and caught his eyes. "So . . . what happens next?"

He looked at his watch. "Rehearsal, right? Ten o'clock?"

She hadn't considered that he might want to come back for more. "Dayne . . . Ashley knows, and Rhonda will be there."

"Shhh." He put his finger against her lips. "I'll stay in the back. No one will figure it out. I promise." He hesitated. "Besides, I'm still thinking about that set-painting position. Ashley and I would work great together."

For a second, she thought he was going to kiss her. But he glanced at the Flanigans' front window and grinned at her instead. "I'll see you at practice."

She watched him drive off, and then she jogged up the driveway.

Bailey was waiting for her just inside the front door, her hands on her hips. "That was Dayne Matthews, wasn't it?"

"Who? The guy I . . ." The words died on her lips. She walked the rest of the way inside, shut the door, and leaned hard against it. "Did your mother tell you?"

"No, she wouldn't say a word. But, Katy, it was so obvious. I mean—" she gestured toward the front door—"he was Dayne Matthews. I've seen him in a ton of movies."

"So he walks in and you recognize him just like that?" She had a feeling there was more to Bailey's figuring it out.

"Well—" Bailey allowed a small grin—"that and the stuff I heard you talking to my parents about last summer."

"Bailey Flanigan!" Katy gave her a playful push. "How come you never said anything?"

"I thought the whole Hollywood thing was just about the part, honest. I mean . . ." Her cheeks darkened. "I didn't know the two of you sort of . . . you know . . . liked each other or something."

This was exactly what Katy hadn't wanted, for anyone else close to her to know how she felt about Dayne. He was a movie star, for goodness' sake. Regular people didn't fall for actors like Dayne Matthews—not for real, anyway. She sighed and rubbed the back of her neck. "Dayne and I became friends. That's really all it is, Bailey."

Her eyes danced. "But, Katy, the way he looked at you! I think he's in love with you, seriously."

"He isn't." Katy took Bailey's hands in her own. "Love is for people who share the same faith most of all. The same goals and dreams and futures." She shook her head, trying to convince herself as much as Bailey. "Dayne isn't that person for me, and . . . well—" she pictured Kelly Parker again—"I'm not that person for him."

She hugged Bailey and gave her a half-stern look. "Don't tell anyone, okay? People won't understand. They don't know I auditioned for a movie." She paused, studying Bailey's eyes and seeing understanding there. "Okay?"

"Okay." Bailey ran off for the stairs and looked over her shoulder. "But Connor figured it out too."

"Oh, boy." Katy ran her hand through her hair. "No one else, though?"

"And Tim Reed." She gave Katy a sheepish grin. "I called him after you left."

"Great." Katy tossed her hands in the air. "I'm taking a shower. Let's leave in twenty minutes. We can talk about it on the way to rehearsal."

She raced to get ready on time, thinking over the new reality. Enough people knew about Dayne now that it would be hard for him to come to rehearsal this morning unnoticed. Still, he hadn't seemed to care. The kids would keep their distance, and Katy trusted Bailey. Now that she'd asked her to keep quiet, the girl wouldn't tell anyone else.

As Katy dried her hair, she studied the mirror, and her words played again in her mind, the ones she had told Bailey: *"Dayne isn't that person for me, and I'm not that person for him."* It was a fact. It was something she'd been telling herself ever since seeing Dayne in Bloomington.

Now if she could just get herself to believe it.

CHAPTER TWENTY

DAYNE WAS SITTING IN THE BACK of the Bloomington Community Church sanctuary, watching Katy take command of the kids milling about the stage and the first few pews, when his cell phone rang. He half expected it to be Kelly. He hadn't talked to her since he arrived on Thursday, and by now he knew she was mad at him. She hadn't wanted him to go, so she would punish him by keeping her distance.

The trouble was, Dayne had hardly noticed.

He looked at the caller ID and frowned. It was the director, Mitch Henry. He probably wondered where Dayne was, since his advice had been to stay away from Bloomington until he absolutely had to be there.

Dayne walked out the back doors of the sanctuary to the lobby. He found a quiet corner and flipped his phone open. "Hello?"

"Okay, Matthews, where are you?"

"On a deserted island." He tried a laugh, but it died before it reached the mouthpiece. "Hey, Mitch, don't blow a gasket. I'm in Bloomington."

"Doing what?"

Dayne looked across the lobby as a few late kids burst through the double doors and sprinted down the aisle. "Taking in a little local theater."

"Matthews—" Mitch's tone was defeated—"I told you to stay away from her. Isn't that what I told you? Don't mess with her. It'll only hurt you both, right?"

"I remember something about that." He turned his back to the lobby, in case any other latecomers walked in. "But to be honest, the details are a little hazy."

"Tell me you haven't spent any time alone with her. I'm serious. Kelly Parker was in here this morning, and she's furious. Told me she had no idea where you were and that you hadn't called her for three days." Mitch grabbed a fast breath. "Is that true?"

"I haven't kept track." Dayne straightened, feeling the humor fade from him. "Look, Mitch, I wanted to see her. I did, and nothing came of it. There isn't a gossip-rag photog within a hundred miles of this place."

"What about Kelly? You live with the girl. Remember her, the gorgeous lady half the guys in America would love to get their hands on?" He sighed. "I need chemistry in this film. Katy Hart wouldn't take the role, so we gave it to Kelly. Now the chemistry has to be there or I'll have a flop on my hands." He hesitated. "You know, Matthews, this isn't just about you. This is my first big break as a major director, and I want the film to sing."

"It isn't a musical." Dayne felt himself relax. He could work with Mitch Henry—everything would be okay.

"You better make it one." Mitch calmed a bit. "You're sure about the paparazzi? No one followed you there?"

"No one."

"Well, I can tell you this much." In the background there was a tapping sound. Dayne could picture Mitch sitting at his desk, pencil in his hand. "They'll be there Tuesday at the latest. You can't give them anything, Dayne, not a single minute with the girl. Got it?"

"You know, Mitch, for a type-B personality you're pretty demanding." He kept his head low, so his voice wouldn't carry into the sanctuary.

"Type B?"

"See . . . gotcha there." Dayne laughed. "Come on, calm down. I know my limits."

There was silence for a minute, and Dayne could almost see the steam coming from the director's head. "Okay, listen. If you won't stay away from her for Kelly or for me, then think of Katy Hart."

It was the first time Mitch had his attention. "What about her?"

"The trial's coming, Dayne. You want her name linked with yours all over the tabs? Remember what they said before? 'Dayne Matthews and Mystery Woman Attacked at Beach.' Well, the minute they get a good shot of you and Katy Hart, the mystery will be over. All of a sudden you're living with one girl and having an affair with another one—a sweet, small-town girl who does Christian Kids Theater for a living." He whistled. "If you don't think that'll make for some juicy copy, you don't know the business."

Not until that moment had Dayne considered this possibility. Yes, he knew their names would eventually be linked over the trial of the deranged fan, and that until this point, Katy's name had been a secret from the press. That didn't bother him so much. It was the other part, the part about her being the teacher of a Christian Kids Theater.

He felt like he'd been sucker punched, but somehow he straightened and drew in a slow breath. "Mitch, it's been great as always."

"Stay low, Matthews. And call Kelly, send her a dozen roses. Something to make it up to her. I need the two of you at the top of your game."

"I will be—don't worry." Dayne kept his tone light, but his heart and mind were nowhere near light. He finished the call, folded his phone, and slipped it into his pocket. He felt like a thundercloud had descended over him, and as he made his way back to his seat, he barely noticed the rehearsal going on at the front of the room.

He dug his elbows into his thighs and covered his face with his hands. Mitch was right. There was no end to the lengths the paparazzi would go to find a story. And what could be more irresistible than the idea of his having an affair with Katy Hart? Girls like her didn't come along every day; that's for sure. The press would want to know where she worked and what she did. They'd tramp across the front pages of their gossip rags the idea that she was thought to be a young woman with high morals, a teacher of Christian principles.

Yet she was traipsing around hidden places, having an affair with Dayne Matthews, who meanwhile still lived with his leading lady, Kelly Parker. They'd probably start following Katy around too, hoping to catch her going to church or doing some other such thing. That way they could call her a hypocrite.

The possibilities turned his stomach. He leaned back and searched the front of the room until he found Katy. She was placing kids in a single line, explaining how they each needed to hold on to the shoulders of the person in front of them.

"Once you have your balance, kick one leg up behind you." She waved someone over—Rhonda, no doubt. "Watch; it's like this." Her hands went on Rhonda's shoulders, she kicked her leg up behind her, and the two of them hopped forward. "See? You're supposed to look like a long line of commuters making your way through New York City."

The kids put their hands on the shoulders of the kids in front of them. But as soon as they balanced on one foot and started hopping, a boy near the back tripped and fell onto the girl in front of him. The fall started a slow-motion domino effect, and in a matter of seconds, all the kids landed in a heap on the floor.

"Okay." Katy dusted her hands off and looked at Rhonda. "It needs a little work, but it'll be great."

"We can't do it," one boy yelled out.

"Yeah, it's too hard." Another stood beside him, arms crossed. "Everyone keeps jumping on each other's feet."

A chorus of agreement echoed across the stage as the kids untangled themselves and stood up. One little girl was clearly more shaken up than the others. She had her head down, and even from the back of the room, Dayne could hear her crying.

Katy noticed, too, and went to her. "What is it, Maggie?"

"S-S-Sarah Jo." The girl's crying got louder, her sobs more pronounced. "I m-m-miss her."

The other kids realized what was happening. One of the boys sat down cross-legged and looked at Katy. "Sarah Jo would've helped us bring this together. She had really good balance."

"Yes." Katy looked at the sad faces around her. "She had good balance; that's true." She put her arm around Maggie. "But this number doesn't need one very balanced person." She held out her arms, and the kids instinctively drew closer, forming a cluster of standing and sitting kids around her feet. "Everyone has to be balanced together."

"But Sarah Jo should be here, Katy. She should." Maggie's face was stained with tears, and several of the older kids hung their heads.

"Sarah Jo *is* here." Katy made a fist and pressed it to her heart. "She's in our hearts and minds, in our memories. We can't ever forget that." She bent down and hugged Maggie. "We're doing our best on this show for her and little Ben, remember?"

There were a few hushed responses, but most of the kids said nothing.

In the quiet that followed Dayne felt like an intruder, an outsider who shouldn't be privy to this type of private moment. Still, he couldn't tear himself away from it.

One of the teenage boys offered a suggestion. "Maybe if we stop for a minute and pray. Just so we can focus on what's really important here." He looked at Katy and then at the other kids. "This is about a lot more than the show. It's about coming together."

Without further prompting, the kids formed a circle and joined hands. Katy looked like one of them as she took her spot between two of the little girls. Once their heads were bowed, the teenage boy prayed loud and clear. "Things happen for a reason, Lord. We've been saying that again and again since the accident. And no, we don't always see that reason or understand it. But we believe—" his voice broke, and for a few seconds he paused—"we believe You're here. And that You have Sarah Jo and Ben safely with You." He exhaled hard. "Now please . . . let this show bring You glory. Let it be something we can perform in the memory of the friends we lost."

When the prayer was over, Dayne watched them get back in line. At the piano, a friendly looking older woman picked up the melody. The kids put their hands on the shoulders of the person in front of them, and like a single body, they each raised their left foot behind them and hopped forward on their right. Not a person swayed or fell over.

When the number ended, Katy raised her fist in the air and whooped for joy. "See . . . you can do this! You can and you will, and it'll be the best show ever."

Dayne was awestruck at what he'd just seen. It was more than genuine theater and the brilliance of Katy's ability with the kids. It was something that had to do with the prayer the boy had spoken. Almost as if the kid was right, and God Himself really was here, working some sort of miracle right in the middle of the rehearsal.

Watching Katy with the kids drove Mitch Henry's point home, forcing him to make a decision. Never mind what he'd told her earlier when they were on their run. What they'd shared together—the time and laughter, the intimacy of being close enough to kiss—all of it was wonderful. He'd told her the truth; he'd remember every minute forever.

It wasn't pretend—he'd been right about that. But he was wrong about the rest. He couldn't promise that he'd find a way back to her. Not when he had no idea how to start life over, and she had so much to lose. He watched her for the rest of rehearsal, never taking his eyes from her for more than a few seconds.

He noticed Bailey Flanigan looking at him and at the boy who had prayed. It didn't matter if they knew. This would be his last CKT rehearsal. He could joke about painting sets and being here for opening night, but none of it was ever going to happen. Not if it meant putting Katy Hart's privacy and reputation and her job with these kids at risk.

The closer the rehearsal came to ending, the worse he felt. He had to tell Katy. Waiting would only make things harder for both of them. Besides, the media could arrive in town any day. Paparazzi had a way of sniffing out stories, and they might expect Dayne to come in early. Even just for a few days of privacy. It was the photogs' job to make sure that never happened, that Dayne never had a chance to do anything they didn't chronicle for all the world to see.

He gritted his teeth and watched as Katy finished with the kids. He moved to the far side of the room so none of them would notice him on their way out. When everyone was gone, even Rhonda, Katy made her way up the aisle, set her bag down, and held her hands out to him. "That was a tough one."

"I saw." He stood and gave her a quick hug, nothing too long or lingering. "Hey, Katy, I talked to my director."

Something changed in her expression, as if she had some idea of what was coming. "Just now?"

"A while ago." He leaned against the pew and slipped his hands into his pockets. "He wants me to stay away from you."

"I'm sure." She nodded, but she couldn't hide the pain that flashed in her eyes. "He's just looking out for you."

"Not for me." Dayne wanted her to understand everything he was feeling. "I'm not worried about me, Katy. He isn't either, not really."

"Sure he is." Katy tried to laugh, but the sound fell short. "You're about to star in a film with a woman you're living with, Dayne. If anyone sees me with you that throws the whole picture into a tailspin."

He brought his lips together in a thin line. She understood more than he thought. "But it's more than that."

"What?" She picked up her bag and held it to her chest. "Don't tell me he's worried about what the paparazzi would do to me. I have no skeletons."

"You will when the press gets finished with you." He said the words so softly, even he could barely hear them. "Katy, they'll make it look like we're sleeping together. They'll flaunt the fact that you're a Christian drama teacher and make you look worse than Madonna in the process. I've seen them do it." He took one hand from his pocket and touched her arm. "I can't watch them do it to you."

She held her body stiffly, her expression steeled against the emotions he knew must be tearing at her heart. "I have a meeting with the older kids this afternoon, and tomorrow's church." She looked into his eyes, and he felt her find the deep places, the places she had found back in California. "So I guess this is it."

He wanted to laugh at the idea, stand and shout that the thought was ridiculous. Of course this wasn't it. Katy Hart was the only woman who had ever touched him this way, the only one he'd cared about because of her inside more than her outside. He didn't break eye contact with her. "How can you say that?"

"Because it is. Did you just hear yourself? Your director wants you to stay away from me. You even said that being together could ruin everything for you and me both." She gave a sad shake of her head. "I get it, Dayne. I'm right. This is it."

He took his other hand from his pocket and clenched his fists. "I hate this." His tone was carefully measured. He was too sad to get very angry. "Let's get in your car and drive to Canada or Alaska."

She touched his shoulder. A sad smile played on her lips. "They have movies there too."

"I'll see you again before I go." He worked the muscles in his jaw and took a step closer to her. "The director's right. I won't do it if it means you'll get caught by the paparazzi. But if there's any way . . ." He let the sentence die. Who was he kidding? Once filming started, he'd be watched every moment. Even more than in Hollywood, where movie stars were a common sight.

She leaned in and kissed his cheek. "Good-bye, Dayne." She motioned toward the front of the sanctuary. "I'm going to go over the script." She searched his eyes one last time. "I enjoyed every minute of being with you."

"Katy . . ." He caught her arm before she could turn away. "Don't give up, please. I'll find a way."

"Good-bye." Her voice was a whisper, and already he could see tears welling in her eyes. She pulled away, turned, and headed back down the aisle.

He wanted to run after her, grab her, and tell her it was all a crazy joke. Of course they could spend time together. No one would ever tell them what they could or couldn't do, right? They were two adults, after all.

But his feet wouldn't let him go. His feet and his heart. Because no matter what he wanted to tell himself, Mitch Henry was right. He cared too much for Katy Hart to let the media swallow her whole. And as he walked through the back doors of the sanctuary, through the lobby, and out to the parking lot toward his car, he hurt worse than ever before.

By the time he got back to his hotel, he realized why it was so hard to walk away from her. It was because he not only cared about Katy Hart.

He loved her.

CHAPTER TWENTY-ONE

KATY HAD LIED TO DAYNE.

She had no intention of going over the script. All she knew was that if she followed him out to his car, she might follow him anywhere he asked her to go. And since the film crew was still two days from arriving, they might both be able to talk themselves into spending another afternoon or evening together.

But all of it was pointless. And so she pretended to have work, pretended she might be able to study the script after he left, when all she could do was close her eyes and let the tears come. Guys weren't supposed to be this difficult, were they? But Dayne wasn't just any other guy, and she'd known that from the beginning.

After a few minutes she pulled herself together, dried her eyes, and drove home to the Flanigans'. Jenny saw her as she walked in through the second front entrance, the one that led straight up to her little apartment.

"Katy!" She was at her side instantly, taking hold of her shoulders and trying to read the reason for her red, swollen eyes. "What's wrong, honey?"

It took a few seconds for Katy to find her voice. "I won't . . . see Dayne again."

"Why?" Jenny didn't look completely upset by the thought, but her concern was deep all the same. "Did something happen?"

Katy sniffed and clutched her bag a little more tightly. "Life happened. The world of make-believe ended today."

Jenny hugged her, and they stayed that way for a while. When Katy pulled back, Jenny brushed away a stray tear on her cheek. "God has a plan for you, Katy. You believe that, right?"

"I do." She dragged her fingertips across her cheeks. "But why did Dayne have to come here? Why did we have to find each other at all?"

Jenny thought for a moment. "I don't know. But God does. Maybe you need to talk to Him."

"I will." Katy turned toward the stairs. "Thanks, Jenny. Hey . . . I invited the older kids over at four o'clock for a Bible study." She frowned. Her sadness over Dayne made even talking about this almost too difficult. "They're still so angry, Jenny. We need to pray about that too." She blinked back the hint of fresh tears. "At least they're willing to meet with me."

"I'm so glad. Every time Bailey talks about the drunk driver, it's like she becomes somebody different. Someone cold and set on revenge. Jim and I can be in on the study if you want."

"I would." She managed a laugh. "After today, I'm not sure I can lead a prayer let alone a study."

The time in her room was brief. She fixed her hair and makeup and stayed in constant prayer. It was right, what she'd done by releasing Dayne. Maybe she would see him again sometime over the next couple weeks. Or maybe not. Maybe never again. Either way she was glad they'd spent time together. She still wanted to research Kabbalah, because she'd said she would and she wanted to keep her word.

Her time alone with Dayne was over. With every passing minute, she hurt a little more about the fact, but she knew it was the right thing. Why risk having the story blow up in the gossip rags? For what, when he was going to return to Hollywood and Kelly Parker when the two weeks in Bloomington were over?

She forced all thoughts of Dayne and the last two days so deep they wouldn't surface. At least not for the rest of the afternoon. Out her window she watched the first car pull into the Flanigans' driveway.

Fifteen minutes later, they were all gathered in the family room—Katy and Jenny and Jim and ten of the older CKT kids, including Bailey and Tim Reed.

"We love the idea of a Bible study," Tim spoke out first. "But what's the real reason you have us here, Katy?"

She steadied herself. The day had already brought so much emotion. "The real reason is a guy named Jeremy Fisher."

"The drunk driver?" Bailey sat up a little. Anger colored her expression. "That's funny, 'cause we want to talk about him too."

There were a few nods around the room, and Tim gave Katy a defeated look. "We think it's wrong. What he did, the fact that he'd driven drunk so many times before. We want to make sure it doesn't happen again."

"I know." Katy looked to Jenny, but she was whispering something to Jim. "You want to see him punished."

"Punished hard." One of the girls at the end of the sofa slapped her hand on her knee. "He should've been in jail, not out on the streets that night."

"That's probably true. I'm sure he'll serve time for what happened to our friends." Katy paused. *God, soften their hearts, please.* "The thing is, guys, I don't think the Lord wants us to put our energy into seeing Jeremy Fisher punished. That's a job for lawyers and judges and juries."

"We want a new law, Katy. That's what we've been talking about." Bailey stood, her voice impassioned. "The Sarah Jo Stryker law. If someone drives drunk once, they get a year in jail. Do it twice, and you lose your license forever." She looked around the room and took notice of the approval from the others. "We wanted to write it up today when we were together."

"Then we'll spread out into the community." Another girl's voice was just as fervent. She sounded angry and indignant. "We'll have petitions everywhere, and we'll get signatures."

"Right." One of the boys beside her raised his fist in the air. "This is America. You get enough signatures, you get on the ballot. Then the voters can decide if someone like Jeremy Fisher should've been allowed on the road at all."

"And while we're at it, we'll get signatures for this case too." Bailey sat back down, but her intensity was still at an all-time high. "We want him to serve a life sentence. He took two lives, so serving one life seems like the fairest thing."

"Guys . . ." Katy slid to the edge of the chair and looked around the room. "Listen to yourselves." She held the Bible on her lap, but before she opened it, an idea hit her. "I want to tell you a story, okay?" She made sure she had their attention. "Once there was a boy who grew up around here. He was an only child, and he liked bike riding with his mother and playing catch with his dad."

The room quieted, and she was glad. She had their attention. "Each Christmas the family would go to church and read the story about Christ's birth from the gospel of Luke. The boy got older, and he went to Clear Creek High—" she looked at Bailey—"same as a lot of you."

At the other end of the room, Jenny and Jim linked hands.

"The boy tried to make good choices, but his football friends were a bad influence on him. His parents had an idea. 'Try something new,' they told him. Band or chess club. Maybe drama."

Katy's voice was clear, the story strong on her lips. "Drama sounded pretty good to the boy. He loved being in the limelight, loved the way it felt when he was carrying the football down the sidelines, pushing himself toward the end zone. He wasn't much of a singer, but his parents encouraged him anyway. There was a new community theater group in town, a Christian group. Surely such a group would have a place for this boy. They were Christians after all. And Christians were accepting, right? So what if his voice was a little off?"

Tim Reed hung his head for a moment, and Katy wondered if he knew where she was headed with the story. She glanced around the room. "The boy decided to audition for the next play. If he made it, well, he'd still play football. But he'd have a new group of friends at least. Kids who didn't want to drink or drive fast or sleep with their dates. He could hardly wait for tryouts."

Katy felt a wave of emotion, but she refused it. She had to finish the story, had to get it out while she still held their attention. "So the boy showed up for tryouts, only he couldn't quite get the melody, not anytime through the song. The whole thing—every note of 'Take Me Out to the Ball Game' was just a little off-key. Cuts were made that weekend, and the boy didn't get a part."

A few of the girls made quiet sounds of disapproval and regret.

"But that wasn't all that happened that week. Four days later, the boy's father got a notice in the mail. See, he's an army reservist. The government needed him in Iraq, and he had a week to report. One week. During that time, the boy's parents argued more than usual, and a month after his father left, he noticed that his mother was gone more than she was home. When she announced that she was leaving on a vacation, he already knew the truth. She wasn't coming back."

Katy nodded, feeling the way the boy must've felt. "That was okay, he told himself. She could go. He still had his father. Only his father e-mailed and said his first leave wouldn't be for six months." She hesitated. "About that time the football friends realized something that made them crazy with joy. The boy lived all by himself now. He was sixteen, so he could do whatever he wanted, right? They cheered him on, congratulating him on his good fortune. And every night of the week they brought over cases of beer and had parties."

She could tell by the faces around her that the kids could see where she was headed. A few girls had tears on their cheeks.

"It didn't take long before the boy realized something. He realized that drinking was an escape. Even after the parties were over, getting lost in a six-pack of Budweiser was better than facing the truth that he lived alone, that his mother had walked out on him without so much as a hug good-bye. Pretty soon the nights weren't enough. He was an adult after all, so who needed high school? Besides, the kids at Clear Creek didn't understand him. And the ones who might've—the drama kids involved in that Christian theater down the street—well, they'd rejected him too."

Even the boys looked disturbed. Katy's voice stayed strong and compassionate as the story continued. "One season blended into another, and the boy began to worry. Drinking wasn't an option anymore—it had become a lifestyle. He got a ticket for driving drunk and then another. When his father came home from Iraq for a month, he tried to get help for his son. 'Don't do this,' he told the boy. 'You'll ruin your life. You have to stay away from the stuff.' And for a while, the boy did stay away. But when the boy's dad went back to Iraq, the loneliness set in again and so did the drinking. Night after night after night, right through the spring and summer and on into the fall."

Katy looked at Bailey. Her expression was softer than before, but her eyes were dry. *Please, God . . .*

She took a quick breath and finished the story. "It all ended late one horrible night. That was the night the boy drank at a club with a bunch of football friends. But they were smart enough to get rides home with people who hadn't been drinking. Not this boy. With no one waiting at home for him, he figured he could make it back without getting in trouble." She shook her head. "But that's not what happened. He was too drunk to drive, and he crossed the yellow line. On the other side, a van full of kids was coming home from a night of pizza and ice cream." She swallowed a lump in her throat. "A van with Sarah Jo Stryker and Ben Hanover inside."

Katy folded her hands and let the story sit for a moment. There was nothing more to say, because they all knew the ending from there. They'd all lived it.

Sniffling came from several of the kids, and a few minutes later, Katy held her hands out toward them. "See, guys, I'm not sure we need a petition if we're going to come together and talk about Jeremy Fisher." She lifted the big brown book in her lap and handed it to the girl closest to her. "Maybe we need a Bible."

Tim looked at her. His eyes were soft and open again, the way she was used to seeing them. "Is it true, Katy? The part about CKT—did he really try out?"

"He did." It was something she'd found out late last night. Bethany Allen, the area coordinator, had pulled her aside after the late meeting and told her. She'd been cleaning out computer files when she came across Jeremy's name and the notes explaining why he wasn't cast in the show.

"I think I remember him." One of the girls hugged her knees to her chest. "He was a nice kid. Curly brown hair, sort of tall. I remember he was off-key in his song."

"He tried like three times, I think." Another girl folded her hands. "When he left, no one said anything to him." She looked at the others. "Probably because no one knew him."

They were quiet again, the reality of Jeremy Fisher's life settling in on them.

Bailey was the first to stand up. She looked at Katy and then at the others. "I'll go get the Bibles."

And in that moment, Katy knew wherever the journey led them, God would see them through. Because for the first time hatred and anger and revenge weren't having the last word when it came to Jeremy Fisher.

Love was.

❧

The cell where Jeremy Fisher now lived was colder than usual. He couldn't stop shivering, couldn't stop wondering what his father would think if he knew his boy was in jail. He didn't know yet, but he would know soon. By now there would be a week's worth of unanswered e-mails. Eventually he'd call the school and find out the truth.

Or maybe he'd already done that. Whatever happened when his father found out, he deserved it. The old man would probably disown him. Maybe he'd stay in Iraq a few years longer and climb the ranks, since he had nothing to come home to.

Jeremy twisted his hands together and winced from the pain. He'd rubbed the skin raw between his thumbs and the rest of his fingers. Too much hand wringing, too much worry. Not about himself, but about the families of the kids who died. Drama kids, right? Wasn't that what he'd read? Kids who might've been his friends if things had turned out differently. What were they doing now, and what did they think of him?

They probably wanted to take him out in a forest somewhere and shoot him cold. He wouldn't blame them. It was what he deserved. Jeremy ran his hands along the sides of his arms and tried to ward off the chills. Was any place as cold as this? He didn't think so, but then the whole cold thing had become part of the pattern.

He'd think again and again about what he knew of the accident, how he'd been driving drunk and veered over the yellow line and pretty much decimated a van full of kids. When that thought sank in, the way he tried to get it to sink in every few minutes, he'd think about how worthless he was, how he had no reason to live. And then he'd imagine the families of the kids taking him to some remote place and blowing his head off.

Everyone would feel better then.

When the thoughts came full circle, he would realize how cold he was. That's where he was in the cycle of things right now. Freezing cold, man. Colder than fall mornings on the football field. The cell should've been heated, and even if it wasn't, it was only mid-September. So where was the cold coming from?

That's when it hit him. The cold wasn't coming from outside. It was coming from inside, deep inside his heart and soul. He was worthless, and that meant he had nothing but ice on the inside. He banged his head back against the cement-block wall. Worthless, worthless, worthless. He never should've been born.

There was a sound in the hallway, and someone walked toward his cell. "Fisher?"

"Yes?" For an instant, he had the craziest thought. Maybe his mother had found out about his arrest, and she'd come to talk to him, to apologize to him for leaving. They would let him out for a few minutes so he could hug her and tell her how sorry he was for letting her down, for doing the unthinkable. Then she'd promise to stay by his side and help him through whatever lay ahead.

A stout-looking prison guard shouted at him, "Fisher, you've got a visitor." The man stepped aside and someone came into view. But it wasn't his mother. It was a woman, a beautiful woman. About ten years older than he.

She waited until the guard took a few steps back. Then she gripped the bars of his cell and gave him a partial smile. "Hello, Jeremy."

"Hi." He'd seen her somewhere before, but he couldn't figure out where. Maybe it was just his imagination. "Are you a lawyer?"

"No." She looked straight into his eyes. "I'm not a lawyer."

That's when he noticed that she had something in her hand. "What's that?"

"The deputy said I could give it to you." She slipped it through the bars. "It's a Bible promise book." She waited until he had taken it from her. "Have you seen one before?"

"Yes." A memory flashed in his mind. He and his parents walking across a gravel parking lot into a church service. That day, everyone was given a little book. The pastor called it the same thing: a Bible promise book. Scriptures broken into topics, if he remembered it right. He blinked and the image faded. "I had one a long time ago."

"Well, now you have a new one." She hesitated, and he expected her to look uncomfortable. If she was some church girl come to do him a good deed, then she'd done that. It was time for her to back away and say some sort of awkward good-bye. But she didn't. "Open it to page seventy-seven."

He narrowed his eyes at her. Who was she, and why did she care if he read something from page seventy-seven? Still, she was the only one who had come, and if she wanted him to turn the pages, he would. It was the least he could do. He ran his thumb over the cover and opened it. Inside, some words were written: *Jeremy, don't ever stop believing.*

Tears came rarely for Jeremy, but he felt the sting of them now. He rubbed his eyes and flipped the pages until he arrived at the spot she had told him about. There, underlined, was a verse.

"Can you read it out loud, Jeremy?" Her voice was soft, kind. She stayed at her spot, clinging to his bars.

"Sure." He found the beginning and coughed twice. "'For I know the plans I have for you,' says the Lord. 'They are plans for good and not for disaster, to give you a future and a hope.'" When he looked up, something happened inside him. For the first time in a week he felt warm. "I never heard that before."

"I was afraid of that." She tilted her head, her eyes sad again. "God has a plan for you, Jeremy. Even now."

"You know—" he hung his head—"you know what I did?"

"I know." She sighed. "That's why I came. I have some kids who might want to visit you one of these days. I wanted to make sure you were okay with the idea."

"Kids?" Jeremy's heart beat hard and fast. Suddenly he remembered where he'd seen her before. It was at the audition more than a year ago, the one for *Charlie Brown*. The woman had been in charge of the group. He licked his lips, trying to keep his mouth from drying up altogether. "What kids?"

"Friends of the kids who died. Theater kids." She frowned. "I can't be sure that they'll come, but I'm praying."

"And you want me . . . you want me to tell you that's okay?"

She nodded. "You have to give permission before I can bring them here."

Jeremy sorted through his options and realized he had just one. "Sure, of course." He closed the Bible promise book and set it down on the bench beside him. "Bring whoever you want."

At that, the woman smiled. She reached out her hand. After several seconds, he did the same and their fingers touched. "I'm sorry, Jeremy." She let her hand fall back to her side. "I wish you would've gotten a part in *Charlie Brown*."

For a long while, his words stuck together. But finally he said, "Yeah, me too."

She told him good-bye, and then she was gone.

After she left he looked at the Bible promise book and picked it up. He turned once more to page seventy-seven and read the verse again. God knew the plans He had for him, huh? Well, those plans looked pretty bleak right now.

The friends of the kids he killed wanted to come see him. Probably so they could spit at him and yell at him and tell him how much they hated him. Maybe they'd scream or throw things at him. That's what he expected, anyway, and if they did, well then, that was okay.

Whatever they threw at him, he deserved it. And not even a Bible promise could change that.

CHAPTER TWENTY-TWO

ASHLEY WAITED UNTIL THEY WERE IN THE CAR after church before spilling her feelings.

"Can I be honest?" She buckled her seat belt and watched as Landon helped Cole into their Durango.

When Landon was in the seat beside her, he shot her a quick smile. "Always, Ashley. Nothing less than honest."

She grinned. "I know. It's sort of a figure of speech."

"Okay." He started the engine. "So what's on your mind?"

"My dad." She uttered a quick groan. "The man's driving me crazy."

Landon steered out of the parking lot and onto the main highway toward home. "Is this story leading to the idea of going to your dad's house?"

"Yes." She winced. "Is that okay?"

He chuckled and changed lanes. "Of course. I just like to know where I'm driving."

"You're driving straight, Daddy." Cole gave a toothy grin first at Landon, then at her. "Right, Mommy? Daddy's driving straight."

"Thank you, Cole," said Landon. "You can sit back now."

"Okay."

Ashley hid a short laugh. Then she looked at Landon. "I think he's spending time with that Elaine Denning again. Remember her? The woman he would go hiking with over the summer?" She said the word *hiking* as if it were akin to chewing tobacco. She worked to soften her tone some. "I mean, they were in a group but still, remember?"

Landon took her hand, keeping his eyes on the road. "I remember."

"Well, she was trouble back then, but she's more trouble now."

"Says who?" Landon turned onto the road that led to her parents' house.

"Kari. She talked to Dad yesterday and she called me this morning. Dad let it slip that he's been talking to Elaine on the phone at night, and guess what else?"

"They're eloping?"

"Landon!" Ashley jerked her hand from his and scowled at him. "That isn't even a little funny."

He chuckled again but gave her an apology with his eyes. "Sorry. I was just pretending to be you."

"What's that mean?" She was shocked. Didn't he see the harm in her father spending time with a widow? The woman might be after his money or his house—anything. She nudged him. "Whadya mean, pretending to be me?"

"You know, believing that every phone call from a woman is the same thing as a wedding proposal." His eyes sparkled, and she was struck by how he still left her breathless. How could she have made things so difficult between them for so many years?

She gave him a demure smile and took his hand again. "I'm not crazy, Landon. The woman's been going with Dad to the farmers' market of all things. Two Saturdays now."

"So maybe they *will* elope." He moved away from her fast so she couldn't punch him. "Kidding. Just kidding."

"Daddy?"

"Yes, Cole?" He tried to look more serious as he caught Cole's look in the rearview mirror.

"I think you should keep your eyes on the road. That's what you always tell Mommy."

This time Landon licked his finger and pretended to score one point for Cole and Ashley. He looked straight ahead and nodded. "Good idea, Cole. That's just what I'll do."

Ashley raised her eyebrows at him. "The point is, Mister Kidding, my dad is seeing a lot of her, okay? And it's way too soon for him to be spending that kind of time with a widow."

"Would it help if she were a guy?" Landon turned into her parents' driveway, pulled up to the house, and cut the engine.

"Why do you ask?" Ashley was anxious to get out, anxious to talk some sense into her father.

Landon studied her. "Because maybe he just needs a friend. I doubt he's doing anything wacky like falling in love, Ash. You know your father. No one could ever take your mother's place, not with him."

Some of the frustration and concern that had built in Ashley's mind lifted a little. "Still . . . I wanted to come over so I could talk to him. Then maybe he could come to our house for dinner."

"Because you miss him." Landon leaned across the gearshift and kissed her on the lips. "Or because you don't want him home alone where he might get the idea to talk to Elaine?"

"Landon Blake . . . why do you have to know me so well?"

"Because. That's part of loving you." He kissed her again. "You were busy this week with the funeral and theater stuff." He gave her a teasing look. "Busy getting a ride home from movie star Dayne Matthews. You know, that sort of stuff."

"It was a simple ride."

"With America's biggest heartthrob." Landon laughed. "Anyway, you were busy. Your father spent the time talking to Elaine, and now you're worried. You don't want his Sunday open too."

"Exactly."

"Hey, guys—" Cole leaned up between the seats—"can you kiss in the house? I have to go to the bathroom."

They all laughed and climbed out of the SUV. In the process, Ashley whispered to Landon, "Know-it-all!"

He pulled her close and kissed her cheek. "Only when it comes to you, Ash."

Inside, Cole rushed to the bathroom, while Ashley and Landon found Ashley's father sitting in his favorite recliner with his feet propped up, watching a football game and drinking a glass of iced tea. "Rams and Colts!" He raised his glass. "Colts are winning."

Cole returned. "Yeah, Papa, because Colts are the bestest team, right?"

"C'mere, big boy." Her father set his drink down and held his hands out to Cole. "You're right about the Colts. This year especially."

They watched a few minutes of the game; then Ashley went to the kitchen and poured water for her and Landon and Cole. "Care if I make Cole a sandwich?"

Her father raised his voice loud enough for her to hear. "Make us all one. I have some chicken salad in the fridge."

She opened the refrigerator and spotted the deli container on the top shelf. Ashley felt a twinge of sorrow. On summer Sundays, her mother had always made chicken salad. Only she would boil the chicken, chop it, and add fresh onion and red peppers and shredded cucumber, and she'd serve it over a tossed salad.

A sigh left Ashley's lips as she took the container and lifted the lid. So much of life would never be the same again without Mom. Ashley made a plateful of sandwiches and returned to the family room. They ate and made small talk while Cole cuddled on his grandfather's lap. The game kept Cole's attention, and Ashley was surprised to see that he could follow the action.

Once in a while her dad would say, "What kind of play do you think they'll run next?"

She wasn't even sure whether the Colts were on offense or defense, but Cole would grin and say, "A pass play, Papa. Maybe a screen."

"Or a bootleg pass, right, Coley?" Landon gave an approving nod at their little boy.

Ashley was amazed. Had Landon and Cole been studying plays in their spare time? Maybe when she was upstairs painting? It was just one more way the two of them had bonded in the year since the wedding. She put her hand over her abdomen. "This new baby better like football."

"Yeah, Mommy, and he better be a boy too." Cole caught her look and made his eyes big. "Just kidding." He gave a single laugh and looked at Landon. "Like Daddy, right? Us boys like to kid around."

Her father tousled Cole's hair. "That's what boys do best."

Only at halftime did Cole lose interest and ask Landon to go outside with him. "There's a snake near the porch, Daddy. I promise. Maybe if we go together we can catch it."

"Okay." Landon took Cole's hand, and the two headed for the patio door. "Let's walk really quiet."

Cole held his finger to his lips. "And talk quiet too. Paul at school says snakes get scared of loud noises."

"Right." Landon sent Ashley a look from the doorway, one that said he would give her the time she needed to talk to her father.

Ashley mouthed the words *thank you*. When they'd closed the sliding door behind them, she turned to her father. She waited until the next commercial; then she slid to the edge of her seat. "Hey, Dad, can I talk to you about something?"

"Sure." He looked at ease. Not at all like someone about to be caught in some hidden activity or relationship. "By the way, how've you been?"

"I feel great." She put her hand over her midsection. "I'm starting to show. At least I feel like it."

Her father gave her a skeptical look. "You look flat as a board still, but I understand. Your mother used to feel that way too. Tight across the middle, like she was all of a sudden huge."

Mention of her mother took the wind out of Ashley's concerns. If only her mother were here right now. They could be comparing notes on pregnancy, and she wouldn't have anything difficult to say to her father. Elaine Denning would simply be a distant friend, someone who had faded out of their lives years ago.

"Anyway, honey, sorry. I didn't mean to distract you." He took a few swallows of his iced tea and set the glass back down. "What were you going to say?"

Ashley felt funny now. Maybe she shouldn't bring it up at all. Kari had said it was no big deal. In fact the entire situation seemed to bother her more than anyone else who knew about it. Of course, her brother, Luke, didn't know yet. And she and Luke had always seen eye to eye. She thought about her time in Paris. Well, almost always.

Her father was waiting. "Well . . ."

"Okay, Dad, it's this." She used her hands to talk whenever she was nervous. Now she forced them back onto her lap. "I talked to Kari, and she says you've been seeing Elaine Denning."

"Hmmm." He allowed a quiet laugh. "I thought that's what this might be about." He leaned forward and released the footrest on his chair. Then he crossed the room and took the spot next to Ashley. "I'm spending time with her, yes. She and I are at a similar place in life, Ashley. Our kids are raised, and the loves of our lives are gone." He hesitated. "We're both lonely."

Alarms rattled the control panel in her subconscious. "But what's it mean, Dad? That you and Elaine are . . . that something's happening between you?" She was afraid, but her tone sounded more frustrated. "I guess I don't get it."

"There's nothing to get." He patted her knee. "Elaine's a friend, Ashley. Someone I can talk to and buy vegetables with." He lowered his face and peered past her fear. "That's okay, right? I can have a friend, can't I?"

"You don't need her." Ashley sounded like a hurt child, and she offered a small smile in his direction.

"What other friends do I have?"

Ashley's answer was quick. "Me. I'll go to the farmers' market with you."

"Honey—" he studied her eyes—"you have your own family. Landon and Cole and your new little one. You're busy most of the time, and that's okay. It's the way it's supposed to be."

"Mom should be going to the market with you." Ashley shifted her lower jaw to one side. "That's the way it's supposed to be."

"You're right." Her dad exhaled, but he didn't sound as tired as he had a month ago. "But she isn't here, and I still need a friend."

"Well . . ." Ashley blew at a wisp of her hair. "That's all it is? Really?"

"Really." He smiled at her and helped her to her feet. "Let's go see if they caught their snake, okay?"

She wanted to ask more questions, maybe how he felt when he was with Elaine or what exactly they talked about. But her father seemed finished talking, and his answers had calmed her nerves considerably. Who was she to deny him a friend? It was like Kari had said. Their father was a social person, someone who thrived on people and interaction. He had work, yes. But he needed something more. Elaine was a Christian, someone who shared his morals and beliefs. She and her husband had raised their children much the same way Ashley's parents had raised the five of them.

A friendship couldn't hurt too much.

She took a deep breath as she followed her dad to the patio door. "Knowing Landon, they've probably caught three by now."

Sure enough, Landon and Cole had a couple of garter snakes in a cardboard box. "They're the biggest snakes, Papa. Bigger than Jessie's fish the other day."

Ashley and Landon exchanged a smile. No doubt their son was

competitive. He still talked every day about how having a pretty fish was more important than having a big one.

"Hey—" Ashley's dad pointed to the stream behind the house— "I built a new footbridge. Did I show you?"

"A new bridge!" Cole hopped around in a circle. "I bet we can catch frogs off it, Papa. We can spot 'em and jump in and catch 'em." He clapped his hands. "Just like that."

"Let's go see." Her dad led them down a trail through the grass toward the place where he'd built the bridge.

Ashley marveled at him. Spending his days diagnosing patients and proving himself to be one of the most brilliant doctors in the area. But in his evening hours, he was busy building footbridges for little Cole. She smiled. "It's perfect, Dad."

"What'd it take you?" Landon took the lead and walked over the bridge first. "A whole afternoon?"

Landon and her dad had a running commentary on who could pull together the fastest home-improvement jobs. Landon always took longer, so now he liked to guess at how quick her dad was.

"Two afternoons and one evening." John pointed to a pile of lumber a few feet away. "I have enough to make it wider. One of these days you and Cole come over and we'll make it a two-lane job."

"Oh, boy!" Cole danced over the bridge to the other side of the stream and back again. "Let's do it right now, Papa."

Ashley could've watched them interact forever. But her dry lips were killing her. The past week had been cool and windy, and she tried to carry ChapStick with her wherever she went. This morning, though, she'd gone to church without it. "Hey, guys, I'll be right back. I need to find something for my lips."

She headed into the house and took a drink of water first. Then she walked upstairs to the guest bath near her parents' bedroom. She sifted through the two drawers on the far side of the sink but found nothing. Her mother used to keep a stock of extra tubes of ChapStick or toothpaste or lotion in the drawers. Whatever she thought a guest might need. Now the drawers were mostly empty except for a few loose buttons and an old hairbrush.

She drifted into the hall and into her parents' room. Surely her father would have something in his medicine cabinet or in one of the drawers in his bathroom. She went through the cabinet and spotted a tube of ChapStick right away.

She made an *ahhh* sound as she rubbed it onto her lips and stuck the tube into her pants pocket. She could get her dad a new one and a few extra while she was at it. Just to keep the guest bath stocked the way it should be.

Her lips feeling much better, she walked out of the bathroom and was about to breeze past her parents' bed when she saw her mother's box of letters sitting on the floor, with a few sheets of paper scattered next to it. A surge of joy came over her. Her father must've been starting the scrapbook project! Maybe it was a surprise, something for Christmas.

That must be it, because he hadn't mentioned working on it. She moved a little closer, and for a moment she thought about taking a peek. What would it hurt? He was going to copy the letters for all of them to read, anyway. Couldn't she sit down and look through a few of them? Just knowing that they had belonged to her mother made her want to touch them.

She eased herself onto the edge of her parents' bed and peered into the box. It was full of letters with her mother's handwriting. She reached for a letter on top, but something else caught her attention. On the floor beside the box was a manila envelope, and spilling out from it was another envelope with one word written on it:

Firstborn.

It was definitely her mother's handwriting. Ashley frowned. Why would her mother write a special letter to Brooke? And why would it be here instead of at Brooke's house? Then she considered something. Maybe the letter was intended for Brooke, but it never made it to her. Her father must've been going through the letters when he found it. He probably set it aside so he could remind himself to give it to her the next time she stopped by.

Well, she could do that one favor for her father. Besides, she'd probably see Brooke before he would. She took the envelope and tucked it under her arm. Then she reached into the box of letters. But as soon as she touched the one on top, she was overcome by guilt.

Her father had asked her to stay out of the box. Going through the letters was something he wanted to do alone. She pulled her hand from the box of envelopes and stood up. Fine. If he wanted to go through them, she would let him. She would resist the urge to read them here, now, all by herself.

She took the letter marked *Firstborn* and returned to the kitchen. She slipped it safely inside her purse, making a mental note to let her dad know what she'd done. He'd be glad she found it, glad she was saving him the hassle of getting it to Brooke, where it belonged.

As she headed outside, she felt good about herself. She was right to resist reading the letters today. It was one way of respecting her father. And with all he was going through—fighting loneliness and trying to make his way with a new friend in his life—respecting her dad was the least she could do.

That and an occasional favor to help him out.

CHAPTER TWENTY-THREE

THE FILMING WAS UNDER WAY, but off camera nothing was going right.

Dayne grabbed a paper cup of lukewarm coffee from a portable dispenser and downed it in one gulp. They were smack in the middle of Main Street, not far from the Bloomington Community Theater. An old park lay sprawled out on one side, and a row of brick shops lined the street on the other side.

The scene was between the female lead—Kelly Parker—and her father. They were supposed to be running errands. Kelly was supposed to keep trying to tell her father she was leaving, that she'd taken a job in New York City. But time and again they would run into someone her father knew.

It was one of the movie's early scenes, meant to show the relationship between the main character and her father and the fact that she feels both fondness and frustration about living in the same small town where she grew up.

The setting was perfect, and even the weather had cooperated. Sunshine streamed down on them despite a forecast of clouds and rain. But Dayne couldn't shake the feeling of being caged, locked onto the location no matter what his heart wanted him to do.

He hadn't done much but stay in his hotel Saturday and Sunday, and early Monday Kelly called his cell phone. She had arrived in Bloomington before the rest of the crew and wanted to see him. They spent the day walking around the location, checking angles and areas of interest, and talking about everything but the most important thing.

Finally Monday night she'd brought it up. "She must love living in a town like this."

There was no point lying about it. He nodded. "Katy Hart, you mean?"

"Yes." They were sitting across from each other at a diner near the back of the Holiday Inn. Occasionally someone would approach them and ask for an autograph. But the paparazzi still hadn't shown up. Kelly pushed her fork around the inside of a baked potato. "So . . . did you see her?"

"I did. We hung out for a couple days."

"What exactly . . . ?" Anger tightened Kelly's mouth. She pressed her fingertips into her eyebrows and massaged them. When she dropped her hands to the table, she looked a little more controlled. Control was important to Kelly. "What does that mean—you hung out for a couple days? You mean you've been here having a tryst while I get ready for this movie of ours?"

"It wasn't a tryst." He was quick to defend Katy, but he had no intention of being honest. People in Hollywood weren't honest, just careful. He took a bite of his burger, chewed it, and swallowed. "Katy's not like that. We just talked and hung out."

"Just . . . ?"

Dayne sighed. "What do you want from me, Kelly? I care about her. You know that. You know I offered her the part. But nothing happened between us, okay?"

"Why should I believe you?" She was losing her edge again. "You *see* a girl and you sleep with her, Dayne." She waved her hand at him. "You spend time here where she lives and you expect me to believe nothing happened?"

He pushed his plate back, slammed his napkin down, and stood to leave. "Believe what you want, Kelly."

They didn't talk again until the meeting Tuesday morning. It was held in a private banquet room at the Marriott, where everyone was staying except Dayne. He'd arrived early to go over the location map with Mitch Henry, but there was no missing Kelly's arrival. She was dressed in tight black pants and a form-fitting turtleneck, and even people who had seen her a hundred times and worked with her on previous films turned to appreciate her beauty.

Dayne saw her walk in, but her body caused him none of the usual thrill, and he turned away just as quickly.

"Talk to her, you idiot," Mitch hissed at him. He folded the marked-up Bloomington map. "We're finished here. Go on."

"Fine." Even then Dayne had felt caged, boxed in. Forced into a life that he no longer wanted. He took a seat near the back of the room, and Kelly spotted him. Her eyes told him she wasn't interested in fighting.

"Hi." Her word was almost too soft to hear, but she took the seat next to him. For a long time she looked at him, her eyes big and childlike. "I'm sorry."

Dayne felt the tension from deep within. He shifted, hoping she couldn't tell. He didn't want another inquisition. "Me too."

She put her hand on his knee. "I shouldn't have pushed you last night. If you tell me something's true, I have to believe it."

"That'd be nice." He gave her a partial grin, one that told her things were okay between them. People were still milling around, and there was an air of excitement in the room. It was always this way at the beginning of a shoot. He put his hand over hers. "The movie's going to be great."

"That's what everyone's saying." She leaned in and kissed him. "It's important that we're okay, you know?"

A few months ago, he would've assumed she meant for her own well-being. Back then she'd been very needy, so bothered by the paparazzi that she wouldn't leave her house without him by her side. But that had been changing in the weeks leading up to the film. She'd been out with her friends several times, and more than once the rumor mill linked her with his buddy Marc David.

When the dust settled and everything came to an end after filming *Dream On*, Kelly Parker would be just fine. He touched her hair. "We're okay. Don't worry."

But now it was Wednesday, and he wasn't sure he'd last two weeks here in Bloomington, minutes from Katy Hart. But he might as well have been on the other side of the world. Police tape cordoned off the area being used by the film crew, and along the perimeter were easily a hundred people with cameras. Some were locals who had come to see what all the fuss was about. Others were serious fans, no doubt.

A group of teenage girls moved along the yellow tape, trying to stay as close as they could to him. They carried an enormous cardboard sign that read "We drove four hours, Dayne Matthews. Give us a kiss!"

Another group of fortysomething women held a spot as close as they could get to the food table. Whenever Dayne breezed past for a bagel or a cup of coffee, they'd scream his name and act faint. They had a sign too. Theirs said "Desperate Housewives. Desperate for Dayne."

Brother.

He wanted to duck under the tape and run until he found Katy, wherever she was this morning. Instead, he had to be aware of everything happening around him because a number of the people surrounding the taped perimeter were members of the press. The Bloomington paper was out and would stay on location every minute of the two-week shoot. Same for the Indianapolis papers. Both towns had television reporters standing by for possible live updates every hour.

But that wasn't all. The paparazzi were here too. He recognized half a dozen of them, faces that had trailed him through the streets of Hollywood and hidden in bushes while he shared a sandwich with a friend. The bottom-feeders of the journalism pool.

Every move he made this week would be captured and chronicled for the gossip magazines. Was he in love with Kelly? Were they struggling? Was there tension? What did their body language suggest? Why didn't he have that certain special look in his eyes the way they used to when they talked?

The cameras would be clicking nonstop, and every photo needed a caption. He had an act to keep up for the fans also. If he smiled and waved and let them take pictures with him, the press would sing his praises: "Dayne Matthews Gives Fans Something to Cheer About!" But if he dared grab a sandwich without winking at the desperate housewives, he was doomed: "Dayne Matthews Snubs Fans at Location Shoot."

For now he was trying to stay in the middle of the cordoned area, as close to Mitch Henry as possible. That way everyone would assume he was busy talking work. If he was half the actor everyone thought he was, then certainly he could convince them he was caught up in the filming. He didn't want anyone to know the truth.

That he wanted to be anywhere but here.

"You with us today, Matthews?" Mitch checked his clipboard and shot him a quick look. "Where're all the flashy Hollywood smiles the fans are used to?"

"I'm giving them." He turned to the teenage girls and waved at them. They screamed and jumped, hugging each other and waving back. "See? Everything's fine."

"It's not fine." Mitch sounded disgusted. "But it's going to be for these scenes. I'll see to that."

Dayne was up next, so he had no time to think about leaving. The sunlight was just right for the scene when he comes to the small town looking for Kelly, trying to understand why she'd come back home, hoping to talk her into returning to New York. It was a scene from the last half of the movie, but this was where it needed to be filmed, and with everything else lining up perfectly, Mitch had slated it next on the schedule.

Kelly was across the street in another cordoned-off area, talking with the actor who played her father. They'd finished one of their scenes. The others needed different lighting, so they'd wait until later in the day for those.

"Okay, Matthews, make the rounds." Mitch nodded to the fans standing around the tape. The number had doubled since earlier that morning. "I need you on the set across the street in five."

"Right." He took a step away from the director, and already the girls behind him were screaming. With a practiced grin, he saluted Mitch and turned toward the food table. Along the way he spotted a few regulars from the paparazzi crew, and he stopped and smiled for them.

They went crazy, snapping a continuous stream of pictures.

"Hey, Dayne, how are things with Kelly?" one of them cried out. Normally the photographers said nothing. But in a setting like this, Dayne was trapped. He had to feign kindness toward them; otherwise the fans would think he had a bad attitude.

"Kelly?" He made the okay sign and gave a subtle raise of his eyebrows. Two of the photographers had been on hand the night last summer when she tried to kill herself. "Things are perfect." He waved at them, the smile never leaving his face. "Thanks for asking."

The gossip rags hated it when things were perfect. They hated it when Dayne smiled at them, which was one reason he intended to do it all day long. They wanted an off moment—a chance instant when he might sneeze or snarl or spill his Coke—anything that would make for interesting copy.

He kept smiling, making his way down the line. A little girl held out an autograph book and a Sharpie. He took them and patted her on the head. "What's your name, sweetheart?"

A few feet away, a woman screamed, "Oh, my goodness! He called my niece a sweetheart!" Another scream. "I'm gonna die! I can't believe it."

The little girl looked embarrassed by her aunt. She gave Dayne a toothy smile. "My name's Rachel."

"Okay, Rachel." He moved the pen quickly across the page, the way he'd done thousands of times before. Then he handed the book and pen back to her. "Be a good girl, okay?"

"Okay."

The girl's aunt was jumping, her chest flopping around. "Dayne . . . sign my shirt! Come on, Dayne, over here!"

He pretended not to see her. A few more feet down and the teenage girls wiggled their way to the front of the tape. "Dayne! We need a kiss!" All five girls wore low-cut tank tops and tight jean shorts. The temperature wasn't quite sixty degrees, so they had to be freezing. Still, they waved their poster at him, more hysterical the closer he came.

"A kiss, please, Dayne!" The tallest of the group grabbed his arm. "Come on, we drove four hours!"

Was that all it took? If someone drove four hours then he owed them a kiss? Why would they want a kiss from him anyway? They didn't know him and would never see him again. Besides, not one of them looked a day over eighteen. In the corner of his eye he saw the paparazzi still shooting, their cameras following him everywhere he went.

He waved at the girls and smiled. "I came two thousand miles!"

They screamed and hopped around, as if maybe that was the most brilliant thing they'd ever heard. "Please, Dayne, take a picture with us!"

A picture he could do. He took three cameras from the girls and handed them to one of the gofers walking around inside the cordoned area. He positioned himself with his back against the tape, so the girls could form a group around him. Every one of them was trembling, squealing as the man tried to figure out the first camera.

Two of the girls had their arms around Dayne's neck, and one leaned in close to his ear. "Wanna have a little fun later tonight? We're staying just down the street."

Dayne kept smiling. "Okay, everyone look at the camera."

The gofer held it up and looked at the group. "One . . . two . . . three."

While the gofer was getting the next camera ready, the girl on the other side of Dayne slid her fingers partway down the back of his jeans. He jerked a few inches forward, and the girl giggled. "Sorry." She kissed him on the cheek. "I can't control myself."

He pretended to help the gofer get the next camera ready, but really he needed an excuse to keep his distance. When it came time for the picture, he kept himself just out of reach.

"We love you, Dayne!" the group chimed.

"The best fans are right here!" he shouted. The whole time he kept smiling, as if he was having the time of his life, hanging out with Midwestern teenagers, trying not to be molested by them. Where did the lines blur, anyway? His director wanted him to be friendly with the fans, but teenage girls sticking their hands down his pants? Grabbing him and kissing him? What if they were underage? What would the tabs say about that? When the last picture was snapped, he put four feet between him and the girls and waved at them.

By the time he arrived at the food table, he wasn't hungry.

"Dayne!" the screams came from all around him. The housewives waved at him, leaning over the tape and reaching for him. "Come on, Dayne. We're desperate!"

He walked up to them, his arms open wide, and gave all four a group hug. His ears rang by the time he pulled away. He grabbed a few grapes from the table and returned to Mitch. "There. You happy?"

Mitch didn't look up. "Very. The tabs got every minute. Dayne Matthews—America's heartthrob." He wrote something on his notepad. "You played the part perfectly."

"That's why they call me an actor."

"Exactly." Mitch looked at his watch. He picked up his bull-horn and aimed it at the people across the street. "Okay, attention. We're picking up with scene eleven, like we discussed. Everyone not in the scene get back to the staging area. If you're in it, take your places. I want to roll in two minutes."

His announcement started a shuffling of activity, though no one looked to be in a hurry. Dayne stared at the cast and crew, head-ing in different directions, chatting and laughing, surrounded by an air of privilege and confidence. The crowd outside the yellow police tape was still growing: more cameras, more waving, more screaming fans, more chaos. Wasn't it like this for every film, every time they shot on location outside Southern California?

So much money and time and energy . . . for what? For a two-hour film no one would remember in a year? His eyes glazed over, and he remembered the Saturday morning rehearsal with the CKT kids, the way Katy had circled her students around her, comfort-ing them and teaching them at the same time. Katy Hart's work with the kids—now that was important. Something everyone in-volved would remember.

"Dayne?" One of the gofers nudged him. "Mitch called for you." He pointed across the street. "We're shooting scene eleven."

"Right." Dayne tried to smile, but the corners of his mouth wouldn't go up any higher. The smile from earlier was still in place. He nodded at the guy. "Thanks."

Across the staging area, Mitch gave him a friendly wave, but his eyes told another story. The director was furious with him. Because of the paparazzi, none of them could show their real feel-ings, and that was something else that bugged him.

Dayne slipped a few of the grapes into his mouth and sauntered across the street to the area where the scene would be shot. Any other line of work allowed people to get upset. At a marketing meeting or in the midst of an advertising campaign, people could have concerns or doubts or harsh words, and it would all be in the line of work. In the movie industry, even what went on behind closed doors eventually wound up in the rags. On a day like this, the first day of shooting for Dayne Matthews' next big film, every wary eye would be looking for a problem. That way they could gleefully tell the public that there was "trouble on the set" or "differing opinions between the director and the stars."

Kelly was waiting for him, watching him as he stepped onto the sidewalk. Her smile came easily. "You look distracted."

"Nope." He could feel the cameras trained on them. His arm came around her waist, and he pulled her close for a kiss. He could be honest later. She stayed in his embrace for a few seconds, their faces inches apart. "Everything's great."

"Ready for action?" She pulled him close again, her eyes flirting hard.

The bullhorn squawked into action. "Okay, you two—" the voice was Mitch Henry's—"save it for the film."

Dayne gave her one more practiced kiss, waved at his director, and straightened. Even this part felt scripted, and he could only guess how happy Mitch must've been making the announcement. It gave everyone in attendance—paparazzi included—a reason to think that *Dream On* was just a fictitious extension of the real-life love story playing out between Dayne and Kelly.

The whole thing was a joke. A sarcastic laugh simmered in Dayne's gut. The cameras might not be rolling, but the acting had started long ago. Not that it was Kelly's fault. She meant well, and for a time, he'd enjoyed her company. Or maybe he'd only felt sorry for her. Either way, she didn't deserve to be in a relationship with a guy whose attitude was so lousy.

It was one more thing they'd have to work out later.

People were taking their places. The scene would have Kelly and Dayne walking down the street, talking. Kelly's character was confident and friendly, greeting people she knew, familiar with the layout of the street. Dayne's character would lag a little behind her, baffled at how different this town was from the landscape of Manhattan. Halfway down the block, Dayne was supposed to get sick of her ignoring his questions. In a teasing manner, he was then supposed to grab her by the shoulder, pull her into an alleyway, and kiss her.

"Remember what I told you," Mitch barked through the bull-horn. "This one might be outdoors, but it's one of the steamiest scenes in the movie. Let's get it right."

A round of hoots and applause went up around the perimeter of the tape. Dayne grinned at Kelly, and based on her reaction, his expression must've convinced her that everything was okay. She gave his hand a quick squeeze and took her place. They'd run through the lines a dozen times already, so there was a chance they'd get the take clean the first time. That was Dayne's goal.

A makeup artist ran in and powdered his forehead and his nose, while a stylist patted his hair with a sheen they used for outdoor shots. All of it had already been done, but touch-ups were a constant part of the work. Beside him, Kelly got the same treatment.

Around the set a hush fell over the crowd.

"Okay, everyone." Mitch sounded exuberant. "Quiet on the set."

Dayne took his position. He could feel Kelly at his side, and he wondered how much of his director's upbeat tone was wishful thinking and how much was his attempt at convincing everyone that the film was going to be a huge hit. He took a quick breath. *Okay, Matthews*, he told himself, *make it count*. He closed his eyes and imagined that he was a New York businessman accustomed to getting his own way. Only now the girl he loved had run out on him, and he'd come to her small hometown to find her, to talk some sense into her because, of course, things would work between them.

Yeah, he could be the part. No problem.

He opened his eyes, and there—standing across the street near a tree outside the cordoned-off area—was Katy Hart. Next to her stood Jenny Flanigan and the choreographer, Rhonda. All three of them had Starbucks drinks in their hands, and they looked content to stay in the background. Jenny and Rhonda were talking, but Katy was quiet.

She had her eyes trained straight on him.

Even from fifty yards away, he could feel her in his arms, hear her voice the way she sounded a few days ago. He wanted to call for a break and run to her, but it was impossible. If he looked at her another second longer, Kelly would catch on and spot her too. Then even drawing on the best of their talent they wouldn't be able to pull off the scene.

Dayne swallowed hard and looked away. He leaned close to Kelly. "Ready?"

"Ready." She smiled at him. "Remember, let me take the lead."

He nodded, but all he could think about was Katy. She had to know he couldn't talk to her, yet she'd come. Did it mean she wasn't willing to give up? Or had the others merely brought her along because they were curious?

The sun was hitting them from the east, and Mitch had moved closer, his director's chair positioned in the middle of the street a few yards away. Still, he used the bullhorn. "All right, let's slate it."

One of the assistants held a black chalkboard in front of the camera and said, "Scene eleven, take one."

Kelly set out at a relaxed pace. A few extras strolled by from the other direction, and Kelly waved at them. "Mr. Grover, Mrs. Grover."

Dayne twisted his face in disbelief, looking over his shoulder as the couple passed and taking awkward steps to keep up with her. "What is this place?" He held his hands out at his sides. "You know everyone, or what?"

She spun around, her expression pleasant but determined. "That's the idea." She flipped her hair over her shoulder and kept walking. "Not that you New Yorkers would know anything about that."

"Hey . . ." He took a few quick steps and reached for her hand.

When she turned around, her eyes were impatient, perfectly so. "I'm here because I want to be here. Can you understand that?"

"Yes, but . . ." He had a line, and he searched his brain trying to find it. "Yes, but you . . ."

"Cut!" Mitch flew off his chair and stormed the remaining distance toward him. Not far off, the paparazzi fought for position, snapping pictures all the while. The director kept walking until he was two inches from Dayne's face. "You don't know the lines?"

He glanced for a second to where Katy was standing. She had her back turned, and he figured she must've known. How could he concentrate with her watching him? This had rarely happened to him in all his days of acting. He could be dating one girl and playing the boyfriend role for another. He could even do a bedroom scene with an actress while a girlfriend watched.

But none of them had become part of him the way Katy had, the way she always would be.

"Matthews!" Mitch was seething now. "Get focused!"

A fine layer of his spit hit Dayne on the cheek. He wiped it off, but he didn't dare smile. "Sorry. I know the lines."

"You better." The director spun around and returned to his chair.

Kelly shot him a weak smile. "Distracted by my beauty, huh?" she whispered.

"Yeah." He made a face. "What can I say?"

The scene was slated again, and this time they got all the way to the part where Dayne was supposed to take hold of Kelly's shoulder and pull her into an alleyway. He did just that, careful to keep his expressions in line with his dialogue. But as he pressed her against the brick wall and moved in to give her the kiss that was supposed to take her breath away—the one that should take away the breath of every female who would watch the movie—he tripped over his lines again.

This time he walked away and tossed his hands. Before Mitch could yell at him, he grinned at the director. "She's making me nervous," he shouted loud enough for everyone around the perimeter to hear. "I think I have a crush on her."

Dayne's pronouncement was enough to send a ripple of giggles along the rows of fans. Even the paparazzi smiled as they snapped his picture and noted for the record that the on-screen chemistry between Dayne and Kelly was so strong it was messing with Dayne's ability to remember his lines.

Except that was a lie, of course. Dayne knew it and Mitch knew it, and at that point, Kelly had to know it too. Dayne crossed the street, and as he did, he looked off to the side at Katy. She was watching him again, and her eyes held an apology. He gave her the slightest shake of his head and hoped she would understand. No, he couldn't talk; no, he didn't want her there watching him; and no, this wasn't what he wanted.

But he had no choice.

She seemed to understand, because from the corner of his eye he saw her say something to Jenny and Rhonda. After a minute the three of them turned and left. By then he was midway through a brief conversation with Mitch and Kelly.

"Whatever's going on in your head, Dayne, get it out." Mitch was beyond angry. For the first time he looked worried. "This kissing scene has to be one of those they talk about in chat rooms across the country." He took hold of Dayne's arm. "You know that kind of kiss, Matthews?"

Katy's face came to mind. Dayne blinked and nodded. "Yeah, Mitch. I know it."

"You should." Kelly was still smiling, trying to keep the moment light. After all, everyone around them thought he was simply too smitten with Kelly to keep up the pretense of the scene. She tapped her finger on his chest. "That's how you used to kiss me."

Mitch waved his hands. "None of this used-to stuff." He pointed at the alleyway across the street. "Go kiss the girl, Matthews."

He put his arm around Kelly as they walked back to their spots. "Sorry. It's just taking me longer to get into character."

"How about if I don't look too deeply into that one, okay?" She leaned up and kissed his cheek. "Let's get it right."

"We will. I promise."

Dayne kept his word this time. With Katy gone, he could focus all his anger and longing, all his frustrations on the scene. The kiss came out fantastic, filled with the kind of passion and rage and impossibility that marked the best on-screen moments.

When they were finished, Mitch stood up and clapped. "Perfect, people! That's what I'm talking about!" He directed the bullhorn toward the fans. "How about that? What do you think?"

The people cheered and screamed their approval. Some of the women called out Dayne's name. "Kiss me like that, Dayne!"

"We love you, Dayne!"

"We're still desperate, Dayne!"

Kelly had her admirers too. A group of guys playing football in the park had come over and found a spot along the tape. They hooted at her and tried to get her attention. "You need a real man, Kelly Parker. Take one of us!"

Dayne didn't care about any of it. The only thing that mattered was he'd found a way to pull off the scene. Not because of his acting skill or because he'd been able to get into character. Not because of Mitch Henry's harping, either. But because he'd forced himself to look at his leading lady and see the face and eyes of someone else altogether.

A young drama instructor who had just walked away one more time without looking back.

CHAPTER TWENTY-FOUR

KATY DROVE HOME FROM REHEARSAL still mad at herself for going to the location shoot two days ago. She had known from the beginning that it was a bad idea, but Rhonda wouldn't give up.

"You mean he was sitting in the sanctuary for two whole rehearsals and you never introduced us?" She was half-furious, half-crushed. "Then you have to take me to the location shoot, Katy."

She talked it over with Jenny, and the two of them decided it couldn't hurt. They would stand on the perimeter and watch the happenings. If Dayne wasn't too busy, they'd say a quick hello and Katy could introduce Rhonda.

But that wasn't how it turned out at all.

Of course they'd shown up just when Dayne and Kelly were trying to film a love scene. Katy knew that part of the script well. It was a turning point, the time when the female lead realizes that she can't win. She wants to stay in her small town, but she wants the male lead more.

The kiss was supposed to show her passion for him, her struggle about what the future held. But as soon as Dayne spotted Katy, she had the feeling things weren't going to work out.

"He saw you," Rhonda had whispered.

"I know." Katy had turned around. "Let's go. This is awkward."

"It's not awkward; it's amazing." Rhonda took a step closer and motioned to Jenny. "Come on, we're too far back."

The next few minutes told Katy she was right. Dayne was making mistakes she could only blame on herself . . . and why not? They had left things without any real solution, no closure. Of course her presence would distract him.

She turned into the Flanigans' driveway, parked, and climbed the stairs to her apartment without being noticed. Before another night went by she was determined to research Kabbalah on her computer. It was something she'd told Dayne she would do, and she wasn't going to fail him. Not on this. He would leave Bloomington soon. But his faith, his salvation weren't anything to mess with.

She had a feeling neither was Kabbalah.

Now she had to find the reasons why, the proof that would help him find his way to God—the God of his adoptive parents.

She tossed her bag on the bed and pulled a letter from her pocket. Tim Reed had handed it to her as practice was ending, and she hadn't had a chance to read it until now. She opened it and smiled at the boyish printing.

> Katy,
> Just wanted to thank you for making the Bible study a weekly thing. I think we all need it.
>
> Tim

Her heart hurt in a good way when she thought about how the CKT kids were coming together. That first night, after she'd told them Jeremy Fisher's story, they had read about the Prodigal Son. It wasn't fair, a few of the kids pointed out, and Katy had to agree.

Why would a father throw a party for the bad son, the one who had made all the wrong choices? the one who had come home empty-handed? Especially when the father had never thrown a party for the good son? But that wasn't the point of the story, and by the end of that evening the kids seemed to understand.

The point was, the father loved his kids. Both his kids. Every day was a party for the good kid, because he had a pure uninterrupted relationship with his father. Not so for the bad son. Every day of his absence was another day of darkness. In that sense, of course the father would celebrate when he looked at the horizon and saw his lost son finally returning.

"What right did the good son have for being angry?" Katy had asked them. "Maybe his father wanted him to celebrate the bad son's return also. Think about that."

The kids had done what she asked, because several of them mentioned it over the next few rehearsals. One day when they met for Bible study before practice, they'd looked at verses on love. By the end of the hour it was clear what was happening. God was working in their hearts. They might not be ready to forgive Jeremy Fisher just yet, but it was coming. She could feel it with absolute certainty. God was working a miracle in their group, and in time it was going to be clear to all of them.

Katy sat down at her computer, signed on, and waited for the search line to come up. She typed in *Kabbalah* and hit Enter. Thousands of possibilities came up, the first of which were official websites for the organization. She clicked the top one and waited.

A mystic blue page filled the screen, and at the top it read: *The wisdom of Kabbalah teaches its students how to attain the upper world and the source of existence. By finding purpose, all men can achieve perfection and learn to enjoy the limitations of time and space.*

Katy read it again and one more time after that. Still, she was confused. Dayne had talked about an upper world, but it wasn't something she'd heard before. And what was the idea that all men could find perfection? Only Jesus was perfect, and people couldn't find that righteousness without dying to self and living for Him. The Bible's teaching on perfection smacked in the face of the teachings of Kabbalah.

She scrolled farther. One summary of the teachings said that Kabbalah was the ultimate source of fulfillment in this world. *Kabbalists live a life governed by one law, the general law of the universe,* one teacher had written. *This law has one single objective—to make us equal to God.*

A chill ran down her arms. She checked two more sites and found statements about how Kabbalah could teach a student to become his or her own god. She read about the six hundred and thirteen impure desires and the one hundred and twenty-five spiritual steps.

After thirty minutes of research, Katy was sick to her stomach. The teachings felt more like a cult than anything, and she tried that as another search.

Kabbalah and *cult,* she typed in.

Another long list of possibilities appeared, and she tried the first. It read: *Media alert—Kabbalah is part of the pop culture, but it is also a destructive cult!*

Her heartbeat quickened. No matter if she ever saw Dayne again, she had to get this information to him. She scanned the page, and the sick feeling in her stomach grew worse. Leading cult experts likened Kabbalah to cults that were sinister, deceptive, and destructive.

Leaders at the centers will make outrageous claims, one expert said. *Then they try to take huge sums of money from new recruits, convincing these people that only by giving can they make their way through the myriad of spiritual steps required to reach fulfillment.*

It's hogwash, another wrote. *The centers use control tactics and other tricks typical of cults. If someone you know or love is caught up in Kabbalah, get them out.* The expert went on to say that the answer was to have a high level of personal responsibility.

Katy wanted to throw something at the computer. Personal responsibility wasn't the answer to spiritual lies. The truth would only be found in Scripture. That's when the idea hit her. She would copy the information on Kabbalah, print it out, and buy Dayne a Bible. Then she'd put the two items together and get them to him before he left. Her personal feelings were nothing compared to the seriousness of what he was about to be involved with.

As she turned off her computer, she remembered the words that had blown across her soul when she prayed for Dayne the week before: *Make the most of every opportunity.* Maybe that's the reason he'd been brought into her life. She felt silly for letting her feelings get involved, childish for kissing him. She was there for one obvious reason—to stop him from doing something he would regret forever.

Otherwise he might never know the truth.

⚘

John and Elaine walked the last aisle of the farmers' market, enjoying the comfortable banter they'd found together. They had a standing date now to spend Saturday mornings together, and John had done everything he could to calm the fears of his kids. They all knew now, even his two youngest adult children, Luke and Erin. He'd told them all the same thing.

Elaine was his friend, and having a friend in this season of his life was important.

If he'd thought Elaine was looking for anything other than friendship, he would've ended things with her immediately. But now that his life had a new purpose—to find his firstborn son—he needed a friend more than ever. Especially since no one but Elaine knew about his plans.

He carried a bag of fresh-picked apples. She held a small paper sack with more blueberries, her favorite. They'd been talking about the letters, how John had sorted through them and decided that if Elizabeth wanted to find their oldest son, then he would fulfill her wish or die trying.

Elaine pointed across the park. "Hey, what's happening over there?"

John peered over a family setting up a picnic. The days were still warm, still sunny enough to spend outdoors. But the leaves were picking up color, and the sun set earlier every day. Fall was setting in and winter wasn't far behind it. When he saw the white panel vans and trucks and a film crew, he remembered. "That's where they're filming that Dayne Matthews movie."

"Right." Elaine tried to get a glimpse, but she was too short to see much. "I read about it in the paper."

"Ashley came by the other day. She loves this kind of stuff."

Elaine raised her shoulders a few times. "If you've got the time, let's take a look."

"Sure." John swung the bag of apples over his left shoulder and turned onto a sidewalk that would take them closer. "I don't remember the details, do you? I think it's a love story."

"It is." She smiled. "*Dream On*, I think. Stars Dayne Matthews and Kelly Parker. The gossip magazines say they're living together. I guess the interest is up because of what they have offscreen."

"Hmmm—" he smiled at her—"I didn't know you read those."

"I don't. Just the covers when I'm in line buying groceries. You can get most of it without turning a single page."

John laughed. They were closer now, and he led her to a spot near one corner where they had a front-row view of the happenings. Dayne Matthews was standing next to a man with a bullhorn. Across the street, Kelly Parker and an older man were talking in front of a row of small businesses. People stationed around the edge of the cordoned area had their hands up, warning the spectators that filming was going on.

After a few minutes, the man with the bullhorn yelled, "Cut, got it! Perfect! You people amaze me."

The crowd of onlookers clapped, and someone a few feet from John and Elaine called Dayne's name. He turned around and smiled, and for the briefest instant, John sucked in a quick breath. "My goodness."

"What?" Elaine shifted her blueberries to her other arm and tried to follow his gaze. "That's Dayne Matthews."

"I know." He shook his head. "Dayne's a client for one of the attorneys at the firm where Luke works. More than a year ago, Luke told me that everyone at the law firm thought they looked alike." He stared at the movie star. "They were right."

Elaine squinted, studying Dayne. "Sort of." She gave a slight nod. "I can see the resemblance."

The man with the bullhorn was asking everyone to quiet down again, and John motioned toward the parking lot. "Let's get going." He whispered, "I'm not much of a star gazer."

She laughed, and they were quiet as they walked to his car. The whole way, John thought about the letters and the fact that he had the rest of the day to finish going through them. Clouds were gathering overhead, and more rain was expected. It would be the perfect afternoon to light the fireplace and sort through the box. He'd know about Elizabeth's thoughts, and at the same time he could select the best letters to copy for Ashley and the other girls.

The conversation with Elaine was pleasant on the way home, but it felt good to drop her off and have the silence. Even though the silence could be lonely, it was sometimes the best sound of all. Because in that silence, he could always find his way back to yesterday.

At home, he put on the kettle and went to his room to retrieve Elizabeth's letters. A new setting would be better to sort through the letters this time. He grabbed the box of letters and the manila envelope with the three letters inside. He glanced inside the manila envelope, but something wasn't right.

It contained only two envelopes.

Suddenly his heart began to thud hard against the wall of his chest. Where had it gone? He saw the ones for himself and the kids. But the one for their firstborn son was gone.

It had to be here. He set the manila envelope on the bed and checked the floor. It had been here the other day, and no one had touched the area since. Of course, the cleaning lady had come yesterday. Maybe that was it—maybe she'd set it somewhere to keep it from being sucked in by the vacuum.

He moved the box of letters off the bed and looked underneath it. Then he dropped to his knees and lifted the bed skirt. It had to be here. Other than the housekeeper, no one had been in his room, and he hadn't moved it.

Or had he?

He stood and stared at the box. Was he so caught up in the memories and emotions the other day that he'd buried the letter marked *Firstborn* in the box with the others? He clutched the manila envelope and lifted the box onto his hip. That had to be it. He must've slid it down somewhere near the bottom so no one would find it.

For the next hour he sorted through the contents of the box, placing letters in piles on the kitchen table according to who wrote them and when they were sent. By the end of that time John was certain of one thing:

The letter was missing.

Ashley had been over, but she wouldn't have taken it, would she? But if not her, then who? The thought made him sick. But even worse was the idea that the secret he and Elizabeth had kept for so many years was about to become public knowledge. And after that, nothing between him and his kids would ever be the same again.

It was too much for John to take in, and as he ate dinner alone and tried to pass the time all evening, he finally convinced himself that the housekeeper must have moved it. She would've been cleaning and not known if the envelope belonged with the box or somewhere else. In her doubt, she would've set it somewhere safe, somewhere he might find it. Yes, that had to be it.

If Ashley had seen it or taken it, she would've called him by now. She wasn't one to sit on something so life altering. The thought brought him comfort. He'd talk to the cleaning lady as soon as he could. He would ask her where she'd put the envelope, and all would be well. By the time he turned in, he was sure that was the answer.

In fact, he had no doubts whatsoever.

CHAPTER TWENTY-FIVE

THE CHEMISTRY BETWEEN KELSY BOUCHEY and the rest of the *Annie* crew was beyond what Katy had hoped for. Kelsy was the perfect Annie, singing with a soulful earnestness that made her not only believable but unforgettable. The girl's skill and professionalism reminded Katy of Sarah Jo Stryker, and at times she'd done a double take, looking over her shoulder to see Kelsy where—for a moment—she had expected to see Sarah Jo. Little Kelsy could take a person's breath away with a single song. And since she had a number of solos, the show was already off to a great start.

Katy stood near the front of the sanctuary and raised her hands toward the kids onstage. "Let's do that again. The street-people scene needs work."

Rhonda hopped into the center of the action and helped position kids where they needed to be. Katy took a seat, her notepad balanced on her lap. It was Saturday morning, and more than a week had passed since she'd seen Dayne or allowed anyone to bring up his name.

All her focus was on the play. In the orphanage scenes, she'd worked in some special blocking to highlight Kyle Lanham. He was onstage now looking adorable as always, playing the role of one of the orphans, since they didn't have a little girl his size who could pull off the vocals. They'd renamed him Wally, and the other orphans were constantly fawning over him. The boy had complained about his role at first. If he was the only boy people might think he was a girl, he said. Because of that, Katy shifted a few other boys into those scenes.

Kyle's mother had pulled Katy aside at the last practice. "No matter what Kyle tells you, he loves the attention." She patted Katy on the back. "Thanks for trusting him with the part."

"He's playing it perfectly." She hadn't had as much time to get to know the new parents with this show, but she liked Kyle's mother. "Whatever you're doing at home, keep it up."

Now they were putting the final touches on the blocking for the street scene. Kelsy was supposed to come in stage right with her newfound dog and ask the group of shabby street people whether anyone was looking for a dog, and for that matter, whether any of them had given away a little redheaded girl nine years earlier.

Katy had debated a long time about whether to use a real dog. That had always been the plan, but with the tragedy of the accident and the lost rehearsal time, it seemed like more than they could pull off. Still, the rest of her creative team had wanted a real dog, and a brief audition was held at the end of the first rehearsal. They picked a dog named Mister, a golden retriever with a slightly earnest expression. In auditions, the dog was able to come and sit on command. With the other dogs generally wandering around the room and sniffing each other, Mister was the obvious dog for the part.

The next hurdle was whether to call him Mister or Sandy, the way the script called for. Katy's creative team agreed that somehow the dog would have to learn to come to the name Sandy.

Everyone who knew the story of Annie knew that her dog's name was Sandy. Period.

They'd kept the dog out of rehearsals until today, and so far they'd run into one problem after another. The first and most obvious was the fact that Kelsy Bouchey, for all the talent she brought to the role, was deathly afraid of dogs. It had taken half an hour for Nancy Helmes to get the child to sit still long enough for the dog to come up and lick her hand.

Now Kelsy was willing to let the dog walk by her side, but she was still jumpy around him. The cast members were all in their places, and Kelsy stood off in the wings, with Mister on a leash at her side.

"Okay, let's take it from the end of the song."

One of the older girls in the middle pretended to dole out soup to the cold, shabbily dressed street people lined up on either side of her. Katy surveyed the line of faces. "You don't look cold, guys. Come on."

Immediately, the street people began blowing on their fingers and rubbing their hands together.

"That's it, and look interested in each other. You're in a soup line, but you'd be making conversation."

The kids started talking with each other.

"No, wait!" Katy stood and waved her hand. "Silent conversation, pretend conversation."

A few of the older kids hid a round of laughter, but the noise dropped. The girl in the middle held an imaginary ladle and looked down the line. "Another day, another bowl of soup."

Katy looked at Kelsy. "That's your cue, honey."

"I know, but the dog's smelling my shoe."

"That's okay." Katy took a few steps toward her. "Dogs do that. Just pull on his leash and bring him onstage."

She tugged at the leash and walked to the middle of the group of street people. "Hi, everyone. Hey, did anyone lose a dog?"

The street people responded with a mix of quiet no's and head shakes.

"Well, then . . ." Kelsy took another step toward the people.

"Open up, Kelsy." Katy was back at the front pew, getting what would be the front view of the scene. "We have to see your face at all times."

She nodded and turned her shoulders toward the front of the room. "Well, then, did anyone give up a little redheaded girl nine years ago?"

A few more lines of conversation followed, and then the scene went into a reprise of the earlier song. When it was finished, on came Bryan Smythe, the new CKT heartthrob and one of the kids attending the weekly Bible study at the Flanigan house. He scattered the street people and then approached Kelsy. "Hey, little girl, what's your name?"

"Annie."

"Hmmm." He gave her a stern look. "This your dog?"

"Yes, mister."

At the sound of his name, the dog did a happy circle around the two of them, wagging his tail and hanging his tongue from his mouth. In the process the leash wrapped around Kelsy's and Bryan's legs, and the two of them teetered and tipped and finally toppled onto the stage with the dog between them.

Mister hovered over Kelsy and began licking her nose.

"Help!" Kelsy screamed.

"Don't panic!" Bryan tried to push his way between her and the dog.

Kelsy's arms were flailing. "Get him off me!"

Katy put her head in her hands. She walked up to the kids and helped them get untangled. "Okay, so let's cut the word *mister* from the scene."

Again a round of giggles came from the kids who were now watching from either side of the stage.

"Yes, it's all very funny." Katy smiled at them. They were right;

it *was* funny. But they still needed to find a way to make it work. "Remember—" she took the leash from Bryan and pulled the dog to her side—"we open in six weeks, and so far the dog scene's nothing more than a comedy routine."

She handed the leash back to Kelsy and showed her and Bryan where to stand. "Let's take it from the part where Bryan asks you if this is your dog."

Bryan did as he was told. The kid had two parts in the play. Police officer in this scene and the one where he has to return Annie to the orphanage, and the rising star in the NYC song, mostly because he was amazing at belting out the solo in the middle of the number.

Bryan gave Kelsy a stern look. "This your dog?"

"Yes . . ." Kelsy shot a glance at Katy. "Yes, sir."

"All right, then what's his name?" Bryan pretended to have a billy club in his hand, and he tapped it against his open palm.

"Uh . . ." Kelsy looked at the dog. "His name's Sandy. That's it, Sandy. Because of his nice sandy color." She smiled at Bryan. "He's my dog, all right."

"I guess we can see about that." Bryan walked the dog across the stage and turned to face Kelsy. He unhooked the dog's leash and held him by the collar. "Call him, and if he comes to you, then he's your dog. If not, he goes to the pound." He paused. "Okay, kid. Call your dog."

Kelsy gulped, just the way Katy had told her to. She crouched down and looked at the dog. She held out her hand and said, "C'mere, Sandy. Come on, boy. Come, Sandy."

From her place in the pew, Katy held her breath. The next part was the riskiest of all.

Bryan released the dog, but instead of going to Kelsy, Mister trotted to the center of the stage, sat down, and stared out at the pews. He headed back past Bryan, down a set of stairs, and into the aisle to one of the mothers sitting four rows back.

Again there was laughter, and Katy raised her hand. "I have an idea." She ran onstage, knelt at Kelsy's side, and hung her tongue from her mouth. Then she crawled on all fours to Bryan and looked straight at Kelsy.

Bryan picked up on it. "Okay, kid," he said between bouts of laughter, "call your dog."

Kelsy held out her hand and said, "C'mere, Sandy. Come on, boy. Come, Sandy."

Katy shook her behind as if she were wagging her tail; then she hurried on all fours straight to Kelsy. The parents in the audience broke into applause, and Katy jumped to her feet and took a bow. "If we can't get Mister to do it, I'll be the dog." She rushed back to her seat. "No need to panic."

Mister's owner was here this morning, watching her daughter play one of the servants. She came up and sat next to Katy. "I think I know how to make the scene work."

"You do?"

"Yes." The woman gave her dog a disdainful look. "Raw hot dogs."

Katy felt herself frown. "For . . . ?"

The woman grinned. "For Mister. He loves raw hot dogs." She pulled a bag from her purse, and inside were a few mottled brown sticks of meat. "I can tear them into pieces, and Kelsy can hold them. Mister will come to her for sure that way."

It all made sense in an instant. "Of course. Great idea." Katy reached for the bag of hot dogs but changed her mind. "Would you do that? Tear them up for us?"

The woman agreed. She sat in the pew ripping apart the hot dogs, while Katy went to Kelsy and explained the newest idea.

Kelsy shook her head. "Hot dogs make me sick." She wrinkled her nose. "They're slimy and gross."

Next to her, Bryan gave them a look that said he agreed with her.

Katy put her hands on her hips. "It doesn't matter what you think of them, honey. Mister likes them."

The dog's owner came up with the plastic bag containing what was now a cup of ripped-up hot dogs. Kelsy was right; they didn't look very tasty.

Katy took them and handed them to Kelsy. "Put them in the pocket of your coat. We'll make sure you have a coat with pockets in the show. That way you can reach in and grab a few pieces when you need Mister to come, okay?"

They ran the scene again, and this time when Kelsy called the dog, he came to her at a full run, knocking her down. He snatched the bag of hot-dog bits and ran toward the back of the sanctuary.

It was two o'clock, time to wrap things up. Katy watched the dog head through the back doors of the sanctuary. She turned to the kids and tossed her hands in the air. "Okay, so we pray about the dog. Every one of us, all right?"

The kids were grinning, all of them except Kelsy. Bryan was helping her to her feet, but she had a disgusted look on her face and she held her hands out in front of her. Bryan led her offstage and signaled Katy that he'd help her wash up.

"Okay." Katy took a deep breath. "Like I said, if we don't get the dog to work, I'll wear the collar."

The kids filled in around the stage, and they had five minutes of conversation over what they could improve, what they still needed to work on. Then they prayed and Katy dismissed them. The older kids were planning to meet later that afternoon at the Flanigans' for another Bible study.

Katy was glad. It gave her a purpose, a reason to stay busy so she wouldn't think about Dayne. The problem was, she needed to think about him. She'd bought him a Bible and printed out the notes on Kabbalah. The two items were in a bag in her car. Now she had to get them to him without showing up on the set or calling him—two things she'd promised herself she wouldn't do.

When the kids were gone and Mister had been caught by his

owner and returned to her car, Jenny Flanigan approached Katy. Bailey and Connor and Tim Reed milled about near the back of the sanctuary, clearly waiting for Jenny. She touched Katy's shoulder. "Hey . . . how're you doing?"

"Good." Katy laughed. "The dog thing'll come together eventually. I have a good feeling about it."

"No, Katy." Jenny searched her eyes. "I mean about Dayne. They're finishing soon, and you haven't mentioned him."

"I know." Katy bit her lip.

"We're stopping by there on our way home. The kids want to watch the filming."

She wanted to go too, wanted to blend into the background and watch Dayne up close. Just so she could remember what it had been like being with him. But since she wasn't allowing herself to do that, she had an idea. She reached for her notepad. "Can you do me a favor?"

"Anything." Jenny's concern rang in her voice. They hadn't talked much about Dayne in the past week, but it was clear Jenny understood that things couldn't be good between Katy and him.

Katy scribbled fast on a piece of yellow lined paper. She tore it from the pad and folded it six ways before holding it out to Jenny. "Can you give this to Dayne? Tell him I couldn't come, but I wanted him to have this."

"I can do that." Jenny took it and stuck it in her pocket. She hesitated. "You sure you don't want to come?"

"No." Katy felt her eyes well up, and she exhaled through pursed lips to stop herself from getting emotional. "I have work to do before the older kids come by this afternoon. Just . . . just give him the note."

"Sure." Jenny gave her a hug. "It'll be okay, Katy. I'm here for you if you want to talk."

She nodded and took a step back. Jenny started to head up the aisle as Katy remembered one last thing. "Wait!"

Jenny turned around.

"Make it look like you're a fan, okay? Tell him to read it later, so no one thinks anything of it."

"I will." She nodded toward the kids. "I think we'll be getting a few autographs. I'll blend right in."

Katy watched them until they left the sanctuary. She wanted so badly to go with them, to see how Dayne was doing and look into his eyes. That way she wouldn't have to ask, because she would know within her, the way she knew what he was feeling every time they'd been together. For a moment she considered running after Jenny and forgetting all the reasons why she had to stay away. But then she remembered the note. If they could get it to Dayne, she wouldn't need to go to him out on the street location.

Because he would find her.

⚘

Jenny Flanigan felt as if she were on a mission. She waited until she was in the car with Bailey and Connor and Tim Reed before telling them what Katy had said.

"Are you kidding? We have a secret note to pass to Dayne Matthews?" Bailey was sitting in the seat beside Jenny, and she squealed, barely able to sit still.

"I feel like we know him or something." Connor buckled his seat belt, his voice almost as excited as his sister's. "Maybe he'll ask us to join him on the other side of the tape."

"Guys—" Jenny kept her tone even as she pulled out of the parking lot—"Katy wants us to act like fans. Yes, you've met him, and yes, he's been to our house. But that doesn't mean we know him."

"You mean, like ask him for his autograph, that kind of thing?" Tim was eager too, but being a teenager, he was playing it cooler than the others.

"Right." Jenny looked in the rearview mirror at Connor. "Katy doesn't want anyone wondering about the note. We really have to pull it off, okay?"

A round of okays filled the car, and from the backseat Tim whispered, "Wait'll I tell the guys about this."

Jenny laughed. She had to admit it was fun, going to the on-location site for a Dayne Matthews film, with a mission to find the star and pass him a secret note. "Say whatever you want to your friends, guys. Just don't mention the note. Katy was serious about that part."

They headed downtown and parked near the theater. It wasn't much of a walk, and the closer they got to the area where they were filming, the harder it would've been to find an open spot. A light rain had fallen earlier, and the ground was damp.

"I hope they're still filming." Bailey walked next to Tim, leading the way.

"They will be." Connor nodded. "I read it in the paper. They need a bunch of different weather shots to make it feel like a small Midwestern town." He held his hand out and looked at the clouds overhead. "They're probably glad it rained."

Another block, and the cordoned-off area came into view. The crew had left the area for a couple of days so they could shoot at a farmhouse they'd rented just outside town. Now they were back near the park to wrap up the shots that hadn't come together before.

Jenny felt in her pocket and made sure the note was still there. She was tempted to read it, but she wouldn't. If Katy wanted her to know, she'd tell her later. For now she needed to focus on getting it into Dayne's hands.

"It isn't crowded." Tim glanced over his shoulder at Connor. "I bet we talk to him right off."

"I hope so." Bailey squinted at the commotion in the center of the cordoned-off area. "He needs that note."

Jenny held her finger to her mouth. "Enough about the note. It's our secret from here on out, all right?"

They all nodded and followed Bailey and Tim to a spot along the police tape. It looked like the cast was in the middle of a break or a meeting. Dayne Matthews and Kelly Parker and two other actors were talking with the director.

Bailey folded her arms in front of her. She kept her voice low, so only Jenny and the boys could hear her. "How're we going to do this?"

Jenny wasn't sure. The rain had definitely thinned the number of spectators, but still they needed to get Dayne's attention. She tapped Connor on the shoulder. "You're the youngest." She looked at Dayne and back at her son. "Let's move a little closer, and then you call out his name."

Connor lowered his brow, nervous. "Then what?"

"Here." Jenny handed him a pad of paper and a pen. She'd found them in the car just after they parked. "This way it'll seem like you really want an autograph."

"Okay." Connor shrugged. "I really *do* want one, so I'm not faking or anything."

Jenny smiled at him. She loved Connor's transparency.

Bailey and Tim continued to lead the way, working past a few groups of damp, subdued, probably die-hard fans. At the first opening along the police tape, Bailey moved in and the others followed. The meeting with the director looked like it was breaking up. Dayne was saying something to Kelly Parker, as the two pulled away from the others.

Jenny nodded to Connor and whispered, "Now!"

Connor didn't hesitate. He held up the pad of paper and pen. "Dayne! Over here!"

The screaming fans were gone for the afternoon, so Dayne heard Connor right away. He turned and at first he looked like he might only wave, but then his eyes met Jenny's and something changed in his expression. He leaned in and said something to Kelly, then pulled away and headed in their direction.

He must've felt like Katy, afraid to do anything that might

cause suspicion among the photographers still crouched along the police tape. He went first to the fans at the far end of the tape and worked his way toward them. It took five minutes before he reached out for Connor's pad of paper. He wore the same smile he'd had for the other fans as he signed his autograph and handed the pad back to Connor, but his eyes told another story.

No one was standing within hearing distance of them, and he looked at Jenny. "How is she?"

Jenny pulled the note from her pocket, then reached for Connor's pen. She handed both items to Dayne, along with a blank sheet of paper from the pad she'd given Connor. "She wanted me to give you this. Sign the second sheet so no one will know about the note."

He nodded, as if she'd asked him a question about the film. Then, in a manner that was as relaxed as it was practiced, he took the blank piece and scribbled his name across it. He handed it back to Jenny and said, "Where is she?"

"Getting ready for a Bible study."

The photographers were watching them, but no one was taking pictures. They'd probably seen Dayne do this all week long, take a few minutes and tend to the fans who waited for him along the police tape.

Bailey and Tim each took a piece of paper from the pad and handed them to Dayne. Jenny was proud of all of them. No one would've guessed they weren't an ordinary group of fans.

"This part's not an act." Bailey's cheeks darkened, and she bounced a little. "Can you sign these too?"

"Sure." Dayne smiled at her. "You knew who I was the other day, didn't you?"

"Yes." She grinned at Jenny. "I told Katy it was obvious. Of course you were Dayne Matthews."

He kept smiling, kept playing the part of the doting actor, giving time and attention to his devotees. "What about you?" he asked Tim. "We haven't met, but I've seen your work."

Tim looked stunned. "You have?"

"Yep." He signed the final sheet of paper and handed it to Tim. "You're good, Tim Reed. Keep it real, okay?"

"Okay." Tim's mouth hung open. He glanced from Bailey to Jenny and then back to Dayne. "Hey, thanks."

Dayne nodded to him; then he looked at Jenny again, and for the first time, his familiar smile faded. "Tell her something for me." He smiled again, pretending to be engaged in a casual conversation.

Jenny played along, shifting her position and cocking her head as if she had the most curious thing to ask him. "What should I tell her?"

"Tell her I miss her." With that, he made a subtle move of his hand, tucked the note from Katy into his pocket, and continued on to the next group of fans.

Bailey clasped her hands together and did a partial knee bend. "Oh, my goodness, I can't believe that just happened." She bounced some more and took hold of Tim's forearm. She kept her voice low enough that no one on either side of them could've heard her. "He remembered you, Tim. Can you believe that?"

"I know." He let out a quick burst of air and ran his fingers through his hair. "I mean, he was at rehearsals the other day, but I don't think I had much of a part."

"He was at *Charlie Brown*." Jenny smiled at the kids.

"He was?" Connor was a little louder than the others. Jenny raised an eyebrow at him and he lowered his voice. "How did we miss that?"

"Katy told me he snuck in on the last night of the show. He sat in the back and watched the ending, and then he left." She turned away from the taped-off area and motioned for the others to follow her. "I guess he was doing research for his location work."

"That's so cool." Bailey looked at Tim again. "Maybe he can get you a break in the movie business."

They were still talking about it when they reached the car. None of the kids could get over how well Dayne had played it off, how he had treated them like any other fans, even while he talked about CKT and Katy Hart. But the part that stuck out to Jenny was something more hidden, something only she had picked up on. Since Katy had mentioned that she'd been to Hollywood to read for a movie starring opposite Dayne Matthews, Jenny and Jim had worried about her. When it became clear that she had feelings for Dayne, they were even more concerned.

They saw the headlines at the supermarket checkouts. Dayne was a reckless playboy, a selfish guy who would use whatever girl walked into his life and never think twice about it. Even after he'd been to their house the other day, her prayers for Katy had been singularly focused. *God, keep Katy away from Dayne Matthews.*

But now she would have to change that prayer. From here on out, she would pray that God have His way with whatever had grown between Katy and Dayne. Because this afternoon she'd seen a human side to Dayne Matthews. Human and vulnerable and very much concerned about one girl and only one girl. Not his leading lady, no matter what the tabloids said or whom he was living with. That girl wasn't Kelly Parker.

It was Katy Hart.

CHAPTER TWENTY-SIX

DAYNE WATCHED THE FLANIGANS and Tim Reed leave. He forced himself to keep up the act, to keep making his way along the line of fans, talking to them, answering their questions. Things had settled down among the spectators, and only rarely did he have screaming girls along the police tape anymore. The fans who remained were chatty and personable. He needed to give them more time, more one-on-one attention.

But with Katy's note in his pocket, he was dying for a moment to himself. When he reached the end of the line, he waved back at Kelly and Mitch and motioned to his trailer. They nodded, understanding that he probably had to use the restroom or freshen up. He kept his pace slow even as he headed up the trailer steps and shut the door behind him.

He quickly jerked it from his pocket and opened it.

> Dayne,
> I need to talk to you. The paper says you finish at five. Meet me at the Lake Monroe trailhead at six o'clock.
>
> Thinking of you,
> Katy

His hands trembled as he read it two more times. So she hadn't forgotten about him. Every day, every hour he scanned the perimeter where they were shooting, hoping to see her somewhere in the background. But she hadn't been by since that first day, and he hadn't called her.

He'd barely had a minute to himself, but it was more than that. Kelly was with him now. They hadn't slept together—he couldn't, not after the time he'd spent with Katy Hart. Whenever Kelly suggested that he move into her room at the Marriott, he would ward her off with excuses about working on his lines and needing his space.

But he had to pretend things were okay because of the film. The act he was playing for the press and the fans was one he continued after the cameras stopped. He was kind and touchy around Kelly, kissing her often and letting her think everything was fine. A few days ago, she stopped asking about Katy and whether he was thinking about her.

Which meant he was a better actor than he gave himself credit for.

Now he looked at the note again and made a plan. Kelly had talked about their having dinner with Mitch, but that was impossible. Whatever it took, at six o'clock he would be at Lake Monroe waiting for Katy.

He tucked the note back in his pocket, stepped out of his trailer, and joined Kelly and Mitch in the middle of the cordoned-off area. Then he worked with Kelly on one more scene.

As soon as Mitch gave word that they were finished, Kelly came to Dayne and put her arms around his waist. "Still up for dinner?"

"Not tonight." He watched disappointment change her expression.

"Why not? Mitch is looking forward to it."

The lies were adding up, and Dayne was starting to hate it. Lying used to come easily, but not anymore. Maybe it was part of his interest in Kabbalah, letting go of negative emotions. He narrowed his eyes and looked up. "My agent sent me a script, something he wants me to get back to him about first thing in the morning." The lie took root. He looked at his watch. "I've got three—maybe four—hours of reading ahead of me at least."

She pouted, but her eyes told him she believed every word. A gofer brought each of them a bottle of water, and she took a few steps back. "Things were good today."

"Very good."

Mitch walked up, and Dayne repeated the lie. It was easier to tell this time around, but as he was getting to the part about his agent wanting the script read by morning, one of the minor stars in the film, Hawk Daniels, approached them and put his arm around Kelly. He whispered something in her ear, and she . . .

Dayne took his eyes from Mitch and studied Kelly. Yes, she was blushing. She was whispering to Hawk and blushing.

Mitch was watching too, and he rolled his eyes. He plastered what was obviously a fake smile on his face, and in a voice intended for their small group alone, he inclined his head toward Hawk and Kelly. "Don't give the bloodsuckers something to write about. Please."

Hawk nodded at Dayne. Then he grinned once more at Kelly and went on his way.

"Huh." Dayne gave Kelly a look. "Good friend?"

She tried to gather herself. "*New* friend." She took hold of Mitch's hand. "Looks like you and I are having dinner by ourselves."

"Oh, good. Next thing you know *I'll* be in the tabs."

They said their good-byes, and Dayne rode back to the Holiday Inn with one of the gofers. The ride was quiet, because Dayne kept playing the scene with Kelly and Hawk over in his mind.

Was she seeing him?

Any other season in his life and a scene like that would have bothered him. But not now. Watching them had given him something he hadn't felt for a long time when it came to Kelly Parker.

A sense of peace. Maybe that's why she hadn't pushed the issue of spending more intimate time together this week. Maybe Hawk had replaced him. Knowing what was bound to come when they were finished filming the movie, Dayne could only hope so.

He thanked the gofer and found his rental car. The paparazzi must've gone to dinner. They were lazier in Bloomington than they were in LA. Photos were snapped all day during the shoot and in any off moments when the stars were having casual conversation or taking pictures with fans. But so far the photographers hadn't followed them around at night.

There was an assumption on a location shoot like this one: work hard during the day and turn in early each night. After all, they'd given the press no reason to sense a scandal. And what interesting thing could the stars of *Dream On* possibly do in Bloomington, Indiana?

Dayne climbed into his car and smiled. If they only knew.

The closer he got to Lake Monroe, the more nervous he felt. He had only a few more days in Bloomington, and since Katy had kept her distance, he hadn't expected to hear from her again. Not that he wasn't constantly thinking of a way to see her.

But as busy as his filming schedule was, there hadn't been a chance. Until now.

He pulled into the lake parking lot, cut the engine, and looked around. Katy's car was parked a hundred yards away near what looked like a private boat club. She must've walked the longer distance so he wouldn't be tempted to park near her, just in case he was being tailed by paparazzi.

The sound of frogs filled the evening air, and he looked over his shoulder. No one had followed him. He climbed out and shut the door, feeling his heartbeat all the way to his fingertips. This was exactly the thing Mitch Henry had forbidden him to do. *"Don't see the girl, Matthews. Stay away from the girl."*

He shut the words from his mind. No one would ever find them here.

The night was warmer than it had been all week, probably because of the low clouds. A fine layer of mist hung over the lake, and the air was thick and humid. He looked down, something he did without thinking anymore. His way of keeping as much privacy as possible, even here where he couldn't see another person anywhere. He found the trail, and as soon as he was in among the trees he spotted her.

She was standing against the trailhead sign, watching him. Beside her on the ground was a brown paper bag. He slowed down. How could he have stayed away from her? Even from fifty yards away he could feel his heart respond to her. Whatever this was about, the news must be good. The last time they were together, she told him she didn't see any way to make things work between them.

But now . . . why else had she asked him to come?

He closed the distance between them and ran his tongue over his lips. His mouth was dry; he was anxious about what she wanted to say. When he was a few feet from her he stopped and looked into her eyes. "Hi."

"Hi." Emotions must have warred in her heart, because her expression went from cautious joy to fear and back to joy again. She moved the toe of her tennis shoe in a circle in front of her. "Thanks for coming."

"Katy . . ." He couldn't pretend about how he felt. Not when they were alone in the fading sunlight on a wooded trail, a world away from anyone or anything but the two of them. He ordered himself to hold his ground, not to take her in his arms until he heard her out. "Did Jenny give you my message?"

"That you miss me?" She smiled. "Yes."

His lips parted, but he couldn't find the words. Finally he nodded. "I do. I . . . I've thought about you every day."

"Yeah." A hint of sadness played in her eyes. "Me too."

He could feel his knees shaking, and he marveled at himself. No one had ever done this to him, made him feel like a kid with his first crush. He could have just about any woman he wanted, and for most of his adult life, he'd done just that. But this was something so different. Like he'd woken up and realized who he really was. "So—" he brushed at a mosquito circling near his face—"how's *Annie* going?"

"We've got a derelict dog." She made a funny face. "If he doesn't work out, I told the kids I'd wear the collar and leash."

He chuckled and shifted his position, not sure whether she wanted to walk or stay where they were. "I bet the kids liked that."

"They did." Her voice was soft, musical almost. "I think they're hoping the dog'll stay bad." She nodded up the path a ways and picked up the brown bag. "Let's walk." She glanced past him, back toward the parking lot. "Just in case."

"Okay." Dayne wasn't worried. The paparazzi wouldn't have a clue where to find him. Still, Katy had more to lose than he did. He followed her another twenty yards down the trail. She stopped and leaned against one of two trees that stood only a foot apart from each other. He gave her a questioning look. "Here?"

"This is good. I don't want to be too far from the cars."

He thought of something then. Maybe it wasn't only the paparazzi that had her nervous. It was late in the day, and the sun was setting. She was remembering the time they were together this close to dark, when the knife-wielding fan had jumped out at them. No wonder she wanted to stay out of sight, but not too far from their cars. He leaned against the tree opposite her, the toes of their shoes touching. "How's the Bible study going?"

"Very good." Her tone was suddenly passionate, and he was reminded that CKT wasn't only a job for Katy—it was a calling. She looked up through the tree branches at the pink-streaked sky overhead. "The kids' hearts are changing, Dayne. I see it more every time we get together."

"I'm glad." He didn't want to rush her, but he had to know. "So . . . why are we here?"

She still had the brown bag in her hands, and now she set it down and pulled something out, a few pieces of paper stapled together. "I did the research, like I said I would."

"Research?" Was she talking about the film or something else?

"On Kabbalah. Remember, I said I'd look into it?"

"Oh, that." He brought his hands together and felt his bare wrist. Mitch hadn't wanted him wearing the Kabbalah bracelet during the filming. One other bit of information they could deny the media. "What'd you find?"

Her eyes were more serious than he'd ever seen them. "It's bad stuff, Dayne. Some people say it's a cult."

"Really?" A sick feeling rumbled in his gut. "How come?"

"Well, let me ask you." She handed the papers over to him. "Has anyone from the Kabbalah Center talked to you about making a large donation, something about money taking you through most of the spiritual steps?"

Dayne felt the blood leave his face. How could she have known that? He flipped through the pages. On them were two topics: *The Bible and Kabbalah—Some of the Differences* and *Why Some People Think Kabbalah's a Cult.* He looked at her. "You did this? You took the time to put this together?"

She nodded. "I told you I would."

"Thanks." He was suddenly winded. How close had he come to writing a seven-figure check to the Learning Center? It was something he had planned to do when he got home. He shook his head to clear his mind. "I'll read it when I get back to the hotel room."

Her eyes held his for a long while. "I think you need to go back, Dayne."

"Back to the hotel?" He'd just gotten here. She couldn't have only wanted to give him the notes and then be on her way, could she?

"No." She stared into the loneliest, most confused part of him. "Back to your roots, to the faith your adoptive parents tried to teach you."

He brought his lips together and for a moment said nothing, only peered through the trees at the darkness falling over the lake. Finally he shrugged. "Where should I start, Katy? No one in Hollywood thinks like that. No one I know, anyway."

"Start with the photograph—the one your birth mother gave you." She slipped her hands behind her. "You said there was a letter on the back, something you've never read."

"Right."

"So . . . go find it. Read it. The way back has to start somewhere for all of us."

"The way back?" He loved this about Katy, the fact that she could talk about real things. Not just scripts and dinners and how the press might view them.

"The way back to God, Dayne. He's the reason you're here, the reason we found each other in the first place. So that you'd have a reason to go back to the beginning."

"But . . . I don't know; the guys at the Kabbalah Center talked about finding freedom and peace, getting rid of negative feelings." He leaned his head back against the tree. "Doesn't that sound good to you?"

"It sounds like something only God can take care of." She touched his arm. "God and you."

He pressed his fingers to his chest. "See, I have all this . . . I don't know—anger—I guess." The frogs were louder than before, and he raised his voice. "I told you about my adoptive parents, but I didn't tell you how I feel now. I'm angry at them." He waved his hand at another mosquito. "They picked God over me. Now I'm supposed to go looking for God?"

She eased her fingers around his wrist. "You have to search. The answers are out there, Dayne." She reached back into the bag and pulled out a book. No, it wasn't a book—it was a Bible. She handed it to him. "I got you this. So the search would be easier."

"Oh." He made a quiet sarcastic sound and then regretted it. Her sincerity was touching, but that didn't make her suggestions any more plausible for him. "I won't find the answers at the Kabbalah Center—" he held up the Bible—"but I will find them here?"

"Yes." She had no doubts whatsoever; that much was clear from her tone.

The path was getting dark. They had only a few more minutes of daylight before they'd have to go back. "Why, Katy? Why the Bible?"

"Because it's the only thing on earth that is the authoritative Word of God. Any search for truth has to start there, right? Because God's the author of truth."

Dayne let that roll around in his mind. He'd never thought of it that way. God being the author of truth. He looked at the Bible, then at her. This wasn't the time to have a debate. He'd missed her too much to waste their time that way. He slipped the Bible and the document on Kabbalah back into the brown bag. "Thank you."

"Meaning we aren't going to talk about it." She searched his face, his eyes.

"Not now. We don't have much time, Katy. It means a lot to me that you'd do this, though. The research and the Bible." He paused. "Really, thank you."

She nodded and looked at something on the ground near her feet. After a while her eyes found his and she spoke straight to his soul. "What you said earlier . . . that you missed me . . ."

"Yes."

"I missed you too." There was shame in her voice, and it cut him deep. Was he that bad for her that she hated the idea of missing him? He studied her, waiting for her to finish. She stood straighter, no longer leaning against the tree. "I tried not to miss you, but I did. I couldn't help it."

They'd been talking for twenty minutes, and the whole time he'd wanted to take her in his arms. Now he couldn't take another breath without reaching for her. He put one hand around her waist and the other along the back of her head. "Come here, Katy. Please."

She came, but he could sense her reluctance. Only after they drew together in what was now a familiar embrace did he feel her relax in his arms. "Dayne . . ." She pressed the side of her face against his chest and clung to him. "How come I can't just walk away?"

He kissed the top of her head and whispered, "Maybe you're not supposed to."

"But I *am* supposed to." She looked up, and there was alarm in her eyes. "If there's no future for us—and there isn't—then I need to be your friend. Nothing more. Nothing that would—"

He lowered his face to hers and kissed her, silenced her the only way he knew how. Not by his kiss so much, but by showing her how wrong she was. They could never be only friends—never. Fate might not give them a chance to be together, but there was no point lying to each other.

The kiss grew and became two kisses and then three, and Dayne felt himself falling, losing control. She must've sensed it too because her breathing came faster, and in a sudden rush she pushed back from him, her eyes wide. "We can't, Dayne. No." She took a step toward the parking lot, her eyes clear and determined in the fading light. "I promised myself this wouldn't happen. It's not . . . it's not why I wanted to see you."

He felt a ribbon of anger tie itself around his soul. "And what was, Katy?" Her kiss still burned on his lips. He didn't want to fight with her, not now. But he had to make his point. "Was it this?" He lifted the brown sack and held it out to her. "You came to warn me away from Kabbalah and turn me back to God?" He set the bag down and gave a single laugh. "Is that all this is for you?"

"Of course not." She moved away from him. "But I have to answer to that same God. And right now I can't think of a single good reason why I should be standing here in the woods kissing you."

Her words were like so many knives stripping away everything wonderful about the way he'd felt a few moments ago. He stared at her, baffled. "Not one good reason, Katy?" His voice was much softer than before, the control back. "We care about each other, right? Isn't that enough?" She shook her head and backed away in the direction of the parking lot. "No, Dayne. It's not enough. In a few days you'll leave here and walk out of my life forever. And what then? What am I supposed to do with my feelings for you?"

"What am I supposed to do with mine?" He thought of something. "Don't forget the trial. We'll be together again whether you like it or not."

"That isn't the point." Her eyes filled up, and she looked away. "It's like I said before. What we have here or at the football stadium or out jogging—it's all pretend. Your life doesn't have room for me, Dayne."

He looked at her, looked beyond her fears. "And yours has no room for me, either."

"Exactly." She spoke the word with finality and defeat. Her tears spilled onto her face and shone in the dusk. "We found each other so I could show you the way back to God." She pointed to the brown bag beside him. "I did that." Another step backward. "Now I have to go."

"Katy . . . wait."

She shook her head and turned away. Then she ran back down the path, sprinting as if she were terrified he'd come after her. Not because she didn't trust him. Because she didn't trust herself. He could see that now. The humid air filled his lungs, making the ache in his heart worse. He picked up the brown bag and waited. After a minute he heard an engine start up and the sound of a car driving away. She didn't have to worry. He wouldn't go after her, not if she didn't want to be caught.

Stars were piercing the dark sky by the time he reached the parking lot. He slid the bag onto the passenger seat and drove all the way back to the hotel in silence. When he reached his parking spot near the back entrance of the Holiday Inn, he saw a lone photographer sitting in a car nearby.

The man leaned through the window and snapped a round of pictures.

Dayne stared at the guy and uttered a sad-sounding laugh. "You people never give up, do you?" He said it loud enough for the photographer to hear him.

"It's a job," the guy said. Then he held up his camera and clicked again.

"Well . . ." Dayne smiled and waved. He wouldn't give the guy the satisfaction of a single usable photo. No frustrated looks or angry eyes, nothing. He took a step closer, the smile frozen in place. "You're too late this time, buddy. You missed the story."

With that, he took his brown paper bag and headed into the hotel. Only then did the shock wear off a little, enough so that he could think about what Katy had said. How he needed to find his way back to God, and that maybe she had been brought into his life to show him the way. But there was something Katy didn't understand, no matter how many times he tried to explain it to her. The God she was trying to point him to? That same God had taken everything important from him—his birth parents, his adoptive parents, his chance at a family.

He thought about the rest of what she'd said, how she owed it to God to stay away from him, to let him go. Didn't it just figure? God had taken everything else. And now He'd taken the thing that hurt him most of all.

He'd taken her.

CHAPTER TWENTY-SEVEN

EVERYONE ELSE WAS READY, but Ashley still had curlers in her shoulder-length hair. Landon wouldn't mind. He knew that every now and then she ran a little late. Besides, the dinner tonight at her father's house was nothing out of the ordinary. Just a time for all of them to get together and catch up.

They would talk about *Annie* and the sets and how the kids were coming along in their grief over losing their friends. Dayne Matthews and his movie crew had gone back to Hollywood, and they'd probably touch on that, and about how much calmer the town was without the commotion of a film team in the middle of town.

She'd spoken to Katy twice since they left, but she was quiet about Dayne. Whatever had come of their time together, she wasn't talking about it. Almost as if she wanted to forget she'd ever known him.

That wouldn't come up at dinner, because Ashley hadn't told anyone but Landon and Kari about Katy's connection with Dayne Matthews, and they knew the matter was private. But the family was bound to talk about how the farmers' market would be saner now, and maybe her father would give more details about his friendship with Elaine Denning.

They'd all be there, after all. Dad had said they'd call Luke and Erin and talk to them on speaker. That way it would feel like they were all together again. Those two and Landon and Cole and her, Kari and her family. Brooke, of course . . .

Ashley set her lipstick down. Brooke! Of course Brooke would be there. She gasped and jogged down the hallway to the kitchen. She'd forgotten all about the letter, the one she'd found in her parents' room. Here she'd been trying to do her dad a favor by getting it to Brooke sooner than he might've, and now it had sat in her purse for three weeks. Way too long! She grabbed her bag and scurried to the bedroom. Her dad probably wondered what had happened to the letter. She hadn't even remembered to tell him she took it!

Ashley . . . you're so scatterbrained, she chided herself and took a seat on the edge of the bed. What if it had fallen out? Her purse was never exactly in one safe spot. Sometimes she'd leave it on the floor of her car or tossed onto the backseat. The letter was obviously something special, written by their mother just for Brooke.

Her heart skittered about anxiously as she dug through the side pocket. It didn't settle back to normal until her hand made contact with the envelope, stuffed near the bottom of the bag. She pulled it out and frowned. It was bent in half, with a smudge across the right corner.

How could she be so careless? The letter had stayed in her father's possession since her mother's death, in the box on the closet shelf, no doubt. And now she'd let it get all tattered. If it weren't for her mother's writing across the front, she'd put it in a new envelope.

She stared at it a little longer. Her curlers hung on either side of her face, and she gave them a little shake. They were still warm against her cheeks, which meant she had another five minutes at least before she could take them out. So . . . what had her mother written to Brooke, anyway? And why just to her firstborn? Was there something special, some words of wisdom she wanted to give Brooke that the others didn't need?

The possibility seemed strange, not at all like her mother.

A memory came back to her, the hours just after her mother's funeral. Her father had gathered Ashley and her siblings together and read them an important letter their mother had written to them. All five of them. In that letter, their mother had addressed them each by name.

So why a sealed envelope marked *Firstborn*?

Ashley turned the envelope over in her hand and noticed another smudge on the back. Cole's Teddy Grahams probably. They were spilled throughout the same side pocket, and a few of them had morphed into a mass of fine cracker dust. Ashley brushed at the spot with her thumb as the memory from after her mother's funeral lingered.

Her dad had put the letter—the one addressed to the kids— back into a single manila envelope; only there had been two more smaller envelopes inside it, right? The details were getting clearer now. She had noticed the other envelopes and asked him about them. "What about the other letters, the ones still in the envelope?"

Yes, she definitely remembered asking him about it. And he'd said the others were for him. Ashley blinked and ran her fingers over the sealed edge of the envelope. That didn't really make sense, either. Why would Mother write one letter for her children and two for her husband? Ashley tapped the letter with her pointer finger.

Suddenly another few pieces from the past came into focus. The letter had been on the floor next to a manila envelope when she found it three weeks ago. So maybe it was the same manila envelope.

She studied the letter in her hand. Perhaps this was one of the letters her father hadn't pulled out, one of them he said was for him. A strange queasiness made its way through her veins. Why would her mother have something special to say just to Brooke? And why wouldn't her father have shared that letter at the same time, while they were all gathered together? He could've at least given it to her.

She breathed out and realized that her heart was pounding.

"Ashley . . ." It was Landon, calling from another room. "Are you ready?"

"Almost," she yelled, all the while staring at the letter, barely able to breathe. "Just a minute."

Panic and fear sat on either side of her, poking at her, laughing at her. *This is ridiculous.* She set the letter down on the bedspread and felt her curlers. They were cool now; she could take them out. If she sat here long enough her imagination was bound to run away with her. It was what made her a good artist.

She would put the letter back in her purse, give it to Brooke tonight, and never think about it again. Her legs tightened and she started to stand, but instead she dropped back down on the edge of the bed. Was her father hiding the letter? She picked it up again and held it closer to her face, trying to see past the white envelope. Maybe he didn't want anyone to read it, even Brooke. Maybe that's why it had been in his room with the other letters.

She recalled her father's reaction, the way he'd sounded stern when he found her in their closet looking through her mother's letter box. Maybe this firstborn letter was the reason he hadn't wanted her looking around her mother's letters in the first place. All because of something terribly important, terribly private that she'd written to Brooke.

Was there something shocking surrounding Brooke's birth, something none of them knew about? Even Brooke? Ashley slid the tip of her fingernail beneath the sealed flap. What would she want Brooke to do if things were turned around, if Brooke held a possibly ominous letter intended for her? In that case it might be better if Brooke read it first. That way, whatever the letter held, her sister could break the news to her gently.

No, Brooke would never buy that argument.

Ashley bit her lip. Of course, she could hardly hand Brooke a letter with Cole's graham cracker crumbs smeared across it. Even if it did have their mother's handwriting across the front. The letter needed a proper, clean white envelope, an envelope like the kind they kept downstairs in the computer desk. She worked her fingernail beneath the flap, just enough to lift a small curl of paper. Brooke wouldn't want a letter from her mother in a dirty envelope. And, oh yes, she'd read the letter in the process.

The moment it all came together, nothing in the world could've changed her mind. She ripped the envelope open and pulled out the letter. Her heart was galloping now, taking her imagination with it. But before she could think up another reason why her mother would write a letter to only Brooke, Ashley unfolded it, held it out, and began to read.

My dearest firstborn, my son,

My son? Ashley stopped there. What was this? All this time she'd thought the letter was from her mother, but maybe not. Obviously not. Her mother's firstborn wasn't a son; it was Brooke. In an instant, her gaze darted down the full page of text to the signature at the end, and only then did the room begin to tilt.

In her mother's handwriting, the letter was signed *Your mother, Elizabeth Baxter.*

Ashley couldn't draw a breath, couldn't make her lungs work right. She looked at the first line again and frowned at the piece of paper. Maybe her mother was delusional when she'd written it—that's why she'd written something so crazy. She let her eyes find the beginning again.

My dearest firstborn, my son,
If you are reading this, then you have found me. . . .

The room tilted harder. Ashley gripped the edge of the bed with her free hand and squeezed her eyes shut. The words were far too lucid to be a mistake or some kind of delusional rambling. It was an actual letter written by her mother to a firstborn son, someone who apparently was looking for her. So that meant it wasn't a mistake. Ashley wasn't dreaming or trying to find her way out of a nightmare.

But then it must be a mistake; it had to be. Her mother didn't have a firstborn son. Of course not. Ashley bent over her knees and forced the air from her body. After three tries, she was able to suck in a quick breath. If the letter was accurate, if it was really written by her mother, then . . .

The information hung over her like a shifting hillside, the small pebbles slipping, sliding in around her feet. It didn't make sense, couldn't make sense. She was shaking, adrenaline speeding through her veins, alerting her sinews and fibers, every muscle and nerve, of the certainty that nothing—nothing in all of life—would ever be the same after this single moment.

But even if the information buried her, she had to know, had to read the letter and understand the details for herself. There would be no moving forward otherwise. Her body permitted her another small bit of air, and she held the letter up again. When her hand shook too hard to read the words, she lowered the paper to her lap and hunched over it.

My dearest firstborn, my son,
If you are reading this, then you have found me. Or you have at least found the others. Son, I have prayed for the chance to tell you this information in person, but time is running out. I can't go peacefully to be with the Lord until I make every effort to reach you. Even if the only way I can do that is through this letter.

Each word was another small rock, falling and tumbling around her, making it difficult to move, to think, or even to fathom the gravity of what might lie ahead. The first part of the letter could lead to just one conclusion, but it was a conclusion Ashley didn't dare consider, wouldn't let herself think about. Instead she tightened her grip on the edge of the bed and forced herself to continue.

> Your father and I have thought about you with every passing year. Every birthday and Christmas, the fall when you must've started school, the year you would've graduated. You were always in our hearts, just a mention away. We had no choice about what happened, dear son. My parents sent me away, and a woman took you from me even when I screamed for her to bring you back. This is the part you must know. We never wanted to give you up. Never.

What? Ashley blinked twice and read the words again and then another time. *This is the part you must know. We never wanted to give you up. Never.*

The avalanche came then.

This new definition of the past, this new reality about who and what the Baxters were came tumbling and sliding, burying her beneath it, suffocating her, leaving her no way out.

When it was finally over, when the earth had stopped crumbling in around her, she knew this much: the landscape that made up her life—all of their lives—would forever be changed. An eerie silence filled the room, a silence where Ashley couldn't move or think or feel her heartbeat. *God, how do I deal with this? Help me. Please, God.*

I'm here, daughter. Run to Me.

Ashley leaned back and stared at the ceiling. He was here, God Himself. His Spirit was around her, helping her, holding her. *You're here. I can feel You, God. I want to run to You. Lift me out of this; carry me, Lord. I can't do it without You.* And at that instant, she felt her heartbeat slow a little. God was the answer in all of this, wherever the rest of the letter took her. Wherever the rest of her days took her. He was all-knowing, all-seeing. Her mother's letter wasn't taking Him by surprise. No, the earth could break apart and swallow her whole, and He would be waiting to catch her.

The only way out was to trust God, believe that He would help her hold on. And that meant grabbing hold of the most obvious detail and never letting go, no matter how much it hurt.

The detail was this: her parents didn't have five children. They had six.

She looked at the line again. *We never wanted to give you up. Never.* She held on to the idea and continued reading:

> After you were gone, they told me to forget about you. They said I'd be better off if I convinced myself you had never been born. Your father and I prayed that you would be adopted by a Christian family, people who would raise you to share the faith that has always been so important to us. We tried to convince ourselves that you belonged to God, that He had found a family for you, and that somehow the social workers had been right. You were never ours in the first place. But we were wrong. My deepest regret in all my life is that I didn't fight harder to keep you.

Two tears fell onto Ashley's jeans, and she dabbed the backs of her hands against her cheeks.

> The way you felt in my arms the day you were born is something I will never forget. Your fuzzy blond hair and blue eyes, wide and alert, as if you knew our time was short. I didn't think I'd ever know that feeling again, the warm weight of my newborn son against my chest. But God gave us more children. Five more. And last of all He gave us a son, a boy we named Luke. Watching Luke grow up has always filled my heart with a mix of joy and sorrow. Because he looked just like you. When he turned one and learned to walk, I knew what you would've looked like as a toddler. It was

the same when he lost a tooth and learned to ride a bike and graduated from high school. Every milestone was a reminder of all I'd lost with you. All I'd missed.

Sobs built up in Ashley's gut, and she pressed her free hand to her stomach. That could've been Cole just as easily. If her parents had forced her to give away her firstborn son, she would've felt the same. No wonder her mother had always had a special love for Coley.

"Ashley . . . honey, what's taking so long?"

She couldn't answer Landon. Instead she found her place in the letter and blocked out everything but her mother's words.

> And so I've begged God for just one thing. That somehow in the midst of my final days I might have the chance to see you again, to hold you one more time. One last time. I want to know that you're okay, that you were placed in a warm and loving home. If you have a wife and kids, I want to know about them.
>
> I was sick one other time, and I tried to find you. The records were sealed, and we were turned away. So I know that it'll take a miracle now, but that's okay. The God we serve is in the miracle business. Our lives have been a testimony to that.
>
> My prayer for you is that you would know God, that you would have a relationship with Him. Also that you would know the love of family—our family. You might belong to other people, but you will always belong here with us too. Because whenever I think of my precious children, I don't see five—I see six.
>
> I always will. I love you, Son. If I don't get the chance to hold you here, then I have to believe God will let me hold you in heaven. And there we won't ever have to say good-bye again.
>
> Your mother,
> Elizabeth Baxter

Ashley heard footsteps as she finished reading, and when she looked up, Landon was in the doorway.

"Ashley?" His voice was softer, without even the slightest bit of impatience. "What is it, honey?" He walked to her and put his hand on her shoulder. "What's wrong?"

Where could she begin? She wiped at her tears again and held out the letter. "I . . ." She shook her head. "Read this."

Landon looked confused, but she couldn't think of how to explain it to him. She slid over and he took the letter, lowering himself to the spot beside her.

"It's from my mother." She sniffed and took hold of his elbow, leaning her head on his shoulder. "The envelope says *Firstborn*."

He hesitated, and for a moment she thought he was going to ask questions, try to get the story out of her. But something in her expression must've convinced him to read the letter, and that way, whatever he might want to know would somehow be answered. He held the letter in front of him and started to read it to himself. After only a few seconds, he stopped and let the letter drop a few inches. He stared at her, his mouth open.

"Yes." Ashley sniffed. "Keep reading."

Landon did. He read the whole thing, and then he put the letter on the bed and took her in his arms.

She felt safe there, and she wished she could hide in his embrace and never have to face the things she'd learned in the last fifteen minutes. But even now God was giving her strength, helping her climb out of the rubble of truth. She sat up and found his eyes. "Can you believe it?"

"Not in a million years." Landon looked out the window, his expression flat, shocked. "Your parents are pillars, Ashley. As long as I've known them, they never even fought." He gave a single laugh. "I mean, they were having Bible studies for kids back when we were in high school." He put his hand on her knee. "And they never told you?"

"They never told any of us." She massaged her forehead. "I have *two* brothers, Landon. Somewhere in the world I have a full-fledged brother I've never met."

Landon picked up the letter again. "It sure looks that way."

She did a sad distant-sounding laugh. "No wonder." Her gaze shifted to the framed photograph of Cole sitting on the dresser. "I couldn't understand why Mom never gave up on me." She narrowed her eyes, seeing back to seven years ago. "I was the black sheep, but she never had anything but love for me."

"That's how she was." Landon's words were soft, a caress that soothed the tremors in her heart.

"But it was more than that." She looked at him. "Don't you see, Landon? She was the black sheep too. She was just like me."

"Mmm." He nodded. "Maybe that's why she was so compassionate. Because she'd been there."

"And it's why she was so wonderful with Cole." Her voice cracked. "Because she had to give *her* little boy away. When I got back from Paris I told her I wasn't thinking of doing that." She shook her head. "Mom never said another word about it. She helped me every way she could, the way her parents didn't help her and Dad."

"I'm sad for her."

Ashley looked at Cole's picture again. "She never found him, her firstborn." Another trail of hot tears spilled onto her cheeks. "It was her last prayer, but it never happened. She didn't get to hold him again, didn't get the miracle."

The sadness of that drew them together, and Landon hugged her close again. "I'm sorry, Ash."

She kept her crying quiet, deep inside her. Eventually she found control again, and she drew a series of quick breaths. "Landon—" she nuzzled her cheek against his—"maybe we're supposed to find him for her."

"Maybe." He picked up the letter, studying it. "Where'd you get it?"

"In my dad's room." She raised one shoulder. "I thought it was for Brooke. I took it to give to her. As a favor, to save him the trouble."

"Hmmm." He winced. "Did you tell him?"

"No." She raised her hands. "I forgot about it until just now."

He took hold of her fingers and searched her eyes. "What're you going to do?"

"Well . . . I have a thousand questions." She felt her determination building. It wouldn't really be a confrontation. More of a reality check, another way of letting this new picture of her parents' past become believable. She eased the letter from Landon's hands. "But right now there's only one thing I can do."

"What?"

She held up the letter. "Get this back to my dad."

✤

Dinner passed in a blur. When the meal was finished, they put the telephone in the middle of the table, dialed Luke and Reagan, and placed the call on speaker mode. The couple was cheery and upbeat as they caught everyone up on the latest with Tommy. Luke's tone changed some when he explained that they couldn't come for Christmas like they'd hoped, but that the reason was a good one.

"We're bringing Malin home from China earlier than we thought!" Reagan squealed. She and Luke had decided to adopt a little girl from Beijing. "We just found out yesterday. She'll come home in late December or January."

"That's wonderful, honey." Ashley's father moved closer to the speaker. "Maybe all of you can make it back to Bloomington for spring break. By then you'll be adjusted to each other."

"Yes, Dad. Definitely." Luke's voice was thick, more emotional than usual. "I can't believe it's really happening."

"Well—" her dad grinned in a way that stilled his trembling chin—"Tommy will make a wonderful big brother."

Ashley added her congratulations, but she was barely listening. She kept watching her father, trying to see past his happy smile and joyful eyes. Had it always been so easy? Keeping a secret the size of an elephant from all of his kids? Weren't there times when he looked around the table and wondered where his firstborn was? how he was doing? Ashley swallowed back the questions. Of course there were times like that—there had to be. He'd just kept them hidden, same as her mother.

The phone call came to an end, and they placed one to Erin and Sam. Their four girls were thriving, advancing in every area at their own pace.

"We're all getting over colds around here." Erin laughed. "We can never have just one or two sick kids, but all four have to get it at once."

"I remember those days." Her father gave a sympathetic laugh. "You kids were the same way. The worst was when you all had chicken pox. Your mother was a saint."

Ashley studied him again, and her thoughts ran far beyond the moment. *A saint, Dad? Mom was never a saint and neither were you. None of us ever are, right?* All any of them could do was try their best and let God make up the difference.

Erin announced that their family was coming for spring break, same as Luke and Reagan. "He called me the other day." Excitement sounded in Erin's voice. "They should have their little girl by then, so we'll all be together."

Ashley stared at the black phone in the middle of the table and thought of her brother, the one she'd never met. *Not all of us, Erin. Not all of us.*

The call lasted another few minutes, and when it was over, Brooke and Peter pushed back from the table and talked about needing to get up early for Hayley's physical therapy. The child was still making progress, and Brooke was particularly happy about the way her speech was coming along. Verbalization was the last step to recovering after a brain injury, Brooke explained, and Hayley could say ten or eleven words now.

Kari and Ryan agreed that it was best to get going too. "Little Ryan is sleeping through the night now." Kari put her arm around

Ryan and gave him a crooked grin. "We don't want to mess that up, do we?"

It took another ten minutes for the group to gather the kids' sweaters and shoes and say their good-byes. Ashley worked alongside her sisters, helping Cole with his new hiking boots, the ones he had insisted on wearing, just in case they took a hike after dinner.

But neither she nor Landon had any intention of leaving yet. When the others left, Landon took Cole into the family room. "Cole and I need a little ESPN. Sunday nights aren't the same without Chris Berman's *NFL Primetime*."

Her father was standing in the entrance, leaning against the far wall where he'd stood while he said good-bye to the others. Now he gave Ashley a curious look. "I thought you needed to get home?"

She had the letter in her back pocket, where it had been all night. "No, Dad." She nodded toward the stairway. "I need to talk to you."

"Okay." At first his lighthearted demeanor remained. But then she was almost sure something deep and anxious flashed in his eyes. "My room?"

She nodded. "Please."

He led the way upstairs, and when they were inside, Ashley shut the door. The box of letters was on the dresser, right out in the open. He dropped down on the corner of the mattress. She thought about sitting down beside him, but she couldn't. She could barely breathe or move until she got past this.

Her father's face was lined with concern now. Whether he knew what was coming or not, Ashley couldn't tell, but he was worried. No question about that. He studied her. "This seems serious."

"It is." She took a few steps closer, so she stood right in front of him.

Some of the color left his face. "You're okay, right? Everything with the baby's fine?"

"I'm fine." She reached back, pulled the letter from her pocket, and held it out to him. "I found this in your room a few weeks ago. It was in an envelope marked *Firstborn*."

He stared at the letter and then lifted his eyes to hers. She noticed him take hold of the bedpost, steadying himself. Fear and anger crossed his expression, but anger won out. He narrowed his eyes. "I asked you not to go through your mother's letters." Pain threw itself in the mix of emotions racking his voice. He pointed at the box. "Those belong to me, Ashley. It was very important that no one else go through them."

She had expected this, so she didn't react. Instead she stood there motionless, watching him, waiting.

He snatched the letter from her hand. "Where's the envelope?"

"Back at my house."

"You took it from my room and opened it?" He hesitated, shocked. "Why, Ash?" The anger was fading. Panic took the lead, and his breathing grew faster, shallower. "Why'd you come in here and take one of her letters when I clearly asked you not to?"

"I'm sorry." Her voice was indignant. Maybe she was wrong to take the letter, but that's not what this moment was about. "I was getting ChapStick, and I saw it as I walked past. The letter said *Firstborn*." She looked past her father's pretense and fear and shock. "I thought it was for Brooke."

"So . . ." He swallowed hard and seemed to hold his breath, probably desperate to learn that somehow she hadn't actually read the letter. He slumped a little, his voice quieter than before. "Did you . . . did you read it?"

For the past hour Ashley had pictured herself being mad at him or, if not mad, at least hurt. How could her parents have kept this secret all their lives? And how was it fair that none of the Baxter kids had ever had a chance to know about their lost brother, let alone meet him?

But now, watching him, she felt no anger or pain, except for him. He'd never intended for her to find out, so this was as much a shock for him as it was for her. She put her hand on his shoulder. "I read it, Dad."

He held her eyes for a moment and then opened the letter. In a hurry he scanned the page before lowering it to his lap. When he looked up at her again, his eyes were full. "You know . . ."

"Yes." Her knees felt weak. "We have an older brother."

Her dad placed the letter on the bed beside him. Then he made a fist and brought it slowly to his forehead. "He was supposed to be our secret."

"Mom . . . she wanted to find him."

A shaky sigh came from him. "I know. I'm . . . I'm trying." The lines around his eyes and mouth made him look five years older than he had at dinner. "I'm talking to private investigators." Defeat filled in the crevices along his forehead. "Did you tell the others?"

"Only Landon." Her own anger was still absent. She hadn't expected him to look so broken. "They have to know, Dad. You need to tell them."

He reached out and took her hand. "I want to find him first." His tone was quietly intense, begging her to understand. "Then I'll get everyone together and tell them. Can you let me do that?"

Ashley hung her head. He was asking her to keep the truth a secret from her siblings, something she hadn't expected. Now that she knew, she figured he'd tell them right away. Tonight even. "Wouldn't it be easier if everyone was looking for him?" Her voice was thick, her throat tight. "Helping Mom get her last wish?"

"No." He picked up the letter and pressed it to his heart. "This part of our past belonged to just the two of us. I want to find him for her. Just me." He looked at the box of letters. "I'd already decided I was going to do it. That's why the letters were down."

Defeat joined the other emotions vying for Ashley's attention. "You could spend your life searching for him. Brooke and Kari and Erin and Luke . . . they all need to know." A sob filled her throat, and she waited until she could find the words. "He's our brother, Dad. One of us. We should've found him a long time ago."

His expression twisted and without any words he pleaded with her. "We'll all be together at spring break. I'll tell them then."

"Even if you haven't found him?"

"Yes, no matter what." He gave a small shrug. "We always thought it would hurt less if you kids didn't know about him."

Ashley shook her head, her words more of a quiet cry. "It hurts more."

In all her life, she'd seen her father cry only a few times. When each of them got married, when it was clear Mom wasn't going to make it, and when they lost her. But now, tears filled his eyes and spilled onto his leathery face. He never blinked, never took his eyes off her, and twice he swallowed, struggling as if he wanted to say something but couldn't.

"Ashley." His voice was a choked whisper. "I'm sorry."

Her legs couldn't hold her up another minute. She took the place next to him on the bed and put her arms around his neck and held him. She hadn't expected to cry, not when she had so many questions. But the questions didn't matter as much now. She—and one day her siblings—would have a lifetime to talk about the answers, to hear the details of their parents' past: how they'd gotten in trouble, how they'd survived the ordeal of being apart, and how they had given up a child.

Right now—if she could find the strength to speak—she needed to tell him something else. Because if anyone could understand what her parents had been through—why shame and regret and pain would've kept them quiet about the past for so many years—it was her.

He was saying it again. "I'm so sorry, Ashley. We never meant to hurt you kids with this."

"I know, Dad. It's okay." She rested her forehead on his shoulder. "I love you. We're all going to be all right. God will help you find him. I have to believe that."

Her father's tears came harder, and Ashley understood the reason. Now, in addition to everything else ripping at his heart, he was feeling relief. All his life, he and her mother must've worried about how their kids would handle the news about their older brother if they ever found out. And now she was letting him know that nothing could tear at the soul of the Baxter family.

Not even something this big.

As she held him, Ashley was struck by the fact that this was what her parents had done for her seven years ago. They had held her and welcomed her and let her cry about the past. They had forgiven her. Now, in some ways, the tables were turned, and she knew what to do because it was what they would've done. What they had done. This wasn't a time to push him or criticize him or force him into a decision he didn't want to make.

It was a time to forgive.

CHAPTER TWENTY-EIGHT

THE DRIVE TO THE STORAGE UNIT was a long time coming.

Dayne had thought about going there ever since Katy had brought it up at the lake that day. The thought had been on his mind through the rest of the location shoot in Indiana and during the long days of filming back at the studio. Every night he told himself that the next day he would drive to the San Fernando Valley, to the rented space where his past was boxed up and locked away. The spot where one box contained the paperwork and documents associated with his adoption, along with a framed photograph of Elizabeth Baxter.

But every day he'd found another reason to stay away. Too busy or too distracted or too much to think about. He was good at convincing himself that another day would work better.

Now, with filming of *Dream On* almost completed, he had no choice but to go. He'd accused Katy Hart of running, but he'd been doing the same thing ever since he returned from Bloomington. Running from his relationship with Kelly Parker and from the shallow conversations on the set. Definitely running from the people at the Kabbalah Learning Center. They must've remembered his schedule, because the calls started coming a day after he returned home.

"We know how anxious you are, Mr. Matthews," one teacher told him. "We're looking forward to having you in class. The upper world isn't something you can reach without the teachings; you know that, right?"

For the first few days, he answered the phone when they called.

"Have you made the decision yet about your donation? About how much you'd like to give?" It was another teacher, one of the suited guys from his visit before the Bloomington trip. "I think we talked about passing through half the spiritual laws, you know, being free of the materialism and wealth of this world. Detaching from all impure thoughts."

Dayne stopped at a light and tapped his steering wheel. He wasn't sure what it was about Kabbalah. The teachers who called weren't saying anything different, but ever since talking to Katy, he heard it with fresh ears. Detaching from impure thoughts by writing a check? He wasn't ready to chuck the entire thing, but he had doubts now—doubts where before he'd had only a strong desire to follow.

What was that? How did something like that change?

The light turned green, and he made a quick start. There were no paparazzi behind him now. In fact, they seemed to have laid off some, one of those things that went in spurts. He was still a major player in the gossip rags, but other scandals—a major Hollywood couple on the outs and a pregnant former teenage pop queen who'd left her unemployed husband. Yes, the magazines would always have something to write about.

When he left home this afternoon, a guy in a Volkswagen had been parked outside his house. He followed Dayne for five blocks, but Dayne had lost him on the freeway. It felt good to be alone. The guy never would've known what he wanted to see at his storage unit, but he didn't want anyone speculating.

Traffic was busy on Ventura Boulevard, and Dayne was glad for his black-tinted windows. It gave him the peace he was always looking for, even for only a few minutes, because the public couldn't climb in the SUV and read his thoughts or decide where he wanted to drive. They could know where he lived and whom he dated. Or worse, whom he couldn't. But they would have to leave him alone in his black Escalade.

Another red light. Dayne switched the radio off—nothing but commercials. Ahead was a billboard with Kelly Parker's face twenty feet high. She was the new spokeswoman for a cosmetic company, a deal that doubled her income overnight. He looked at the ad and smiled. He was glad for her. She seemed more confident these days, less bothered with the press, less worried about what they thought. She wasn't starving herself like before, either. Another sign she was doing well.

But life with her was emptier than ever. He noticed a pack of gum on the console; and he slid a piece from it, opening it and popping it in his mouth in a single movement. He was pretty sure she was seeing Hawk Daniels on the side. The chemistry he and Kelly had to work at on camera seemed to come easily for Kelly and Hawk.

She'd spent the previous night at a friend's house, one of many recent girls' nights out. Dayne leaned on his armrest and stared straight ahead. He didn't care; she could do what she wanted. They were almost done shooting the movie, and then they could make decisions about the future.

Or at least about their future.

His future—as well as his past—well, he'd never had much say in that. Not about who his parents were or how they'd raised him. Acting was something he'd chosen, but he hadn't planned on the public responsibility that went with it. His life was planned out for him by his agent and directors, the studios and marketing departments. He couldn't cut ties and move to Bloomington. He couldn't convince Katy that they might have a chance together someday. He definitely couldn't make contact with the Baxter family.

But he could leave Kelly Parker, and someday soon he would. He'd stayed with her because it was easier, better than a breakup in the middle of filming. A breakup like that would put him back on the front page, where he'd been last July after the arrest of the stalking fan. Wait and do it after, and it would be relegated to an inside story, half a page at the most.

He laughed, but the sound was tired and defeated. See how he was? Measuring his time and days, his decisions in relationships by the response the tabloids would have to it. The situation was ridiculous, but he knew no other way.

The storage place was just ahead, and he turned left into the parking lot. He had a key, so no need to mess with the front desk or any other person on-site. He pulled his vehicle up to the door of his own unit and cut the engine.

Maybe that's why he was here today. What had Katy said about the photograph of Elizabeth Baxter? That the way back has to start somewhere for everyone, right? He worked his gum as he climbed out and walked to the storage door. Nothing else in his personal life was working, so why not?

He unlocked the door, went inside, and spotted the box right off. It was still in the middle of the unit, where he'd left it last time he'd been here, more than a year ago. He went to it and pulled up another box for a chair. Then he opened the one with the adoption documents inside, and there on top was her picture.

She looked sweet and gentle, the same as she'd looked in the hospital that evening in Bloomington. He lifted the wooden frame carefully, as if it contained something of the woman herself. He rested it on his knees and studied her image. Bits of his conversation with her came back. When she'd understood who he was, she apologized to him. There, in the stuffy quiet, he could hear her voice as fragile and shaky as it had been that night.

"We missed you. . . . You belonged with us. . . . I never stopped missing you, never stopped loving you."

When she had hugged him, he felt whole in her arms, all the questions answered, all the pieces in place. She'd told him that she'd tried to find him, and he'd explained about the private investigator he'd hired. One of the best parts was that she didn't know about his fame. He was just a guy who walked into her hospital room until he told her he was her son. Then that was the only part that mattered. She asked about his job, and she seemed happy that he was an actor. But not because she recognized him or knew him for his public persona.

But those parts of the conversation weren't the most distinct now. It was the last part, when she'd looked deep into his eyes and told him to find God. The same God who had taken so much from him. There she was, this woman who would've raised him if she'd had the chance, telling him basically the same thing Katy had told him: *"Find God. Find your faith."*

He held the photo closer, trying to remember every word. They'd spent an hour together, and she had talked about God from the beginning. Apparently she'd been praying every day for a miracle, that God would bring him to her. Her voice played again in his soul.

"Things didn't work out the way I wanted them to; we couldn't all be together here. But in heaven we can all spend eternity together."

Dayne closed his eyes. What he would have given for more time with Elizabeth Baxter. She had loved him all his life; he believed that. Every birthday and Christmas and milestone, she'd thought about him and wondered about him. Same with her husband, John.

Then there was the part he remembered more often than the rest, especially since his talk with Katy at the lake. Elizabeth had been grateful that her prayers were answered, that she could see him before she died. But when she learned that he didn't share her strong faith, she'd grown misty-eyed.

"I thought I wanted to see you because I needed to tell you I never forgot about you, never stopped loving you. But maybe it was so you could find a heavenly father in God."

He opened his eyes. There it was again, the same message. The hope that he might take his anger and confusion and frustration, his lack of privacy and lack of free will, and turn it all into a search for God.

Dayne set the photo back on his knees and exhaled hard. "I'm not sure I'm ready," he whispered. "I'm not even sure it's what I want."

While he was speaking, he was turning the frame over, sliding his fingers beneath the metal fasteners at the back, working slowly since the frame was old and the back hadn't been removed for decades. Finally, the black backing shifted and he eased it off the wooden frame. He set it on the box beside him, and suddenly there it was. Elizabeth had indeed written a note to him, in faded blue cursive, on the back of the photograph.

His heart slipped into a rhythm he didn't recognize, and he wiped his palms on his jeans. With great care, he lifted the photo out and ran his fingers over the lines on the back. Her handwriting was familiar to him in a way that didn't make sense. He read it as easily as he read his own.

> Dear Son,
> I don't know where you'll be when you read this or if you ever will. You are hours old as I pen these words, wrapped in my arms the way I want you to stay forever. If you do find this, I hope you know that we wanted to keep you. You are a part of us, and you always will be.

Dayne's eyes blurred with tears. He blinked and found his place again.

Your father and I made a mistake, but you, Son, are not a mistake. We have been forgiven, and wherever you are, I pray you, too, have been forgiven. Everyone needs forgiveness, and only Jesus can take care of that. If you find Him, Son, then one day you will find us too. Here or in heaven, it won't matter. Then we'll be together forever, just the way we are right now. And we'll never have to say good-bye.

I love you always.
Mommy

It was the last part, the last word that seized Dayne's heart and broke loose a wave of sorrow. She had been his mommy, and someone had taken him away. Yes, his adoptive parents had been wonderful, but he never saw them enough, never felt like he was part of a family with them. Elizabeth, though, had wanted him all the days of his life—wishing for him, hoping for him, searching for him.

And now it came down to this sweet, simple message.

He read it again, and something began coming to life within him. When he was at boarding school in Indonesia, he and his friends would play basketball, sometimes when the rest of the students were sound asleep. One of the boys had a copy of the key, so they'd slip inside and turn on the lights. But then they'd sit there in the semidarkness waiting, because the gym lights didn't come on quickly or instantly. They took time warming up, bit by gradual bit, until finally the room was fully lit.

That's the way he felt now, sitting in the storage unit.

The words his mother had for him contained something he hadn't considered before. He had been to the Kabbalah Center a number of times and heard teachers talk about impure thoughts and spiritual laws and having oneness with God. They talked a lot about reaching the upper world.

But they never talked about forgiveness.

His birth parents had obviously done something they were ashamed of. They had been a couple of innocent kids, madly in love, and intent on avoiding a sexual relationship until they were married. His private investigator's research had told him that much. But they'd made a mistake, allowed themselves an opportunity, and Elizabeth had gotten pregnant.

In her world, there had been consequences for that kind of problem, and so Elizabeth had been sent away. But here was the thing, the part that was still coming to light in his heart: Elizabeth wasn't consumed with her parents' role in what happened. She wasn't caught up in anger and condemnation toward them, even though she could've been.

She was more interested in being forgiven herself. Forgiven for going against what she knew to be real and true and right.

He looked up at the white metal ceiling and saw her face again in his mind, the way she had looked in the hospital bed. Yes, she was sad and full of regret. She wanted more time with him, a chance to introduce him to the rest of the Baxter family. But she had an unwavering peace.

In the face of death and sorrow and loss, she had a peace that he had searched for all his life. He looked at the back of the photo and read the letter once more. The lights were fully on now. Elizabeth had peace not because she had found oneness with God. Not because she'd written a check or dodged the impure thoughts.

She had peace because she was forgiven.

Dayne examined his life, the life he'd lived since his adoptive parents were killed in the plane crash. He'd gone to UCLA and studied drama, but his choices had been far different than they'd been at the boarding school. He had girls staying the night in his dorm from midway through his freshman year on.

There weren't enough hours left in the day to go through the list of people he'd used and walked on, the people he'd cheated or betrayed. Even now he was living a lie, sharing a bed with Kelly Parker when his heart and soul and mind were never anywhere near her.

He'd lived a life contrary to everything his missionary parents had stood for, everything they'd lived and died for. He'd slept with married women and—in his early days—certain female casting directors just to get the edge on a part. Of course he didn't have peace. Deep in his soul he'd always known that he was living wrong. But in his circle it was the way of life, a normal condition of Hollywood stardom.

It was hot in the storage unit, and a drop of sweat slid down the side of his face. Whether he could live a life for God or find God, the way Katy and Elizabeth Baxter had talked about, he wasn't sure. But in that moment he was convinced of a few things. He was done with Kabbalah. When he got home he would pack up everything he'd gotten from the center and toss it in the trash. There could be no oneness with God, no upper world, without forgiveness. He could see that now.

That wasn't all. When he got home, he would tell Kelly as gently as possible that it was over. He would remain her friend, the way people did after a Hollywood breakup, but nothing more. She was one of the few people he could still seek forgiveness from, and he'd do it before the day was over.

But the most important thing was this: he knew he wouldn't have the peace he was looking for until he had complete forgiveness. Forgiveness for every wrong choice he'd ever made. He couldn't go back and find all the people he'd hurt, all the women he'd used, and all the people he'd stepped on over the years. The only way to find forgiveness was to take it from the only one offering it.

The very God he'd spent a lifetime avoiding.

Dayne closed his eyes and tried something he hadn't done since he was in boarding school, back when he was forced to do it. He lifted his silent voice to the heavens and prayed to the God of his adoptive parents and his birth parents. The God of Katy Hart. *God, I need forgiveness. I've . . . I've made a lot of bad decisions, and I'm done with them, finished with them. I'm sorry, God.*

The sweat on his face became tears, and he held his breath, clinging to his composure. *I need Your peace, and I need to see my parents again in heaven. I can't do it.* He spoke the next part out loud. "I don't know how, God. So please . . . please forgive me."

A subtle wind blew across his soul. *My son, I forgive you. I have loved you . . . with an everlasting love. With unfailing love I have drawn you to myself.*

The words were so real, so clear that Dayne stood and turned a slow circle, staring at the corners of the storage unit. He still had Elizabeth's picture tight in his hands, but where had the response come from?

Finally he sat back down on the box and looked at her photo again. He'd been raised in the faith, hadn't he? The response could've come from only one place. From the same God he'd been talking to. The words were from a Scripture verse he'd known a lifetime ago. He hadn't given them any thought for twenty years, but now they were strong and real and vivid. Life-changing words.

Suddenly the truth welled up inside him. For every wrong thing he'd ever done, he was forgiven. Jesus Christ had seen to that by dying on the cross. Wasn't that the message he'd heard a hundred times growing up in the boarding school? That same forgiveness was his—now. The way it belonged to Elizabeth and John, the way it belonged to all people who asked for it. Maybe he had found God, without really looking at all. There was more to it, of course. The changes wouldn't happen overnight, but this was a beginning. He remembered what Katy had told him at the lake the last time he saw her.

"The way back has to start somewhere for all of us."

That's what forgiveness was—a start. The response that had filtered through his heart was proof. *My son, I forgive you. . . . I will never leave you . . . never.* Because with those words came something Dayne hadn't known for all of his adult life, something he'd craved and sought after regardless of the fame and money and adulation. The one thing he couldn't get from a bank account or a movie role or a learning center or a relationship—even a relationship with Katy Hart.

Complete and all-consuming peace.

CHAPTER TWENTY-NINE

DRESS REHEARSALS FOR *ANNIE* were scheduled to start in two days, and as Saturday's practice wrapped up, Katy could only stand back in awe. Not just because of the event she and the older kids were going to take part in after practice.

But because the show was going to be beautiful.

The kids were turning in better rehearsals every day, and Katy was running out of things that needed improving. Even the kids in small roles were improving themselves without being asked.

Kelsy Bouchey had come to her a week earlier and asked for pointers, anything that would make her performance a little stronger, more memorable.

Katy had given the little girl a hug and looked into her eyes. "Honey, you're doing a great job. I wouldn't change anything."

"But—" she was as serious as she'd ever been—"Sarah Jo Stryker wanted to be Annie." She gulped. "And I want to make Sarah Jo's parents happy. It has to be perfect."

Katy had to swallow back a rush of tears. She crouched down so she was on Kelsy's level. "I can't give you anything else, honey.

You're doing a great job. But maybe you could ask Jesus to give you something more. That way you'd know this show was more special."

The sentiment had been echoed throughout the cast. Some of the boys had talked about hitting a new level with the full-company ensemble scenes, since little Ben Hanover had wanted so badly to sing and dance in a play. In honor of Ben, they'd taken to wearing Peter Pan hats during some of the rehearsals.

Alice Stryker was doing much better now, her injuries from the accident mostly healed. This morning she'd stopped by practice and sat in the back of the sanctuary. A few kids gave her hugs, but for the most part people gave her space. She held a handkerchief below her eyes the entire time she was there. Katy approached her on the break and told her that the kids were dedicating their show to Ben and Sarah Jo.

Alice sniffed and worked her throat for a moment, her eyes red and swollen. When she could find the words, she said, "Thank you, Katy. I . . ." She focused on the front of the sanctuary, where the kids were huddled in groups, sharing snacks and laughter and lines from the play. "I wish I had one more chance to watch her rehearse." She looked at Katy. "Because that's what I would do. I would watch." The tears spilled freely down her face. "I never really watched her sing."

Katy didn't know what to say. She hugged the woman for a long time and then dabbed at her own eyes. "Come to opening night, please. We've saved the front row for you and your family and the Hanovers."

Alice nodded, but she made no commitment. She lifted her hand and gave Katy a little wave. Then she gathered her purse and her damp handkerchief and left through the back door without another word.

That had been an hour ago, and now practice was finished and the kids were waiting for a word from her. She gave a few final instructions to Nancy and Al Helmes and Rhonda regarding the upcoming dress rehearsal.

"I can't wait for opening night." Nancy Helmes smiled at the others, her eyes glistening. "I have a feeling it'll be a time to remember."

"Even the dog's doing great." Al chuckled. "Who'd have thought?"

Rhonda grinned. "I still think it would've been fun to see Katy in a dog costume."

"It's all about the raw hot dogs." Katy brushed her knuckles against her shoulder and cocked her head back. "I got the premium brand. The dog's been perfect ever since."

"I think it's more about having a premium God in charge." Al raised his brow at her, but his eyes held the teasing they'd come to love.

They all laughed.

Katy carried her notepad to the front of the sanctuary and through the sea of kids seated on the floor. "Okay, another excellent rehearsal." She studied the earnestness on the face of one child after another. "Let's pray that everyone will stay healthy during dress rehearsals and that we can bring together the props and costumes before opening night."

Tim Reed raised his hand. He was sitting next to Bailey Flanigan and several of the older kids. He waited until Katy recognized him; then he stood and said, "Let's pray about something else." He glanced at his peers. "We heard that the Hanovers might not come. I guess . . . it's been really hard for them." He looked at Katy. "We think it would help everyone if they came. So maybe we could pray about that too."

Katy nodded. "Good idea."

They talked for a few more minutes, and then they prayed before Katy dismissed them. As they started to leave, she looked at the older kids. "The kids from the Bible study are meeting out back. The moms who are driving are already out there waiting."

It was the moment she'd been waiting for all week. Al Helmes was right about the reasons things were going so well. God's presence had been with them from the beginning, working one miracle after another in their midst. Kids knew their lines and their blocking, the music sounded heaven-sent, and the sets were finished a week early.

But nothing onstage would ever compare to the miracle God was about to work this afternoon. The Bible study had grown in number and depth over the weeks. They'd talked about Jeremy Fisher's life and how they might've been in the same place if they'd been him. The kids began to see that anger and hatred and revenge could never be part of the solution, no matter how guilty a person was. Then they looked at the book of John and talked about what Jesus meant when He said, "In this world you will have trouble. But take heart! I have overcome the world."

After the weeks of Bible study, the kids had made a decision—all on their own. After the last regular rehearsal they would take a trip to the jail.

The kids were quiet as they piled into three vehicles. Katy watched them, struck by the maturity in their eyes and faces. There was none of the usual giggling and teasing and silliness. They were kids on a mission, preoccupied with the enormity of the task that lay ahead of them.

Katy took the passenger seat in the first van, the one driven by Jenny Flanigan. They said little until they turned into the jail parking lot and Jenny turned to her. "Of all the things you've done with these kids, Katy, this will always be the one that mattered most."

"I didn't do it." Her heart raced in anticipation, but she managed a smile. "I just helped give them a chance to let God do it."

Katy led the group through the parking lot and helped them check in at the front desk. The jailers were expecting them and had already placed Jeremy Fisher in a room big enough to hold their group.

"He won't be wearing handcuffs," a guard explained to her.

"He's not considered a risk." The man's face was stern. "Not when he's sober, anyway." He looked down the line at the group of quiet kids. "I'll have two officers outside the room if you need anything."

Katy took a step forward. "Thank you."

The adults were also invited to visit Jeremy, but many of them didn't want to. It was something for the kids, they said. Others thought it was too soon for such a connection to be made. Katy didn't question their reasons. She was only grateful that the kids had decided to come.

Katy waited with an officer near the door until everyone was ready. They followed the man through a series of doors and into a space the size of a high school classroom. At the front was a table, and at the table sat a thin, scraggly-looking kid with nervous eyes as big as Frisbees.

Katy had been here before, so she took the lead. She went to him and held out her hand. "Hello, Jeremy." She waited until he made eye contact. How must he feel? "I told you I had some kids who might want to come." She turned and pointed to the group huddled near the door. "Here they are."

Jeremy gave a quick, furtive glance at his visitors, but he shifted his attention back to Katy. "I . . . I deserve this." His hands and arms trembled, and his words seemed to stick in his throat. "I told you they could come, so they can go ahead. I'm ready."

A strange feeling rattled the doors of Katy's heart. "What do you mean, you're ready?" She twisted her face, confused. "Ready for what?"

He gulped and ran his tongue over his lower lip. "These are their friends, right?" His voice was a shaky whisper. "Friends of the kids I . . . the kids that died."

"Yes." Katy looked back at the group. They were still near the door, waiting for the go-ahead from her. She turned back to Jeremy. "These are their friends, the kids I told you about." She still didn't understand. "What are you ready for? What do you deserve?"

"For them to tell me off." He ran his hand through his curly hair. "They're mad at me, and this . . . this is their chance to tell me how they feel, right?" He gave a weak shrug. "Isn't that what this is about?"

A knowing came over Katy, and she wanted to cry and laugh at the same time. Jeremy Fisher thought the kids constituted a verbal firing squad, and even still he'd been willing to meet with them. Katy didn't say anything in response. She only stood a few feet away, faced the others, and simply nodded.

The group came forward and formed a line.

The first to reach him was one of the girls. She put her hand on Jeremy's shoulder. "We know you didn't mean it to happen." Her voice was clear, but a stream of tears ran down her cheeks. "If you would've been in CKT you would've known how nice they were, Sarah Jo and Ben. And maybe you wouldn't have been drinking." She never took her eyes from him. "But I know you didn't mean to kill anyone, Jeremy."

As she spoke, Jeremy sat a little straighter. He looked from her to Katy and back again, his expression surprised, then shocked as if to ask, *What is this? Where are the verbal bullets?*

Several kids came up after that, talking to Jeremy one at a time and telling him things that were similar to what the first girl had said. The moms watched in the background, dabbing at their eyes, as the procession continued. With each CKT teen who spoke, Jeremy's shock faded a little more. Instead he slumped in his seat and wept, nodding and listening to the words being spoken to him but unable to say anything in return.

Tim Reed was next. He reached out and shook Jeremy's hand, but when the handshake was over he didn't let go. "Sarah Jo sang with me over the summer." He smiled at the memory, his eyes watery. "She was amazing, man. One-in-a-million voice. I know she would've wanted to live." He released Jeremy's hand and patted his shoulder. "But she would've forgiven you." He looked at the other CKT kids, then back to Jeremy. "That's why we're here. We forgive you too. Now get your life right with God and make something of yourself. Don't let their deaths be in vain."

Jeremy nodded, his cheeks red and wet. Tim shook his hand one more time and then joined the others near the door.

Next in line was Bailey Flanigan. Katy's heart went out to her. The loss of Ben and Sarah Jo at the hands of a drunk driver had been one of the two most difficult things Bailey had ever experienced. Her anger toward Jeremy Fisher was easily the other.

Bailey walked up to Jeremy, and for a moment she said nothing, just looked at him. A bit of the old anger remained in her expression but only for an instant. Then her eyes softened, and everything about her face and demeanor changed.

She took hold of Jeremy's hands and spoke in a voice that was clear and kind. "I wanted to hate you, Jeremy Fisher. I thought you were selfish and careless and unfeeling. You drank way too much, and then you went out and killed our friends." She hesitated. "I wanted them to punish you, lock you up and never let you out. But God changed how I felt." Her voice cracked, and only then did her eyes well up. "Hate won't bring back Ben and Sarah Jo." She sniffed. "It won't make you more responsible or less dangerous. Only God can do that. And God tells us hate isn't the answer. Love is. So I didn't come here to hate you. I came here to tell you I'm praying for you to change, to find faith in Christ, and to feel our forgiveness."

Then Bailey did something that took Katy's breath away. She leaned in and hugged Jeremy Fisher. When she drew back, he looked like a lost little boy. The pain of his mother's leaving and his father's being in Iraq, the emptiness of drinking, and the horror of the accident—all of it was on his face. But there was something else there, something that hadn't been there before.

A thin ray of hope.

Only one more CKT student remained, the one who had called Katy only last night to ask if she could come. The one that tugged at Katy's heart more than all the others combined.

Brandy Hanover.

Since the accident, she'd had three operations on her leg, and she still wore a full-length cast. She inched forward with the use of her crutches.

Jeremy watched her, and a deep fear filled his eyes, as if he knew who she was and if he'd had the chance, he would've bolted from the room and run from her.

Near the door, the other kids were sniffling, many of them crying openly.

Brandy made it to Jeremy Fisher's side, and for a long time she only looked at him. Then she handed him something, and Katy squinted to see what it was. Only as Jeremy took it did she get a good look. It was a school picture of Brandy's brother, Ben, the last one he'd ever taken. Katy had seen the picture before. It would appear in the *Annie* program on a memory page, alongside a photo of Sarah Jo.

"That's my brother, Ben." Brandy glanced at the picture. It was an adorable shot, showing Ben's impish grin and his missing front tooth. Brandy's tears were like many of the others'— quiet and controlled, leaving her the ability to speak clearly. She looked at Jeremy. "I thought you might want to know about Ben." She paused, but only long enough to balance on her crutches and wipe her cheeks. "Ben loved singing and dancing and Peter Pan. He couldn't wait to try out for CKT." She sniffed, but her voice stayed strong. "He thought Neverland was a real place, and he used to run into my room with his Peter Pan hat and bug me by singing as loud as he could, 'I can fly . . . I can fly . . . I can fly.'"

Jeremy leaned back and shaded his eyes with his hand. Tears streamed down his face, and his body jerked from a series of sobs.

Brandy put her hand on his shoulder. "I'm not telling you this to make you feel worse, Jeremy." She shifted her position, putting her broken leg out to the side. "I just want you to know him."

She waited until Jeremy put his hand down and looked at her. Jeremy's voice was thick, but he managed to say, "Go ahead."

Brandy took the photo of Ben and smiled at it. "He was the slowest one in the morning. He would wait till the last minute to comb his hair or wash his cereal bowl." She handed the photo back to Jeremy. "He always drank the last of the milk before I had a chance. But at night he'd sit on my knee when Mom read Dr. Seuss to us. He loved *Horton Hears a Who!* When I was in a play, no one ever clapped louder." Rivers of tears spilled down her cheeks. She put her hand over her heart and looked straight into Jeremy's eyes. "Nothing's the same without him. I miss him so much."

Jeremy looked at the picture in his hand and then up at Brandy. His face twisted in a mix of sorrow and horror and regret. "I'm sorry."

"I know. I forgive you, Jeremy." Brandy took the photo back and studied it for a long moment. Then she put her hand on Jeremy's and brought her face closer to his. "Please . . . don't drink anymore. Okay?"

Katy rubbed her fists across her own cheeks and drew a deep breath. It was her turn, but she couldn't imagine how she was supposed to close the moment, not when she couldn't even speak. She watched Brandy hobble over and join the rest of the group. That's when it hit her. If an eleven-year-old could do what Brandy Hanover had just done, then she could pray. Even if she sobbed through the entire thing.

"God—" she put one hand on Jeremy's shoulder—"we're here because we've loved and we've lost. We lost Ben and Sarah Jo, but—" she steadied herself—"but we don't want to lose Jeremy too. So we ask with one voice, one heart, that You will awaken Jeremy to Your truth and Your salvation. To Your forgiveness. And in the meantime let him know that everyone in this room will be praying for him."

Jeremy was weeping too hard to speak. They looked at him one last time; then he leaned forward and buried his head in his hands. He stayed that way, his shoulders shaking, as they left the room.

Katy would be back to talk to him, back to see if he was ready to make a decision to follow Jesus. But even as he wept, Katy had the strongest sense that the others would see Jeremy Fisher again, and that when they did, he wouldn't be merely the drunk driver responsible for killing a couple of CKT kids.

He would be a fellow believer.

CHAPTER THIRTY

NO FORCE ON EARTH could've kept Dayne from keeping his promise this Friday night in November.

He landed in Indianapolis and rented a car the smart way, the way that gave him a clear path to Bloomington without worrying that the paparazzi had followed him. He pulled into town thirty minutes early and drove to the theater parking lot. Darkness had already fallen, and Dayne was glad. No one would notice him; no one would expect Dayne Matthews to be driving around the Bloomington Community Theater now. Not when he was still finishing reshoots for *Dream On* at the Hollywood studio.

A quick glance at the parking lot and he found Katy's car. She would be inside, going over a hundred last-minute details. He parked and rolled down the window. The air was much colder than it had been in September, but it smelled faintly of burning leaves and damp wood, the way home would always smell to him.

He thought about his last meeting with Katy at Lake Monroe, how confused and shortsighted he'd been. So much had changed since then. The peace he'd found in the storage unit had remained.

He'd apologized to Kelly Parker, and the two had remained friends. She rebounded quickly, moving straight from his Malibu house to the one belonging to Hawk Daniels, just down the road. One day he hoped to tell Kelly a little more about the changes happening in him. But first he needed to understand them himself.

The people from the Kabbalah Center had stopped calling, and every day Dayne would open the Bible Katy had given him and find that God's Word spoke to him.

Mitch Henry, the director, had noticed the difference. At first it worried him. "Don't lose your edge on me, Matthews. I need you in top form through the whole film, through editing and retakes and all of it."

But after a while, Mitch had come back to him, surprised. "Whatever's happened to you, keep it up. You're a different person on camera. Transparent and real. The audience is gonna love it."

Dayne was glad about that, but it wasn't what drove him. The peace, the forgiveness—that's what kept him going back to the Bible as often as he had the chance. There were passages he didn't grasp and changes that still needed to come. But he was a different person today than he had been the last time he was in Bloomington.

He only wished for a chance to tell Katy.

But he couldn't, because he couldn't stay long. He had to be back on the set at noon tomorrow, so he'd booked a red-eye back home tonight. His return flight to Los Angeles left in five hours. He would watch the show and be on his way. Because he was finished lying to people. And this was something he'd promised Katy.

He left his car and walked across the lot toward the theater. He wore his sweatshirt and baseball cap again, the disguise that best hid who he was. The plan was simple. He'd ask for a balcony seat, and since so few people ever sat in the balcony, he'd have a good chance of not being recognized. That and a good view of the stage.

The crowd was thick near the door. He kept his face down, occasionally glancing at the far wall where no one was standing.

When it was his turn to pay, he pretended to be caught up in a search through his wallet.

"Just a minute." He riffled through it, staring straight down. "Yes, here it is." He handed the woman the exact change, then dropped a few dollars on the floor. He was picking them up while the woman handed him a balcony ticket. Without looking up, he took it and thanked her, still stuffing the loose bills into his wallet.

"You're in luck. I gave you front row." The woman had a smile in her voice. "You should have a good view from up there."

He thanked her again, but he was already facing the stairs. On his way up he took a program from a basket, avoiding the ushers stationed at the door of the main-floor seating area. He found his seat and settled back, taking in the view around him. The woman was right. He could see the entire theater, the people filing in and trying to find their seats while the smell of popcorn drifted up.

All of it filled his senses and made him long for the chance to return again and again. At a time when he wouldn't have to hide in the balcony. He looked at the stage and imagined what the sets and backdrop would look like. His sister Ashley Baxter Blake was supposed to be amazing, and now he could hardly stand waiting five more minutes until he could see her work.

The commotion was picking up, so he shifted enough to see the main-theater seating again. So far he hadn't seen Katy, not that he expected to. She would be busy behind the scenes. He only hoped he could see her before he left, even from a distance. He spotted Ashley walking in through the far side entrance. Next to her was a tall man, and next to him was a blond boy, maybe seven years old. The boy was familiar, and Dayne realized why. He'd seen all of them as a group the evening when they left the hospital, the day that he'd seen Elizabeth.

Dayne leaned forward and studied them. His nephew bounced along, taking hold of the man's hand and tugging on Ashley's sleeve. Dayne squinted, trying to see the child's expression. He looked happy and bubbly, like he'd be a kick to hang out with.

Something else too. The boy resembled him, like pictures he'd seen of himself at that age.

Was this always how it would be? Clandestine moments and stolen glimpses, no relationship, no connection with the people who were his own flesh and blood, his family? Ashley led her husband and son to a row of seats near the middle of the theater. As they worked their way in, another brunette stood, then one with hair that was a little bit lighter. Dayne felt his breath catch in his throat.

These were his other sisters—he recognized them too. Then a man with two little girls came down the aisle. The littlest one used a walker, but her face was all lit up, probably excited about the show. Dayne marveled at the scene, took in every second of it, mesmerized by their faces and actions, the fact that they felt so familiar to him.

If he could only bound down the stairs and go to them, tell them the truth and not worry about the fallout. He sat back in his seat, his eyes riveted on them. He had nothing to worry about, but that wasn't all that mattered. For the Baxters, they had everything to lose—a sense of privacy and decency that would be marred forever if they were ever pictured in the tabloids. And once they were there, they'd never have the same existence again.

He wouldn't risk it—not now or ever.

Moments like this were all he would ever have, and they would have to be enough. Ashley was laughing about something, hugging the one he figured was Brooke. That's when he noticed something else. Ashley was pregnant. The thought was bittersweet—happiness for her and her husband and little boy and bottomless sorrow because this child would be one more family member he'd never know.

The lights faded to dark then, and the orchestra began the overture.

Dayne glanced at his watch. He had just two hours before he had to leave.

❧

Katy raced through the greenroom putting out last-minute fires.

"I don't have my eyelash curler!" It was one of the orphans.

"Hold tight." Katy zipped across the room and led one of the makeup moms to the girl. She made it another five feet toward the door when another orphan popped out from the group and held her hands up. Her tattered skirt was covered with dirt.

"I was putting on my dirt smudges, and the whole jar spilled." Her face was pale, even through the stage makeup, terrified at what might happen now that she'd spilled on her dress minutes before the performance.

Katy bent down, brushed off the skirt as best she could, and smiled at the girl. "You're an orphan. It works. Don't worry about it, honey."

Connor Flanigan waved at her from across the room. He held a mustache in his hand. "My spirit gum's all dried up. I need a mustache for the third scene."

"You're right. Bert Healy has to have a mustache." She made a frantic search of the dressing room table and found a bottle. Spirit gum was the safest glue for theater work. She dabbed some on Connor's lip, pressed the mustache into place, and patted his head. "Go get 'em!"

Finally she made it to the stairs, raced up, and found her usual opening-night spot—in the box on the left side of the theater. From there she could see the wings and the stage and much of the audience reaction, all except the balcony. The way it was situated, she could see just the tops of the heads of people in that section.

She took her seat and exhaled, catching her breath. The theater was already dark, and the orchestra was playing. Everything was in order. Now it was up to the kids. She squinted at the first row near the stage and wondered if the Hanovers and the Strykers would come. But it was too hard to tell in the dark.

Not until the overture ended and the lights came up did she see for herself what she'd been hoping for. The kids' prayers had been answered. There in the front row was Alice Stryker, her husband, and their little boy, Joey. Next to them were Mr. and Mrs. Hanover and Brandy, her casted leg sticking straight forward.

Between them was an empty seat, the one where Ben would've sat.

Katy gripped the armrests. Her heart swelled within her, and she blinked back the wetness in her eyes. *Thank You, God. Thanks for getting them here.*

This was the point during the evening when Katy's curtain warmers would come out, usually a few CKT kids in costume, ready with a cute skit about turning off cell phones and waiting until intermission to order popcorn. This time, Tim Reed walked out in front of the closed curtain, carrying a cordless microphone. He was dressed like Oliver Warbucks, but he didn't have his bald cap on, and he didn't attempt to stay in character.

He smiled at the audience and welcomed them. In a straight-forward manner he gave them the theater rules and explained that there would be souvenirs and refreshments at intermission and after the show. Then he hesitated, and for a moment he looked at the Hanovers and Strykers in the front row.

His eyes lifted to the audience again. "Most of you know that we experienced a tragedy in CKT this session. We lost two kids, two of our friends, in a car accident. One of those was Sarah Jo Stryker, and the other was Ben Hanover." He motioned to the front row. "We're honored to have both their families here tonight."

A hush fell over the crowd as Tim said that last part. Katy held her breath as she watched their faces, the sadness and shock as the audience reacted to the thought that the two families hit hardest by the tragedy were, in fact, in their midst this very night.

A few seconds passed, and then Bryan Smythe's parents stood and began to clap. Not a wild cheering, but a sedate, slow clapping that expressed camaraderie and sympathy. The moment the clapping began, others joined in, and with Tim still standing in front waiting to finish, the entire theater wound up on its feet, showing their support for the Hanovers and the Strykers.

Katy could see both families. They huddled in their own groups, arms around each other, moved deeply by the outpouring from the crowd.

When the clapping finally died down, Tim took a step toward the audience and said, "And so we dedicate this show to the Hanovers and the Strykers." He moved back, gesturing toward the curtain as it opened. "CKT proudly presents *Annie*."

The night could've ended right there, and Katy couldn't have felt more satisfied. But from the opening number, Kelsy Bouchey turned in a performance far beyond anything she'd done in rehearsals. Katy remembered their conversation, how the girl wanted to make her role as Annie something special for the Hanovers and the Strykers. Now she was doing just that.

Scene after scene, the performance was amazing, better than anything Katy had ever seen on an opening night. The dancing was sharp, music right on key, and the singing was powerful enough to move her to the edge of her seat. The show was everything they'd prayed it would be, a moving testimony to life and hope and especially to the memory of two very special kids.

When it was over and the kids came out for curtain call, it was to a standing ovation that lasted through all the bows. Many of the kids had tears on their cheeks, and several made a point of waving to the Strykers and the Hanovers. As Oliver Warbucks's servants bowed, they each pulled Peter Pan hats from behind their backs and placed them on their heads. When Katy glanced at the Hanovers and the Strykers, they were smiling, their faces wet with tears.

"Okay," she whispered. "Here goes."

Normally she stayed in her box through curtain call, but the kids had something different planned tonight. She darted out of the box, down the stairs, through the greenroom, and up the stage stairs. All the kids were onstage, so she came through the middle with a dozen kids who'd worked crew for the show. Once the crew members had taken their bows, and with the applause still ringing, the group directed their hands toward the lighting and sound booth, then toward the orchestra, and finally up toward God, who had brought it all together in a way Katy had only dreamed about.

When they were finished, the orchestra would normally have played a finale version of "Tomorrow," the main song from the play. But this time the music was different, something the kids had requested.

Katy reached out and took the hands of the kids on either side of her. As she did, the kids all across the stage held hands, and at the right time they started singing "How Great Thou Art."

The audience seemed to realize that something special was happening, and every member stayed on his or her feet, singing along with the kids.

Katy scanned the audience, her heart overflowing, and finally she looked up to the balcony. Her mouth hung open for a moment, and she took a step forward so she could see him better. It was Dayne! He'd come, just like he said he would, and now his eyes held hers, speaking straight to her soul, reminding her of feelings that had never gone away. She wanted to go to him or shout out or wave, but she could do none of those. The moment was deep and beautiful, a showering of love and faith for all of them, but especially for the two families who needed it most.

She kept singing, the corners of her mouth raised in a smile despite her damp eyes. *Do you hear me, Dayne? Do you see me telling you that I still care, that I haven't forgotten you?* She never looked away, and neither did he. As the song ended, she mouthed the words *thank you*.

He made a subtle nod in her direction, and his lips formed the words *you're fantastic*.

They were singing a second song now, "I Love You, Lord." Katy wanted to go to him, but even as she tried to think of how quickly she could get to the balcony, he looked at her. Then he gave her the slightest wave and turned to leave.

He couldn't be going, could he? He wouldn't have come so far only to leave without talking to her, right? She watched him exit the balcony, and after a minute she saw him leave through the back side entrance of the theater. He really was leaving. He'd come just for the show, and now he was gone.

Tears splashed onto Katy's cheeks, and she wondered how long before the kids and she would find themselves in another season of laughter. The kids' voices were building toward the last part of the song. "'Take joy, my King, in what You hear: May it be a sweet, sweet sound in Your ear.'"

Katy's tears came harder, but she smiled through them. She cried because she wished with everything inside her that Sarah Jo was on that stage singing with them and that Ben Hanover was in the seat between his mother and father. She cried for the painful loss they'd all suffered and for the lessons they'd learned regarding Jeremy Fisher. For the way all of CKT had come together since the accident.

But she also cried because of Dayne Matthews and feelings that maybe weren't pretend after all. She had tried her hardest to put aside thoughts of him, but he was still there when she woke up and when she lay back down to sleep at night. She wondered how he was doing and whether he'd read the letter on the back of the photo of his birth mother and if he'd found the wisdom to walk away from Kabbalah. Twice a week she'd catch herself checking messages, looking for his phone number.

And so the tears were for that too. Because she couldn't imagine closing the door on a guy who would fly across the country to see her students perform on opening night. Her feelings for him were real, same as his were for her. But that's all they would ever share—distant, unfulfilled feelings. Her tears fell even after the song ended, because the truth was clear. With Dayne, real love had never really gotten a chance to bloom.

Whatever was between them, it had started in the dark shadows of the Bloomington Community Theater. And tonight, even though they would see each other again at the trial in Los Angeles, whatever they shared had ended the exact same way. He had gone back to his world, and she needed to let him leave. Her life was here, where she belonged.

Her role as director of CKT had always been the job she felt God alone had given her. But now as she watched the families in the audience come together, hugging and congratulating the cast and crew, showering the Hanovers and the Strykers with love, it became clear that working with these kids was so much more than a job.

It was a calling. And she would stay with it as many years as God allowed.

AUTHOR'S NOTE

There is mention in this novel of a religious group called Kabbalah, along with a place called the Kabbalah Learning Center in Los Angeles, where Dayne takes religious classes. Though Kabbalah is a real religion, there are two sects of Kabbalists—one rooted in Old Testament Judaism, and the other rooted in a combination of Old Testament Judaism and a set of unique teachings. Since the latter of these Kabbalah sects is currently drawing great interest from the Hollywood community, I chose to include it in the fictional story line of Dayne Matthews.

I did a great amount of research in order to keep my details factual. However—as with any organization—I could not use all my information. It is possible that some of the information given to me or found through research is not exactly represented in the way certain people might view it. In addition, I chose to portray this group through the lens of Christianity and biblical truth.

The Kabbalah Center in *Forgiven* is in no way intended to exactly duplicate any specific Kabbalah center. Certainly any similarity between my characters and real-life characters is entirely coincidental.

A WORD FROM KAREN KINGSBURY

DEAR READER FRIENDS,

Thanks for traveling with me through the second book in the Firstborn series. From the beginning when I imagined five books about Dayne Matthews and Katy Hart, I knew forgiveness would be one of the issues I'd have to deal with. The reason? Forgiveness is such an integral part of living the Christian life. Without Christ's forgiveness, all of us would be doomed to eternal death. By accepting it, we can experience eternal life.

The difference between the two is all the difference in the world. That was something Dayne needed to experience. At the same time, the idea of a tragedy in the world of CKT required forgiveness also. I used tragedy for several reasons. First, because the CKT in the Firstborn series is a picture of any small group of faithful people, and with faith, tragedy can bring people together.

And tragedy is a certain part of life.

One of the promises Christ gave us in the book of John is that, "In this world you will have trouble" (John 16:33). Hundreds of you write to me every week, and I can tell you there is no shortage of troubles, no lack of tragedies. Many of you struggle with loveless or faithless marriages or with a spouse who doesn't share your beliefs. Some of you aren't sure where your next house payment will come from, and others are estranged from a mother or father, a son or daughter. And a number of you are in the middle of the tragic loss of someone you love.

The key to Christ's promise that we would have trouble in this world is the end of the verse: "But take heart! I have overcome the world." The way the second half of the promise was lived out after the fatal car accident in *Forgiven* was this: dozens of kids learned how to come together, and even more, they learned to forgive. They learned that together they could survive any tragedy by clinging to God and their faith and each other.

I pray that is how you and I would go through tragedy as well.

Finally, Ashley needed to forgive her parents for hiding the truth about the child they gave up. It was a quick decision because Ashley realized that her parents were guilty of the same mistake she'd made in the events that led to her son's birth. The example that Ashley gave by immediately forgiving is one we could all learn from. My husband once told me, "Karen, I'm not going to fight with you ever." He explained that in the end he wasn't ever leaving me, and he wasn't going to live a life of anger at me. Therefore, he might as well forgive quickly and completely. That way we'd have more happy days together.

What a great idea. We would do ourselves a favor to follow that thinking. The more quickly you forgive, the more quickly you recognize what Dayne did: forgiveness leads to peace. When we find ourselves anxious and unhappy, doubtful or worried, we ought to ask ourselves who we need to forgive or how we need to be forgiven. Unwinding the tangled mess of unforgiveness and making peace with the people in our lives will give us the peace we're all looking for.

Beyond that, maybe you're one of those considering faith in Jesus Christ for the first time because of something you read in the stories of Dayne and Katy and the Baxter family. If so, then realize this: though the people in *Forgiven* are fictional, the God they serve is not. He is alive and active and working in your life, whether you know it or not. If you don't have a saving relationship with the living God, contact your local Bible-believing church and find out more about Him. Please know that I am praying for you and all my readers every day, that God will use these stories to draw you closer to Him, the way He uses them to draw me closer.

There are still three books to come in the Firstborn series: *Found*, *Family*, and *Forever*. I hope you have the chance to read those books also.

On a quick note, my family is doing well. We're enjoying the Christian Youth Theater, which the kids are still involved in, and

Little League, soccer, and basketball that keep us busy with our four youngest boys. As always, I covet your prayers for my family and me and for the ministry of writing Life-Changing Fiction.

By the way, stop in and visit my website. It's undergone some changes, and now there are many interactive links that give you the chance to leave comments, ask for prayer, or connect with other readers.

As always, I love hearing from you. Drop me an e-mail at Karen@KarenKingsbury.com or go online to my website www.KarenKingsbury.com.

Until next time . . . in His light and love,

Karen Kingsbury

DISCUSSION QUESTIONS

Use these questions for individual reflection or for discussion with a book club or other small group. They will help you not only understand some of the issues in *Forgiven* but also integrate some of the book's messages into your own life.

1. What is the connection between forgiveness and peace?
2. Discuss a time when you forgave someone or when someone forgave you. Share how that forgiveness made you feel.
3. Besides peace, what was Dayne Matthews looking for when he started attending the Kabbalah Center?
4. Were you surprised about Alice Stryker's car accident? Explain how the accident changed her.
5. When has something tragic and unfair happened in your life or the life of someone you know? Describe the situation.
6. How did you feel toward God after that event? How did Katy and the members of CKT feel toward God? toward the drunk driver?
7. When Tim Reed prayed at the meeting at the Flanigans' house, what did he say that showed his honesty in the matter? How did that help everyone else?
8. When did the kids' feeling toward the drunk driver begin to change? Why did they change?
9. Is Elaine Denning a good addition to John Baxter's life? Why or why not?
10. Explain Ashley's hesitance about her father spending time with Elaine.
11. Why does Dayne have stronger feelings for Katy Hart than for his live-in girlfriend, Kelly Parker? What intrigues Dayne about Katy?

12. What is it about Katy's life that makes her feel she could never fall in love with Dayne?

13. Why does Dayne cause Katy such emotional confusion? Explain the battle going on inside her when it comes to Dayne.

14. Do you know anyone like Jeremy Fisher? What led to that person's downtrodden lifestyle?

15. How have you seen alcoholism or abusive drinking be a negative thing in your life or the life of someone you love?

16. Jeremy Fisher assumed the kids were coming to the jail to condemn him. How did the visit from the CKT kids affect him? How do you think he felt when they were finished?

17. Explain Ashley's reaction when she opened the envelope marked *Firstborn* and realized that her parents had given up a child? What are three ways this helped her to better understand her mother?

18. Should Ashley have opened the letter? How do you feel about her rationalizations to do so?

19. How did Dayne come to understand forgiveness?

20. Did he need to forgive or be forgiven or both? Explain.

Please turn the page for an exciting preview of

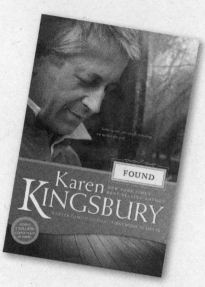

the third book in the

FIRSTBORN SERIES

by Karen Kingsbury

From

F O U N D

by Karen Kingsbury

CHAPTER ONE

THE STORY WAS MORE than any reporter could resist.

A knife-wielding stalker with the delusional belief that she was married to the famous actor Dayne Matthews. The accusation that the same crazy woman had jumped from the dark shadows of Paradise Cove in an attempted murder of an associate of Dayne's. The rescue of that associate by Dayne, the photos that showed him and an unknown woman kissing on the beach earlier that night, and the fact that no one had ever been able to identify her.

Never mind that it was just a deposition. A crew of news vans and photographers surrounded the entrance to the Los Angeles Superior Court this January morning, hoping for a glimpse of the star they couldn't get enough of. Desperate for details beyond what they already knew.

Dayne Matthews sat in the backseat of the rented black Suburban. His attorney, Joe Morris, was driving. They were the only people in the vehicle, and from their position at a stoplight in front of the courthouse, they could see everything. Newscasters and print guys and tabloid photogs scurrying about the scene, searching for the best angle, the fewest shadows, plugging in wires and adjusting lenses as they waited for him to appear.

"They're out in full force." Joe turned the SUV into the parking lot.

"They love a good story." Today's newspaper lay on the seat beside Dayne, and he picked it up. His publicist had spoken with the media and put quite a spin on the facts. The article read: *Dayne Matthews and his unnamed associate will appear in court this morning to give depositions in the case against stalker Margie Madden.*

Dayne chuckled to himself. Katy was coming into court half an hour after him, and she was hardly a mere associate—though that's what the media and the police had believed about Katy since the beginning. An "associate" helping him scout out a location for an upcoming film. Since Katy was an unknown and since they didn't need to release her name until the trial, no one had to know that she was an actress or that she'd turned down the lead role in *Dream On* or that she lived in Bloomington, Indiana. The tabloids had a picture of him kissing an unknown woman earlier that evening on the beach, and he had explained that she was an actress who preferred to stay anonymous. The media had never put the two stories together.

"Let's go." His attorney exhaled hard as he put the vehicle in park. "It'll take a while to get through the throng."

Dayne unbuckled his seat belt and slid toward the door of the Suburban. The explanation he'd given to the press and the police had holes big enough to drive a train through, but none of it was a lie, not really. Katy *was* his associate, in the sense that she'd associated with him in a work setting for a time. And the police didn't care about the tabloid photos of him kissing some woman on the beach. He wasn't on trial after all.

Margie Madden was.

The explanation bought them time. That way Katy could stay

out of the limelight as long as possible. By the time the press heard actual testimony and realized her name, and that she'd been thinking about the role in *Dream On*, the movie would already be released and Katy would be only a small aspect of the story.

Dayne and Joe walked close together, their pace fast and clipped. Joe had flown out from New York City to be here, even though his presence wasn't really necessary. The prosecuting attorney would handle the deposition, and normally witnesses needed no other representation. But Dayne's situation was different. His public persona was at stake any time he did or said anything involving the law. His attorney even planned to have someone out here from the New York office at Dayne's side every moment during the trial.

They were a hundred feet from the courthouse when the swarm of media caught wind of Dayne's arrival. In a rush they pivoted and aimed their cameras. A few nicely dressed newscasters stepped in front of the others, large booming microphones in their hands. The bigger the network, the more likely they were to use his last name.

"Mr. Matthews." A heavily made-up blonde stepped into his path. "Is it true you want the judge in this case to make an example of Margie Madden, and is it true—?"

"No comment." Joe took hold of Dayne's elbow and straight-armed a path through the crowd. "Excuse us."

"Dayne." It was a photographer shouting from a few layers back in the crowd. "Tell us about the associate. Where is she? Isn't she supposed to be—?"

"She's already here." Joe's answer was loud enough for most of them to hear. It was part of the plan, that he would discourage the press from sticking around and waiting for Katy.

The photographer raised his hand and shouted again, "Does she still work with Dayne and in what capacity, since we don't have a name on her and—"

"No comment." Joe kept up his pace. He pulled Dayne along, leaving no room for responses. Dayne sort of liked the help. Maybe if he had Joe around more often, the paparazzi would leave him alone. He stifled a grin at the thought.

The crowd parted easily, and Dayne did his best to look straight ahead, his expression serious. The press would have their requisite photos and footage—Dayne Matthews, Hollywood star, coming to court to give testimony on the crazy stalker who tried to kill his associate. None of them really expected more than that.

Other than passing glances and whispered comments, Dayne and Joe weren't approached again as they entered the building and took the elevator to the eighth floor. Dayne stopped for a minute and looked out the window across the hazy Los Angeles scene. Somewhere out there Katy Hart was back in his city, making her way to the courthouse. Her visit was all he'd been able to think about since Christmas.

"This way." Joe took the lead and headed toward a room at the end of the hall.

They were met by a sharp-looking woman who appeared to be in her midfifties. She introduced herself as the prosecuting attorney. "We have a room set up for you." She gave them a businesslike smile. "Follow me."

The attorney explained the proceedings as they walked down another hallway, but Dayne did little more than give an occasional nod in her direction. Joe would handle the details. All he had to do was tell the story while the prosecutor tape-recorded it. For now he could let his mind wander, let himself think about Katy.

He hadn't heard from her since opening night of *Annie*, but she was there when he woke up and when he lay down to sleep. The past few months had been the loneliest of his life. Not that he hadn't had offers. He was in the middle of filming a romantic suspense film opposite Angie Carr, a dark-haired beauty with exotic looks and a penchant for her leading men. They'd met at several functions but never starred in a film together until now.

On the first day of filming she had poked her head out of her trailer and called to him. "Dayne, come here." Her eyes danced, and her smile held the pout she was famous for. "I have a question."

He was in the middle of three things, including a conversation with his agent. But she was his priority as long as they were still establishing chemistry for the film. He jogged to her trailer, stepped inside, and closed the door behind him.

She stood facing him, dressed in nothing but a transparent negligee. "Hi." She took a step closer. "I need your opinion." Another step. "Will this work for the bedroom scene, the one at the beginning of the film?"

He swallowed and put his hand on the trailer door. "I thought the script called for a nightgown."

She pushed out her lips in a pout most men would have found irresistible. She played with a lock of her hair, dropping her chin and looking beyond seductive. "You don't like it?"

"Yeah, well . . ." He let loose a single chuckle and rubbed the back of his neck. "The film's PG-13, so I'm thinking something less see-through."

She grinned. "Oh, well." One more step and now she ran her finger down the length of his arm. "It works for right now, anyway." She nodded toward the set crew outside. "They'll be busy for an hour before they need us." Her face was so close he could smell the mint on her breath. She dropped her voice to a whisper. "Do you know how long I've wanted to practice a love scene with you, Dayne Matthews?"

He gritted his teeth. "Angie, listen . . ." She was stunning, but so what? Did she want him to take her right here on the trailer floor? And if he did, then what? They'd pretend to be hot lovers for a few weeks, and after that he'd be lonelier than ever. Something else too. The peace he'd found in Bloomington wouldn't last if he went back to his old ways.

With gentle hands, he framed her face and drew her close. Then he kissed her forehead. "The film calls for a few kisses—that's all." He searched her eyes. "We'll have time to practice later, okay?"

She could've gotten angry, but she didn't. Instead she took a few steps back, making sure he had a view of her full frame. "I'll look forward to it." She tossed him a confident smile as if to say she wasn't giving up that easily. "Dinner tonight?"

Since then, Angie's attempts had been relentless, just short of desperate, but he'd managed to keep his distance and still build chemistry with her. Working with her had its benefits. She was a professional, brilliant on the screen and fun off it. But she made him feel empty and plastic, the way all of Hollywood made him feel lately.

He was glad for a day off now, and never mind that he'd spend most of it here in a Los Angeles courthouse. He would've looked forward to a day in jail if it meant seeing Katy Hart again.

The attorneys were still talking as they reached a door at the end of the hallway. Dayne glanced at his watch, then toward the elevator. Katy would be here in fifteen minutes.

"This is perfect." Joe opened the door and led the way into a small room. He looked at Dayne. "You ready?"

"Perfectly." Dayne felt a sudden rush of passion toward the job ahead. The stalker had cost him much. This was his chance to get back at her.

The prosecutor followed them inside. "The deposition doesn't start for twenty minutes." She checked the clock on the wall. "I'll grab coffee and be back by then."

"I'll come." Joe set his portfolio on the desk and nodded at Dayne. "Want anything?"

"I'm fine."

The attorneys left, and Dayne took one of the seats. In the silence he could almost hear his heart beat. Would Katy still have feelings for him? Would the electricity, the emotions that had existed between them still be there after they'd been apart so long? He tapped his fingers on the table. The minutes couldn't drop off the clock fast enough.

He should've brought his Bible, the one Katy had given him.

That would've passed the time. He had been reading it lately, taking in a little more of the message every night. Not that he was ready to hit the nearest church or claim himself born again, the way some of his athlete friends had done recently. But the God of the Bible was the same God claimed by his parents, the Baxters, and Katy Hart. Because of that, He was the same God on Dayne's mind more often now.

He was about to step outside and check for Katy when he heard a knock. The attorneys would've come in without waiting, so maybe it was . . .

He stood and opened the door, and before he could take another breath he was looking into her eyes. The same clear blue eyes he'd connected with from the balcony of the Bloomington Community Theater back in November.

"Hi." Katy was breathless. She looked over her shoulder, nervous. "I've never seen so many cameras."

"They didn't know it was you, did they?"

"No." She exhaled, finding her composure. "I slipped past."

He let her in, closed the door, and suddenly they were alone, face-to-face as if no time at all had passed between them. "Katy—" he reached out and took her hands—"you look wonderful."

The faintest blush tinged her cheeks, and she shifted her gaze to the floor. When her eyes found his again, he had the answer he was looking for. The connection was still there. It was in her eyes and in her expression and in the way she ran her thumbs along the tops of his hands. "I didn't think we'd have any time alone."

"We won't have much."

Her smile told him everything she was feeling. But at the same time it cried of resignation. Because here they were again, their emotions leading the way, and yet their time would be measured and counted by the events around them, by the parameters of his world.

"How are you, Dayne?" Katy didn't blink, didn't seem to want to lose a moment of whatever minutes they had together.

"I'm good." He grinned, wanting desperately to keep things light. How was it fair that this visit would end up amounting to little more than another sad good-bye? "What are you working on?"

"*Robin Hood*." She stifled a laugh. "It's coming together."

"The kids?" He wanted to know, wanted to soak himself in everything about her. "Are they okay?"

"They are. The older kids are still in the Bible study, the one they started after Sarah Jo Stryker's accident." She made a funny face. "Of course, we should probably spend an extra day a week on practice, the way things are going."

"Blocking, you mean?"

"No." She laughed. "Trying to stay onstage. I'd be happy with that." Katy talked with her hands when she was excited. Now she released his hands and began illustrating her story. "So there's this scene where Robin's supposed to fly in from the wings on a rope, right?"

"To rescue Maid Marian?"

"Exactly." She took a quick breath. "Marian's standing on a fake tree stump, her hands tied, and he's supposed to swing in, land beside her, and save the day."

Dayne chuckled. He could see what was coming.

"Instead—" Katy demonstrated the swinging motion—"he sails in from the wings and knocks her square on the floor."

"Oh." Dayne made a face. "Was she hurt?"

"Her pride, yes. Her onstage chemistry with Robin, yes." Katy gave him a teasing look. "We decided we better just have him run in from now on."

"Sounds good." Dayne saw so much more than her physical beauty. Her enthusiasm and spirit, her joy and excitement for the little things of life. All of it was like getting air after being too long underwater.

"So . . . enough on that." Her tone softened. "How are you . . . really?"

"Well . . ." He found her eyes and held them. "I'm not a Kabbalist."

Her eyes widened, and she looked deeply at him, to the lonely desert plains of his heart. "Really?"

"Tossed it all." He felt his eyes begin to dance. "Some girl said it probably wasn't for me. Told me I needed to find the truth."

"Must've been a smart girl."

"Mmm." He took hold of her hands again, but he kept his distance. "Definitely. In fact, she gave me a Bible."

"A Bible? How interesting." Her eyes twinkled. "What a great idea. You know . . . since, well, it is the truth. I mean, if you're looking for it you might as well go to the source."

"That's what I figured." He felt his smile fade. "It's changing me, Katy. I can feel it."

Her expression softened, and what had been playful became serious. She closed the gap between them and slipped her arms around his neck. "Dayne, I prayed for this . . . for you."

He wouldn't have gone to her, wouldn't have crossed the line he'd crossed the last time they were together. But now, lost in her embrace, he couldn't imagine letting her go. Slowly, he worked his fingers along the back of her neck into her hair. She smelled wonderful, like the flowers in Bloomington.

Too soon she pulled back and searched his eyes. "Did you find Jesus? When you read the Bible, I mean?"

His hands were around her waist but only loosely. He looked beyond her. The question was a good one. He understood forgiveness and peace better. "Have I found Jesus?"

"Mmm-hmm." She angled her head, her soul as transparent as a child's. "When you look past the hurt and sadness of your yesterdays, is He there?"

A part of his heart sank a little. The answer wasn't what she wanted to hear. "Not yet." He released his hold on her waist and took her hands once more. "But I'm looking."

Disappointment never even flashed in her eyes. She gave him her brightest smile yet. "That's it."

"What?" It was all he could do to keep from kissing her.

"That's what I've been praying for." Her eyes glistened. "That you'll look."

The door opened. They dropped hands and stepped back to keep from being hit.

Joe Morris was the first to enter. He stopped and looked from Dayne to Katy. "Hi. You must be Katy Hart."

"I am." She held out her hand to him. Her cheeks were red, but she rebounded quickly. "I understand the deposition won't take long."

"Not at all."

The prosecutor stepped into the room. She greeted Katy and then Dayne. "We need your testimony on record so we can prepare for the case."

Dayne felt the intimacy from a moment ago fade like fog in July. It was no longer a reconnecting, a time to remember why he couldn't get Katy Hart out of his mind. They were in business mode now, and the atmosphere stayed that way for the next hour.

When the lawyers were finished, the group stood and moved to the door. Dayne was about to ask Katy if she wanted to go somewhere, spend some time together before she left. But before he could say anything his cell phone rang.

He checked the caller ID. Kelly Parker. He stuffed his frustration. She rarely called. At least he could politely put her off until later. The two of them hadn't talked much since she'd moved out. He held his finger up to Katy and opened his phone. "Hey."

"Dayne." There was a cry in her voice, one that mixed sorrow and fear. She waited a moment. "I've got bad news. I just found out."

His heart skipped a beat, and he moved to a corner of the room. In the background he heard his attorney start a conversation with Katy. He pressed the phone to his ear. "What is it?"

"There's no easy way to say this." Kelly sighed, and it rattled all the way to his soul. "Dayne, I'm pregnant."

John Baxter was running out of options.

He'd done everything he could to find his firstborn son, everything a person could possibly think of. He'd searched the Internet for information, and he'd gone to adoption sites. He'd made phone calls and connected with people who aided parents in finding their birth children. Now he was down to his last hope.

The chances of finding his oldest son rested completely in the hands of a private investigator. John had hired him a week ago, and now—sitting on his desk—was a message from the man with one simple instruction: *Call immediately.*

He stared at the piece of paper and reached for the phone. Was this it? Had the man found the boy he and Elizabeth had prayed about for so many years? Would he have every bit of information he'd ever wanted in just a few minutes? The possibilities welled up in him and made it hard to breathe.

John closed his eyes and exhaled. *God, meet me in this place. I want to find him so badly, and this is my last chance. Please let there be something to go on—a lead, a phone number, a name. Something.*

He opened his eyes, and they fell on a small frame on his desk. It read: *With God all things are possible. Matthew 19:26.* A smile tugged at the corners of John's lips, and he felt himself relax. *Thanks, God. You always know just what I need.* Whatever the private investigator had to tell him, he wouldn't give up. Not now, not ever.

His palms felt sweaty against the phone's receiver. He took a full breath, picked it up, and tapped out the private investigator's number.

The man's secretary answered and connected him to the PI.

"Tim Brown here." The man was a fast talker, high energy. "How can I help you?"

"Uh . . . this is John Baxter, returning your call." He swallowed hard. "Did you find my son?"

"Yes, John, thanks for calling back." The man's tone became

serious, slower than before. "Listen, something's come up in my research. Something very, very important. We need to talk about it in person."

In person? John wouldn't be able to think straight until he heard the news. "Are you sure? Can't you tell me now?"

"Not something like this." Tim rustled some papers. "Can you be here in the morning? Eleven o'clock?" He sighed, and the sound carried his concern across the phone lines. "This is very sensitive. I think you should know right away."

Three great series
One amazing drama

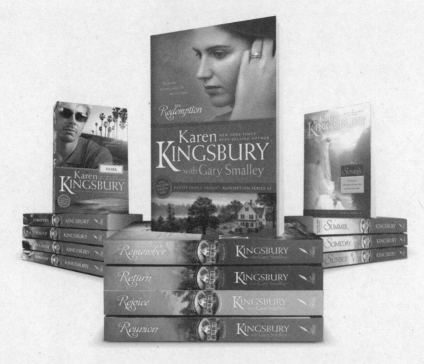

New York Times bestselling author Karen Kingsbury has captured readers' hearts with the beloved Baxter Family Drama, beginning with *Redemption* and continuing through the Sunrise series. Start at the beginning to discover why so many have fallen in love with the Baxters!

Redemption Series
Redemption
Remember
Return
Rejoice
Reunion

Firstborn Series
Fame
Forgiven
Found
Family
Forever

Sunrise Series
Sunrise
Summer
Someday
Sunset

Other Life-Changing Fiction by
KAREN KINGSBURY

REDEMPTION SERIES
Redemption
Remember
Return
Rejoice
Reunion

FIRSTBORN SERIES
Fame
Forgiven
Found
Family
Forever

SUNRISE SERIES
Sunrise
Summer
Someday
Sunset

STAND-ALONE TITLES
Fifteen Minutes
The Chance
The Bridge
Oceans Apart
Between Sundays
When Joy Came to Stay
On Every Side
Divine
Like Dandelion Dust
Where Yesterday Lives
Shades of Blue
Unlocked
Coming Home—The Baxter Family
This Side of Heaven

ABOVE THE LINE SERIES
Above the Line Take One
Above the Line Take Two
Above the Line Take Three
Above the Line Take Four

BAILEY FLANIGAN SERIES
Leaving
Learning
Longing
Loving

SEPTEMBER 11 SERIES
One Tuesday Morning
Beyond Tuesday Morning
Remember Tuesday Morning

LOST LOVE SERIES
Even Now
Ever After

RED GLOVE SERIES
Gideon's Gift
Maggie's Miracle
Sarah's Song
Hannah's Hope

E-SHORT STORIES
The Beginning
I Can Only Imagine